Finding Ida

By Myron Kaufman

Categories: 1) historical, 2) America, 3) immigrant, 4) Jewish

To my grandfather, Abraham Kaufman, whom

I knew not well enough.

Acknowledgements

Although, to the best of my knowledge, the incident on which this novel is based: Abe following the love of his advanced years from Florida to New York, is true, my grandfather didn't talk very much, so I had to fill in the rest of his personal story. While some elements of his, my father's and my own life have made their way into the story, most of the characters and incidents are purely creations of my imagination.

I am grateful to everyone who read Finding Ida in its early versions, especially the Atlanta Green Reading Group and the two critique groups of the Atlanta Writers Club in which I have participated. I especially thank my wife, June, whose tireless reading and rereading, keen editing, and frank comments greatly improved the book.

Table of Contents

Part I - The Old Country

Chapter 1

My name is Abe, and I don't talk a lot. Nothing's wrong with me; it's just that I've spent my life being a Jewish son, brother and husband, and, as you know, in those roles you don't get much chance to express yourself. But now I'm ninety-one, and in recent years I've been a Jewish lover...and a lover must speak up... I guess.

I'll say it. I'll even yell it. "She shouldn't have left me alone like this." Now I have to find her and see if I can get her to come back to me.

I was the youngest child and only son, doted on by my four sisters: Leena, Golda, Freyda and Raisa—or was it Reena? What kind of man forgets the name of his sister? Although, as an excuse, it's been almost eighty years since I saw any of them. Until the Second World War, Leena's letters kept me up on what was happening at home. But then they stopped, and I've had no further news of my family.

I often wonder what my life would have been like, if I had stayed with my family instead of coming to America. Not very good, I suppose. But at least I would have been spared the loneliness I've experienced certain times in my life.

My sisters treated me like a doll, to be dressed, told what to do and scolded. And dolls don't talk—at least they didn't back in those days. Leena spent a lot of time with me, because she had a limp, which kept her from outdoor activities with the other girls.

"Stand still, Avrom," she would say, while she examined me all over. "I'm practicing to be a nurse." Sometimes in my dreams, I can still feel her hands on me. Poor Leena! I hope that during her life, my body wasn't the only one she ever had a chance to run her hands over.

7

When I got older, I went to the school in our town, Zyvotov, in the Ukraine, where I got a prize for being a good student. Papa was the butcher in our little *shtetl*, an important position, and he had a front row seat in the *shul*. We lived pretty well—for Jews that is. The good smell of Mama's stew, slow cooking on the stove, usually filled our house. It didn't smell so good outside—because of the tannery. Nobody liked it, but everyone put up with it, since the tannery provided the leather for the shoes that were the main business of the town. In most houses, but not ours, the grownups and most of the children put shoes together from morning to night.

Our house was one of the biggest in the town. As the only boy, I had my own room—although it wasn't much bigger than a closet. The girls doubled up—or did they all sleep in the same room? I really can't remember.

Elya is the only friend I can recollect from those days. We played soldiers in the alleyways of the *shtetl*. The surrounding woods beckoned us with its secrets, but our parents warned us not to venture there. "Not a step outside the town," Mama said. "Who knows what the peasants would do if they caught a boy with a *yarmulke* on his head?" So, of course, we put our *yarmulkes* in our pockets and tiptoed into the shade of the trees. Each day we went a little further, until one day, a hunter with a gun strode out of the trees. We froze with fear, but he just grunted and moved on. We weren't the game he was looking for. Thereafter, we stayed in the town.

"The Bible says," Rabbi Zev told me, when I was studying for my *bar mitzvah,* "'Thou shalt bind them for a sign upon thine hand, and they shall be as frontlets between thine eyes.'" He showed me how to wrap the leather boxes containing biblical passages around my forehead and hand during my morning prayers. "After your *bar mitzvah*, you will do this every day, except *Shabbos*."

Papa, seeing me at my prayers one morning, said, "Avrom, it's been a while since I donned my *tefillin*. If I can find them, I'll join you." He went back into his bedroom and after a few minutes, returned with his own boxes. They were in such good condition, I couldn't imagine they'd been used much. In fact, I had to remind him how to attach them according to Rabbi

Zev's instructions. Praying with my father each morning for the next few months gave me the feeling of being uniquely important in my family.

About two weeks after my *bar mitzvah*, I awoke one morning to find Papa had already gone to his shop. After that, with my tendency to sleep late during holidays and Papa often being in a rush, both our *tefillin* found their ways into the bottom of drawers.

When I was fifteen, and beginning to notice the girls in our village, Czar Nicholas threw a big fireworks party for the town, supposedly to celebrate the turn of the century. Everyone went out to watch it on a nearby field. That was a big mistake.

To this day, I can't watch fireworks without getting goosebumps from thinking about that night over three quarters of a century ago. While some of the soldiers fired off the rockets, others went through the crowd, grabbing boys for the army. The explosions drowned out the screams of their mothers.

One brute put his hand on my shoulder and spun me around. "Too young," he said and continued his search through the crowd. Elya, who was a year older and four inches taller than me, was taken that night. I never saw him again, but I was relieved when his parents received a letter, in which he said he was serving "in the East."

Mama was horrified. "They'll never take my baby," she said. "He'll go to America. I'll write my brother."

We knew about America from my uncle, Yudel. Yudel was a tailor, but since almost everyone in the *shtetl* sewed, there wasn't much business for a tailor in Zyvotov, and he often peddled shoes in surrounding towns. Once he was robbed on a lonely road. "Why should they buy shoes from a Jew," he said, "when they can just rob him?" When the police wouldn't help him, he decided to leave.

Yudel wrote that America was the golden land, where there was no limit to what a man could achieve, if he worked hard. "Send little Avrom," he wrote. "I'll take good care of him." So Papa scraped together enough money for the train and the boat.

9

I begged Papa not to send me away, but he wouldn't listen. "Avrom, Mama is right," he said. "You can't imagine how horrible war is. But even if there's no war, being in the army is terrible for Jews. They keep them there forever and treat them like *dreck*. I've heard of Jews committing suicide in the army."

I wasn't convinced, but I didn't have the courage to argue with my father.

Following Yudel's instruction, Papa sewed a five-ruble gold coin into the inside of each of my shoes, "to show the authorities in America you won't be a burden on society." He also gave me a ruble in my pocket, in case I had to bribe an official on the train, and some kopeks for spending money.

In late March, Papa hitched up the wagon, and the whole family accompanied me to a nearby town and cried when I got on the train. Papa had bought me a used winter coat. It was at least two sizes too large for me, wrapping around almost to my back and held closed by a heavy belt. The faded circle on its arm indicated it was of military origin. "A soldier probably traded it for a bottle of vodka," he told me. "You'll grow into it, and it will keep you warm."

Each of my sisters gave me a big hug. Leena wiped the tears from her eyes, and said, "Avrom, I'll be very angry with you, if you don't write. This might help you in America." She gave me a small book, *Learning English*. "Study it on the boat."

Mama provided me with a bag of food: bread, cheese and the last apple from the cellar, which she had saved for me. I hugged her; not realizing it would be for the last time ever. Yesterday, five women had looked out for me, tomorrow there would be none. Mama's last words to me were, "Don't trust strangers," and Papa called out, "Don't be a Menahem-Mendl," as I boarded the train.

With these words spinning in my head, I found a seat on the train. I was scared. I didn't really understand why they were sending me away. With the sleeve of my jacket, I wiped away my tears. I didn't know anyone outside our *shtetl*. *If I couldn't trust strangers, who could I trust? And who was Menahem-Mendl?*

10

The train went through Vinnytsia and then after countless stops arrived in Kiev, where I changed trains. I sat huddled in my seat for the more than the full day it took the train to arrive at the Saint Petersburg railway station, which was the largest building I had ever seen. There, after asking directions a half-dozen times, I was able to follow Papa's instructions and look up one of his old friends, Boris Chernovsky. Papa had written Boris about me, asking him to book my passage to New York. Boris had been born in our town, but after getting an engineering degree, he was hired by a company in Saint Petersburg. He and his wife, Sophia, were thin, nervous people without any children. I slept on their couch for three nights, while I was waiting for my ship to depart.

Sophia indulged me with excellent food: omelets for breakfast, thick stews for dinner. "Eat now, you won't get much on the boat," she told me. But I was too excited to eat. I wanted to go out and see the magnificent capital of the Russian Empire, so colorfully described in my schoolbooks, but Sophia said, "It's dangerous out there. Hooligans everywhere. They love to beat up Jews; I wouldn't wear your *yarmulke*, if I were you."

"I don't know what I would tell your father," Boris said, "if anything happened to you here. But if you wait until tomorrow night, I'll take you to see the ice breaking on the Neva. It's a sight worth seeing."

The next evening, as soon as Boris got home, he gave me a big fur hat and we started walking through streets of mud and melting snow. Carriages were getting stuck everywhere. Closer to the river, the streets were paved and the traffic moved more smoothly. In one large square, I stared at a church with a huge dome. "It's Saint Issac's," he told me.

After about an hour, we arrived at the Nicolaievsky Bridge, next to the Winter Palace. A chapel constructed of smooth blue stone, sat at the center of the bridge. Its tulip-shaped dome was topped with a large cross. Three bays were built into its wall, the center one displaying a colorful mosaic of Saint Nickolas surrounded by angels. Nickolas was reading a book. "He's the protector of the poor from the rich," Boris said.

Pedestrians bowed or crossed themselves as they passed the chapel. Even carriage drivers stood up and put their hands on their hearts. "Be safe," Boris whispered to me. "We don't want them to know we're Jewish. Make

11

believe you're crossing yourself." Since being safe was my top priority, I followed Boris's lead.

We stopped a little past the chapel and looked over the side of the bridge. In the center of the river the ice had already melted and the water was flowing rapidly. Large sheets of ice were carried along toward the bridge. Whenever one of these collided with a concrete pillar there was a huge roar, like thunder, and the bridge shook. At either end of the bridge the ice hadn't yet melted and large piles of it had built up against the supports of the bridge. Some of these were almost as high as the wrought iron railing. With their screeching, I was convinced they were reaching for me. Occasionally there would be a rumble as one of them collapsed. For years that ice would attack me in my dreams.

It wasn't terribly cold, but there on the bridge I was shivering. I tightened the belt of the coat Papa had given me. The next day I was going out into a cold, cold world all on my own. I wished I were back in my bed in my village, so I could pull the covers over my head and be away from the scary noises. I stood there shaking for a long time, until Boris said, "Had enough? Ready to eat?" I nodded, and we started our long trek home. When we got to the house, we were welcomed by the smell of the goulash and potato pancakes Sophia had made for my last dinner in the old country.

My ship was departing in the morning. Boris had to work, so Sofia took me down to the port. She loaded me up with a big bag of food: bread, cheese and dried meat. After hugging me goodbye, she yelled as I crossed the walkway, "Take care. Do well in America. Write and let us know you arrived safely."

The ship—I don't remember its name—was a freighter that sometimes carried human cargo. For this trip, its twenty passengers, all Jewish, slept on hay-filled mattresses on cots arranged along the walls of a large windowless compartment. From the smell of the place, I suspected its last occupants were livestock.

Jews are not naturally born sailors, and when the sea was rough and one of us got seasick, almost everyone would throw up. There was only one bathroom, so we had to use the bucket provided with each cot. On a bad night the smell became unbearable. I was sick much of the time, wrapped up in my coat on the cot, and didn't partake of the soup that was provided in a large vat once a day. When the weather turned fair, I sat up on deck and studied the English book that Leena had given me. At those times, I became ravenously hungry and was thankful for Sofia's provisions. I must have lost ten pounds on the trip from my already skinny frame.

On the ship I met the Polovskys, a family that had left the Odessa region after repeated pogroms there. Mrs. Polovsky knew a little English, and would invite me to sit with her family when she taught it to her children. She had two boys and a girl. The youngest, Isak, about four years old, had a horrible cough. The Polinskys were frantic he would be detained when we got to America. "Stop coughing," each of them would tell Isak. That would make him cough even more.

After thirteen days, the captain announced we would be arriving in New York the next day. We were all so excited we couldn't sleep and stood on deck, peering into the distance. Shortly after sunrise, I was the first one to see land in the distance. "Land…America!" I called out. Everyone started to sing and dance.

Passing into New York harbor on a drizzly morning, we were greeted by the Statue of Liberty, with her robes and torch. Since then, I've had dreams where I wrapped myself in those robes. I once took a boat out to Liberty Island and climbed all the way up to the top of her torch.

When we were near the statue, a launch stopped our ship, and a health inspector and some policemen came aboard. "Is everyone up on deck?" the inspector, a short, thin man with a mustache asked in Yiddish.

"Yes," we all answered, although we could see the Polovskys were one person short. The inspector looked us all over and seemed on the verge of leaving the boat, when a cough came from behind the door that led down to our sleeping compartment. We all started to clear our throats and make other noises to cover up the sound of what by now had become a full-fledged coughing attack. It was too late. The inspector had heard it, and he and a policeman descended the stairs and brought a frightened, coughing Isak to the deck.

"We'll have to take him to the hospital," the inspector said, while Isak tried to escape from the policeman's iron grip.

"I'll go with him," said Mrs. Polovsky.

13

"Not allowed," the inspector said. "What's his name? We'll bring him back to you when he's better." None of us were sure he'd ever get better.

The policeman carried a screaming Isak down to the health department boat, while Mrs. Polovsky wailed on the deck. I looked at the Statue of Liberty; she had betrayed us so soon.

We were very disappointed when our ship sailed right past the tall buildings of New York, to New Jersey on the other side of the river. There we were put on a small boat that took us back out into New York Harbor. I gasped at the size of the building on Ellis Island. It seemed bigger than the Railroad Station in Saint Petersburg. When the boat pulled up at the dock, I picked up my canvas bag and joined the crowd. It felt wonderful to have solid ground under my feet again. I was happy, but being only sixteen, understandably nervous. *What would life be for me in this new country?*

Part II - New York

Chapter 2

I may be old, but I'm not stupid, so I know something is wrong as soon as I get back from my walk. Fat Goldfarb is sitting in his usual place: in the rocking chair on the porch of Gluckstein's Sun Spot, our single-room-occupancy hotel, down here in South Beach.

South Beach, Miami, where poor New York Jews go to get away from the cold weather. Most are so involved with stretching their social security, they don't see the beauty of the place before they die.

"So Abe, where did Ida go, with her suitcases and that son of hers?" Goldfarb says. He's so excited, I'm sure he peed in his diaper; his chance at last to get me for taking up with Ida.

That's the trouble with Florida, the weather's so good that a busybody like Goldfarb can sit outside all day and keep tabs on everyone's comings and goings. At least back in New York, bad weather keeps the gossips inside some of the time.

Of course, I don't answer him; I never speak to Goldfarb. But what he said disturbs me, so I hurry up the stairs—the elevator is so slow—and knock on the door of 305. No answer—now I'm really worried.

The hall where immigrants registered was bigger than the Saint Petersburg railway station. The first stop was the money-changing booth. Just as Papa had told me, my two gold Russian coins got me five American silver dollars. Next were the lines for medical exams, boys and men separate from girls, women and screaming babies. The lines were long but moved quickly. Babies cried and parents held on to their children and their belongings. At last I reached the medical station, where a doctor who spoke Yiddish asked me a number of questions. He looked suspiciously at my emaciated chest, but his stethoscope heard nothing, so he passed me through. Some people got stopped by the eye exam, where they were looking for trachoma, a very contagious disease that can make you blind. At the immigration table, the letter from Yudel and his five-year-old photo with an address on the back convinced the authorities that I had some place to stay in New York. My coins showed that I had the means to get there.

It was late afternoon when they put me on the ferry to the lower end of Manhattan Island—the Battery they called it. The weather had cleared, allowing me to size up my new home. The buildings of New York were not as elegant as those of Saint Petersburg. Nowhere did I see grand palaces or churches, although a half-dozen steeples rose above the other structures. But oh were they tall! In one at the tip of Manhattan I counted fifteen floors. I couldn't imagine why it didn't fall over. Then I saw another building under construction. It was built with a frame—I guess that was what held it up.

Rounding the tip of the island, I could see what looked like another city. Later, I learned it was Brooklyn, which had become part of New York shortly before I arrived. Huge towers, each with two pointed arches, stood on both sides of the river. I gaped at the bridge hanging from wires between the towers. It was five times as long as the Nicolaievsky in Saint Petersburg and hung a hundred feet above the water. Ice would never reach up to that bridge!

On both sides of the river the buildings seemed to go on forever. And people—I'd never seen so many people. From a distance it looked like we were approaching a huge anthill, on which a giant had just stepped.

When the ferry docked, many of the passengers were embraced by friends or relatives. No one was there for me. Carrying only a cloth bag with my meager possessions, I felt lost and panicked. How would I find Yudel's place in this great mass of humanity? I didn't even know in which direction to walk. I had worked on my English on the boat, but was it was good enough to get me around?

Someone touched my arm. I turned to see a young man, dressed in black, who looking at my *yarmulke*, said in Yiddish, "I see you're Jewish. We'd like to help you. Follow me." I meekly followed him over to a table, where other Jews were waiting for assistance from a group of men, who a sign indicated were members of the Workman's Circle.

"Do you have a place to live?" a Circle member asked me.

16

"I'm going to stay with my uncle." I showed him the address on the back of the photo.

"Do you know how to get there?" he asked.

"No," I shook my head.

"It's not too far." He turned his head and called, "Schmuel!"

A boy of about twelve extracted himself from a group that was standing behind the table. He wore a *yarmulke* and had the long curly sideburns called *peyes* favored by orthodox Jews. Beneath his black vest, hung the white fringes called *tzitzit*. "Yes?"

"Take this young man to this address—Hester Street, it's near Essex, I think."

"I know where it is," he said, and then turning to me, "Follow me."

As we wended our way through the crowd, I thought of Mama's warning. *Maybe she was wrong. Maybe in America you could trust strangers.*

While we hurried through the streets, Schmuel talked incessantly. He was fluent in both Yiddish and English and seamlessly crossed from one to another, allowing me to learn a few English words on the way. He told me he went to a *cheder*, where they were given off one day a month to do *mitzvahs*. Helping immigrants was his good deed. Schmuel was very mature and self confident; I would have been afraid to march around a city like New York when I was his age. He pointed out the sights to me on the way: the New York Stock Exchange, City Hall with the Brooklyn Bridge in the distance, his *cheder* and his *shul*.

"That's a really bad neighborhood," he warned me, pointing up a street teeming with people. "I'd stay away from there."

After about a mile of walking, the increasing number of *yarmulkes* and black hats and coats told me we were entering a Jewish neighborhood. Finally, Schmuel looked up at a number on a doorway and said, "This is the place. Let's see if he's home." We walked up to the second floor, where he knocked on a door—no answer. "He's probably still at work. I'll make sure he still lives here." Down by the entrance there was a line of mailboxes. Finding Yudel's name on one of them, Schmuel assured me that we were at the right place, and my uncle would soon be home. I thanked him for his

17

help, and told him I hoped we would meet again some day in New York. He beamed; he had done his *mitzvah*.

I was exhausted from not sleeping the previous night, so I laid my bag of possessions down in front of Yudel's door, put my head on it, and in no time was fast asleep. Not being tossed about on the boat was such a joy that I was sleeping soundly when a foot poking my thigh awakened me.

"What do we have here?" a booming voice said.

I sat up and saw a big fella. Except for more pounds and less hair, he looked like the guy in the photo, who I vaguely remembered from our *shtetl*, "Yudel?"

He looked at me. "Avrom, what a big boy you've become. I hardly recognized you."

I looked at him. "I didn't recognize you either—without your hat or *yarmulke*."

"You don't need a *yarmulke* in America," he answered, so I put mine in my pocket. I wanted to be an American. In an instant, out went the traditions of my village and five years of twice a week instruction by Rabbi Zev. "Cover your head in order that the fear of heaven may be on you," was written in the Talmud," he had said. Even though I had an overwhelming desire to fit into my new country, it was a while before I stopped worrying about being scolded, like the people in the *shtetl* would, if they found you bareheaded.

"This calls for a celebration." Yudel gave me a rough slap on the back. "I'm going to go out and get us some dinner. You can wait for me inside." He unlocked his door. "Have a seat. I'll be right back."

When Yudel got back, it was getting dark, so he lit the oil lamp, and spread out our feast: a roast chicken, a container of potato salad, some pickles and a big bottle of seltzer. "Now tell me everything," he said. "How are my sister and all my nieces? Tell me about the town and, of course, your trip."

I talked and Yudel soaked up everything. At one point, the door cautiously opened and a bearded fellow dressed in black with a hat came in. "This is Ansel, my boarder," Yudel said. "Ansel, this is Avrom, my nephew from the old country." Ansel nodded at me and without saying anything went

18

into the back room. Yudel must have been very hungry; he ate most of the chicken, wiping his greasy fingers on his shirt. He was also hungry for news from the old country. "And how is Dora Belchman?" he asked. "Did you ever see her?"

Dora was a neighbor, who my mother had said Yudel had been interested in. "She's married with two children now."

"And is she as slim as she used to be?"

"No, not any more." I jerked my head up in order to keep from dozing off.

"You look exhausted Avrom," Yudel said. "You can sleep in my bed—for tonight."

"Thank you," I murmured.

"Did you bring any money with you," he asked.

I showed him my five coins. He took four of them, "I'll hold these for you."

Yudel steered me into the front room, where I collapsed on his bed. I felt him taking off my shoes, like Mama would sometimes do back home. At last I was in America, and with someone who cared about me. The softness of Yudel's bed felt so good after sleeping on the hard cot in the boat for two weeks that I fell asleep in two minutes.

It seemed like I had just pulled the covers over my head, when Yudel shook me awake with, "Okay, sun's up—time to go to work."

Yudel worked at Henkel's Dress Factory. "It's a good place to work," he said. "Not a sweatshop, like most." He was a tailor—a big *macher*. His job was to take drawings and make them into samples for the skinny models to wear. I was a *nebbish*: a sweeper of floors, a carrier of packages, a doer of any dirty job that had to be done—for which I was paid a whole two dollars a week. Yudel took it and said, "For your room and board." He gave me a quarter to use for clothes and entertainment. "Don't spend it all in one place," he'd say every week with a chuckle. What he didn't know was sometimes when I delivered a package a nice lady or man gave me a nickel.

19

Room and board at Yudel's weren't much. The place measured ten by thirty feet, equally divided into three rooms. I slept on a straw mattress on the floor of the kitchen. Yudel's bed was in the front room, which had the only windows in the place. Ansel had the back room. On winter's nights, my room was heated by the glowing embers of the coal-burning stove. Yudel and Ansel huddled under their covers.

There were four apartments on our floor. The two in the back had an extra room. Each of the other apartments housed at least six people. We all shared one toilet in an unventilated closet in the hall. It usually smelled very bad. "We're lucky now," Yudel said. "Until two years ago, the whole building, all four floors, had to use one outhouse in the back yard." An outhouse didn't sound that bad to me. That's what we had in the *shtetl*. At least fresh air kept it from smelling so awful.

Dinner was bread and Yudel's stew: carrots and potatoes cooked up with the cheapest meat he could buy. For breakfast, he made oatmeal, and for lunch I took bread and a chunk of salami to work. Once in a while there was an egg, an apple or a piece of cheese, and for holidays, he bought a chicken. Although I yearned for Mama's cooking, I never went hungry, which, looking at the bones showing through the skin of some of our neighbors, meant I did better than most. Ansel was ultra-orthodox and never ate any food in the apartment. Yudel told me he had an arrangement to get his meals with an orthodox family.

Yudel talked to me in Yiddish, and I didn't get much opportunity to practice English at the factory. Fortunately, on Delancy Street or Hester Street, near where I lived, English wasn't necessary. My Yiddish and a quarter could get me a shirt and pants from a pushcart—although who knows who wore them before me.

The only time I had any conversation with Ansel was when he returned from a Passover *Seder*, his tongue loosened by the mandatory four cups of wine. Yudel had gone out, so Ansel sat down at the kitchen table and talked to me in Yiddish.

"It's a wonderful place—America," he said. "I've been here less than a year, and already I was able to buy boat tickets to bring my Biddle and Yosef over."

20

"How old is Yosef?"

"He's three now. I don't think he'll remember me."

"Why did you decide to leave your family?"

"Ever since Czar Alexander was assassinated, Christians have been killing Jews in Odessa. I don't know why—the assassins weren't even Jewish. Every couple of years the authorities work up the peasants, and they come around and massacre Jews in some *shtetl*. There's nothing they don't blame on Jews."

Since this was the first year ever I hadn't enjoyed a Passover *Seder*, I asked Ansel wistfully, "How was your *Seder*?"

"Wonderful! The Bimcoffs made a wonderful *Seder*. Reb Bimcoff allowed me to lead parts of it, and Mrs. Bimcoff made a wonderful meal." Ansel gazed up at the ceiling. "She reminds me of my Biddle, Hadar does, a real good Jewish woman. Would never show her hair or her ankles to a man other than her husband. Not like many other Jewish women who come here."

I can imagine what it must have been for Hadar Bimcoff to slave over a hot coal stove in a poorly ventilated tenement in those days. Maybe God could have allowed her to do without her wig and neck-to-foot covering when she was cooking the Passover meal.

On Friday nights, Yudel went to the bathhouse. It cost three cents, so while he was away, I would heat up some water on the stove, climb into the sink and wash myself. This was no easy matter and would have been impossible for Yudel. I don't know what Ansel did, but from his smell, I didn't think he washed very often.

On the first Friday of every month, after his bath, Yudel would meet with some of his *landsmen*, guys from our *shtetl* who had come to New York.

"Come sit with us for a while," he said to me. "We meet at the Vilna tea shop at the corner of Rivington and Ludlow at eight. They love to get news from the old country." When he saw me hesitate, he added, "I'll buy you a piece of strudel."

I couldn't turn down a piece of strudel. "Sure, I'll be there," I said. I would have preferred he returned the money he took from me, but I was afraid to ask him. After all, he could have put me out in the street.

The Vilna was a poorly heated, dingy place with sawdust on the floor. Its only advantage was it had so little business, that for two cents you could buy a pot of tea and sit all night at one of its four tables, which shared the light of a single bulb hanging by a wire from the ceiling. Yudel and three of his *landsmen* were there when I arrived.

"Avrom, let me introduce you to the gang from the old country. This is Nassan and this Pinchas, both sewing-machine operators in shirtwaist factories. They've been in America a while, so I don't think you know them."

Nathan and Pinchas were both in their twenties and, like Yudel, had the well-scrubbed look of a Friday-night bath. In the frigid room, they sat in clean white shirts with their black coats draped over the backs of their chairs. They both stood and shook my hand.

"Most people call me Nathan, now," Nassan said, glancing at Yudel. "You might want to call yourself Abe."

Abe—that had a nice sound to it, and pretty soon I adopted it.

"And this Dovid Fenkel," Yudel continued. "He's been here about a year and sells vegetables from a pushcart. Perhaps you know him from Zyvotov?"

From his smell, I guessed Dovid probably hadn't bathed since he had come to America. He was continually scratching his scalp through a bush of unruly hair, and his black jacket was stained with either his dinner or his wares. I recognized him from the school back in the *shtetl*, where he had been a few years ahead of me. We nodded at each other.

"Let me get you some tea and strudel," Yudel said, getting up and going to the counter.

"How long have you been here?" Nathan asked.

"Only five months."

"It's quite different from Zyvotov, eh?" Pinchas laughed.

"I've never seen so many people," I admitted.

Yudel came back to the table carrying the tea and the strudel I was dying to sink my teeth into. He asked the group, "Moshe's not coming again tonight?"

"I stopped to pick him up," Nathan said. "But he's still in bed with that cough."

"Has he seen a doctor?" Pinchas asked.

"I don't think he can afford one." Nathan said. "He probably doesn't even have enough to rent his pushcart."

"We've got to do something about that," Yudel said. He put a five-dollar bill on the table. Nathan matched him, and Pinchas and Dovid each added a few dollars.

"I'll bring him this," Nathan said. "Maybe it'll help. God willing, he'll be able to do the same for us someday, if we need it, God forbid."

"You see, Avrom," Yudel said, turning his head to me, "You're not alone in America. You can always count on your friends from the old country."

"Now tell us what's new back home," Pinchas said. He had slicked-back hair and a dapper mustache.

I told them about the soldiers grabbing older boys for the army at the fireworks celebration.

"My father wrote me about that," Dovid said. "Once they get you, they can keep you in the army for ten...even twenty years."

"I heard that they won't stop beating you unless you convert to Christianity," Pinchas added.

Although the strudel didn't match what we had in the *shtetl*, now I could better understand why Papa had sent me to America.

At Henkel's we worked from eight to six, Monday through Thursday; eight to five on Friday; and one to seven on Sunday. Saturdays, Mr. Henkel went to *shul*, Yudel stayed in bed, and I explored New York City. The trolleys and the El were for rich people, so I walked. Setting off with some bread and a chunk of cheese or salami in my pocket and a flask of water on my belt, I would walk from morning until night.

At first I stayed in the neighborhood—the Lower East Side—where almost everyone spoke Yiddish. So many people there—you can't imagine.

23

There were more people on one block in the neighborhood than in our whole *shtetl*. You had to push your way through the street. There were more customers waiting on line at the butcher shop than my father saw all day. Pushcarts were everywhere, selling fruits, vegetables, pots, fabrics, underwear, buttons—anything you could want.

One day I was pushing through the crowd on Grand Street, when a man grabbed my arm and started to pull me toward a store.

"No money," I called out, just like Yudel had told me, but that didn't stop the man from pulling me.

"Trade," he said, pointing to my coat.

I didn't know what "trade" meant, and the man didn't follow my protestations in Yiddish. His grip was so strong, I allowed him to pull me down the three steps and into the store, where a bearded Jew was sitting just inside the door in front of a small table on which was box containing coins and a few bills.

"Don't pull the customer so hard, Tony," he said to the younger man in English, and then to me in Yiddish, "My apologies, but Tony got all excited about your coat. It looks like a Russian army coat. I would be interested in buying it from you—say for 50 cents. I'll throw in something else you can wear home."

"This coat was a gift from my father," I told him, "when I left the old country. I could never sell it."

"Such a good young man," he said. "Sit down and have a cup of tea with me. My name is Jakob."

I wasn't in a hurry, so I sat and talked with Jakob for a while. Several customers came in, picked out an article of clothing and stepped behind a partition to try it on. That was an advantage of buying clothes from a store rather than from a pushcart. On the way out they haggled with Jakob over the price. Jakob had a good eye in judging just how satisfied the customer was with the clothing, and usually he was able to add a coin or two to his box. Jacob was a *Litvak*, a Jew from Lithuania, and in between customers we shared stories about the old country.

When I got up to leave, Jakob said to me, "Stop by and have a cup of tea with me, when you get a chance. I'm always sitting right here and I get lonely. I would have had a son your age, but he died of the cholera when he was ten."

I did stop by and visit Jakob occasionally. He became one of my first friends in America.

One pushcart sold Yiddish books. For ten cents I bought a Yiddish-English dictionary small enough to fit in my pocket. It helped me read the signs as I walked around the city. I didn't want any other Yiddish books; I was going to learn English!

I still remember the smells down on the Lower East Side: baking bread and cinnamon in front of the bakery, herring near the barrels in the fish store, roasting chickens by the deli. And everywhere, the stench of human bodies, washed too infrequently.

So much noise, you can't imagine: butchers chopping, peddlers calling out their wares and singing in six different languages, live chickens cackling. It was especially bad down at the end of Delancy Street where they were building a new bridge. The tower to support the bridge was already three times as tall as any of the surrounding buildings, and an army of workers was transporting bricks to extend it even further into the air. This Williamsburg Bridge would be even longer than the Brooklyn Bridge at the tip of Manhattan. That amazed me.

Gradually I got the courage to extend my walks away from the safety of *yarmulke*s and black hats to other neighborhoods. In one, most of the men wore just undershirts, and there was a bar on every block. Tough-looking guys lounged outside the bars, and I was glad I wasn't wearing a *yarmulke* as I passed them. I found if I walked quickly and looked only in front of me, I usually wouldn't be noticed. If one of them said something to me, I would make like I didn't hear it, or understand it—which at the beginning, I usually didn't. What freedom it was to be able to walk anywhere I wanted! Not at all like the old country.

The food they were selling in these other neighborhoods was different from that in the Jewish section, especially the seafood. There were unusual fishes with big whiskers, things that looked like snakes, but I was told were eels, and lots of different things with shells, including ugly creatures called shrimp. I even saw a large slimy thing with eight arms. Ugh, I still can't imagine eating that!

I was fascinated by the part of the city called Chinatown. I didn't remember ever seeing a Chinese person in the old country—and here there were thousands of them. Chinese foods were very strange: grasses, roots, new types of cabbages and squashes covered with bumps. There were stands where you could buy ready-to-eat chicken feet and all sorts of dumplings. If I had some money, I would have sampled all these delicacies. My favorite store in the whole city was in Chinatown. It sold colorful birds with big beaks in cages and many of them could talk. Usually they spoke Chinese, but the red and green one next to the door said, "Ni hao, hello," to anyone entering the shop. The shopkeeper didn't mind my coming in and looking over his birds.

On the Bowery I passed a tall woman with full breasts and blond hair wearing a tight bodice. "Want some, cutie," she asked me in a man's voice. I wasn't sure what she meant, so I hesitated. "Don't worry, for you no charge," she said. It made me shiver.

I even saw people with black skin—who, I was told, came from Africa. They usually had low-level jobs like sweeping up horse dung from the streets or throwing garbage into the carts that circulated throughout the city.

To the west there was an interesting neighborhood. It had narrow streets and crooked alleys, just like in our *shtetl*. Wash hung from lines between the two-story row houses. With most of the pushcarts confined to a couple of market areas, the streets were a lot quieter than they were on the East Side. This Greenwich Village was so like our *shtetl*, I could almost imagine myself being back in the Ukraine.

Up north it was a completely different world. No undershirts up there. The ladies were dressed in stylish fashions, like those made by Henkel's. They held the arms of gentlemen, who helped them down from carriages.

At Thirty-fourth Street they had just opened Macy's, the largest store in the world. Eight floors, I counted them myself, covering almost an entire block. On a cold Saturday in December, it seemed there were more than a thousand people in the store. I started at the top and explored every floor.

When I got to the men's wear section, I could picture myself wearing the stylish clothes. Of course, my money wouldn't go very far in there. Suddenly a large hand grabbed my shoulder from behind. I froze. Just like two years earlier on the fireworks field, it spun me around.

"Let's see what you got under dat coat," a big fella in a vest and jacket said to me. My English wasn't yet too good, so I didn't understand what he wanted of me and just stared at him. He grabbed the belt of my coat and pulled it open, then patted down all my pockets.

"Okay, you got any money?" That I understood. I showed him the 32 cents in my pocket.

He sneered at me. "That won't buy you much here. Get on your way. We don't want gawkers here."

I quickly left the store. It seemed like in America, there were places you weren't welcome if you didn't have much money.

My favorite street was Fifth Avenue—someplace to get away from the noise of the city. The houses were huge; I couldn't believe that just a single family and their servants lived in one of these palaces. I wanted to get a better look through the windows or into the gardens, but the police and uniformed doormen made sure I kept on moving. Fifth Avenue ended in a vast park with hills and lakes. Here I could lie down, eat my lunch and nap before starting home.

In New York there was always something new to see. It aroused my curiosity. I could no longer be homesick for Zyvotov, where I had already explored every corner.

Chapter 3

"Did Ida go out?" I ask Gomez at the front desk, when I come back down to the lobby.

"She gone," he says—not looking me in the eyes, which is always a bad sign. "But she left something for you." He hands me an envelope.

I want to rip it open right there, but I restrain myself, since Goldfarb is standing by the door. I take it up to 407—that's my room— and with shaky fingers open it and read:

"Abe, My son, Bruce, made an appointment for me to see a doctor at Sloan-Kettering on Friday. Since he also made a plane reservation, I have to go back to New York with him this afternoon. Sorry to leave without saying goodbye, but I can't miss the plane. I'll write you. Love, Ida."

My heart drops in my chest.

During my first winter in America, Mr. Henkel installed another row of sewing machines in the factory. One of the new operators was a woman of about fifty—a widow, short and plump, with soft brown eyes and dark hair that hung over one side of her face. Mina had been born in the Ukraine, not far from our village and had come to America about ten years earlier. Yudel immediately took a shine to her, and they would talk while eating lunch together next to the window. My curiosity got me to walk by, trying to overhear what they were saying.

"Avrom, come here," Yudel said. "Mina, this is my nephew, Avrom. Only six months from the old country."

"Such a fine boy," Mina said with a big smile. I think I liked her right away.

She reminded me of my mother, so I asked, "Do you have any children?"

"No, Morris and I were never blessed with children. Maybe it was for the best. How could I have supported them when he died?"

Just then the bell rang; everyone had to go back to work.

For the first time since I had arrived in America, Yudel started to go out at night. Mostly he would eat dinner at Mina's place.

"She's a great cook," he said one night on returning with a smile on his face.

"That's good. I'm glad you're happy," I answered, annoyed at having had to eat greasy salami for two meals that day.

"Here's a piece of chicken she made. You can eat it for tomorrow's dinner."

Suddenly, things were looking up.

"You know, Avrom," he said. "God didn't want man to be alone. That's why he took Adam's rib and made woman." A few weeks later, he told me he and Mina were going to get married.

"Getting married," I stammered. What would happen to me? Would Yudel abandon me like my family did? I was only seventeen years old, with one small carton of possessions and a two-dollar a week job. I could starve to death. "Congrat...ulations," I said.

Yudel must have noticed my reaction. "Don't worry," he said. "I'm going to move in with Mina. She has three rooms. There'll be space for you."

What a relief I felt!

On the Saturday before the wedding, Yudel hired a cart to help us move his bed, one chair, and a half-dozen cartons of clothes, books and utensils. We sold the rest of our stuff to a neighbor for a few dollars. We walked beside the cart as the driver made his way to Mina's place. Mina lived two blocks north of Houston Street. The cart driver helped us lug our stuff up three flights of stairs, and Yudel tipped him a quarter.

Finally, I had a chance to see my new home. So different from Yudel's place; it was an apartment, not a tenement. In the living room, Mina had a soft armchair. We put Yudel's bed against the wall and, with a new spread and some large pillows, it became a daybed—meaning it was a couch during the day and a place for me to sleep at night. In the bedroom, which, like the living room had a window, Yudel and Mina slept in a double bed. There was enough room in there for a small desk, a chair and large chest of drawers.

"You can keep your stuff in here," Mina said, opening a large wooden trunk next to the day bed.

The apartment had a separate kitchen, with a small table and four chairs. Most important, it had electricity. With a lamp next to my bed, I could study my English at night. There was a bathroom right in the apartment, with a tub that you could fill with hot water from the stove. It wasn't Fifth Avenue, but to me, it was a castle.

On Tuesday, Yudel, Mina and I were given the afternoon off with Mr. Henkel's blessing. We walked down to City Hall, where Golda and Naomi, two of Mina's friends, joined us. They were both married, but their husbands couldn't get off from work for the occasion. Pinchas and Nassan couldn't get off from work either, but Dovid, with the bushy hair, showed up while we were waiting. "Someone is watching my pushcart, I'll have to get back," he told us. He smelled and was scratching his head. Golda and Naomi tried to keep their distance from him.

After filling out some papers, Mina and Yudel stood with ten other couples as a judge declared them "man and wife." At this time all the couples kissed. Yudel and Mina were especially passionate, with him lifting her a foot off the ground during the kiss. I realized that that night I'd be sleeping just a thin wall away from their honeymoon bed.

After the ceremony, Yudel, in a rare show of extravagance, hired two carriages to take us all back to Mina's apartment. The newly married couple was in the first, and I was wedged between Golda and Naomi in the second. In the carriage, the women talked over me, and I felt their thighs and, at one time a breast, against me. Being a healthy teenager with natural instincts, by the time we got back to the apartment, I was embarrassed to get out of the carriage.

At the apartment, there was *schnapps* and a wonderful lemon sponge cake that Mina had baked. Following Yudel's lead, I swigged down my drink in a single gulp, which put me into a long coughing fit. Everyone laughed, and I decided I'd better have just one. The grownups suffered no such inhibitions, and pretty soon everyone was getting a little silly. Yudel sang some folk songs from the old country. I hadn't realized he had such a good, rich voice. Even though I didn't know how to dance, each of the

30

women in succession hooked her arm through mine and hopped around the apartment. At about five, things came to an end when Golda and Naomi had to go home and make their husbands' dinner. As they left, Yudel winked at me, and pressing a quarter into my hand, said, "Avrom, get yourself a nice restaurant meal tonight." I was glad to get out of there and made sure not to come back until after midnight.

Mina put her foot down, when she found out Yudel was letting me keep only twenty-five cents of my pay. "The boy has to have fun, not to mention save up some money," I heard her say through the thin bedroom wall. The next week Yudel started letting me keep a full dollar.

Sometimes when Yudel wasn't home, Mina and I would sit at the kitchen table and drink tea. She would tell me about her life. Morris, her husband, had been an accountant in Kiev. When the city officials expelled all the Jews from the inner city, they moved to America. Morris found a job as a bookkeeper, and they were able to move into this nice apartment. A downstairs neighbor was an agent for New York Life Insurance Company and talked Morris into buying a policy. Six months later he had a heart attack and died.

"Without that policy, I would have been out in the street. It gave me time to buy a sewing machine and learn how to use it."

I was sorry that Mina's husband had died, but glad to be living in her apartment.

Chapter 4

I couldn't sleep last night. Besides the usual aches and pains, I missed having her next to me. It's not the warmth. God knows, it's warm enough down here in Miami Beach. Maybe it's the thought that with her, if something happens, I wouldn't just lie here until the end of the month, when they come around to collect the rent. At my age it's dangerous to live alone.

Damn Abe, don't pretend, admit it! She's something special and you miss her...and you can't understand how she just upped and left like she did.

I remember Ida and I first met, as most guests at the Sun Spot do, while waiting for its incredibly slow elevator. I first noticed her figure. Not that I looked her up and down, but even from the side of my eye, I could tell she was unusually trim for someone her age, which I later found to be 77. We both inspected our toes until the door opened. I was by the buttons, so I pressed four and asked, "What floor?"

"Three. Please." She answered in a lively voice. She looked too young for this place.

As the elevator crept up, I thought: It's now or never. So I said, "Abe Sokolovsky, room 407."

She looked up. "Ida Blinsky, room 305, I just moved in." She smiled and held out her hand. We just had time to shake before the elevator door opened and she was gone.

The warmth of her hand remained in mine. It had been some time since I'd touched a woman. I recalled what I could of her appearance: dark grey hair, bobbed with bangs reaching to her brows; glasses, but not the really thick-lens ones; top of her head up to my nose, that would make her about five foot three. A slight aroma of her perfume, not the type that smelled like powder, lingered in the elevator.

In August, Henkel's Dresses, which was on the top floor of a four-story building, got unbearably hot. Sweat poured down the faces of the sewing machine operators. When a young woman fainted, several of the women carried her to the couch in Mr. Henkel's office and had her sip some water. They told us she was pregnant and unable to hold down any food in the morning.

During the half hour allotted for lunch, workers sat by the open windows or climbed out onto the fire escape. I preferred to take the utility stairs two flights up to the roof. There you could usually find a little breeze, but since it was the tallest building on the block, the sun beat down on you mercilessly. At the walls, you could look down on the workers on the surrounding roofs. Yudel often came up there, took off his shirt off and tried to get a little tan on his pallid east-European body. Usually, all he managed was a bright red sunburn.

One day, I hurried up to the roof and got the best spot, sitting in the shade of the chimney. Looking over my recently purchased map of the city, I planned my excursion for Saturday. *Brooklyn: I'd never been there. I could walk over the Brooklyn Bridge. Maybe I could make it all the way to Prospect Park and back.*

I was so engrossed in the map I didn't even notice the pair of small feet poking out from a long blue dress next to me. "Could I share some of your shade, sonny?" the bearer of the feet said.

My glance moved up over her slim figure, corseted in the S-shape of the day, to her oval face, framed by curly, short blond hair. I didn't know what "sonny" meant, so I said, "My name is Abe, not Sonny."

"Mine is Helen," she answered, placing a piece of cloth on the roof before sitting down. "Can't get this dress dirty. A buyer is coming to look at it after lunch." After managing to sit down in her corset, she pulled her dress above her knees and said, "Whew, it's tough to wear a winter dress this time of year."

The chimney didn't provide much shade, so Helen sat close enough to me that our shoulders rubbed. With the contact and a whiff of her perfume, my teenage mind forgot all about the map.

"Abe? That's not what I heard Yudel call you," Helen said.

"He call me Avrom—name from old country. But it Abe now."

"The old country? Where's that?"

"They call it Ukraine—part of Russia."

"How long have you been in America?"

"One year and four months." I inhaled a mixture of her natural smell and perfume.

"Your English is pretty good for being here such a short time."

"Thank you much."

"Whatcha reading?"

"Is map of New York. Every Saturday I walk in city. I plan next trip now."

"A map of New York. I never saw one of those. Show it to me. How do you read it? Where are we now?"

I pointed on the map. "We here—on Essex, between Broome and Grand. This is Manhattan."

I'd never seen anyone get as excited over a map as Helen did. All the places she had visited suddenly fell into their proper relationship. She had me point out a half-dozen streets on the map.

"And this is Brooklyn," I said. "And this is Brooklyn Bridge. I walk to Brooklyn Saturday."

"The Brooklyn Bridge. I've seen it, but never walked over it. Want some company?"

"What means company?"

"Company means I go along with you."

"Sounds good."

"What time are you leaving?"

"I leave eight o'clock."

"That's pretty early. Could you make it nine?"

"Okay."

"Great! Let's meet in front of Katz's. Do you know where that is? Corner of Houston and Ludlow Streets—anyone can point you to it."

"Sounds good—nine o'clock—Katz's delicatessen."

"See you Saturday. I gotta go now and powder my face."

So I had my first date in America. In fact, my first date ever. I looked over at Yudel. He didn't seem pleased. That night, as he and I were

34

walking home, he said, "You know Avrom, that Helen, she's a nice girl. I should say lady; she's almost ten years older than you. But she's a *shiksa*—not Jewish. I hope you don't have any ideas. Your mother would never forgive me."

"Oh no, nothing to worry about," I answered. He didn't need to know about my date.

How well I still remember everything about my date with Helen, three-quarters of a century ago. I was up early, and grabbed some tea and bread for breakfast. I pulled a few hard-earned coins from under my straw mattress and was out on the street before eight. From a pushcart man I bought a small backpack. He wanted twenty cents, but I haggled him down to a dime, just like Yudel had shown me. In a bakery I bought two fresh bagels for a nickel and in the grocery, a three-cent wedge of yellow cheese. My flask was full of water. Then I realized I'd need a knife to cut the cheese. No problem, another pushcart provided a kitchen knife for a penny. *This dating was expensive.* I sure hoped Helen would show up.

When the clock in Katz's window reached a quarter after nine, I was ready to leave on my own. But then I saw Helen. Her blond hair and loose-fitting white cotton dress contrasted with the shabbiness of the neighborhood. Heads turned to watch her cross the street. I hadn't realized she was so beautiful.

"Like my dress?"

"I like very much."

"It's a tennis dress from Henkel's. Mr. Henkel sometimes lets me keep the dresses I model. I think he has an eye for me."

I thought any red-blooded man would have an eye for Helen. I was proud to be walking with her. She was very much a woman and I was still a boy. I had anticipated she would get a lot of attention from men, so I had mapped out a route that kept us away from the toughest neighborhoods.

"It's amazing how little of the city I've seen since I moved here," Helen said peering into the window of a shop that sold beads and jewelry.

"Where you live before?"

"I'm from Connecticut. That's to the north. My parents have a dairy farm—about twenty cows. It's hard work and dull, dull, dull. I had to get

35

out of there. Tell me a little about you. Why'd you come to America all by yourself?"

It was the first time ever I had had a chance to talk about myself to a woman. The whole story poured out of me: my parents, my four sisters, the village, and how things were so bad for Jews in the old country they had to send me away.

"Jewish men make good husbands. Not a religious one for me, of course—but maybe one of those rich buyers who come around to Henkel's." I guessed someone in my financial situation could never even dream of having a girl like Helen.

We walked down Broadway so absorbed in our conversation that the park came upon us suddenly. Beyond the park and City Hall, the tower of the bridge loomed. It was even wider and longer than I remembered from my first day in America.

Brooklyn Bridge was a very popular destination for New Yorkers on a warm Saturday in summer. Crowds of people moved along the wide avenue leading to it. Halfway up, the pedestrian walkway separated from the main road and ran above it. A policeman stood by a toll box to insure each person paid his penny before proceeding. I dropped in my two cents. The roadway, with carriages, carts and a trolley ran about twenty feet below, and each time a heavy cart or the trolley passed, the walkway would shake.

By the tower, the walkway opened out to a large platform, where about fifty people stood around. From here you could look down on the tops of the surrounding buildings. Women were leaning out of windows to hang out their laundry. On the rooftops, people beat rugs or just sat around reading and sunning themselves. On one rooftop, I saw pigeon coops. Looking over the side, you could see a half-dozen barges coming up the river. Up here, there was a fresh breeze and the smell of salt water replaced the odor of decay in the city.

"We're up so high," said Helen, "I think I'm getting dizzy."

"Not good to look down. Hold on to railing. Breathe like this." I took some deep breaths. It made me feel powerful to help her.

Helen calmed herself, and after about five minutes, I asked, "You want walk across bridge?"

36

She looked across at the other tower, which seemed a long way off. "I guess I can do it. But you'll have to hold my hand. I'm a little scared."

Well, that didn't seem like much of a chore. Hand in hand we started off on the walkway that crossed the main span of the bridge. Since it was about ten feet across, I really didn't think there was much chance that Helen would fall off. After about fifty feet, I guess she didn't either, since she dropped my hand and edged over a little closer to the rail. "Just think, if I hadn't seen you looking at that map, I might have never seen this view."

We stopped again on the platform at the tower on the Brooklyn side. Although I was too excited to eat, the position of the sun told me it was lunchtime. "You want eat? I have bagels and cheese."

"Just a little bit."

I cut off two pieces of the cheese and broke one of the bagels in half. We stood against the rail, eating and washed our food down with water.

"We'd better head back," Helen said. "I've got fair skin; I don't want to burn. It wouldn't do for a model to get sunburned. You don't have to worry; you're dark."

I looked out at Brooklyn before we left. The houses stretched for miles, but I could see a number of wooded areas. To the right, the elegant houses perched on cliffs looked dangerously close to falling into the water. Some day, I'd have to come back and explore that side of the river.

On the way back, Helen asked me, "Abe, now that you're here in America, what are your plans?"

My plans? That was a question that I had never considered. It never came up in the old country. There, if you were a Jew and your father was a butcher, that meant you would be a butcher in the same village—if the peasants, or the Cossacks didn't burn the place down. Most likely you'd never travel more than fifty miles from home. You weren't even allowed to live in a big city like Kiev.

"I want... learn English... become citizen... see New York ... America... even whole world," I stammered.

"I don't know about America or the world, but I'd like to see some more of New York. Let me know when you're going again." That sounded nice. I guess it meant my date had been successful.

We were passing in front of an Irish bar. Three men stood outside, surrounded by the odor of stale beer. One of them put his fingers in his mouth and gave a whistle. Another said, "Hey babe, come on in here. Let us buy you a drink. Dump that greenhorn."

I was so embarrassed, the blood rose in my face. "Greenhorn" was the worst thing you could call a …greenhorn. They had just spoiled the most perfect day of my life. But what could I do? Any one of those guys could have torn me apart.

Helen held my arm and pulled me along. "Don't let them get to you, Abe. They don't mean anything by it. You don't want to get in a fight and get hurt."

It was good advice that Helen gave me. In all my years walking around New York, I managed to walk away from a lot of potentially violent situations. Only once did I get into a fight…and yes, I got whipped.

About a month later, Helen and I went on another outing. She brought our lunch in a little basket and I dropped nickels in the turnstiles of the Third Avenue El. It was my first trip on the elevated railway. The train was pretty empty because it was Saturday. I took a window seat with Helen sitting next to me. The train made a clackety clack. Like the greenhorn I was, I pressed my nose against the window to reassure myself that we were traveling on rails and not just through the air. On that warm morning, windows in the apartments next to the tracks were open, and I got a fleeting glimpse of life all the way up the East Side.

We got off the train at 109th Street and walked a few blocks west to Central Park. I carried the basket of food Helen had prepared. She skipped along by my side. "You very happy?" I asked.

"Yes," she said holding up her left hand that sported what looked like a diamond ring. "Didn't you notice my ring? I'm engaged."

"Engaged—what that?"

"That's when you've told someone that you'll marry him, and he gives you a ring to seal the deal."

"Seal the deal?"

"To make sure he doesn't just want to use you, then back out."

"Oh. Who lucky fellow?" I asked, trying to hide my jealousy.

"His name is Ben Hartman and he's from Cincinnati, Ohio. His father owns a small department store there, and he comes to New York to buy ladies' clothing."

Ben Hartman—that sounded Jewish. It looked like Helen got her wish: to marry a rich Jew. I was heartbroken. I guess I always knew that there couldn't be anything serious between us, but this closed off all possibilities.

"You know him long time?"

"Not long. I met him when he was here about a year ago. He comes four times a year, and when he was here a couple of weeks ago he asked me to marry him—but only if I would convert to Judaism."

"You will become Jew?"

"I said yes. No big deal. I'm not religious. Haven't been to church in a couple of years. I've started taking lessons from a rabbi."

"Welcome to Jewish people." It was funny. Here, I was becoming less and less Jewish since I'd come to America, while Helen was becoming a Jew.

"Look, who knows—this might be my last chance. I'm twenty-five and not getting any younger. Ben is a great guy and really rich. I've seen some photos of his parents' house in Cincinnati. It's huge! We won't live there, of course. We'll have a house of our own." I didn't know why Helen was trying to explain her decision, it seemed perfectly reasonable to me.

We walked in silence through the tree-shaded lanes of the great park until we found a bench where we sat down and ate. Helen beamed as she displayed the contents of her lunch basket.

"Look at these sandwiches I made," she said, holding up small squares of crust-less bread. "They're like the ones they served at a party Ben took me to. Cheese, no meat—the rabbi says Jews don't mix meat and milk. I'm going to have to learn to be a Jewish society hostess."

"You move to Cincinnati? I miss you," I stammered.

"Oh, that's sweet. Don't worry; I'll see you again. Ben says I've got a great eye for women's styles. He's going to bring me with him whenever he comes to New York...until I have babies, of course."

"That is good."

Helen handed me a sandwich and a slice of raw carrot. It wasn't much to eat. I finished it quickly.

Helen looked down and said, "Abe, do you mind if I ask you a personal question?"

"Personal question, what that?"

"I was wondering if you ever kissed a girl?"

"Kiss a girl? Sure." I assumed my sister, Leena, counted.

"How about in America? Have you kissed a girl in America?"

"No, not in America."

"I'm sure you'll kiss lots of them, with those deep brown eyes of yours."

Then Helen looked into my eyes and said, "Abe, I'd like to be the first girl you kiss in America. Would you like that?"

"Like that very much."

Helen turned her face and leaning towards me, gave me a kiss of such gentleness, that I can still remember how her lips felt against mine after all these years. The kiss was long, but not sexual. I think it said: *If only you were a little older…and rich…who knows what could happen between us.*

I let her do the kissing. After all she was almost a married woman.

After eating, we continued walking west of the park. On high ground, overlooking the Hudson River, large blue signs announced that the buildings belonged to Columbia University. One was a large library with a concrete dome. It reminded me of Saint Issac's Cathedral in Saint Petersburg. The library was at one end of a quadrangle of attractive buildings built from brick and stone. Students wearing ties and jackets were walking around, and a few of them gave Helen an admiring glance. I felt very proud to have just kissed her… I mean to just have been kissed by her.

We passed by a manicured grass-covered field, where students were kicking a ball around. Behind them, I could see a track, where a running competition was going on. Staring through the wire fence, it occurred to me how different my life was from that of these students. America offered you opportunity, but it was very difficult to reach the good life.

A few blocks north we came across the red brick buildings of Barnard College. A number of the girls were wearing dresses similar to Helen's, but none of them were as pretty as her.

We returned to lower Manhattan by the West-Side El. Our walking had exhausted Helen. She sat close to me on the train and rested her head on my shoulder. Pretty soon her regular breathing indicated she had fallen asleep. I breathed in the lingering smell of her perfume and her hair tickled my face. I was sad thinking that this would probably be our last outing.

Chapter 5

Two weeks have passed and Ida hasn't written. I can't stand not knowing what happened to her. Why couldn't she wait around to say goodbye and tell me whether she'll ever come back? It isn't right she left the way she did. I could send her a letter—Gomez gave me her son's address, where they're forwarding her mail. But what good would that do? If she were going to write, she would have already. I could call, but to tell you the truth, I've never liked talking on the telephone; it makes me freeze up.

No, what I've got to say to Ida has to be said face-to-face. I've made up my mind: I'm going up to New York to find her and try to get her to come back. Her son's place will be a good place to start looking. Don't know what will happen after that.

I spoke to Gluckstein, that gonif. He wouldn't refund any of my rent for the month. I packed all my stuff in two suitcases and a carton and left it in the room. If I'm not back by the end of the month, he'll put them in his storage room and charge me ten dollars a month. If he doesn't get his money, he'll sell it all. He made me sign a paper agreeing to that.

October in New York: it's going to be chilly up there and I'll probably have to do a lot of walking. Lucky I've kept the overcoat and hat I used to wear when I lived up there. I'll carry them and pack a suitcase with shirts, underwear, toiletries, and of course my scrapbook, which I always take with me.

Most guys my age wouldn't be up for this job. But I'm so healthy it's scary. Wear glasses, of course, and talk a little too loud, as those whose hearing isn't perfect usually do. Only been under the knife once: for a hernia, if you don't count those things they took off my skin. I got them from walking around in the sun. I only take one pill a day—for my blood pressure. Of course I put my teeth in a glass most nights—but what guy my age doesn't?

Maybe it's because I've lived a healthy life: never smoked and hardly ever drank. I walked long distances all my life, and, in my early days, I played basketball. I think I was happiest when I was playing basketball.

Down the block from Henkel's, at the corner of Hester and Essex Streets, there was a park. It didn't look like Central Park, or any park you see today. It had no trees, and not a single blade of grass grew there. Any that tried were soon trampled by the hundreds of people who milled about at all hours. It was just an open space of packed earth, where most of the day sunlight could reach the ground because it wasn't blocked by buildings. It had swings and climbing bars for children and stands where older people could sit, either in the sun or the shade. Bands sometimes played there on weekends. And on the southern end of the park, marked off by ropes was a basketball court; we would call it a half court today.

Nowadays, the park is very different and run by the city. It's called Seward Park. I've gone back there a number of times. On its tree-shaded paths, women push baby carriages and people sit on benches. The park has a large fountain centered on a mosaic map of the neighborhood. There's equipment for children, a jogging track, tennis courts, and yes, it still has a basketball court.

Sometimes on Sunday, before work, I joined the groups of men who watched the basketball games in the park. Those games were very different from what you see on TV today. The ball was at least twice as heavy, and it was often lumpy. As you can imagine, this didn't make for good dribbling, especially when the ground was wet. The ball was usually moved around with lightening-fast passes that could easily dislocate a finger. Players maneuvered for position when they didn't have the ball. They wore neither uniforms nor special shoes. On Sunday, many of them had just come from church and were in their best clothes: including vests, jackets and hats. Even though some of the players were good two-handed shooters, scoring was a relatively rare event and an occasion for applause and hollering from the fans. Ten baskets won a game, which typically took between fifteen and thirty minutes. The winning team won the right to "defend the court" against new challengers.

Between games, onlookers like myself had a chance to take a few shots. One Sunday, I amazed myself when one of my shots went through the hoop. I was basking in my success, when a player who was organizing a challenging team called out to me, "Hey kid, wanna play?" I was supposed to be at work in ten minutes, but that was an invitation I couldn't turn down.

I soon learned that sinking a basket was a lot easier when you're unguarded than when a hand is being waved in your face. Also, retrieving the ball after someone's shot is a lot harder than it looks. The fella I was playing against was slow, but at least fifty pounds heavier than me. I couldn't keep him from pushing his way under the basket. Twice the ball was thrown to him there, and once he scored. I could only make feeble attempts to block his shots.

I was fast and quick, but whenever I tried to run to the basket an elbow or foot would block my way. Once I found myself on the ground. Getting up, I assessed the situation; I thought I knew how to handle it. The next time our team had the ball, I started to dart around my defender's right side. Predictably, his right foot came out to trip me. Then I quickly changed direction and went the other way, bumping him as I passed. He had to hop to keep from falling, and by the time he regained his balance, I had received a pass under the basket and banked the ball through the hoop. The crowed clapped their approval. "He put one over on you, Gilly," one onlooker called out.

I was hooked. I knew I'd be back to play every Sunday morning. I was late for work, but what could I do? You can't quit in the middle of a game. It took about another ten minutes before we lost ten to six. As a member of the losing team, I could leave, while a new group of challengers took to the court. I hurried into Henkel's, covered with sweat and dirt. Yudel didn't notice my being late.

From then on, I got to the park much earlier on Sunday—usually about ten. The players in the early morning games were usually my age or younger. I began to develop good moves and a soft shot. Towards noon, the older, more burly players would show up and challenge us for the court. At first they usually won. But after a while, a team made up of guys my age found that we could often beat them with skill and quickness. We called

44

ourselves *the Kings of the Court*. I kept a fresh shirt at work, so when I arrived, I could wash up and make myself look presentable.

I was the child that Mina had never had, and she always was looking for ways for me to get ahead. "You should check out the courses at the Educational Alliance on East Broadway," she said. "The rich German Jews set it up to help out us immigrants. They think that they're much better than us because they've been here a while. But I hear lots of young people go there."

Having overheard her talking to Yudel, I knew that by "young people", she meant "a nice Jewish girl." But what had I to lose? So one day after work, I stopped off at the five-story Alliance building. The activities for the week were posted on a bulletin board near the door. Classes were held six days a week, morning until night. Two of them, *Speaking English* and *Becoming a Citizen*, caught my eye. A sign said that tea was in progress on the roof garden, so, not realizing there was an elevator, I hurried up the six flights of stairs.

It wasn't much of a roof garden—just a few plants in containers. Two pots of tea and some cups were laid out on a table next to a plate of pastries. Around the table stood a dozen people, ranging from my age up to mid-thirties.

"Welcome to the Educational Alliance," said a blond fellow, a little older than me, as I approached the food table. "Can I pour you some tea?"

"Yes," was all I could manage after running up the stairs. He didn't look or sound Jewish.

"My name is Ira Nussbaum. Have one of these pastries. They're called ruggela."

"I am Abe Sokolovsky." The pastry, browned dough wrapped around a mixture containing nuts and raisins, was fantastic.

"Let me make you a nametag. Let's see: Abraham Sokolovsky."

"Not Abraham—Abe—or Avrom."

"Avrom means Abraham—the patriarch of the Jews—in English." He ignored my protest and continued writing out the tag. Then he gave it to me to put on my shirt with the attached safety pin.

I wasn't sure what a patriarch was, but I knew I didn't like this guy. "How long have you been in America, Abe?"

"One year and half."

"Are you interested in any classes? I think you could use *Speaking English*"

"Yes, sounds good."

"That's fine. The young lady over there will help you sign up. We also keep a list of jobs, if you're interested."

"Thank you—have job."

"And Abe—we're starting a new basketball team. Do you play?"

I couldn't believe my ears: a Jewish basketball team. Suddenly my opinion of this place rose.

The Educational Alliance began to play an important part in my life. Wednesday evening I took Speaking English. Mina said my English was improving every day.

Monday and Thursday I practiced with the Alliance basketball team. Basketball in the Alliance gym was very different from that in Seward Park. The wooden floor and round ball made dribbling a more important part of the game. The Alliance must have had lots of money, because each of our seven players was given a pair of sneakers and a grey uniform for games. My tank top shirt had an E and an A on the front and the number six on the back. The team was called the Maccabees, after very famous Jewish warriors, but that name was too long to put on the shirt. Since it was pretty cold in the gym in winter, I wore the shirt over a long-sleeve pullover. We all had to sign a paper that said if we left the team, we would return the shoes and uniform.

The Maccabees were all Jewish immigrants from Eastern Europe. None of us had been in America longer than five years. Two of us, the Bregman twins, had big bushy beards. We were all still full of the idea we could achieve anything in this country, and we had the energy and drive to match our aspirations.

Izzy Spivak was the star of our team. He talked a lot. During games, he would talk to the opponents—sometimes succeeding in getting them to lose their cool. "What's the matter fat boy," he said to the player guarding him. "Getting tired?" Izzy got more than his share of elbows in the

46

face, but he also scored a lot of foul shots. He was my best friend for most of my life. Izzy wanted to be a lawyer and kept at it for ten years until he reached his goal.

Another Maccabee, Paul Horowitz, went on to be a big-time politician in the city. In later years I'd come across his name in the newspaper. I think he ended up in jail.

Our coach, Jake, had recently graduated from Springfield College in Massachusetts, where basketball had been invented about a dozen years earlier. Jake tried to teach us basketball as it was played at Springfield. This involved three players on the outside passing the ball around, while the two strongest and tallest players moved around under the basket, trying to get free for a pass. I played outside, and if the man guarding me backed up to help inside, I would take my two-handed shot. Unfortunately, the Bregman twins, the tallest players on our team, were only five-foot ten and didn't provide much offense close to the basket. In our first two games we got beaten pretty badly.

It didn't take long for us to get impatient with Jake's patterned style of play, and we began to develop our own approach. One of our outside players would dart to the basket and I would follow him. Izzy would throw me a perfectly placed bounce pass, and often I would score. Instead of bringing the ball down the court slowly and "setting up", we would race down to get a shot before the defenders got back. Fortunately for the team, Jake realized it would be easier to temper our natural enthusiasm, rather than try to straitjacket us into his style. He worked on conditioning, running us up and down the court. Gradually with our wide-open style of play, we began to hold our own. Jake impressed upon us that in the gymnasium, unlike in the park, basketball had rules and a referee. Elbows, knees and feet were not to be used...or at least not, when the referee was looking.

We played a couple of other Jewish teams, either at the Alliance or at Prospect Hall in Brooklyn, and beat them regularly. We also played YMCAs from around the city. One of these, the 23rd Street Y, was a powerhouse. They had been undefeated for two years, until losing to the New York Knickerbockers for the city championship the previous year. They had a player who must have been at least six-foot five. "Hey freak-man—escape from the circus?" Izzy asked him. The guy knocked Izzy to the ground and was called for a foul. Our defense was very good in the first half, and we went into the locker room behind only 15 to 17. Their coach must have given them some good tips during the intermission, because they came out and beat us by more than ten points.

One evening after a game, a boy of about sixteen, wearing a *yarmulke*, came up to me. "Do you remember me?" he asked.

I looked at him closely. "I don't think so."

"From your first day in America."

Then it came to me, "Schmuel, I didn't recognize you without your *peyes* and *tzitzit*. Are you still at the cheder?"

"No, I go to public school. I've decided I'm going to be a doctor."

There was something about Schmuel that made me sure he would reach his goal.

In my second year on the team, we were invited up to Columbia to scrimmage with the College team before they started their regular schedule. It felt good to be playing at Columbia instead of just looking though the fence, like I did with Helen. They were very good and beat us soundly. It was too bad there were no athletic scholarships in those days. If there were, I probably could have been one of those Columbia College boys.

We were minor celebrities in the lower East Side. A Yiddish paper, *The Forward*, reported on all our games, and the big ones even made it into the *Times*. For a team of short Jews, we did pretty well, and our success was the object of much speculation in the press. Somewhat later, Paul Gallico, sports writer for the *News*, wrote something like, "The reason, that basketball appeals to Jews with their Oriental background is that the game places a premium on an alert, scheming mind, flashy trickiness, artful dodging and general smart aleckness." When Mina showed me that article, I thought it was so funny I cut it out and saved it for a number of years. Another sportswriter suggested that Jews were better at basketball because they were short, and short men are quicker and have better balance. He should see the teams nowadays.

Chapter 6

Such a little lump my hand felt in her breast as I held her while we were sleeping. If I had known that such a little lump could have separated us like this, maybe I wouldn't have mentioned it to her. That's ridiculous! Of course, I would have told her—that's what you do when you love someone.

She was panicked and made an appointment with her doctor the next week. He said it might be cancer and referred her to Jackson Memorial—probably the best hospital in Florida. "We can fight this thing together," I told her. So who does she trust—Jackson Memorial and me or that son of hers who she's given control of all her money, and who doles it out to her like she's a teenager?

I've had a lot of experience with cancer, having taken care of my wife, Sarah, in her final days. The doctors up in New York really dropped the ball on Sarah's diagnosis. With the war on cancer that Nixon declared back in '71, maybe now they'll do a better job with Ida. Nixon was my least favorite president, especially at the end, with Watergate and the coverup. However, if a president had to declare war, I can't think of a better enemy to declare it on than cancer.

But I still don't know why Ida couldn't have waited around to say goodbye to me or at least telephoned or written.

Last night I ate at Hoffman's Cafeteria, where I had met Ida for the second time. It brought back my memory of that meeting. She had been sitting at a corner table that evening almost two years ago, when I approached her carrying my tray. She was reading a book—a real thick one. In my experience, retired folk in South Beach either never read, except for newspapers, or they read incessantly. I don't read; I walk, so I thought she was out of my class. But, hey, life is short—especially at my age—so I said, "Ida? Ms. Blinsky?"

She looked up from her book and said, "Yes?"

"It's Abe—from the elevator—in the Sun Spot."

She blinked her eyes once or twice before saying, "Oh, yes—please, sit down."

"Are you sure that's okay. I see you've finished eating."

"Of course…I didn't move down to Florida to be in a hurry. I've got lots of time."

So I sat. The book she was reading was Gone With the Wind. Since I had seen the movie, I was able to talk about it—or, at least, listen to her talk about it.

And then we talked a little about our lives. Like myself, Ida had moved to South Beach after her spouse had died. "I got a little tired of everyone feeling sorry for me—inviting me to dinner as an act of charity— and I was supposed to beat my chest about how I missed Sam. To tell you the truth, he was pretty hard to live with—even before he got stomach cancer."

I knew well how difficult it could be living with a dying person.

"Almost all of Sam's money was tied up in our house. My son sold it, paid off the mortgage, and sends me a little to live on every month."

Mina kept a scrapbook of newspaper clippings about our games, and she and Yudel watched some of them at the Alliance building. Yudel was my loudest fan in the stands, stamping his feet and shouting, "Go Avrom!" Of course, no one knew he was referring to Abe Sokolovsky.

One day on our walk to work, Yudel said, "You know, Avrom, basketball is fine and nice, but it's only a game. It won't help you save any money, get a wife and raise a family. I think, during lunchtime, I'll show you what I do. A tailor can always make a living."

Since it was winter, I didn't mind giving up my lunch hour. Yudel showed me how he traced a pattern on a piece of transparent paper, which he cut out and pinned onto fabric. He outlined the pattern with special chalk and cut the fabric to its shape. With pins he roughly fashioned the fabric into the shape of the dress, then sewed the seams together on his sewing machine. Unlike the production Singer machines in the factory, Yudel's sewing machine was driven by foot power. "It gives me more control," he said.

The next step was the tricky part. One of the models—there were two after Helen left—tried on the dress. For the best presentation to buyers, it had to fit perfectly. The most popular style of the day was a dress that followed every corseted curve of a woman's body. Yudel pulled the dress tight on the model, then pinned together some loose material and made a few chalk marks.

One day at lunchtime, he was adjusting a blue dress on Rose. "You do this one, Avrom," he said. My hands shook as I held the loose fabric at Rose's waist. She was a tall thin brunette. I knew she had a child and a bruiser of an Irish husband. I reached for the chalk. "No, this one you have to pin," Yudel instructed.

Pin! That made it even more difficult. Not only did I have to worry about touching Rose, I had to worry about sticking her. Sensing my nervousness, Rose smiled at me and said, "Don't worry, I'm a model. Being touched and stuck is part of the job." Her comment put me at ease and allowed me to finish.

Yudel was amazed at how fast I picked up the "tricks of his trade." It made him think maybe he wasn't irreplaceable. It helped I was his nephew. "I guess tailoring runs in our family, Avrom." One day he came to me and said, "Mr. Henkel wants to talk to you in his office."

I had never been in Mr. Henkel's office. So I was sweating when I knocked on the glass of his door, afraid he was going to scold me for being late two weeks earlier?

"Come in, Avrom."

Mr. Henkel's office was decorated with photographs of models wearing Henkel's dresses. Even though I wanted to see whether Helen was in any of them, I didn't let my eyes stray in that direction. One of the first telephones I had seen sat on Mr. Henkel's desk, and a heavy safe stood in one corner. I wondered what he kept in that. A large table for laying out patterns, several chairs and small tables, and a couch completed the furniture. I had heard female employees joke about "Mr. Henkel getting you on his couch," but I couldn't believe that, since he was a bearded observant Jew, and Yudel had told me he had a wife and three kids. During working hours, anything going on in here could be seen through the glass of the door.

"Avrom, it's been a while since we've talked. Have a seat. How are things going for you in America?"

"Good, thank you." Actually, we hadn't ever talked.

51

Mr. Henkel stroked his beard. It was short and well trimmed, very different from the large bushy ones seen on most observant Jews. "I've heard some good things about you. My son saw a Maccabee basketball game. He recognized you when he came to visit me here and says you're very good. Did they play basketball where you came from?"

"In the Ukraine? No." His basketball talk put me at ease.

"Would you like some tea?"

"Thank you." Why not? I thought. Being seen drinking tea with the boss would raise my status at Henkel's.

Mr. Henkel stood up. He was no taller than five foot two. He walked over to the sideboard, giving me a chance for a quick look at the photos. I was almost sure the one by the window was of Helen. I wanted to get a better look at it, but Mr. Henkel returned with a small plate of cookies and a cup of very strong tea. He placed both on the small table next to my chair.

"Yudel told me you have talent as a tailor."

"Yudel's a good teacher."

"Avrom, I won't beat around the bush: You seem like a young man with ambition. I would like to propose something to you."

A young man with ambition—that sounded good to me. "What is that?"

"You may have noticed that lately most of Henkel's dresses come with belts. It's becoming more and more difficult to make those belts in our factory. It takes up too much space."

He hesitated and looked at me as if I should know what was coming—I didn't. "Yes?" I asked.

"The pajama company on the second floor is going out of business. I've rented their space. Henkel's Dresses will be expanding into half the space, and in the other half, I want to set up a new company, Henkel's Belts. It will make the belts for us and maybe even for other dress companies. Louis Rosso will be in charge. He can use someone with talent as a tailor. Are you interested?"

I was silent as I thought about the tips I would lose by not delivering packages. The seconds ticked by.

"It's a good opportunity. You'll learn a lot. Of course, you'll get a nice raise...say, to four dollars a week."

I've always wondered if I'd gotten that raise, if I had answered right away. Maybe that was the trick to getting things—just keep your mouth shut. "Yes, I would like job. Thank you Mr. Henkel."

"Very good. I think you're making the right decision. Louis will get in touch with you." We both rose, and Mr. Henkel extended his hand to "seal the deal," as Helen had said.

I turned to leave the office, but before I could reach the door Mr. Henkel added, "Avrom, would you like to join my family and me for *Shabbos* dinner this Friday? I think they would like to meet you—especially my son."

That was totally unexpected. I wasn't sure I would enjoy it, but what could I say except, "Yes, I would like that much." I left the office, not having a chance to drink much of my tea, but taking a cookie with me. I wasn't able to get a good look at Helen's photo, but I resolved it would be mine, if the opportunity arose.

Yudel almost "flipped," as they say, when he heard that I had been invited to Mr. Henkel's house for *Shabbos* dinner. "He never invited me, not even when Mina and I got married."

"I think his son is a basketball fan and wants to meet me."

"Maybe, I should learn to play basketball."

I didn't think that was a good idea. Yudel had developed quite a potbelly since he married Mina. He got out of breath just walking up the stairs to her apartment. He might have a heart attack on the court.

"Dinner at the Henkel's," Mina said. "You're coming up in the world. But you don't have anything to wear. We only have three days to get you some new clothes."

"Oh, I know a place on Grand Street," I said, telling her about Jakob's store.

Mina laughed. "I said new clothes, not something already worn and shiny. We'll go to Levy's on Delancy Street."

At Levy's, I picked out a shirt and pair of pants, a navy sport jacket and my first tie—all never having been worn before. Yudel lent me three dollars. "With your new salary," he said, "you'll be able to pay it back next week." The next day at work, he took in the jacket in the back, so it was a perfect fit.

When Friday evening came, I dressed in my new clothes, which weren't quite warm enough for a March evening. However, Mina told me that wearing my Russian army coat was out of the question. The Broadway trolley let me off at 76th Street, where the Henkels lived in a six-floor apartment building that extended over half a block. A uniformed doorman stopped me. "Your name, sir?" he asked. It was the first time that I had ever been called "sir." It must have been my new clothes.

"Abe Sokolovsky."

"And you are here to see?"

"Mr. Henkel."

He pressed one of many buttons on a big brass panel. A minute later, a voice asked, "Yes?"

"Mr. Sokolovsky to see you," he answered. I heard a scratchy response. "The elevator is over there." He pointed across the marble-floored lobby to where another uniformed man was standing. "It's apartment 43 on the fourth floor."

I had been in elevators before when I delivered packages to stores, but never in one as elegant as this. Its interior walls were mirrors separated by ornate brass panels. "First door on your left," the operator said when the elevator reached the fourth floor.

There were only six doors on the floor, surprising, considering the size of the building. I pressed on the button outside the door; lovely chimes sounded inside. I heard footsteps approaching.

"Avrom, welcome to my humble abode," Mr. Henkel said when he opened the door.

It didn't seem so humble to me. I stepped into a long hallway, with a ten-foot ceiling, whose only purpose seemed to be to provide a mat for wiping shoes, a rack for hanging coats and hats, and a mirror for a last check before leaving the apartment. Back in the tenements, there would be at least two beds in there. The smell of dinner cooking made my mouth water.

"Come into the living room. Like a scotch?"

"Yes, thank you." I wasn't quite sure what a scotch was, but was eager to shed my greenhorn image.

The living room was like no room I had ever been in. It contained two couches, at least a half-dozen chairs, three tables and lots of empty space. And what chairs and couches! At Mina's, a chair was something you sat in; I wasn't sure I could sit in these chairs. On their wooden frames, elaborate vines had been carved and coated in gold. Their upholstery was a light blue tapestry, showing a hunting scene.

"Have a seat." I carefully sat, and Mr. Henkel went over to a dark wooden cabinet, also decorated with golden vines, on which there were a number of bottles. He brought over two small glasses, each containing an amber liquid. I stood; toasting, I surmised, was always done standing. This was to be a test of my manhood. I hoped I would do better than I had at Yudel's wedding party, where I had failed miserably, coughing for a least three minutes after downing the liquor in a single gulp.

"*Le'chayim*," Mr. Henkel said, and with a snap of his wrist, poured his drink down his throat.

"*Le'chayim*," I answered, following his lead. For a second, I thought everything was going to be all right. Then a terrible burning hit my throat. I tried to hold back a cough and made a noise like a death rattle. Tears poured from my eyes. Trying to hide my condition from Mr. Henkel, I turned back towards my chair, coming face-to-face with a short, smiling, grey-haired woman.

"So, this is the young man you told me about, Isaac. I'm Miriam Henkel." She advanced, holding out her hand.

A tear rolled down my face, while I shook her hand. I wiped it off with my other hand. I hope she hadn't noticed. "Pleased to meet you," I answered as soon as I had regained my voice. "I am Abe Sokolovsky." At least the Henkels would know I wasn't an alcoholic.

"Megan will be serving dinner in a few minutes. I'll make sure the children are ready." She disappeared back into the hallway; I returned to my seat.

55

"So you call yourself Abe now," remarked Mr. Henkel. He seemed a little hurt at not having known.

I tried to recover with, "That's what most people call me here."

Mr. Henkel sat back in the dark blue velvet couch. He stared off into the distance for a few seconds. "Avrom...Abe, tell me—have you ever heard of a man by the name of Samuel Gompers?"

"No, I don't think so."

"I'm sure you will. He's a very dangerous man. He's trying to turn the workers against the factory owners—getting them to form unions." Mr. Henkel then launched into a long discussion of the relative importance of capital and labor. I wasn't sure what capital was, but I resolved to learn more about it. "Some employers treat their employees very badly," he continued. "I'm glad Henkel's is not among that group. Don't you agree?"

"Oh yes, Henkel's is a very good place to work."

"Do you have any suggestions how things can be improved? How I can increase worker satisfaction?"

I thought for a moment. It's not very often a worker can make a suggestion to the boss. I would be letting down my coworkers, if I didn't suggest something. "It gets very hot in summer. I've seen big fans in windows of other factories. They could help cool things off."

"Excellent idea! I'll get some by this summer."

"Dinner's ready," called Mrs. Henkel, and Mr. Henkel led me across the hallway into the dining room. Under a large, cut-glass chandelier, two of his children stood behind chairs at a dining-room table that sat at least a dozen. "Abe Sokolovsky, I'd like you to meet Ruth and Samuel," Mrs. Henkel said. "Samuel is a big fan of yours. You can sit now children."

Ruth, a bouncy twelve-year-old, gave a little wave of her hand and sat down. Samuel held out his hand and shook mine with gusto. "Call me Sammy," he said, "I watched you in a couple of Maccabee games."

Mr. Henkel took the chair at the head of the table. "Sit next to me, Abe."

"Where's Leah?" Mrs. Henkel asked.

"She was in her room," offered Ruth.

"Go tell her we're starting," said Mrs. Henkel. "We need her to light the candles." Ruth pouted, but got up and left the table.

"How long have you been playing basketball?" asked Sammy.

"About two years."

"Do you practice much?"

"Whenever I can. I work you know." I looked at Mr. Henkel. We both smiled.

"They've started a team at the Uptown Y," Sammy said. "I hope I can make it. I'm pretty short."

"A team needs some short players," I answered. "They're usually quicker than the big guys."

Ruth returned, followed by her sister, who looked about sixteen years old. Leah had the Henkel short stature. She weighed about 180 pounds, which wasn't so unusual for women in those days. She gave me a lovely smile on entering the room.

"Leah, this is Abe Sokolovsky," her mother said. "Please light the candles."

"Hi, Abe," Leah said and went over to the buffet.

Mr. Henkel passed me a *yarmulke*, "You'll probably want this," he said. Both he and Sammy donned theirs. It was the first time I had worn one since the day I got off the boat from Ellis Island.

Leah put a small lace doily over her mid-length dark hair, struck a match and lit the two candles, each in a large brass candleholder. With her eyes closed, she waved some of the warmth of the flames towards her and then in a beautiful soft voice sang, *"Beruch atah Adonai..."* The Sabbath prayer, which my mother used to sing, brought tears to my eyes. Everyone was looking at Leah and didn't see me wipe them off. *".....lehadlik ner shel Shabbat,"* she concluded.

Leah sat down at my right and we got down to the serious business of the meal. Mr. Henkel said the blessing for the wine and we all drank from the goblets in front of us. Then he said the prayer over bread and cut pieces of challah and passed them around the table. Megan served the first course, a rich barley soup. The few strands of red hair hanging out of her white maid's cap aroused my interest in getting a better look at her, but I decided that was a bad idea; I fixed my eyes on my plate and the Henkels. While we were eating the soup, Megan loaded the table with platters of roast chicken, pot roast, baked potatoes, carrots, and another vegetable I had never eaten but had seen called asparagus on stands around the city.

Over dinner Leah talked about poverty in the tenements and a recent article in the *Times* that reported on malnourished children being taken away from their parents by city officials.

"If they didn't drink away all their money," Mr. Henkel said, "they'd be able to feed their children."

"I don't think so," Leah answered. " Some of them make so little, that after paying the rent, there's nothing left for food.   Don't you think so, Abe?"

"Yes," I said. "Down on Hester Street, where I used to live, lots of people looked like they were almost starving." Leah looked happy to have me on her side of the argument. Mr. Henkel gave me an incredulous look.

Dessert was a delicious apple strudel, and following the after-dinner prayer, Mr. and Mrs. Henkel, Leah and I retired to the living room to continue our conversation.   After a short while, Mrs. Henkel looked pointedly at her husband and said, "Isaac, I know there's a book you want to finish. Why don't we give the young people some time by themselves? I'm sure they have better things to do than talk to us."

I looked at Leah; her cheeks were red. After her parents left, she said, "Would you like to go for a walk, Abe? I could show you some of the sights of the neighborhood."

I hesitated because I remembered it had been getting cold when I arrived. But knowing she wanted to get away, I said, "Sure."

"Okay, let's go," she answered, and we rose.   From the large closet in the hall, Leah removed an expensive-looking, fur-trimmed coat.   Then she looked at me. "Oh, I see you didn't bring a coat. Let me get you one of daddy's sweaters." She seemed a very thoughtful person.

It was cold when we left the building and turned up Broadway, but Mr. Henkel's woolen sweater kept me warm.

"I'm sorry, Abe."

"Why are you sorry?"

"My mother keeps inviting young men like you to our home and parading me in front of them. She thinks that if I'm not married by the time

I'm eighteen, I'll be an old maid and never give her grandchildren. It really embarrasses me."

"Don't be embarrassed. I enjoyed meeting you and loved hearing you sing the blessing. I haven't heard it since I left the old country."

The street lamp reflected in Leah's dark eyes. "Daddy told me your family is back in the Ukraine. Who do you live with here in America?"

"My uncle, Yudel, and his wife Mina. They're very nice but not religious: no *shul* on Saturday or candles at Friday night dinner."

"Too bad. You'll have to come for Friday night dinner with us again."

"I'd like that," I said after a hesitation.

I think she picked up on my wavering, "You don't have to worry about mama pushing me on you. I'm not interested in getting married for quite a while. I'm only seventeen. Next year when I graduate, I'm going to learn to be a nurse, and then I'm going to work with Lillian Wald in the tenements. I'll probably move down to the Lower East Side."

"I've seen some of Miss Wald's nurses down there. I hear they're wonderful."

"Oh yes, there's such a need. Not only for sickness, but also to teach families about sanitation and healthy eating."

At 74th Street, a huge darkened building illuminated only by the moon and a single street lamp loomed above Leah and me. I stood at the corner and counted fifteen floors. Each of its hundreds of windows was decorated, either by carved stonework or a wrought-iron railing. The corners of the building were curved and led my eyes up to circular towers extending from the roof. A massive stone arch decorated the main entrance of the building, which was closed off by a steel construction fence.

"It's the Ansonia," Leah said. "When it opens next month, it'll be the grandest hotel in the world. Mr. Dodge-Stokes had it built. He's into clocks and copper. The whole top floor is going to be his apartment. And listen to this: he was brought up on a ranch and plans to raise cattle on the roof."

"Cattle on the roof? How will he get them up there?"

"It has a huge elevator."

I pictured a stampede, with cows flying off the roof onto Broadway. What a city: down on the Lower East Side some people lived ten to a room, while up here, Mr. Dodge-Stokes could have a cattle ranch on his roof. I should've been angry at the inequity, but in my youthful exuberance, I focused on the possibilities of this great, new country. Maybe some day I too could live on upper Broadway, if not on a ranch like Mr. Dodge-Stokes, perhaps in an apartment like the Henkels.

We walked around the block and returned to the lobby of Leah's building. We parted with a pledge to be friends and keep in touch. Leah said I could return her father's sweater at work on Sunday. I was glad, since it was getting quite cold, and I had a long trip home.

Leah wasn't interested in getting married, and neither was I. Even with my raise I couldn't manage it. However, I had the normal urges of nineteen year-old male. Izzy had introduced me to Rivka, who ran a "house"—actually one floor of a tenement down on Broome Street. For fifty cents, Rivka served you tea, and you could spend up to an hour with one of her girls. "You don't want to use a twenty-five cent house or a street girl," Izzy advised me. "It's too easy to catch something. At Rivka's they're clean Jewish girls—rabbinically inspected." Indeed some of the men waiting in Rivka's living room could pass for rabbis.

For my first time, Izzy spoke to Rivka, and she passed me on to Colette, who was much in demand. Colette, in her early twenties, had arrived from Hungary three months earlier. She didn't speak any English, so we conversed in Yiddish. "Rivka tells me it's your first time, so I'll only inspect you a little," she said. Colette had a charming way of looking shy as she undressed. She was the first woman I'd seen naked—except for peeking at my sisters in the old country—and I was totally in awe of her small-breasted pale body. I hate to admit it, but I was so excited that I didn't get beyond her taking me in her hand for the inspection. It would have been very embarrassing to go back out and see Izzy so quickly. Fortunately Colette let me stay in her room for the entire hour, kissing and hugging her. "You're sweet," she told me, as we left. "It's the kissing and hugging that girls like most." I made use of that information the rest of my life, and came back to see Colette several times, where we went beyond hugging.

60

Summer came, and I didn't notice any fans in the windows of Henkel's Dresses. Maybe Mr. Henkel had forgotten my suggestion. He would certainly remember before long. Anyway, I wasn't working up there any more. I was downstairs at Henkel's Belts.

Chapter 7

First, I need to find a place to stay in New York. My money won't last long, if I have to stay in a hotel. I think I'll call my grandson Michael, who stayed at my apartment one summer when he was in law school. He brought me up to date on his family with a New Year's newsletter a couple of years ago, and I've sent him a couple of postcards. But I haven't really kept in touch with him.

I don't like using the telephone in the lobby. It's too close to the porch, where Goldfarb sits, listening in. But it's better than getting a bunch of change to use a payphone or going to one of those places where they have booths that the Latinos line up for.

"Can I use the phone for a long-distance call?" I ask Gomez.

"Sure, Mr. Sokolovsky. Make your call. I'll let you know the charge when you're finished."

Yeah, they charge an arm and a leg. That's why I don't make long distance calls very often. I hope Michael still has the same number. It's been at least five years since I last called him. Nine o'clock—that shouldn't be too late to call.

"Hello."

"Hello, Susanna. Is Michael home?"

"Who is this?"

"This is Abe, Michael's grandfather."

"Abe? How are you? We haven't seen you since our wedding."

"I'm fine. Is Michael there?"

"I'll get him; he'll be excited."

I hope I can keep the chitchat to a minimum—don't want to run up a big tab.

"Gramps! How's it going? Haven't heard from you in ages. Everything okay?"

"Everything's okay. Listen. I'm coming to New York. Got some business. Can I stay with you for a couple of days?"

"Of course. When are you arriving? Can I pick you up at the airport?"

"I'm coming by bus—to the Port Authority, on this coming Saturday morning. I'll take the train to Jamaica."

"Are you sure you can do that? I could come in and pick you up at the Port Authority."

"No problem. See you Saturday."

"Tell me what's been going on with you these last few years."

"It's a long story. I'll tell you on Saturday. There's someone here waiting to use the phone," I lied.

"Okay. We'll be waiting for your call."

I'm glad that didn't take too long. "Okay, Gomez, what's that going to cost me?"

About two weeks after my dinner at the Henkels', I came home from basketball practice and Yudel said, "Sit down, Avrom, I've got some bad news for you."

I sat down at the kitchen table, tilted my head and stared sideways at him, afraid to look directly into his eyes.

"A letter came from Leena today—bad news." Yudel always opened my letters from home. He handed it to me. My hand was trembling, as I read the Yiddish,

Dearest Avrom,

It is with great sadness that I tell you Papa died yesterday while chopping up a side of beef. He had seemed to be healthy and happy until that day. We started our Shiva today.

Being his only son, you always had a special place in Papa's heart. It pained him to send you to America, but he knew what a horror the army was for Jews. It gave him great pleasure to see how well you were doing in the new world.

Mama is holding up well, but it would cheer her, if you wrote and sent her a picture.

> *Golda, Freyda and Raisa are married and Golda's and Raisa's husbands work at the butcher shop, so the business will carry on. They each have a boy and a girl. Freyda's husband is a rabbi. He gives Hebrew lessons in the village. They don't have any children yet. I teach in the village school. So far I am unattached.*
>
> *I'll write more when things settle down.*
>
> Love,
>
> Leenitchka

"God be willing," Yudel said, "we can all go so painlessly."

I was overwhelmed with guilt because I had written so rarely. My father had worked such long hours, I hadn't got to know him very well, and now I would never have a chance. I wondered whether he had ever regretted sending me to America. I had hoped to impress him with my success in this new country.

I tried to remember Papa's last words to me, as I jumped on the train. "Don't be a Men…," he had said. But I couldn't remember the name. Now that it had slipped from my mind, I was too embarrassed to ask Yudel what he had meant.

That night I slept with the Russian army coat Papa had bought wrapped around me. It made me feel closer to him.

I resolved to write immediately and keep in closer contact with my family from then on. I did send a letter the next day and then one about a month later telling about my job and including a picture of the Maccabees, with the player's names at the bottom. Each time I had a little success in my job or in basketball, I would think, *too bad Papa couldn't know about that.*

Unfortunately, with my busy schedule: English course, basketball and the new job, it was easy to slip back into my old not-writing habit. The job, in particular, was becoming very demanding.

I was assisting Louis in setting up the new belt factory. Mr. Henkel had made it clear he wanted expenses kept to a minimum, so wherever possible we had to buy used equipment and furnishings. The pajama factory had sold everything when they moved out; all we had was a big open space.

64

"Walk around the neighborhood," Louis told me. "There's always signs for 'Going Out of Business Sale.' If you find something, run back and get me right away."

Louis was right. Over on Forsyth Street, I found a shirtwaist company that was liquidating. I ran and got Louis and he came running with the big wad of bills Mr. Henkel had given him. For twenty-six dollars he bought five large tables and two heavy-duty sewing machines. He got a receipt to give to Mr. Henkel. We carried it all downstairs. "I'll wait here," he told me. "I don't want anyone to take our stuff. You run and get the large cart."

I ran back to Henkels and got their large flat cart and pushed it the five blocks to Forsyth. We loaded it with the sewing machines and two of the tables. "Take this stuff back to Henkels and have someone watch it," Louis told me. "Come back and we'll get the rest." The cart was a lot harder to push loaded up. It took me over an hour to get back. I could see Louis pacing back and forth when I turned the corner. "What took you so long?" he asked. My face reddened with anger, but I didn't say anything. We loaded up the three remaining tables and I pushed them on the cart, while Louis strolled along beside me. I began to think I wouldn't be happy working with him.

Over the next few days, Louis and I made the rounds of shops that sold second-hand equipment. I pushed the cart, and Louis walked beside me, eyeing all the girls. He was Italian and married—a big, handsome fella in his mid-thirties. Many of the girls returned his glances. At one place we bought a four-foot long, heavy-duty shears for cutting leather, at another a riveting machine for installing eyelets.

Louis explained the intricacies of the belt business to me as we walked the streets. "Most belts are just a tube of the same material used for the dress. We cut two strips that the operator sews together with their good sides facing each other. They use a long tool to pull the tube inside out and then fold the ends over and sew them."

That seemed simple enough to me.

"But," Louis continued, "More and more they're using belts with buckles, where the material is sewed to a backing—either buckram or leather. We'll need woodworking machines to make dies for complicated shapes and a press to use them."

I paid careful attention. Louis knew his stuff, and some day his information might be useful. We got a few more items, and then he told me, "We've got enough for a start. You take the stuff back. I'll see you in about an hour."

Too bad Louis was leaving. I could have used his help lugging the stuff up the stairs. Louis's mind always seemed to be "somewhere else." I wondered where he was going, but didn't dare to ask.

We spent about a week setting everything up, hiring an electrician to wire up the machines. Louis had me build a partition for an area next to a window, where we installed a large exhaust fan. "That's where we'll spray the latex cement on the backing," he told me. Meanwhile, he went out to buy a supply of leather, buckram, buckles, eyelets and thread.

Our first order from Henkel's Dresses was simple: straight belts of dress material stitched on to buckram backing—twenty each in three different colors and four sizes. Louis showed me how to use the shears to cut the buckram to the required width and length. With a die he shaped the end of the strips. The dress material was cut an inch wider. The two operators we borrowed from Henkel's Dresses sewed the material to the buckram. We pressed eyelets into the strip at marked positions and a buckle was sewn in place. I had the task of finishing: removing all loose threads and inspecting each belt. The whole job took less than two days. "With some practice, we'll be able to do it in half the time," Louis said.

For more complicated styles, we traced patterns on wood and cut it to shape, screwing sharp metal around its edge. The resulting die was used to cut the buckram or leather. We kept the dies, in case the designers wanted to use the same shape at a later time. Some belts had bows, which had to be shaped and sewn by the operators. Velvet and similar materials were glued to the backing as well as sewed.

I was learning a new trade and working very hard. I often had to go in on Saturday and rarely had a chance to walk around the city. I also had to give up basketball. Several times I missed practice, and when I did show up,

I was too tired to do my best. At the end of the season, I told Jake I wouldn't be playing on the team next year. He didn't seem to mind; there were a number of talented younger players waiting for spots. With some sadness I returned my shoes and uniform. Izzy also left the team at that time. He was starting school at City College.

Shortly after I left the Maccabees, I had a letter from Leena. She ended it with: *You look very sexy in your basketball suit. I see from the picture you are now called "Abe." However, you will always remain my little Avrom.*

Love

Leenitchka

Chapter 8

The Miami bus station hasn't changed much since I moved down here in '70, six years ago. Neither has the bus trip to New York—still twenty-two hours. Thank God I can sit back while someone else does the driving. Never had a car or learned to drive; there's always been a bus or train to get me to where I wanted to go.   Those tourists with their fancy automobiles had quite a shock a few years ago when the Arabs cut off the oil supplies. A lot of them came down here for their winter vacations and couldn't get gas to go back north.

Too bad I can't afford to go by plane. I don't have much money—a little more than a thousand left in my savings account, not much to show for a life of frugal living. But hey, I've got my health—knock on wood. They say: if you've got your health, you've got everything—and I agree with them, especially since I can live on my Social Security. God bless Franklin Delano Roosevelt! And Goddamn cheating bosses, thieving bankers and ungrateful children!

Maybe I'm stupid for giving up the warmth of Miami for the uncertain weather in New York—not knowing how many years, or even months I have left. But this business with Ida just won't let me rest. I have to find out why she left the way she did, and whether she felt something for me or I've been living under a delusion these past two years.

I saw Yudel in my dream last night, and he said, "Don't be scared when you have no other choice." He's right: I can't go through the rest of my life without knowing why Ida left the way she did.

My thoughts are drifting back to Ida... To tell you the truth, I never thought I'd take up with another woman after Sarah passed away. However, I found myself hanging around the lobby, so I could catch Ida as she was going out for dinner each night. After about two weeks, it was no longer possible for either of us to pretend out meetings were accidental, and Ida asked me, "Abe, how would you like a home cooked meal? I really like to cook."

I had my doubts about the home cooking. The Sun Spot's policy of no cooking in rooms was listed on the List of No-No's posted behind the front desk. Most of us long-term residents, however, have hot plates in our rooms. We hide them when the maid makes her weekly visit. "On a hot plate?" I asked.

"No, we can use that small kitchen behind the lobby. It has a two-burner stove and a microwave. You buy the food; I'll do the cooking."

I had forgotten about that room; it was mainly used by the hotel staff.

"That sounds great," I said.

Ida made something called "cock-o-van," chicken breasts cooked in wine, with lots of garlic and cut up scallions; boiled potatoes and frozen peas, with fruit tarts for dessert. We finished half a bottle of wine with dinner. A couple of hotel guests including Fat Goldfarb, attracted by the aroma of the food, had poked their heads around the corner while we were eating.

"So Abe, where do you go every day, on those long walks you take every morning?" she asked me.

I told her how beautiful the sunrise was over the beach, about the park on the beach a few miles north, the opulent hotel lobbies and the strange-looking crowds leaving the clubs early in the morning.

"You must really be in good shape to walk so far," she said. "Some of the younger guys who live here can't walk around the block."

Fat Goldfarb was in that group.

After dinner, Ida said, "No reason to waste these leftovers. Help me take them up to my fridge."

Upstairs, Ida unlocked her door, and we put the food in her mini-fridge. Then she stepped close to me and said, "So, Abe, let's see how good shape you're really in."

And that began one of the best periods of my life.

I went to the Henkels' for Friday night dinner once in April. The weather was perfect for walking that night and I enjoyed telling Leah

69

everything I was learning about the belt business. I don't think I had ever talked so easily to a woman.

Two weeks later, when I arrived home, there was an envelope waiting for me on the kitchen table, a very unusual occurrence. On the card in the envelope was printed: *The class of 1905 of the Julius Sachs School for Girls invites you to their graduation reception, to be held in the School Building of Temple Emanu-El, Fifth Avenue and 43rd Street at 5 p. m. on Sunday, June 7, 1905. R. S. V. P. 49167.* In the lower right hand corner, was hand written, *Hope you can come, Leah.*

I showed it to Mina. "You've really arrived," she said. "That's the fanciest synagogue in the city." And then, assuming I was going, she added, "You'll need a graduation gift, of course."

"What are these letters at the bottom?" I asked.

"That's *Respondez s'il vous plait.* It means: Let us know if you're coming. You can either telephone that number or write to the address.

I was impressed. "Is that French?"

"Yes it is. We R. S. V. P.'d all the time when I lived in Kiev."

The card and envelope were made of such fine paper—almost like linen—I didn't even consider throwing them away; I tucked them in the bottom of my trunk.

I wasn't sure where I'd find a telephone to R. S. V. P. We didn't have one in the belt factory. Mr. Henkel had one on his desk, but I was reluctant to ask to use it. Then I remembered I had seen a telephone booth in City Hall when Yudel and Mina were married. I hurried down there the next day during lunchtime.

A man wearing a suit was in the booth, talking into a mouthpiece and holding something attached to a wire up to his ear. That didn't look too difficult. When he left, I went into the booth and pulled the door closed. The instrument consisted of two parts. On the left was what looked like a candlestick with a mouthpiece on its top and a round piece of metal with holes at its bottom. The earpiece the man had been using hung from a hook on its side. Two metal rods securely fastened the candlestick to a large box on its right. There was a single slot and a lever on the top of the box. Instructions on the top informed me, *Local calls only. Insert five-cent piece*

70

in slot. Lift receiver, then dial number. When party answers, press lever to drop coin and complete connection.

Five cents! I could travel the length of Manhattan on the El for that. It wasn't worth it, but for the experience of using a telephone, I'd go ahead. I wedged the invitation up against the wall behind the box, held the receiver up to my ear and warily dropped my nickel in the slot. The first digit of the number I had to call was a four. I put my finger in the hole of the dial over the four; nothing happened. I put the receiver back on the hook. This would take a little experimenting. Since I was good with machinery, I should be able to figure it out. If not, would I loose my nickel? I hoped not.

With my finger in a hole, I could rotate the dial, but only to the right and only until my finger hit the stop. That must be the way you dialed a number. I picked up the receiver again and dialed each of the digits in turn. A harsh ringing in the earpiece startled me.   "Hello," a woman's voice answered after four rings.

I started to talk and then remembered that I had to push the lever to complete the connection. I did and heard my nickel drop to the bottom of the box. I had been so involved in the process of using the instrument I hadn't planned what I was going to say. "This is Abe Sokolovsky," I stammered.

"Calling about what?"

"Uh...I received an invitation..."

"To the Julius Sachs School graduation?"

"Yes."

There was some rustling of paper.   "Let's see; you're Miss Henkel's guest. Will you be joining us?"

"Yes, I will."

"Very good. And would you like a chicken or roast beef entrée?"

I wasn't sure what an entrée was, but roast beef sounded pretty good to me. I was elated. Besides going to a fancy party, I had mastered the pay telephone. Now there was just the matter of Leah's gift.

What could I get someone as wealthy as Leah, who probably already had everything? I pondered this question as I crossed Columbus Park and entered the streets on the other side. I was amazed how this neighborhood had changed, in the four years since I'd arrived in America.   Then, it had been Mulberry Bend, probably the most decrepit and dangerous

71

neighborhood in the city, with hundreds of destitute tramps living in each tenement. Schmuel, the boy who had directed me to Yudel's place, warned me to stay away from there. Now a new park brought light and air into the area. While quite a few tramps still hung out in the park, the surrounding streets were going upscale. Pushcarts had been removed, and new shops were opening. The sign in the window of one of these caught my eye: *Medical Supplies*, it said. There in the window was a doctor's stethoscope. *Leah wants to be a nurse—that would be the perfect gift for her.* One dollar secured me the shiny new instrument, housed in its own leather case. It had been a very productive lunch hour.

I was so busy, the day of Leah's graduation reception snuck up on me. Mina had picked out a new tie for me from a pushcart. Louis was very impressed when I told him where I was going. "Take Sunday off," he said, looking at me warily; maybe I was a spy planted by Mr. Henkel.

The day was cool, so I left myself an hour to walk to Temple Emanu-El. I had passed by it several times before but had never noticed the Star of David carved into its stone face. In the old country, synagogues were much more modest. Any show of wealth would have incited the jealousy and anger of the locals. On the Lower East Side, the Jews didn't have much money and worshipped in storefronts or small *shuls* in tenements.

Temple Emanu-El's building extended for more than half a block on Fifth Avenue. The main section was taller than the surrounding four-story buildings. Domes sitting on thin columns on either side of the door doubled its height. It reminded me a little of the churches I had seen in Saint Petersburg.

A sign to the left of the temple pointed me along a walkway to the school building. Halfway along, I passed a small door in the side of the temple. It was unlocked and I opened it, stepping directly into the side aisle of the temple. The building was dark, except for beams of multicolored light streaming in through two stain glass windows in the front. Dust particles bounced around in the beams like insects. It took a minute for my eyes to make out the two rows of massive columns that supported the ceiling and led up to the pulpit and ark on a raised platform. I pictured the rows of high-backed benches between the columns and on the other side filled on the high holy days. More than a thousand Jews—most of them rich like Mr. Henkel. Maybe some day I could be a member of this congregation.

I left the Temple and continued along the path. At the school building, I followed a line of well-dressed people up the stairs to the second floor. The afternoon sun brightly lit a large room with windows on three sides. A middle-age woman at a table by the door asked my name. "Mr. Sokolovsky, you're at table eight. Miss Henkel is there already." She attached a nametag to my jacket with a safety pin.

Leah came over and took my arm. "Abe, I'm so glad you could come. Let me introduce you to some people."

I handed her the gift that Mina had nicely wrapped. "Here's a graduation present for you. I hope you'll be able to use it."

Leah flushed, "Oh you shouldn't have." She took the gift. I didn't see any other gifts around and wondered whether I should have taken Mina's advice that it was necessary. "My parents aren't here yet, but I'll introduce you to the other people at our table."

We made our way through the half-filled hall to table eight. "This is my friend, Rachel Steinman," Leah said, "her parents, Mr. and Mrs. Steinman, and her friend Joseph Busan. I'd like you all to meet Abe Sokolovsky." I walked around the table to shake everyone's hand. Rachel was a frail-looking, pretty blond with a limp handshake. I'd seen so few blond Jews, they still surprised me. Joseph was tall and modestly overweight. His handshake was designed to impress, perhaps to subdue. I wondered whether he was, like me, just a friend, or had a more formal relationship with Rachel. The Steinmans just nodded and didn't turn or get up to take my hand. "Abe practically runs one of my father's companies," Leah explained. I was glad Mr. Henkel wasn't there to hear that exaggeration.

"I'm in my third year at Columbia," Joseph loudly announced. "What school did you go to?"

For a moment I was speechless: he certainly wasn't asking about my village school in the old country. But then I saw an out—time to change the subject. "Columbia: we played your basketball team last year when I was on the Maccabees." That got his attention.

"Did you win?" he asked with less bravado.

73

"No, but it was close," I lied, and he forgot about his original question.

"When do we eat?" asked Mr. Steinman.

"It shouldn't be too long," Rachel said.

"I brought something for you," said Mrs. Steinman, handing her husband a roll. "He has an ulcer. The doctor said he shouldn't let his stomach get empty."

From what I could see of Mr. Steinman's stomach, it had rarely been empty.

Leah looked toward the door. "My parents are here." The Henkels made their way over to the table. Mr. Henkel kissed Leah on the cheek. "Congratulations, honey," he said. "Hello everyone." He nodded at each of us in turn. "I don't think I know this young man."

"Joseph Busan." He rose and gave Mr. Henkel one of his impressive handshakes.

"I'm so proud of you," Mrs. Henkel said to Leah. She hugged her daughter and kissed her on her cheek.

We all sat down, and the waiters brought the first course. I was seated between Leah and Rachel. "What are you going to do after graduation?" I asked Rachel after we finished our soup.

"Daddy got me a job at Macy's. I'll be a personal shopper. That means helping rich women shop for clothes."

"Only until we get married," added Joseph, from across the table.

"Of course, darling," said Rachel.

I noticed Rachel wasn't wearing a ring "to seal the deal." Maybe Joseph wasn't as prosperous as he made out.

"Lennard Steinman is one of the biggest furriers in the city," explained Mr. Henkel. "He sells to Macy's and all the big department stores. I'm sure I could get Leah a job like that, but she's set on being a nurse."

"And working in some of the most dangerous parts of the city," added Mrs. Henkel.

"I've been accepted in the nursing program at New York Hospital," Leah announced. "It starts in September."

"I hope you're happy there, dear," said Mrs. Steinman. "Personally, I couldn't stand being around sick people all day—so depressing."

"And," added Leah, "this summer I'm going with five other seniors to Europe. Miss Seligman, our headmistress, will be our chaperone. We sail on the *Deutschland* for Liverpool in two weeks. We'll spend three weeks in England and then go on to Germany and Paris."

"That's wonderful," I said. I'd miss her; although remembering my transatlantic voyage, I wasn't sure I envied her.

At that point our main courses arrived, and we all started eating. The roast beef was a good choice. I had never before eaten such a delicious and tender piece of meat. Rachel also had ordered the beef, but hardly touched it. I considered asking if I could have her leftover, but then decided that that probably wasn't done in polite society.

After dessert, a stately woman stood up at the head table.

"That's Miss Seligman," Leah whispered to me.

Tapping on her water glass with a spoon, Miss Seligman brought the audience to attention. "Members of the class of 1905 of the Julius Sachs School for Girls and your parents and friends, I am so happy to welcome you all to this festive occasion...." Miss Seligman congratulated the graduates and then introduced the trustees of the school who were sitting at her table. Their names: Schiff, Loeb, Sears, Lehman...didn't mean much to me at the time, but I later found out they were among the richest families in America. "And now I am honored to introduce our speaker for tonight, Dr. Julius Sachs. Let me read you just a few of his accomplishments: Professor of Education at Columbia University, founder of the Julius Sachs School for Boys and the Julius Sachs School for Girls, principal of the Sachs Collegiate Institute for Boys and the Sachs Collegiate Institute for Girls, founder of the Franklin School, which later became the Dwight School...."

I was impressed. I had thought that Jews were only famous for becoming rich. Here was a man whose fame was based on giving, rather than getting, money. I later learned Professor Sachs also came from one of New York's richest families. No wonder he wasn't interested in making money.

Professor Sachs' talk was about the importance of the classics: French, German, science and literature, for Jewish girls, who would become the repository of culture for their families. He explained that gender-segregated schooling was important; otherwise, the physical limitations of the girls would keep the boys from reaching their "highest attainment." Girls should be trained—very well trained— to be wives, mothers and perhaps teachers. I looked at Leah. From the look on her face, it didn't seem she appreciated his message.

With my four-dollar-a-week salary, it was heady stuff for me to be rubbing elbows with the upper class. They weren't as much fun as my Maccabee buddies, but maybe they were the route to getting ahead in New York. I had never thought of Leah as anything more than a friend, but maybe I should reconsider that.

Chapter 9

Ida and I learned a lot from each other. I taught her to get up early and see South Beach when it was cool and empty. We'd buy coffee and bagels and eat on a bench next to the beach, watching the sun come up. After walking down Ocean Drive to South Pointe Park, we'd come back by Collins Avenue and watch the storekeepers open the stores. Mainly deliverymen and sweepers were out, with an occasional weirdo, going to wherever weirdoes go in the morning. I'd have to walk much slower than I would on my own, because Ida had circulation problems in her legs. But her doctor said the walking was good for her and even allowed her to reduce the medicine for her pressure.

Ida taught me to read; until I met her, my reading had been confined to newspapers and magazines. She taught me to read books—her favorite books, which she had brought down with her from New York. One that I particularly liked was The Chosen by Chaim Potok, which told about the conflicts between tradition and modernism in Judaism.

The rooms at the Sun Spot were not well suited for reading, having only a bed, a small table with a wooden chair and a vinyl armchair, of the type you find in a lower-class doctor's office. So Ida and I would take our books down to the lobby or out on the porch.

The only problem there was Fat Goldfarb trying to horn in, with "So what are you reading, Ida?" He'd never ask me, because he knew I would just look at him like the piece of excrement he was.

Ida, on the other hand, was always courteous. "I'm reading Ship of Fools, Julian. Have you ever heard of it?"

"Oh yes, I've heard it's a very good book."

Sure he had!

On our morning walks, I would often discuss the books I was reading with Ida

"Are you enjoying Ragtime?" she asked.

77

"Very much. I vaguely remember some of the characters in the book: Stanford White, he was killed over some girl; and Emma Goldman, she was a famous Communist speaker. But why is it fiction, if the characters are real?"

"Doctorow takes real characters and puts them into made-up or exaggerated incidents to drive home a point."

"Is that why he uses names like 'Father' or 'Tateh'?"

"Yes, Father represents a traditional upper middleclass American who has trouble adjusting to the twentieth century."

"What are you reading?" I asked her.

"The Book of Daniel."

"From the Bible?"

"No, it's another book by Doctorow. He's my favorite author. It's about the children of Julius and Ethel Rosenberg, who were executed for being Russian spies."

"I remember that."

"Doctorow tries to imagine what was like for them before and after their parents were executed."

"How could he find out about that?"

"He doesn't. That's why its fiction. In fact, in real life the Rosenbergs had two boys, neither of them named Daniel, while in the book they have a son and a daughter."

"I don't think I'd like to read that." I said.

"Why not?"

"It's a little too close to home."

"Too close to home? Don't tell me you were blacklisted—in the belt business."

"No, but I was put through the mill by an FBI guy once."

"For what?"

"Nothing, absolutely nothing."

The summer went quickly. Henkel's Belts was getting busier. We even got our own telephone. Louis would spend half the day on it, ordering stuff, trying to drum up business and doing God knows what. He managed to get us a few outside orders—mainly from small contractors. Now we kept three operators busy full time and had our own *nebbish*, a sixteen-year-old named Harold, who cleaned up, delivered packages and did some of the finishing. I was busy cutting material, backing and leather and attaching velvet to backing with the latex spray.

One day on the way home, Yudel said to me, "You know Avrom, if you're not getting married, at least you should have your own room. You're too old to sleep in the living room. Mina and I are going to look for a two-bedroom apartment. We'll be asking you to chip in another 50 cents a week."

That sounded pretty good to me. With Mina providing all my food, I had been saving almost two dollars a week. Two weeks later we made the move north to East 12ᵗʰ Street. This time, with all of Mina's furniture, we hired two strong guys to help us. Their horse cart had to make four trips to transfer everything to the new apartment.

Our new neighborhood was mostly middle-class Italian, although recently there had been an influx of central Europeans. The place was in a real apartment house, with an elevator and a small lobby, but no doorman. It was only two blocks from Tompkins Square Park, which had four half-court basketball courts. Izzy didn't live too far from the park, and he would often join me for Saturday morning basketball games. We were among the best players, and our teams usually survived a half-dozen challenges for the court.

One Saturday after basketball, Izzy and I washed up and made one of our rare sojourns to spend some time with Rivka's girls down on Broome Street. I was heartbroken to hear that Colette had been snatched up for a wife by one of the rich customers. Hettie, a big, strong German farm girl took me in hand, and we had "a roll in the hay," as she called it. Izzy and I were leaving the building, when we saw a couple of guys going down the stairs to the basement. Always adventurous, he said, "Let's see what's going on down there."

The man minding the basement door must have thought we were with the other two guys, because he let us in. Three or four rooms filled with cigar smoke led off a hallway. In each, four to six men were sitting silently around a table intently studying their cards. Dollar bills, with some fives mixed in, lay on the tables. One of the players broke the silence. "I'll raise you five," he said. *Five bucks, that was more than I made in a week.*

"Looks like poker," Izzy said. "I'd like to get in the game. Do you have any money?"

I made a point of never bringing much more than I needed to Rivka's. Who knew what could happen while my pants were off. "I only have about a buck."

"Too bad," Izzy said, "I'll have to come back some other time."

"Would you gentlemen like a place at one of the tables?" a pretty girl carrying a tray of drinks asked.

"Not today," Izzy told her.

"Sorry, we don't allow spectators," she answered, motioning with her head towards the exit.

Before leaving, I glanced into the last room. There in front of me was a man's back, with a mole on the side of his neck that I couldn't mistake. I had watched it for hours each day while Louis talked on the phone. I pushed Izzy toward the exit.

"What's your hurry?" he asked me when we hit the street.

"My boss was in there."

"Mr. Henkel?"

"No, Louis, he runs the belt factory."

"He must do all right to play in that game," Izzy said.

I wondered.

In the Fall I saw Leah briefly several times when she stopped at Henkel's Dresses to have lunch with her father. It was November before I finally found enough free time to walk her back to the hospital. First she talked about her nursing studies. "There are about thirty nursing students. Besides me, only one of them is Jewish. We take killer courses and go on rounds with the medical students. They keep us away from the infectious diseases, but I've seen some pretty gruesome cases: patients with huge tumors, severe malnutrition and horrible burns. In the spring, we get assigned as a helper to a nurse. I hope I have the stomach for it."

The conversation then shifted to her European trip. Leah had been most impressed with London. "It's not as busy as New York, but the buildings and parks are much more elegant. I saw King Edward and the whole Royal Guard, about 100 of them, in red uniforms with tall black hats, pass by on their black horses. We need some pageantry like that in America.

"The Victoria and Albert museum," Leah continued, "was very interesting. They've got stuff from the whole British Empire in there, including 3000-year-old mummies from Egypt."

"And what did you think of Germany," I asked.

"The big cities we visited, Bremen and Nurnberg, weren't very interesting, and the people weren't friendly—too busy going about their business and eating those horrible sausages. But the train went through some very beautiful country. I loved Heidelberg. It's an old university town. And Strasbourg is beautiful, although it hasn't completely recovered from the war between France and Germany."

"I imagine Paris was great," I said.

"Yes, I think it must be the most interesting city in the world. It's the center of a new movement in art called Impressionism. I bought a small painting for my parents."

Leah's comments made me realize how little I knew about art or any other "high culture." I resolved to spend a day in one of New York's museums when I had a chance.

"I loved sitting in cafes on the left bank and watching the people." Leah said, and then she added, sort of as an afterthought, "I met a student from the Sorbonne there. His name is Bernard Goldstone. We became romantically involved."

"Romantically involved? What happened to your chaperone, Miss …?"

"Miss Seligman. Oh, she was the one who arranged for us to meet French students."

"Will you be seeing Bernard again?"

"I think so. He's planning to move to New York this summer. French Jews have become very nervous since the Dreyfus affair."

I didn't know what the Dreyfus affair was, but from my experience in the Ukraine, I could imagine. I'd have to check it out at the library.

"I hope Bernard won't keep us from being friends," Leah said.

"Oh no," I answered.

"Well enough about me," Leah said. "What's new with you."

When we reached the hospital, I gave Leah a big hug and hurried back to work. On the way there was lightness to my step. A big weight had been taken off my mind. With Leah being romantically involved, I no longer had to decide whether to court her. I could just enjoy her friendship—for as long as it lasted. I knew I really preferred it that way.

Shortly after we moved into the new apartment Anthony diAngelo, the Tammany ward boss, visited us. "Are all your men folk registered to vote?" he asked. "Tammany Hall is in this ward. It would be very embarrassing if we didn't make a good showing in next-years election." Yudel was already a registered voter. "Make sure your nephew becomes a citizen as soon as he can," he told Yudel.

In April '06, I had been in America five years and was eligible to become a citizen. (Actually, Tammany had ways by which they could even register newly arrived immigrants.) Mina wanted to stay on the good side of her new neighbors and encouraged me to follow diAngelo's suggestion as soon as possible. "You never know, some day we might need Tammany's help," she said.

Naturalization took place at the courthouse next to City Hall. Mina made sure that I knew Teddy Roosevelt was President; Charles Fairbanks, Vice President; Frank Higgins was Governor and George McClellan was Mayor. With the blessing of Mr. Henkel, she and Yudel took off one morning to accompany me to the courthouse. The line of naturalization candidates was long, but moved quickly. Some of them, accompanied by their Tammany sponsors, looked like they were right off the boat.

At last, I handed the clerk my application. Sure enough, he asked me the names of the President, Governor and Mayor and then had me read a few lines on a card. Yudel had to attest that I had been in the country for five years. The clerk then gave me another card on which was the pledge of allegiance and directed us into the next room. There, I stood with about twenty other petitioners in front of a judge and the flag of the United States. Mina and Yudel sat with other guests in the back of the room. After three more petitioners arrived, the judge had us raise our hands and recite the pledge, and there I was—a citizen of the United States of America. Mina and Yudel hugged me, and a tear came to my eye. Now I really was part of this great country.

I wrote home telling the family I was now a citizen. Too bad Papa couldn't have known that.

In late '06, a distinguished-looking gentleman appeared on the scene at Henkel's Belts. He was in his fifties, with a full head of white hair.

"I'm Arthur Hammel, Mr. Henkel's accountant," he said. "He sent me down to do the year-end audit."

For three days, Arthur poured over stacks of invoices and receipts, occasionally calling Louis over for clarification. From what I could hear of their conversation, Louis hadn't regarded keeping records as very important. "You have no right to question my honesty," he told Arthur. By the third day they were yelling at each other. Finally, with a, "I don't have to take this," Louis grabbed his jacket and stormed to the door. Arthur put all the papers in a box and went upstairs.

It seemed like Henkel's Belts was able to operate without Louis. He had spent so much of the time either on the phone or out, supposedly drumming up business, that I was reasonably adept at keeping things going. Orders kept coming down from upstairs, and as long as nothing unusual came up, I felt I could handle them. Still, Louis knew a lot more about the belt business than I did, and I lived in constant fear I would make a mess of things. There was one outside order that we were finishing up, which presented a problem. Who was it for? Where would I deliver the belts? How much would I charge? In vain I searched for some record of the order.

On the third day after Louis left, word came down from upstairs. Mr. Henkel wanted to see me in his office. I was scared. Would he shut us down? I went up and tapped on his door.

"Come in," Mr. Henkel said.

The cold sweat on my hand made it difficult to turn the knob, but when I entered the office, I saw a bottle of whiskey and two glasses on his desk. That didn't seem like a bad sign. "You wanted to see me?"

"Yes," he answered. "Now that you're working downstairs, I don't get a chance to see you very often. How do you like the belt business?"

"I like it; I've learned a lot."

83

"I hear that Louis is often away," he said, "and you've had to take care of things by yourself."

"Yes, Louis goes out visiting customers."

"Let me be direct with you. Arthur tells me there are some 'irregularities' in the books of Henkel's Belts. He thinks Louis has been stealing from me. I would fire him, but I hear he's left on his own."

"I haven't seen him in three days," I said. "I don't know whether he's planning to come back."

"Well, if you see him, tell him he doesn't work here anymore. He can see me about picking up his last week's salary."

My throat felt dry. What would that mean for our little belt company? I didn't have long to wait to hear Mr. Henkel's plan.

"I've been told that you've done a good job keeping things together in his absence. I'd like to make you an offer."

"Yes?"

"You take charge of the inside work at Henkel's Belts: manufacturing, ordering supplies, book keeping and all that. I'll get someone else for outside sales."

I stood there dumbstruck. Mr. Henkel must have interpreted my silence as waiting for the 'rest of the deal.'

"I'll give you the same agreement I had with Louis," he said. "Five dollars a week, and, as a bonus, ten percent of the profits at the end of the year."

A percentage of the profits: would that mean I was a boss? I nodded, "That sounds great!" My face lit up with a smile.

"Let's seal that with a drink," Mr. Henkel said, and he poured two ample shots of scotch into the glasses. We clinked our glasses and said "*Le'chayim*". I had had more experience drinking by that time, so it went off without incident.

"I'll send Arthur down to show you how to keep the books and write checks. I hope you can do a better job at that than Louis. Good luck, Abe." We shook hands, and I left.

I went back downstairs. My head was spinning. I was only twenty-one. In a little over five years, I had gone from a nebbish to a boss, or at least, a ten-percent boss. I didn't know how much my share of the profits would be, but I would work hard to make them as large as possible. I wondered, however, if in my enthusiasm I had accepted Mr. Henkel's deal too quickly. I resolved that next time I'd keep my mouth shut for a while longer and see if he came up with something better.

Louis was gone, but his presence lingered on at Henkel's Belts. While he was still there, he had given me strict instructions to take the number of anyone who telephoned and say he would call them back. I was definitely not to tell them he was out or where he was–if I knew. Now I wasn't sure what to tell them, so I settled on, "Louis isn't here now. I don't know when he'll be back." The list of numbers from both men and women reached two pages. One call was helpful. "Where's my belts," a gruff voice asked. That must be for the outside order. I took down the address and packed up the belts.

Finklestein's Dresses was a small operation on the third floor of a walkup on Broome Street. Six operators were sewing in a small room. Dresses were piled on tables. I shivered: on this December afternoon, the small pot-bellied stove at one end of the room wasn't up to keeping the place at a habitable temperature. Everyone wore a sweater. I guess this was a sweatshop, of which I'd heard so much, although no one was sweating this time of year.

"Where's Louis?" Finklestein asked.

"He left. He doesn't work at Henkel's any more."

"Okay, let me see the belts," he said through the cigar in his mouth. The smell from it permeated the room. I wondered whether the dresses smelled. He laid the package on a table, opened it and carefully inspected three or four of the belts. "They're okay, I guess," he pronounced. You can go.

I just stood there.

"What are you waiting for?" Finklestein asked.

"My money."

"I don't owe you nothing—*zilch*. I paid Louis in advance. Get your money from him."

Silently, I stood my ground. Finally, Finklestein reached into his pocket and took out some bills. "Here's ten—just to get rid of you."

I stood my ground.

"Okay, here's another five," he said. "You won't get another penny out of me. I'll throw you out, if you don't leave."

I felt that I had gotten as much as I could, so I left. I was elated: it was my first triumph in running Henkel's belts.

A few days later Louis dropped in after picking up his last paycheck upstairs. "So you're in charge, eh, kid. I guess old man Henkel is grooming his future son-in-law to take over the business."

I changed the subject, "Hey, that order for Finklestein. Did he pay you in advance like he said?"

"Ha! Of course not. No one pays in advance. Twenty-five bucks— that was the price. Finklestein is a *mascalzone*—a *gonif* you call him. Don't ever trust him—or anyone else. You've got a lot to learn, kid." Louis had a good laugh at my expense.

"What's the old man paying you?" he continued. "Same as me— seven dollars a week, plus twenty percent of the profits? Don't think you'll get rich on that. Well, I guess it'll all be yours some day." With that he turned around and left. Now I really had a problem. Who could I trust: Louis? Finklestein? Mr. Henkel? I just had to keep my eyes open.

Chapter 10

The electronic monitor indicates my bus is boarding. Better get in line now. For a long trip like this, I need an aisle seat. Don't want to be climbing over someone every hour when they're trying to get some sleep.

They packed a nice lunch for me at Wolfy's: a huge corned beef sandwich with mustard on rye, two half-sour pickles and a Danish, with a Dr. Brown's cream soda—that's my favorite. I'll pick up something for dinner when the bus makes a stop.

There's already a line for my bus. Looks like I'll be the only white person on the bus, if you don't count the Mexicans and a couple of guys you can tell are Cubans from the shirts with four pockets they're wearing.

I don't mind being with different types of people. I've spent my whole adult life walking through every type of neighborhood—in both New York and Miami. People are people; they're just as likely to smell bad if they're orthodox Jews as they are if they're black or Chinese.

"Is this the bus for New York City?" a small black woman asks me; she's maybe sixty years old, although you never can tell. Like me, she's dressed nicely for the trip, a green suit, clean, but a little worn—just a whiff of perfume. She's carrying a shopping bag and wheeling a small red suitcase.

"I hope so. That's where I'm going."

"Last time I took the bus," she says, "it overheated. We had to change buses in Greensboro."

"Do you go to New York often?" I ask.

"Whenever I can save up enough from my social security to make the trip. My daughter lives in Manhattan—in Harlem. I've got two granddaughters, ten and six. I love them to pieces."

Social security—she must be a little older than I thought. "How long are you staying?"

"Only about two weeks. I don't want to wear out my welcome. How about you—are you going all the way to New York?"

87

"Yes, I'm going to stay with my grandson. He's a lawyer. Lives in someplace called Jamaica Estates. He has a boy and a girl. I haven't seen them in a while."

By now, about fifty people are lined up for the bus. "Are you traveling by yourself?" she asks. "We could sit together."

"That would be fine, if I could have the aisle seat."

"Of course, I like to sleep against the window. My name is Bessie."

She holds out her hand and I shake it. "I'm Abe."

"Okay folks," the bus driver says. "Let's load up your luggage. No room inside for any suitcases." He opens the bin at the bottom of the bus. Bessie and I wait long enough to see our luggage safely stored and then board.

We take seats near the middle of the bus. A Latino in his seventies with yellowish skin takes the seat across the aisle from me. A few minutes later, he goes into a coughing fit, making no attempt to cover his mouth.

"I hope you don't mind my asking, Abe," Bessie says. "How old are you?"

"I'm ninety-one."

"My father lived to be your age. My husband wasn't so lucky. He died two years ago—at sixty-eight."

"I'm sorry to hear that." For the first time in a long while, I think of my own father; he only made it to fifty-five. I remember him leading a Passover Seder, and, of course, sending me to America.

At the start of '07 I was sitting on top of the world. My salary was more than enough to live on, and I looked forward to getting a share of the profits at the end of the year. Being a boss made quite a difference in my life. Every day there were decisions to be made: not only how to make the belts, but also how many sewing machines to run and what supplies to order.

Mr. Henkel had bankrolled our company with three thousand dollars, which we were to pay back over three years. But when Louis left, the checking account was down to twelve hundred. As a worker, when I left the factory I didn't think about work, but as a boss I thought about it all the time—sometimes even when I was trying to sleep at night. It was a lot for a

22-year old to have on his shoulders. I was trying my utmost to make Henkels' Belts a success; I think I was still trying to impress my dead father.

I also learned an important lesson in 1907: the success of a business depends on more than how hard and well everyone works. When in March, I heard the newsboys call out, "Read all about it—stock market crashes," I didn't think much about it. But a couple of months later, Henkel's business slowed down. I didn't connect the two events. We went from three sewing machine operators to two and sometimes to only one. Fortunately, instead of hiring our own sewing machine operators, we "borrowed" them from upstairs, so I was spared the job of hiring and firing employees.

Walking home with Yudel, I asked, "Why are things so slow?"

"Avrom," he said, "Man plans and God laughs. When you've lost most of your money on the stock market, you don't buy your wife a new dress."

It seemed a successful businessman had to be aware of what is going on in the country—maybe even the world. That meant reading newspapers. Yudel read the *Forward*, which concentrated on the lower East Side. For a broader perspective, I'd have to look at the *Times* or maybe the *New York Post*. Since I didn't mind getting day-old news, I'd check the trash bins as I walked to and from work. Only rarely did I give the newsboy my two cents.

In April, the Henkels invited me to *Shabbos* dinner again. I expected Leah to be there, but when I arrived, Mrs. Henkel told me, "Leah's going to be late. What sort of job is it that doesn't allow a girl to get home for Friday night dinner?"

"Someone has to take care of the patients on Friday afternoon," Mr. Henkel said.

"The Christian nurses could take Friday and Saturday and the Jews Sunday," Mrs. Henkel suggested.

"Good idea," Mr. Henkel admitted. "Let's talk in the living room, Abe."

After our customary drink, he asked me, "What do you think about the financial situation?"

I was glad I had started reading newspapers, and was able to say, "Not too good. Looks like some people were too greedy."

"Yes, I'm glad they aren't Jewish."

"How bad do you think it will get?"

"These things usually don't last too long. I think the situation should improve pretty soon. Don't worry about Henkel's Belts. I won't let it go under. You can pay me back the startup money over five years."

I felt good: not only had Mr. Henkel reassured me about my job and reduced the stress of paying him back, but he had also talked to me like a fellow businessman.

When Mrs. Henkel called us, we moved to the dining room for dinner. In Leah's absence, Ruth lit the candles. She sang the blessing over the candles in a squeaky voice, and then turned around and took a little bow. While Megan served the soup, Sammy and I talked about the Maccabees, who were having a very good season. Sammy had made the team at the Uptown Y, but he wasn't a starter and usually didn't get into the game. He had grown two inches over the past year, however, and thought he might do better in the fall.

We were having dessert when Leah arrived, wearing her white uniform. "Sit down and eat," said Mrs. Henkel.

"I'm not too hungry, I'll just have some soup."

"Soup!" said her mother. "That's no dinner. You've got to keep up your strength. You work so hard."

"Just soup. Maybe I'll have something later."

In fact, I noticed that Leah had lost some weight. She seemed very tired. As soon as she finished the soup, she said to me, "Let's take a walk. It's a beautiful evening."

As we strolled past the now-occupied Ansonia, I wondered, but did not ask, whether the cows ever made it to the roof.

"I was on the birthing ward today," Leah said. "There were so many women having babies the doctor had to run from one to the next. One woman had been in labor for twenty hours, and he had to operate to get the baby out. While he was doing that, Nurse O'Brien and I had to deliver two babies on our own." She smiled thinking about the experience.

"We didn't have a hospital in my village," I offered. "The women had their babies at home."

90

"I'm sure in your village there was a midwife and the women had family to help them. These are very poor women. They haven't been in this country very long and don't have any relatives here. They won't have any help when they get home." Leah was silent for a few moments and then continued, "It's very rewarding to bring a new life into the world, but in a way it's sad. Those women are going to be taking their babies back to such a poor environment. I don't see how they're going to be able to take care of them. Without assistance many of the babies won't live past their second birthday. That's why I want to be a visiting nurse."

I was silent for a few minutes, ashamed at not having realized the plight of those women, who were my neighbors. Then I asked, "When will your friend Bernard from France be arriving?"

"I'm not sure. His mother's been sick lately, and he doesn't think he can leave her."

Leah didn't seem happy about this. Maybe like Helen, she should have gotten an engagement ring to "seal the deal."

"I'm sorry to hear that," I said, and I meant it.

I kept my eye on the company checking account balance. When it reached eight hundred, I began to have my doubts about how large my percentage of the profits would be.

In October, the newsboys called out, "Huntington bank fails." I saw people lined up outside of banks. Mr. Henkel had his companies' money in the Bank of New York. That was no fly-by-night outfit; it was the oldest bank in America. Nevertheless, he sent Arthur down to the bank to withdraw most of the balance. I guess he put the cash in the safe in his office.

The Huntington Bank failure and several others that soon followed didn't directly affect me; my life savings of a little more than a hundred dollars was safely stored in a shoebox under my bed. Mina had much more, and hers was in a bank. One morning she left work to join a long line of people waiting to withdraw their money. Fortunately, her bank wasn't in trouble, and she got all her money out. That evening, holding a stack of twenty-dollar bills, she looked around for a secure place in the apartment to hide them.

91

"You can put them under your mattress," I suggested.

"Under the mattress, that's the first place any thief looks."

She finally decided to store the bills in a bag of rice. She poured the grains into a bowl, put the bills in the bottom of the bag and then refilled it with rice. It should be safe in there, I thought, unless the thief was hungry. For a moment I wondered about the security of my shoebox, but then it slipped my mind.

Everyone was getting nervous. From what I heard, it sounded like the whole banking system could collapse. The newspapers called it a panic, and I guess that was what it was. Even Mr. Henkel's assurances didn't completely alleviate my fear.

Things got worse and worse, until I heard the newsboy holler, "Morgan organizes rescue." Seems like a man by the name of J. P. Morgan and some of his friends had got together enough money to restore confidence in the banks. Now that's what I call rich!

Arthur did his audit toward the end of the year and asked me to bring my bills for December up to Mr. Henkel's office. At lunchtime, I went up with a box of papers. The office was empty, but the door was open. I went in and put the box on Mr. Henkel's desk. When I turned to leave, the photos on the wall caught my eye. There was Helen, modeling a tennis dress similar to the one she wore on our date. I looked around. The workers had either gone out or were sitting by the window. No one was looking my way. I quickly removed the thumbtacks from Helen's photo. Then I rearranged the others to cover the empty space left on the wall. I put the photo under my shirt and left the office. Halfway down the stairs, I felt very dizzy. I was breathing rapidly. What had I done—jeopardized my career for a photo? Well, it was too late to try to return it now.

About a week later, Mr. Henkel called me up to his office. I was sure it was about the photo. Someone must have seen what I had done and turned me in to get on Mr. Henkel's good side. Now I had to pay the piper. I was all ready to apologize when I entered Mr. Henkel's office.

"Well, Abe," he said before I had a chance to speak. "Your first year in charge has been a rough one. Arthur tells me that Henkel's Belts lost money last year."

It was what I expected. Did that mean he was going to shut us down? "I'm not surprised," I said.

"Don't feel bad," he continued. "It's not your fault. Sometimes the economy goes bad."

"Do you think it'll get better?" I asked.

"I'm confident it will. Already Morgan's bailout is restoring confidence. People are returning their money to the banks. I'll keep supporting Henkel's Belts."

"I'm glad to hear that."

"Of course, there won't be any share-of-the-profits bonus this year. But you deserve something." He handed me a sealed white envelope.

"Thanks."

"Keep up the good work." We shook hands and I left his office.

Going back downstairs, my disappointment with the performance of Henkel's Belts was tempered by relief at my petty thievery not having been discovered. On the stairs I opened the envelope. Inside were five ten-dollar bills. I know nowadays that doesn't seem like much—maybe a night on the town for two. But back then, fifty bucks was big money. It was twenty percent of my yearly salary—and on a year when Henkel's Belts lost money. I was satisfied and looked forward to doing much better as soon as the economy recovered.

Chapter 11

"I remember the first time I took the bus to New York," Bessie says as we edge onto the Florida Turnpike. "They didn't have roads like this then. The trip took two whole days. No toilet on the bus, so they had to stop every few hours: at a gas station, or just by some trees, if someone had an emergency."

"Most people take a plane," I say. "That only takes three hours."

"I don't know if I'd do that. Can't figure out what keeps them up in the air. Anyway, I'm not in any hurry. Just as soon meet someone and have a little conversation."

"I hope you don't mind if I eat," I say. "Didn't get any lunch today."

"Eat, that's a good idea. Could you give me my blue satchel?"

I stand up and take my Wolfy's bag and Bessie's blue satchel down from the rack. She rummages in the blue bag and pulls out something wrapped in aluminum foil. "Fried chicken. Made it myself."

"Corned beef on rye. It's from Wolfy's."

"That's a pretty big sandwich," Bessie says. "I've got an idea. I brought more chicken than I can eat. Why don't we eat it now, while it's still a little warm, and later for dinner we can split your sandwich?"

Now, I don't usually do fried food anymore—stomach isn't as good as it used to be—but Bessie's chicken smelled wonderful, and sharing would save my paying for a meal. "Good idea, and I've got some pickles and a soda to go with the chicken."

I wish I could tell you that my expectations were met, and I made big money as part boss at Henkel's Belts. However, my bonus check at the end of '08 was 84 dollars and for '09 was 134 dollars. Nothing to sneeze at, but I was hardly headed for the ranks of the super rich. It didn't have to be that way: Henkel's was one of the first belt companies, and if we had tried harder at the beginning, we could have could have grown much faster. But by '09, we had a lot of competition, and were reduced almost exclusively to servicing Henkel's Dresses.

The problem was the way Henkel's Belts had been set up. Mr. Henkel had said he would have someone working on getting us outside orders, but that never materialized. I followed up with the companies that Louis had gotten orders from, but in the troubles of '07, a couple of them, including Finklestein's, went out of business. Since I was running the factory, I couldn't be out pounding the streets. Also, as I found out, key employees at our customers expected a little "something", maybe a bottle of whiskey or a turkey, for Christmas. I spoke to Arthur about that, and he said those wouldn't be "appropriate expenditures." As a result, we lost most of our outside customers. I hadn't appreciated the importance of everything Louis did when he wasn't in the factory. Maybe he wasn't stealing from Mr. Henkel after all.

So Henkel's Belts was a one-customer company, and that customer set his own price. This gave Mr. Henkel complete control over our profits— and my bonus at the end of the year. I was beginning to feel less like a boss and more like a worker—a very hard working worker. I was stuck at age twenty-four.

"How are things going at Henkel's Belts?" Yudel asked me on one of the few days I left early enough to walk home with him.

"Not too good. Unless we get some outside orders, we're never going to make much profit."

"You need a salesman."

"Mr. Henkel said he'd get someone, but he never did."

"Listen Avrom, It's the squeaky wheel that gets greased. You've got to talk to him."

"I think you're right; maybe I'll go in and see him." I was pretty sure I wouldn't have enough nerve to do that.

A few days later, I was hurrying home, when I passed Cooper Union, a six-story brick building at Seventh Street and Third Avenue. One of the Bregman twins from the Maccabees had studied engineering there. I saw a crowd entering the building. A double line of policemen stood outside. I recognized Juanita, one of Henkel's operators who sometimes worked for the belt factory. "What's going on?" I asked her.

"Samuel Gompers is going to talk in the Great Hall," she informed me.

I remembered Mr. Henkel telling me that Gompers was a "very dangerous man." I thought I should find out for myself if that was true, so I followed Juanita across the line of policemen and entered the building.

The Great Hall of Cooper Union was larger than the gym at Columbia. It was built with arches and columns, like some churches I had seen. The room had more than a thousand seats, all of which were filled when I entered. People were standing in the aisles and in the back of the room. Juanita and I managed to find a place against the back wall. Juanita nodded toward the speaker, "That's Feigenbaum, he's a Socialist."

Feigenbaum was talking about the need to build a new society—pretty boring stuff. When he finished and introduced Samuel Gompers, the President of the American Federation of Labor, the crowd went wild. It was almost five minutes before things quieted down to where Gompers could speak. He was so short that he had to stand on a box to look at the audience over the podium. He looked like a little gnome, but spoke like an angel. He got everyone's attention when he called out, "Our movement is of the working people, for the working people, by the working people."

He spoke about low wages, long hours and horrible working conditions, and although Henkel's wasn't the worst in any of these categories, I could relate to them. Gompers said, "I have never declared a strike in all my life. I have done my share to prevent strikes. But there comes a time when not to strike is but to rivet the chains of slavery upon our wrists." At these words, the crowd let out a roar. Even I was cheering—until it occurred to me that a strike would cut off Yudel's and Mina's incomes—and probably even mine.

After Gompers finished talking, another boring Socialist was introduced. I was one of the many members of the audience who headed for the door. We passed through the police line without incident.

I could understand why Mr. Henkel thought Gompers was a dangerous man: he excited the workers. His ability to move them to immediate action, however, was diluted by the other speakers, who talked in abstract terms about a new society of the distant future.

The next morning, while walking to work, I saw small groups of women shivering in front of buildings all along Ludlow and Grand Streets. A few of them had bandages wrapped around their heads or stood with the aid of a crutch. I saw one young woman with what appeared to be dried blood on her face. The placards they carried said: "Strike for a living wage," or "50-hour week." I was surprised; I hadn't thought the previous night's meeting would have resulted in any action. And I was worried; would I find something similar in front of Henkel's?

When I turned onto Essex Street, I was relieved—no picket line in front of Henkel's. Upstairs, everything seemed normal. Maybe conditions here were good enough the workers wouldn't go out on strike.

At lunchtime, I went upstairs and searched out Juanita. She told me what had happened after I left the meeting.

"A young woman in the audience called out something. A few of the men helped her to the stage. She talked in Yiddish, but they translated for her. She said she was on strike when the boss sent some thugs to beat her up. That was why she couldn't walk. She was such a little girl...I started to cry. All of a sudden shouts came from the audience: 'strike, strike, strike' they called out. That's what everyone was yelling when we left the building and the police swung their clubs at us. I was lucky; I got away without getting hit."

Henkel's avoided the strike, but Mr. Henkel must have paid attention to the placards, since a few days later he announced that workdays would end at five, rather than six. With the half hour off for lunch, the workweek was now less than fifty hours at both the dress and belt factories. In addition, Henkel's accepted the International Ladies' Garment Workers' Union as the bargaining representative for its workers. The local union leader was Rosalyn Henneker, a sewing machine operator. I was irritated Mr. Henkel hadn't discussed any of the decisions with me. In addition, that summer, he finally took the suggestion I had made two years earlier and installed large fans in some of the windows of both the dress and belt factories.

Chapter 12

"Does your daughter work?" I ask Bessie, after we finish the fried chicken, and I go to the bathroom to wash my hands.

"She's a teacher in Harlem, and her husband's an engineer."

"That's great!"

"Yes, God has been good to me," Bessie says. "My grandfather was a slave and then a sharecropper. My father farmed his own land. My husband was a postal worker. And now my daughter and her husband are professionals."

"Did you ever work?" I ask her.

"Yes, I cleaned houses in my home town, Wetumpka, Alabama. It's not far from Montgomery. I took a few years off after I had my baby—to take care of her and to recover. I had a very difficult pregnancy and birth. Couldn't have any more children after that. I'm lucky she turned out so well."

"I'm glad things worked out for you."

"Yes, now I have a nice little house in Brownsville. Have you ever been there?"

"No, but I've seen it on the Miami map."

"It's a good neighborhood. Mixed population: colored, Latinos and whites. It was my sister's; bless her soul. Left it to me when she died. No mortgage. And where do you live?"

"In South Beach. Mainly old people, although some young ones are moving in—mainly weirdos. They're sprucing up some of the old hotels for tourists. The old folks who live in them will have to find another place."

A little later, Bessie says, "Abe, I'm sure you must have seen a lot of things in your 91 years. What has your life been like?"

"Yes, I have seen a lot." And I start to tell her a little of my story.

One morning in the spring of 1910, Yudel was sitting at his table at Henkel's, cutting around a pattern, when he felt a sudden sharp pain in his

98

head. He tried to continue cutting, but he couldn't use his scissors. He tried to stand up, but he crashed to the floor. The workers carried him to the couch in Mr. Henkel's office. Mr. Henkel sent for a doctor and fetched me from downstairs.

"Yudel," I said, joining Mina at his side. "What happened?"

"I don't know," his left hand pointed to that side of his head. "I have such a headache, you wouldn't believe, and I have no strength at all in my right hand and leg."

When the doctor, an orthodox Jew with a large grey beard, showed up, he waived us all out of the office. "Please, ladies and gentlemen, I'll need some privacy while I examine the patient."

Mina and I stood outside, watching as the doctor felt Yudel with his fingers and listened to him with a stethoscope. We saw Yudel motion to where his head was hurting. He tried to move his arm, but could only lift it about two inches. The doctor came to the door and motioned to Mina and me to come back in.

"The diagnosis is apoplexy," he said. "Nowadays we call it a stroke. There's not much we can do for it. Sometimes there's a full or partial recovery…sometimes not. Exercise can help…and prayer. In the meantime he needs plenty of rest, food when he feels up to eating, and two aspirin every six hours. I suggest you get him a wheel chair." He rose and looked around for whoever was to pay him his dollar fee. I saw Mr. Henkel motion him over. Mina and I were panicked.

Yudel couldn't walk home, so Seth, Henkel's shop foreman, and I each put one of Yudel's arms around our shoulders and carried him downstairs to a waiting carriage. When we got home, the carriage driver helped me get Yudel up to the apartment. It wasn't an easy job so I gave him a ten-cent tip.

After Yudel's stroke, life wasn't easy. Mina stayed home to take care of him, so all of a sudden I was the only wage earner in our little family. Even though I doubled my contribution to the upkeep of the apartment, Mina and Yudel were running through their savings at an alarming rate.

We got Yudel a wheelchair. After the first week, I would help him into it before I left in the morning. However, it was too large to get through the bathroom door. He weighed more than two hundred pounds, and someone had to help him get to the toilet. Mina was too small to support him and all the men in the building went to work. I would hurry home to help him at lunchtime. There was hardly enough time for this, so, for a dollar, I bought an old bicycle to speed up my round trip.

Yudel did everything he could to improve things. Although he was in very low spirits, he hated imposing on others. "Look at me, Avrom" he said, with tears in his eyes, "I'm a cripple—such a burden on you. When a father helps a son, both smile; but when a son must help his father, both cry." It was true: he had been like a father to me for the last ten years. Yudel's favorite expression, "Man plans and God laughs," was particularly apt at this time. I think Yudel's Yiddish proverbs kept me from getting too depressed about his condition.

To give Yudel some exercise, I would help him up and he would hop along the back of the couch. After a month or so he learned to lift himself up on the arm of the couch, and, using a crutch, get to the bathroom by himself, so I no longer had to come home at lunchtime. His leg and fingers remained pretty useless, but he regained a little strength in his arm. We had a well-recommended doctor come to the house to examine Yudel. He confirmed the diagnosis and that there were no medicines that could help.

"Man does not always want to hear the truth," Yudel said.

I remembered seeing a shop in Chinatown advertising "Chinese herbal medicines for any condition." One Saturday I went down there on the odd chance they might have something for Yudel.

"For apoplexy, I recommend Dong Quai," the proprietor told me. "Use two spoonfuls to make tea, twice a day. Let it brew for five minutes. Sometimes it works." His perfect English surprised me and I remarked on it.

"My family has been here for sixty years," he told me. "I was born in America. Do you know that America has not allowed immigrants from China for over forty years? The government thinks we're dirty."

On my walk back home, I thought about how similar the plight of the Chinese in America was to that of the Jews in the old country. They were successful, stuck together, had a rich culture and were generally despised.

Dong quai tea tasted pretty awful, but Yudel didn't hesitate to drink it. He thought it was doing some good. "Look, Avrom," he said, as he closed his hand on a glass of water. But when he tried to pick it up, it slipped out, spilling the water all over the table.

A friend told Mina about a company that made linen tablecloths and napkins and would contract with people to sew them on a piecework basis in their homes.

"That would be perfect for me," Mina said. "I could stay home with Yudel and make some money at the same time."

Every Monday after work, I would stop at The Elegant Tablecloth Company on Broome Street, where a half-dozen men were already waiting to pick up bales of material cut to size. Elegant required a ten-dollar deposit for each bale. On Friday morning, after Mina had sewed around each of the cloths, I'd pack them up and return the bale, receiving thirteen dollars after the work had passed inspection. Often money was deducted for less than perfect workmanship. For sewing from morning till night over three days, Mina earned three dollars or less. The bales, although not particularly heavy, were bulky and awkward to carry. For a quarter, I usually hired a carriage for my trip. I never told Mina about that expenditure.

Money was much tighter in our household than before Yudel had his stroke. But with my salary and annual bonus, we managed to get by.

Chapter 13

"I remember back in Montgomery," Bessie says, "colored had to stand in the back of the bus, even when there were empty seats up front."

"I've heard about that."

"And those white bus drivers were mean. You had to pay your fare in the front and then get off the bus and go in the back door. Sometimes the bus would drive off before you got back on."

"That's horrible," I say, remembering how even the nickel fare on the New York subway was a lot for me."

"Have you ever heard of Rosa Parks?"

"The bus lady?"

"Yes, she wasn't the first one to make a stink about it ...two younger girls did earlier that year; it was '55, I think. But when they arrested Rosa for not moving back, we all decided not to ride the buses—not in Wetumpka, it's too small to have buses—but down in Montgomery."

"How did it end up?"

"For a whole year there was a boycott. Dr. King—I'm sure you've heard of him—led it. He was a minister in Montgomery at the time. They arrested him and firebombed his house, but that didn't stop it. Finally the Supreme Court declared segregated buses unconstitutional."

"Firebombed...I hope no one was hurt."

"No, they were able to put it out."

And then I tell Bessie about another fire.

In 1911, Izzy had started New York University Law School. Most of his classes were at night, and to support himself during the day he did "leg work" for lawyers at the Legal Aid Society. This usually involved interviewing housewives about the disrepair of their apartments, or workers about withheld wages or dangerous working conditions. Once every few months he would meet some pretty girls and arrange a double date for us.

102

One day he called me on the telephone at work. "Hey Abe, I met some interesting young ladies, Carla and Marta. Marta is for you. They're both from the Ukraine. Are you available this Saturday?"

"This and every Saturday."

"Great. They work in the building next to the law school. I've got some stuff to do in the library. When they get off from work at five, I'll bring them over to Washington Square Park. Wait for us somewhere near the statue of Garibaldi."

"Will do. See you Saturday at five."

Saturday I played basketball in the morning and walked in the afternoon. By four thirty I was starving and looked forward to meeting the new girls and picking up a knish and hotdog or two from a stand or a nearby deli. I found a bench near the statue and spread a newspaper from the trash over it, so that we would have a place to eat when Izzy and the girls arrived.

I was reading an article about the troubles in Europe, when I heard people crying out behind me. I turned around and saw smoke pouring out a window of one of the upper floors of the building right next to the law school. *Would Izzy be okay? He should be fine; the library was on the second floor of the law school. But didn't he say the girls worked in the next building? Maybe that's where the fire was.* I jumped up and followed the crowds running towards the fire.

The first fire truck to arrive at the scene was one of the new motorized ones. With its bells clanging, it rounded the corner of the park. Pedestrians jumped out of its way. A large crowd was beginning to form, and the horse-drawn fire trucks were starting to arrive. The police were putting up barriers to keep the onlookers away from the burning building. A river of girls was streaming out of the entrance to the building.

I looked up and counted the ten floors of the building. Fire was pouring out of windows on the eighth floor. Smoke was also coming from ninth-floor windows, where girls stood screaming. Up there girls were climbing out onto the fire escape. Then, either from too much weight or bad supports, it pulled away from the window, plunging them all to the ground.

A large ladder truck arrived. The fire fighters swung the ladder against the burning building. But, it only reached to the sixth floor. Four

103

hoses were spraying the building from different directions. But, the sprays all fell far short of the burning floors.

A girl with her hair on fire screamed. She jumped from an eighth floor window. In flames and black smoke she plummeted to the ground, making a *thump* as she hit. A firefighter ran to her with a blanket and put out the flames. But she didn't move. Now, girls and a few men were raining down from the eighth and ninth floor windows: *thump, thump, thump* as they hit the ground. Some of the girls aimed for the ladders below, hoping to grab hold. But none succeeded. Some aimed for a safety net held by a half dozen men. But it wasn't designed to hold so many falling from such a great height. They went right through. The fire fighters called out that the net was broken, and they shouldn't jump, but what else could girls do with flames at their back. Pairs of them stood on the ledge outside the window and, holding hands, stepped into space.

The falling girls hit several of the fire fighters, leading the rest to stand back helplessly, while girls rained down. After a while the whole top of the building was an inferno. I was almost paralyzed by what I had seen. Each girl was someone's wife, mother or daughter, and a huge crowd had collected, with men: Orthodox Jews, Irish, Italians, Germans... screaming the names of women and crying. It was more than I could take; I had to get away from there. I didn't know where Izzy was, but I expected that if I went back into the park and stayed there according to our original plan, he would find me...if he was okay, that is.

I sat in the park and tried to get that horrible scene out of my mind by looking at the trees and birds. It was past dark, when finally I saw Izzy's outline stumbling in my direction. "Izzy, over here," I called out. His face was covered with soot. "Are you okay?"

"Let me sit for a while," he said. He sat on the bench with his head between his legs and coughed repeatedly. Finally, he told me what had happened. "When we heard the call *fire,* we all ran out into the street. But then me and a few other guys realized that the law school building was just a little taller than the one next door, and that might be an escape route. We ran back into the building and took the elevator to the top floor, and then the stairs to the roof."

"That was dangerous," I injected.

"Yes, but we were lucky. In a janitor's closet up there we found some buckets, and lying on the roof, a hose and ladder. We sprayed water and kept the fire from spreading to the Law School. By lowering the ladder to the roof of the burning building, we were able to help a group of girls to escape from the smoke billowing out of its roof. But I didn't see Carla and Marta," he concluded.

"Why were so many girls jumping from the windows?" I asked.

"Because the damn bosses locked the doors. The only way to get up or down was by the elevators. The bosses thought that would keep the workers from stealing stuff. The place was a disaster waiting to happen. The lawyer I was working with at the Legal Aid Society was taking them to court. That's how I met Carla, she was helping me collect data for the case."

"Did any of the girls who jumped survive?" I asked.

"I saw the ambulance take a few of them away. They must have been alive—for now anyway."

Izzy and I put our arms on each other's shoulders and cried. Not in my worst dream, could I have imagined such a horrible thing occurring.

For a while, the fire, in which one hundred forty six people died, was on the mind of all New Yorkers. Who were the owners who locked them in? Surely, as murderers they would be punished. I had to read a newspaper every day, and since people weren't throwing any away, I had to buy it.

Most of the bodies were so badly burned they were hard to identify. The City kept them on ice on one the piers; family and friends filed by, trying to recognize loved ones by a ring or a pin. Finally ten days after the fire, they held a funeral for the unclaimed bodies. It was Wednesday, but everyone took off from work, the bosses knew enough not to try to stop them—or to dock their pay. It was several months later that the two owners of the Triangle Shirtwaist Company were tried. They were both Jews, I'm sorry to say. The jury acquitted them both. They couldn't prove that they actually knew the entrances were locked at the time of the fire.

The Triangle fire made me realize that my job involved more than just making money for Mr. Henkel. As the "boss," I was also responsible for the workers. Thereafter, I always made sure that the exits to the stairs and the fire escape were not blocked. I also invested ten dollars of Henkel Belt's money to buy a large fire extinguisher.

It wasn't too long before the New York State Legislature, over the screams and yells of some of the factory owners, passed stringent new rules to ensure worker safety and wellbeing. After that, safety inspectors made regular visits to the Henkel companies, and new programs, such as worker compensation, were started. I read that Samuel Gompers was one of the members of the committee that made these recommendations to the state legislature.

And then something really bad happened to me: Yudel died.

Chapter 14

Bessie comes down the aisle from the bathroom and says, "I think I got a disapproving look from that couple in the back."

"Which one?"

"Two seats from the back on the right."

I look over my shoulder and see a black couple. The woman quickly averts her eyes. "What sort of look?" I ask Bessie.

"The sort that says, 'Okay, Miss Fancypants, so you got yourself a white husband. What good did it do you? You're still riding the bus with us black folk.'"

That seems funny to me.

"Have you ever been to Disneyworld?" Bessie asks, as the bus pulls into the Orlando station.

"No, I was planning a trip there with Ida—she's a very good friend of mine. But then she got sick and went back to New York."

"Oh, I'm so sorry to hear that. Is that where you're heading now?"

"Yes."

"Well I hope she gets better, and you're both able to go to Disneyworld. I was there with my daughter and her family last year, and it was wonderful."

We have about fifteen minutes in the Orlando station—just long enough to stretch our legs and get a couple of sodas to have with our dinner.

I still remember that day in August 1911, when I got a frantic call from Mina. "Something's happened to Yudel," she said. "He's hanging off the side of his chair. I think he's dead."

"Did you call the doctor?" I asked.

"Yes, he should be here any minute."

I biked as fast as I could all the way home and found Mina sitting on the couch and crying on the shoulder of Mrs. Hirsch, our next-door neighbor. The doctor had come and gone, Mina told me. He had declared Yudel dead

107

and filled out a death certificate. With the help of the two women, he had moved him into the bedroom.

"I was sewing away, talking to him," Mina said. "Then I realized he hadn't answered me in a while. He was hanging over the side of the chair."

"It sounds like he passed very peacefully," said Mrs. Hirsch. "We should all be so lucky."

I didn't feel so lucky. Yudel had been my anchor and compass in America. Besides feeding and housing me, he had started me off at Henkel's and taught me tailoring. His Yiddish proverbs provided me with good advice. Yudel's courage when he was disabled helped me forget my own problems. Most of all, when he was alive, I always felt that there was someone who loved me in this country. Suddenly, I felt very much on my own.

"What do we do now?" I asked Mina.

"I was going to call the Hebrew Free Burial Society."

"The Hebrew Free Burial Society?" I said excitedly. "That's for paupers. We should give him a decent funeral and burial."

"That costs a lot money," Mina said, pulling on her hair. "Over a hundred dollars. Not to mention paying for a cemetery plot and its upkeep. I just can't afford it. I'm almost sixty years old, and I don't know how much longer I can work. Morris's life insurance is almost gone, and Yudel doesn't have any. I'm not sure what's going to happen to me."

"I went to a Free Burial Society funeral," Mrs. Hirsch said. "They do a very good job. Their cemetery on Staten Island is very nice. The rich Jews pay for it all, as they should. If you become rich, you can give the society some money."

Should I offer to pay for the funeral? I thought it over. It would probably cost every penny I had saved in America. Who knew what Mina might be doing now that Yudel was dead? I might have to find another place to live. Reluctantly, I agreed to her plan.

Late the next day two large Orthodox Jewish men came to Mina's place from the Hebrew Free Burial Society. According to Jewish custom, they wrapped Yudel's body in a black shroud without pockets and placed it in a plain pine box. "This is going to be heavy," one of them said. "Can you give us a hand?" I was glad to help out; it was the least I could do for Yudel. We carried the box downstairs to a horse-drawn cart already loaded with two similar boxes.

"The burial will be at noon on Thursday—day after tomorrow," one of the men said. "Here's directions to Mount Richmond Cemetery. It's on Staten Island." He gave me a sheet of instructions, written in English, Yiddish, Russian and German.

On Wednesday I went to work, but my mind wasn't there. As soon as I had made sure that things were going smoothly, I left and wandered the streets. All I could think about was Yudel was gone. He was all the family I had in America and I missed him terribly. Usually I found interesting things to look at as I walked around the city, but that day, my eyes were on the ground and I wasn't even aware of where I was going. When I looked up, I was surprised to find myself down at the Battery. Maybe, I was thinking of getting on a boat and going back to the old country.

On Thursday morning, Mina and I took a carriage to the Battery, where we boarded the ferry to Staten Island. Mina decided to sit inside, but I stood outside against the railing, feeling a fine mist on my face. Off to the side I could see some familiar landmarks: Ellis Island, whose main building seemed a lot smaller than I had remembered, and the grand lady who welcomed me on my arrival in America. Neither could get my spirits up.

The engine of the boat made a grinding sound; after a while it sounded like, "Yudel is dead, Yudel is dead…" Finally I couldn't take it any more, and I ran inside and sat next to Mina. She put her head on my shoulder.

When the ferry docked, we followed the written instructions and boarded a trolley with a dozen other Jews, all dressed in black. After about a half hour the trolley driver announced, "Jewish Cemetery," and just about everyone got off. We were in the middle of the country, with no sign of a cemetery to be seen.

"It must be a mistake," one woman said. "There's no cemetery around here."

I agreed.

A few minutes later a cart pulled by two sturdy horses appeared out of a side road. It was reassuring to see a bearded Jew wearing a black hat driving it. We all climbed aboard and squeezed into the three rows of seats.

The ride to the cemetery was bumpy over an unpaved road, but the air was so fresh and cool I almost forgot where we were going. When a wheel of the cart got stuck in a rut, we all had to get out and push. Finally, we reached our destination and passed row upon row of graves, each marked only with a small brass plaque in the ground. The cart came to a halt in front of a half-dozen freshly dug graves, each already containing a pine box. Behind each was a pile of dirt and a shovel. A young couple stood sobbing over a very small grave. "The rabbi will be here soon," a workman leaning against a tree told us.

Since each grave was already marked with a plaque, Mina and I were able to find Yudel's. I looked down into the hole and said, "Do you think he's really in there, Mina?" She didn't answer.

"Good morning. Let's get started," a young, clean-shaven rabbi said. After a few words in English and Yiddish about souls going to a place of rest, he led us all in the mourner's *Kaddish* in Hebrew. Even though I hadn't been in *shul* for over ten years, I still remembered the prayer. At its conclusion the rabbi threw a shovel of dirt from each pile into the adjacent grave. He motioned to the mourners to follow his example. This procedure, he explained, is so no one is "handing off" the work of the burial. I followed Mina and was proud to help out. Finally, the rabbi pointed out a portable donation box to us all, and asked for contributions to support the work of the Burial Society. I had brought a five-dollar bill with me and dropped it into the box. Mina did the same. When the workman began to shovel the rest of the dirt into one of the graves, we all got back on the cart to begin our return trip.

With my only family member in America gone, I felt adrift. I wrote to Mama, telling her the news: how happy Yudel had been with Mina and how sad I was that he was gone. Maybe God could help me, I thought—but not the God of Temple Emanu-El, I needed the God of my youth, in a small *shul* that might remind me of the one in my village back in the Ukraine. There certainly were enough of these in the Lower East Side. In fact on East

110

Broadway, between Clinton and Montgomery, there were at least a half dozen small *shuls*; everyone called it *Striebel Row.* But I was worried. Wouldn't the men in black hats ask me when was the last time I was in *shul*, like the people back in my village would, especially after I was *bar mitzvahed*?

On the first Saturday after the funeral, wearing my tie and jacket, I headed to East Broadway. On Striebel Row, dozens of men stood around in front of the storefront synagogues. They wore *talises* and the black "nipple" hats popular with the ultraorthodox. Young boys with *yarmulkes* played tag. I was overwhelmed: *which of these shuls should I enter?*

One of the young men, seeing me perplexed, came over and asked, "Are you in mourning?"

"How did you know?"

"When *baalei teshuvah* —Jews returning to the fold—come here, it's usually because they've had a loved one die."

"Which of these *shuls* do you usually recommend to them?" I asked.

"That depends—do you speak Yiddish? Russian? Spanish? Or only English?"

"I speak Russian and Yiddish—although not so much lately."

"Then I suggest Ahavas Torah, that one over there," he said, pointing to a two-story building, a little more prosperous than its storefront neighbors.

"Can I just go in?" I asked him.

"Certainly," he said. "They usually can use help getting the *minyan*. Except for the High Holy Days, of course. No trouble getting ten Jewish men for prayers then. They even sell tickets."

I thanked him and entered the doorway of the narrow redbrick building. Wooden stairs at the right led to the gallery, where I surmised the women would sit, when they came—mainly on holidays. Downstairs, the main room had four rows of benches, accommodating perhaps fifty worshippers.

Directly ahead of me, a door was open, and to its right was a small table on which there were a few *yarmulkes and talises* and a half-dozen prayer books. I took one of each of these and entered the *shul*. There, about thirty black-clad men wrapped in *talises* were standing for the silent prayer. The prayer book, in Hebrew and Yiddish, looked familiar; I thought it was the same one we had used back in the *shtetl*. Praying with those men, I felt grounded once again. When we all stood for the mourners' *Kaddish*, I no longer felt alone. For a number of Saturdays I returned to the small *shul*, putting a dollar in the collection box each time.

My appearance was going downhill during that period. I wasn't getting much exercise and stopped shaving and getting haircuts to connect better with the other men at Ahavas Torah. In addition, I finally lost a front tooth that had been loosened by an elbow in a basketball game several years earlier. Since there were many teeth missing in the Saturday morning congregation and I had already lost one in the back of my mouth, I paid it little attention.

For a while after Yudel's funeral, my mind wasn't on my work. This culminated in my making a really bad mistake at work. In an order of over two hundred belts, I used the wrong backing: buckram instead of leather. Mr. Henkel was not happy, and I was afraid he'd fire me. I had to work more than ten hours on a Saturday, removing the material from the backing with a razor blade. Having missed one Saturday at *shul*, I stopped going altogether and resumed my walks around the city. After that, I resolved to put mind back on my work. My meager savings wouldn't last very long if I lost my job.

Part III - The Bronx

Chapter 15

Crossing into Georgia, I unwrap the corned beef sandwich for Bessie's and my dinner.

"This is a great sandwich," Bessie says.

"Jews like to eat like Irish like to drink."

"We colored folk like to both eat and drink. Harold—he was my husband—was an exception. Never took a drop in his life. Said it was because he saw what liquor did to his father."

"How did you meet Harold?" I ask.

"We met at church. We were both in the choir. How did you meet your wife?" Bessie asks.

I'm glad to tell her about that.

With Yudel gone, things became a little awkward between Mina and me. I guess, having lost two husbands, she was wondering how she would spend the rest of her life. Her friend Naomi's husband had died of a heart attack about a year earlier, and Mina was considering moving in with her. I was beginning to feel like a burden to her.

One evening when I came home from work, Mina was sitting on the couch with a woman about ten years younger than her. The woman had a scrapbook on her lap. "Abe," Mina said. "I would like you to meet Irina Seloko, a friend of mine." Irina was much more stylish than Mina's other friends. Her dark hair, streaked with white, matched her black-and-white silk dress and was set off by long silver earrings. I wondered if every day she dyed her hair to match her dress.

"Hi," I said.

"What a handsome young man." Irina said, waving her hand at me. "Mina tells me that you're an athlete and a businessman."

I blushed. My athlete days were coming to an end, and a less successful businessman couldn't be found anywhere in New York. I looked at Mina. She shook her head and raised a finger to her mouth, telling me to keep my mouth shut.

"I'm so glad to meet you," Irina said, holding out her hand. She had a strong handshake. "Mina also tells me you are currently unattached."

"Unattached?"

"Yes, not seriously involved with a woman."

"Irina is a *shadchan*—a matchmaker," Mina said. "She deals only with girls from good families."

So that was what was going on. Although I hadn't been thinking of getting married, I had been wrapped in loneliness since Yudel's death and wasn't opposed to hearing more from Irina.

"There are wonderful girls out there," Irina said, waving at the window. "Girls who can cook, sew, keep house and drive away loneliness. All my girls come with a substantial dowry, and many of them earn their own money."

"That sounds interesting," I said.

"Sit down and let me show you some of the beauties in my scrapbook."

"I'll make tea," Mina said, and vacated a place for me on the couch. Irina took my hand and guided me down next to her.

I inhaled Irina's perfume while she turned the pages of the scrapbook on her lap. A photograph of a girl was mounted on each page, opposite a sheet of paper that told something about her and her family.

"Rebecca Horowitz," Irina said of the first. "Her father is a salesman for a hardware supply company."

Rebecca wasn't to my liking at all. With her hair hanging over one eye and exaggerated eyelashes, she looked like one of the kewpie dolls I had seen in store windows on my walks around the city. Not the type of girl I wanted to spend the rest of my life with.

Actually, *What type of girl did I want to spend the rest of my life with?* I had never considered this before. I guess I wanted one who looked like Helen but was intelligent and self-assured like Leah. Probably I should have been thinking, at least a little, of her parents and how they could advance me financially, but at that moment my eyes and my brain just focused on the photos. Just the possibility of having a wife banished my loneliness. Irina was turning the pages much too fast. I wanted to sit with her scrapbook and leisurely contemplate being married to each girl.

"Here's the tea," Mina said, putting two cups and a plate of biscuits on the table in front of us. She squeezed in on the other side of Irina to get a look at the pictures, moving Irina even closer to me. Periodically, Mina made a comment, like, "Isn't that a pretty one?"

Most of the girls were fifteen to eighteen years old. They married them off young those days. Some of them were overweight, advertising the ability of their families to feed them well. I passed over those.

A photo of a pretty and intelligent-looking girl caught my eye. Irina spied my interest and said, "She's a lovely girl and very well educated. Her father's a rabbi."

That ruled her out. I had decided the religious life was not for me.

"If you see one you like," Irina said, "I'll arrange a *shidduch*, that's when you meet the young lady and her parents, and they decide whether you're a suitable match."

In my enthusiasm, I had never considered that I could be rejected, either by the girl, or by her parents, which they might do when they discovered how little this businessman actually made.

About half way through the book, a photo of a girl with short dark hair caught my eye. Unlike most of the others, she didn't show a sugary-sweet smile. The set of her chin and the intensity of her eyes suggested strength and intelligence. Irina was already turning to the next page, when I stopped her with, "What about that one?"

"That's Sarah Polinski," Irina said. "A very intelligent girl—an artist. Her father owns a bakery in the Bronx. She's a little older than the others."

She didn't look that old to me. "How old?" I asked.

"Twenty-five."

That was one year younger than me. "That's not too old."

"I should tell you," Irina hesitated, "Sarah has a limp."

A limp immediately made me homesick, thinking of my sister, Leena, who I hadn't seen for so long. More than before, I wanted to meet the girl with the intelligent eyes.

"I'd like to meet her," I stammered.

115

"That's wonderful," Irina gushed. "I'll arrange the *shidduch*. Mina should come too. While you talk to Sarah, Mina can talk to her parents. They'll want to know something about your family...to judge what sort of 'stock' you're from."

Irina rose and said, "You can keep that beard if you want, but I suggest you get a haircut. And you should do something about that tooth in the front. Here's the card of a dentist who can fix it. Make sure he puts in a white one."

The *shidduch* was arranged for the Sunday after the next. I wanted to impress Sarah, so I shaved, had my hair cut and went to see Dr. Blumstein, the dentist Irina had recommended.

"The metal ones last longer," Blumstein told me, "but the porcelain and ivory ones look better."

"It has to be white," I said.

"Let me see what I have," he said. He measured the space in my mouth. "It's good you came to me before the other teeth got pushed over. It's a much more difficult job then." Then he took teeth out of box and compared each one's size and color with those in my mouth. "This one looks the best. It will cost you twenty dollars."

I had brought some money with me, and gave him the go-ahead. The ivory tooth had a pin extending from its bottom and wires that Blumstein wrapped around the teeth on either side. He tapped the pin into my jaw and tightened the wires. "There, good as new," he said. I had my doubts, but I paid him anyway. It should at least get me through the shidduch, I thought.

Things were slow at Henkel's Belts, so I closed the factory on the day I was to meet Sarah. Mina and I took the Third Avenue El, crossing the Harlem River into the Bronx and getting off at 179 Street. We walked two blocks to Washington Avenue and turned down to 175th Street. This part of the Bronx had changed a lot since I walked here a half-dozen years earlier. The last few farms were gone, replaced by wide avenues and open squares.

The Polinski's building had six floors, and their bakery was one of the shops on the ground level. They lived on the second floor. The bakery was open on Sunday. I inhaled the aroma of freshly baked bread as we passed its open door, where two young girls were serving customers in the store.

"Smells wonderful," said Mina. "I wonder if Sarah can bake."

The entrance to the building was next door to the bakery. I hadn't been nervous until we started to climb the stairs, when suddenly I began gasping for breath. *What was I doing?* Mina felt my hesitation, and said, "It'll be all right." She held my hand. Upstairs there were four doors in the hall. Irina had told us the Polinskis lived in apartment number one. Mina pressed the bell, while I hung back with apprehension.

Irina, who had said she would meet us, opened the door. "Abe, Mina, come right in."

Light streamed through the two front windows of the modestly furnished living room. A couch, two upholstered chairs and at least six wooden chairs were arranged around the room. Someone was standing by each of these, except for an old woman who sat in one of the chairs. Let's see, I thought, the bearded man in the suit, with a pot belly and a *yarmulke* not quite covering his bald spot, must be the father; the woman in the loose grey dress, looking like she was getting ready to hug me—that's the mother. The others, two men and four women, all inspecting me carefully: siblings, cousins, aunts, uncles? I didn't know. And standing at the side of the couch, in a blue dress, with a smile that completely put me at ease —was a girl—no a woman, who looked just like the one in the photo.

Irina introduced me to everyone in the room. I immediately forgot their names. She saved Sarah for last. "And this is Sarah Polinski," she said. "The young lady I told you about."

I looked at Sarah. She smiled, held out her hand and took a few steps toward me. Sarah wore an oversized open, laced-up boot, which supported her right foot that was severely turned in. She walked with a very profound limp. Her mother grimaced with a look that said, *Did she have to do that right now? Couldn't she have stayed seated for a while?* But Sarah's limp didn't bother me at all. "Hello Abe," she said. "Come sit with me." Her hand was warm, and I followed her to the couch.

"Would you like some tea and cake?" Mrs. Polinski asked.

"Yes I would."

"We've heard a lot about you," Mr. Polinski said.

117

"I heard you play basketball," said a short, sturdy man a few years younger than Sarah.

"This is Sarah's brother, Benjamin," Mrs. Polinski reminded me.

"Glad to meet you," I said. "I used to play for the Maccabees."

"That's a very good team," Benjamin said.

I was surprised that the Maccabee's reputation had reached all the way up to the Bronx.

Mrs. Polinski, an attractive and energetic woman, brought tea and cake to a small table in front of the couch and then said. "Let's all go into the kitchen and give the young people a chance to get to know each other." Mr. Polinski helped his mother get up and they all walked into the kitchen. *The Polinskis must have a very large kitchen, if all these people would fit.*

After they left, Sarah said to me, "Abe, you've probably guessed that I'm not good at walking, dancing or hiking."

I laughed and told about her about my sister Leena, with whom I spent so much of my early life.

"Was her foot turned like mine?" Sarah asked excitedly.

"No, it was her hip that caused her trouble."

"Was she able to go to school?"

I told Sarah how when Leena was young, Papa pulled her to school in a wagon, but when she got older she insisted on managing the trip on her own. "Fortunately, it wasn't too far."

"I also went to school every day in a wagon," Sarah said, "Polinski's Bakery's wagon, pulled by a horse. I was the envy of all the kids."

"I hear you're an artist," I said.

"Yes, in school, instead of recess, they let me spend extra time with the art teacher. One of the things she taught me was how to make wood engravings. I use them to illustrate children's books. Let me show you some of my masterpieces."

She rose and limped off down the hall, returning with three small blocks. Very excitedly she said, "These are for a book, *Annie Goes to the Zoo*. She sees all the different animals. I go up to the Bronx Zoo and sketch the animals and then come back here and make the engravings."

118

I recognized a bear and an elephant on two of the blocks, but the animal on the third, with a neck about two stories high, I had never seen before. "What's this one?"

"That's a giraffe. I'll have to take you up to the zoo some day to see all the strange animals from other parts of the world."

"I'd like that."

"Too bad you don't play for the Maccabees any more," Sarah said. "I would have enjoyed watching one of your games. Do you still play?"

"Sometimes on Saturday I join a pickup game in Tompkins Square Park, but nowadays I get most of my exercise just walking around the city. I love doing that." I flushed. *I probably shouldn't have said that.*

Sarah picked up on my embarrassment. "Don't worry, Abe, I certainly wouldn't expect to join you in all your activities. You wouldn't have to stop walking, if we married."

I was relieved. We'd been so involved in conversation, I hadn't had a chance to try the piece of chocolate cake Mrs. Polinski had set in front of me. "This cake looks great," I said, and after forkful, "Yum, it tastes as good as it looks."

"It's from the bakery," Sarah informed me.

While I was eating, Sarah said, "Irina said you're in the belt business. Tell me about it."

I was glad that Irina hadn't said I owned the business. I explained to Sarah the deal that I had with Mr. Henkel—six dollars a week and a share of the profits, which hardly ever materialized.

"Six dollars a week," Sarah said. "That's not too much. I think Mr. Henkel is taking advantage of you." A furrow crossed her brow. She thought for a minute and then said, "Abe, I think I'd better tell you this right now."

Uh oh, I thought.

"I don't want to marry a *shlemiel*, who everyone takes advantage of. Before I agree to marry you, I want you to show me you can stick up for yourself. Ask Mr. Henkel for a raise. He might say no, but I'm sure he'll respect you more for asking. Come back next Sunday and let me know how it went."

119

I reddened with embarrassment. I guess I knew Mr. Henkel was taking advantage of me, but I never thought it would be so obvious to another person.

Since I was smitten with Sarah and didn't want to lose my chance to marry her, I decided I'd better approach Mr. Henkel for a raise before I lost my courage. Monday at lunchtime I tapped on his office door. "Come in, Abe," he said. "It's been a while since we've talked." Shaking just a little, I entered the office. "How are you doing since Yudel died?"

"It took me a while to get over it. He was the only family I had in America."

"Maybe it's time for you to think about getting married and starting a family," Mr. Henkel suggested.

He had given me the opportunity I needed. "That's what I came to see you about, Mr. Henkel. I've met a young woman I'm quite serious about. But in order to marry her, I need to make more money. My share of the profits hasn't been as much as I expected."

"Yes, I've noticed Henkel's Belts hasn't been doing too well," Mr. Henkel said.

I gulped. *Would he decide to shut it down?*

"Why do you think that is?" he asked.

"I think we need a salesman. If we got outside business, we could offset some of the fixed costs. Also that would allow us to decided on a fair price to charge."

"Don't you think I'm paying you enough for the belts?" Mr. Henkel said. He seemed hurt at the suggestion, and I quickly backtracked.

"Oh no, I'm sure you're paying a fair price for materials and labor, but without outside customers, I don't know what we should be asking for overhead and profits."

"Hmm...I never considered that. Let me think it over... Is that all?"

I panicked. Mr. Henkel had put me on the defensive, and I was on the verge of leaving without asking for a raise. I couldn't go back to Sarah before I did that. I pulled my stomach in and said, "I think I should get a raise; two dollars a week would be about right."

"Two dollars a week. Let's see. How much do you make now?"

"Six dollars."

"Well, a two-dollar raise would be a third. That's a lot at once. How about a one dollar increase, and we'll see what we can do about getting your profits up."

"O...kay." We shook on it, and I turned to start to leave his office, when he said. "By the way, did you hear that Leah is engaged?"

That stopped me in my tracks. "That's wonderful. Who's the lucky guy?"

"His name is Paul Stokes. He works with Leah. They're a team, Leah says. They visit families in the tenements; she works with the women and he works with their husbands."

"Is he a nurse too?"

"No, he's a college graduate, New York University."

"It's nice they work together."

"Yes, but I don't think they'll make much money at it," Mr. Henkel said, with a sigh.

"When will they be getting married?" I asked.

"I'm not sure," Mr. Henkel said, and then he dropped his bombshell. "Paul's not Jewish. I don't know whether they'll try to have a Jewish or a Christian wedding, or just go down to City Hall, like Yudel did."

Mr. Henkel didn't seem happy about the whole thing. "I don't know what will happen if Jewish children don't marry Jews and bring up their children Jewish," he said. "Soon there won't be any more Jews. I guess that's why they call America a melting pot."

Melting Pot—I remembered passing a theater where that was written on the marquee, but never realized what it meant before. I considered telling Mr. Henkel about Helen, a non-Jew who was going to convert to Judaism and bring up her children Jewish. That would help even things out. But then I remembered the photo I had taken off Mr. Henkel's wall. My being good friends with Helen might remind him of the theft. I decided to keep my mouth shut.

"When I invited you to my house," Mr. Henkel said, "I'd hoped that you and Leah might become more than friends."

What could I say about that? I just nodded my head.

"Leah was always a headstrong girl. She'd only do what she wanted." Mr. Henkel thought for a moment and then asked, "Is your fiancée Jewish, Abe?"

"Yes, she is."

"And how did you meet her?"

"A friend of Mina's—she's a *shadchan*—introduced me to her."

"Leah would never have let me do that," Mr. Henkel said, slowly shaking his head and walking back to his desk.

I decided it was time for me to leave.

My head was spinning. All in all it seemed like I'd been successful. Maybe Mr. Henkel would attempt to get some outside business for us and we'd be able to set a fair price. I was glad Sarah had pushed me to ask for the raise. One-dollar-a-week wasn't much; I hoped she'd be satisfied.

It was lucky I approached Mr. Henkel for a raise on Monday, because on Tuesday morning the headline across all the newspapers was "*Titanic* Sinks." Mr. Henkel didn't come in that day or the next. On Thursday I met him as I was walking down the stairs at lunchtime. His face was ashen as he told me, "Abe, most people don't realize it, but there were a lot of Jews on the *Titanic*. They even had a kosher table in the dining room. I don't know whether you remember the Steinmans, they sat at our table at Leah's graduation." He held the railing to steady himself.

I did remember that day. "The furrier?"

"Yes. He's the one. Lennard and Rebecca were returning from a month's vacation in Berlin, Paris and London. It was the first real vacation they took in ten years. We've learned they're not accounted for."

"That's horrible!"

"And I've heard of at least ten other New York Jews who were probably lost...including Issador Strauss and his wife. He ran Macy's." Mr. Henkel continued. "I just can't believe that something like this happened." He shook his head back and forth, as he continued up the stairs.

Taking my lunchtime walk on that sunny Spring day, I thought about the *Titanic*. A dozen or more Jews didn't match the numbers killed in any of the pogroms in the old country. Leah had said that Jews died of disease and malnutrition on the Lower East Side all the time. But this was different:

These were prosperous Jews who were safe in America. Their only mistake was venturing across the ocean when they didn't have to.

That night Irina and Mina were sitting in the living room when I returned from work. "Thank you for introducing me to such a lovely girl...I mean, young lady," I told Irina.

"I'm glad you liked her," she said. "I spoke to the Polinskis about her dowry."

In my enthusiasm for Sarah, I had completely forgotten the matter of a dowry.

"They are willing to be very generous," Irina said. "But Mrs. Polinski feels that because of Sarah's disability, it is important that you live in the neighborhood, so she can help Sarah out."

"That sounds right," I said.

"They'll find you a nice apartment—in the Bronx, of course—and pay the rent indefinitely. They'll furnish the apartment and in addition give you two hundred dollars. And, of course, you'll get free bakery products," Irina ended with a laugh.

"It sounds very good," I said, and then, remembering my last date with Helen. "Should I give Sarah a ring...to seal the deal?" I had no idea where I would get the money for a ring.

"A ring would be good, but not necessary," Irina said.

Mina thought for a moment before saying, "You know Abe, I have a ring from my marriage to Morris sitting in a box in the bedroom. It's not a very big stone, but I can't think of anything I'd rather do with it than give it to you to give to Sarah."

I was overwhelmed. How lucky I'd been in America to meet someone like Mina who would do that for me. Mina didn't wear the ring anymore, but she was giving up something that could always by sold in case of an emergency.

The following Sunday, without Mina for support, I cautiously walked up the stairs to Sarah's apartment. Mr. and Mrs. Polinski met me at the door.

"Come in Abe," Mrs. Polinski said, "Sarah will be a few minutes. Have a seat on the couch."

"Will you join me in some schnapps?" Mr. Polinski added.

"Of course," I said, by this time confident of my ability to handle the ritual without breaking into a coughing fit.

"*Le'chayim*," Mr. Polinski said. I tossed the brown liquid down my throat, bringing only a few tears to my eyes. *Gee, I'm getting to like this stuff.*

"Tell me about your family back in the Ukraine," Mrs. Polinski said.

Talking about my village was one of my favorite pastimes, although I must admit, even by that time, some of the details were getting fuzzy. I told the Polinskis about my family and my father's butcher shop. Mr. Polinski nodded in approval—a fellow shopkeeper was something he could appreciate. "I hope some day to meet your father," he said. He flushed when I told him my father had died a few years earlier. Mrs. Polinski gave him a look that said, *Look what happens when a Jewish husband opens his mouth; he sticks his foot in it.*

When Sarah limped into the living room, Mrs. Polinski said to her husband, "Come, Saul, join me in the kitchen. I'm sure Abe and Sarah have a lot to talk about."

"How are you, Abe?" Sarah gave me a radiant smile. *That would be a wonderful smile to be greeted with every day.* She sat down next to me on the couch.

"Wonderful!" I said and I meant it. I spoke about my week, including having played basketball in the park the previous day. Then, with some nervousness, I told her about my conversation with Mr. Henkel.

"That's very good, Abe. I knew Mr. Henkel would respect you more, if you asked for what you were worth. Don't be upset about not getting the full amount you asked for. You'll ask again in not too long." I was relieved.

Sarah reached out, took my hand and looked me straight in the eyes. "Abe, I would very much like to marry you," she said. "But before we go ahead, there's something I have to tell you. I could keep it secret, but there are some secrets that can just ruin a marriage." She squeezed my hand. "Do you want to hear this?"

"Of course," I answered. I couldn't imagine anything that could cool my desire to marry her.

Sarah hesitated and then said, "Abe, I'm not sure how to say this…but, if we marry, you'd not be the first I'd ever been with."

I was surprised. I had always thought that "good" Jewish girls protected their purity, although, in truth, I had suspected that Leah had been intimate with her French boyfriend. "Do you want to tell me about it?" I asked.

"Not the details—but it's just that ever since I can remember—and since I was born, I've been told, my mother has given me a forlorn look that said, 'I know with that foot, I'll never be able to find a husband for her. She'll never give me grandchildren and I'll have to take care of her the rest of my life. And what will happen to her after I die?' With that message, I felt if I were ever to have any intimacy, it would have to be outside of marriage. If I had known that you were coming along, I would have waited."

I was sad about not being able to be Sarah's first, but I understood. "It's okay, I'm not so pure myself." I didn't tell her my only experiences had been with prostitutes.

Sarah gave me that beautiful smile again and said, "Well, it's settled then. I'll have daddy arrange our wedding."

"That's wonderful." I reached into my pocket and brought out the little blue velvet bag that Mina had given me for the ring. "I have something for you." I shook out the ring out of the bag.

"Oh, it's so beautiful." She held out her hand and admired the ring. Miraculously, it fit perfectly.

"How did you know my size?"

This didn't seem like the time for the truth. "I just guessed."

"You're so sweet," Sarah said and then "Abe, you can kiss me now."

Now, I had had some experience kissing. Most of the girls at Rivka's would let you kiss them, but these were professional kisses, designed to get you in the mood and involved a lot of tongue in your mouth. Although the girls would feign excitement, the kisses were for your benefit. I decided I'd better stay away from that type of kiss and go for the incredibly gentle kiss I remembered from my second date with Helen. I leaned toward Sarah and our lips softly touched for a few seconds. When we broke contact, she moved closer to me, threw her arm around my neck and kissed me passionately. There was a hunger in her kiss I had never before experienced. Two thoughts ran through my mind: *What if someone came in from the kitchen? And, this is looking like it will be a very interesting marriage.*

Chapter 16

"Your Sarah sounds like a strong woman," Bessie says.

"Yes she was."

"A lot of colored women are strong...because their menfolk need encouragement."

"Is that so?"

"Yes it is. Except my Harold, he didn't need any encouragement. Knew just what he wanted and kept after it. It wasn't easy for a colored man to get a postal job in Montgomery in the twenties. He only got it 'cause he was a veteran."

"A government job was good to have during the depression," I say. "A lot of Jews were school teachers."

"Working in the post office in Montgomery wasn't too good. Most whites didn't like the idea of a colored person touching their mail. They'd hide the colored in the back doing the sorting."

"That seems pretty stupid."

"Sure was. The white postal workers didn't like mixing either. The bathrooms and lunchrooms were segregated. It didn't change until Roosevelt made that Farley fella the Postmaster General."

"Interesting," I say. I hadn't realized Roosevelt had done things for blacks.

I thought about what Bessie said. I guess it was true: Sarah encouraged me to speak up, and that was one of the reasons I married her.

Izzy, of course, would be my best man. The sign on the door of his new office said, *Issador Spivak, Attorney at Law.* I was shocked to see him; he was pale as a ghost. Big chunks of his hair had fallen out, and he had a terrible itchy rash. "It's the Salvarsan," he told me, as he scratched his arm, "A new drug for treating syphilis—contains arsenic."

"How did you get syphilis?"

"There's only one way." He laughed. "When Comstock and his Society for the Suppression of Vice shut down all the houses on Broome

127

Street, I started patronizing other places. I guess they weren't as careful as they were at Rivka's."

"That's too bad," I said, and then, "Guess what—I'm getting married. I want you to be my best man."

"That's fantastic! Of course I'll be your best man…if you don't mind how I look."

"Not at all."

"I think when I recover from the effects of this drug, I'll try marriage myself. I don't want to get another case of the syph. How did you meet your fiancée?"

I told him about Irina, the Polinskis, and the marriage settlement.

"*Shmuck*! What do mean they'll pay the rent forever?" Izzy said. "Nothing is forever. People die; they lose their money. They should have bought the apartment for you."

In later years, I wished I had taken his advice, but at that time I was happy to have gotten as much as I did. I couldn't wait to marry Sarah.

I invited the Henkels to the wedding. Mr. and Mrs. Henkel couldn't make it, but Leah said that she and Paul would be there. I looked forward to meeting her fiancée.

Sarah and I met with rabbi Mendel before the wedding for a "discussion", in which Sarah pledged to keep a kosher home. He also explained the *ketubah*, the marriage contract that I would sign at the ceremony. I would be committing myself to provide food, clothing and shelter for Sarah and to have sex with her. No problem there: I could hardly wait. "You also need a gift to give the bride at the wedding," the rabbi told me. "It's usually a gold wedding ring." The next day I bought one for five dollars.

Mrs. Polinski—Hannah, she insisted I call her—wasn't eager to have Sarah walk down a synagogue aisle, so Mr. Polinski—Saul, he said, following his wife's lead—had the trash cleared from the lot behind the bakery. "It's the perfect place to have a wedding," he said, "when the weather is nice." The *chuppah*, a small white canopy supported by four white poles, under which the bride and groom stood during the ceremony, was set up. A small table covered with a gold and white tablecloth was placed under the *chuppah*. On it was the *katubah*, a decanter of wine and two wine glasses. Everyone in the building donated chairs for the occasion.

Our prayers it wouldn't rain were answered with a hot sunny Friday afternoon in April of 1912. I donned the *kittel*, the white gown worn by the groom. Instead of the smell of flowers, our wedding had the smell of baking bread, which, to tell you the truth, I think is more appropriate for starting a household in the city.

I waited in the back of the bakery with Izzy, who had shaved his head for the occasion. Sarah was in the adjoining room, but I wasn't allowed to see her. An accordionist played Jewish music, quietly while the guests were being seated, and then with more gusto, which was the signal for me to exit the back door. Every chair was filled up, and people hung out of windows and sat on the fire escape. I followed Izzy to the *chuppah* and stood on the right of the rabbi. Sarah escorted by her parents followed almost immediately and stood to his left. She was radiant in her white gown, and her smile ensured me that everything would be good: with the ceremony, the wedding, and our life together.

The first order of business was the signing of the *ketubah*, which was written on white parchment paper, the margins of which Sarah had artistically decorated with drawings of flowers and religious symbols. Sarah and I both signed our names at the bottom of the Hebrew document; Izzy and a man who lived in the building signed as witnesses. The rabbi then explained the contract to the audience, much to my embarrassment.

After blessing the marriage in both Hebrew and English, the rabbi poured wine into one of the two wine glasses. He handed the glass to Sarah, who drank from it and passed it to me. She was so happy; I hoped I could keep her that happy the rest of her life. Now the rabbi gave me the signal that it was time for my big line. Izzy passed me the gold band. Sarah held out her hand. I slipped the ring onto her finger, saying in Hebrew and English, "Behold, you are betrothed unto me with this ring, according to the Laws of Moses and Israel." We were now officially married.

The rabbi recited seven blessings in Hebrew, filled the second glass and handed it to Sarah. She drank a little from it and then passed it to me to drain the rest. The rabbi took the glass, wrapped it in a cloth napkin and placed on the floor for me to break with my foot. This was supposed to be the "last time the groom could put his foot down and assert himself." I was nervous; what if I couldn't break the glass? But it shattered and all the guests shouted "*Mazel tov*"—good luck. I put my arms around Sarah and kissed her. With all the guests looking on, she restrained her passion.

Usually at this point the bride and groom run off to a secluded spot for some time alone, but Sarah and I remained in front of the *chuppah*, while various guests came up and congratulated us. Sarah had a lot of relatives living in New York. They had all migrated from Russia to America in the 1880s, after a massacre of Jews, resulting from a rumor that they had been involved in the assassination of Czar Alexander II. Some of them passed me an envelope, saying "Something to get you started." I hadn't expected that.

Meanwhile from the back of the bakery, long tables were brought out and stacked with delicious foods and wine. Hannah came over to us and said, "Come to the table for the toast." We walked to where Saul was filling up little cups with whiskey and each man took one. Izzy stepped forward and delivered the toast—wishing us enough boys to start a basketball team—and some girls too. We all downed our whiskey.

Leah came up with Paul in tow. "So this is your beautiful bride," she said.

"This is Leah, Mr. Henkel's daughter," I explained to Sarah. "And a very good friend."

Leah introduced Paul to us. He was thin and blond and wearing a short-sleeved shirt and trousers, no jacket. *Maybe because he's not Jewish, he doesn't know to dress up.*

"I hope we'll be able to keep seeing you," Leah said to Sarah. Sarah smiled at Leah, and I was happy; it looked like they might become friends.

Hannah dragged Sarah and I over to the banquet table to say the *kiddush* over the wine and the *hamotze* over the bread, after which the guests attacked the food like they hadn't eaten for a week. The accordionist struck up a tune and people started dancing—men and women—but of course, not together. Some relatives escorted Sarah and I over to the dance area and had us both sit on chairs. The guests danced around us, and then some of the strongest men lifted our chairs into the air while they danced. This was supposed to make us feel like a king and queen on thrones flying through the air. I enjoyed it, but when I looked over to Sarah I could see her eyes were closed and she was white with fear, as she held on to the chair for dear life. I wanted to call out for them to put her down, but no one would have heard me.

There was wine and food and more wine. The festivities continued until almost sundown, when the horse was attached to the Polinski bakery wagon, and Sarah and I were helped up onto a small couch that had been set up in its back. Hannah came along for the ride, but Sarah ignored her and we kissed throughout the four-block ride to our new apartment, which was in a three-story building at 179th Street and Webster Avenue. The apartment was a complete mystery to us. The Polinskis had rented and furnished it in secret. Hannah pointed to the *mezuzah* affixed to the right side of the doorway as she let us in to the apartment. She watched us ooh and ah over the living-room furnishings.

In the kitchen, Hannah proudly pointed to the refrigerator and said, "It's electric, you don't need ice." She opened its door to show us it was stocked with food, but mercifully spared us describing all the contents. The apartment had two bedrooms: one with the marriage bed and the other with a baby's crib and a small dresser. Then with a look that said, *Get busy and make me some grandchildren,* she gave us the key and left. I was sure she had another key of her own.

Sarah and I were exhausted and tipsy, so by mutual consent we stripped down to our underwear and collapsed on the bed holding each other. We were asleep in no time at all.

We slept entwined and awoke when the room was dark, except for a band of light from the streetlamp coming in at the side of the window shade. "What's that?" Sarah said, reaching down and taking hold of my erect penis.

"That's Oscar," I answered, using a name that one of Rivka's girls had called it.

Sarah laughed, "Would Oscar like to pay me a visit?"

"First Oscar has to use the toilet."

"Tell him to come right back."

When I came back naked, after some acrobatics at the toilet, Sarah's underwear lay on the floor. I lay down next to her, and she took hold of me and said, "I'm glad you came to visit me, Oscar," as she directed him into her warmness. Oscar was happy; he had found his home.

Our wedding night was spectacularly successful. We slept, woke and made love a half-dozen times. Oh well, maybe it was only three. I learned from Sarah what it was like when a woman really enjoyed sex and didn't just fake it, like Rivka's girls did. Although I can't say I wasn't a little jealous not being Sarah's first, I certainly saw the advantage of marrying a girl with sexual experience.

Saturday, Sarah and I ignored the sounds of screaming children and slept late. When we awoke, she made me breakfast: pastrami and eggs and a bagel. Hannah had stocked the breadbox with bagels, which were a specialty of the Polinski Bakery and which, she had told us, symbolized life (as in pregnancy) due to their circular shape. It was reassuring to learn that Sarah could cook.

After breakfast, we went out to explore our new neighborhood on a bright sunny Saturday morning. Hannah had chosen our apartment on Webster Avenue very carefully. It was on the first floor, so Sarah had to manage only four steps. A Jewish market was located down the block, although it was closed for *Shabbos*. Two doors down from the market, we were amazed to find the Tremont Yiddish Theater, advertising its current offering. I had seen some Yiddish plays in the old country and looked forward to seeing one here.

With Sarah holding my arm, we walked south on Webster Avenue, where two blocks down we came across a small park. A sign said it was called Echo Park. We had fun hearing our shouts reverberate between its two large cliffs. Boys were climbing on the rocks to impress girls, who engaged in conversation and ignored them. Climbing was out of the question for Sarah, so we sat on a large rock watching the activities. On the way back to the apartment we walked as lovers, with my arm around Sarah's shoulders and her arm around my waist. We even stopped to kiss once—much to the disapproval of some black hats, who were returning from *shul*.

When we got back to our building, we found a barrel-shaped woman vigorously sweeping the steps. "You must be the Sokolovskys," she said. "Your mother told me newlyweds would be moving in. I hope my kids didn't wake you." She winked at us. "I'm Marie dePaula—apartment two, across the hall from you. The landlord pays me to take care of the place."

Marie was the most upbeat person I had ever met. Her husband had been a trolley conductor who was killed in a horrible accident at the trolley yard, leaving her with four children under seven years old. The Manhattan Railway Company gave her a hundred-dollar death benefit, enough to last her a year. But, by working out a deal with the landlord to keep up the building in lieu of rent, and by baking and selling some of the most delicious Italian cookies I had ever tasted, she was surviving. She gave us a plate of them as a moving-in present, and when she found out that Sarah's father ran a bakery she lobbied Sarah to get him to carry her wares.

I decided the El was the best way to show Sarah parts of New York that she had never seen.

"How could you have never ridden on the El?" I asked her.

"I've led a very protected life. If Polinski's wagon couldn't take me some place, I didn't go."

"Not completely protected," I quipped.

She hesitated for a moment and then said, "Don't tell me little Avrom is jealous. He knew what he was getting into."

It was a sure signal that Sarah was annoyed when she talked about me like I was some greenhorn from the old country. I vowed to repress my jealous feelings and was successful for many years.

On Sunday, another beautiful day, we got on the train and rode all the way down to its last stop at South Ferry. Sarah behaved just like I had on my first trip almost ten years earlier. She pressed her nose against the window and looked into all the tenements we passed. "I'm glad the train doesn't go past our window," she said, and I agreed.

At South Ferry we walked over to Battery Park where the ferry from Ellis Island docked. Sarah had been born in America and had never experienced the crush of people awaiting their relatives' arrival. Because it was Sunday, the crowds were larger than usual. We stayed to see one ferry arrive and the ecstatic greetings it produced. Then we took the El back home for dinner and lovemaking.

I think my honeymoon weekend was the happiest time of my life. I know nowadays all newly married couples want to go away to a tropical island, but I can't see why anyone needs more than the girl he loves and New York City, with all it has to offer.

Chapter 17

"Atlanta station—we'll be here about twenty minutes, folks," the driver announces.

My legs can use some stretching—knees get stiff when I sit for so long; they're used to walking. I read in the health column in the newspaper that things can happen you don't feel when you sit too long—like getting a blood clot in your legs. They can travel to your lung or your heart and kill you. Better get up and walk around.

Bessie's fast asleep, doesn't look like she's going any place. I'll get off the bus by myself. Some fresh air might help.

My watch says five after six; better be back by six twenty, just to be sure. I push the door of the terminal open; the cool evening breeze feels good. Glad it's still light out. I wouldn't want to walk around here in the dark.

Not much to see, mainly the backs of tall buildings, a couple of parking lots and two winos.

I'm back with enough time to grab a cup of coffee. There's an Atlanta Constitution on that bench. Never could pass up a free newspaper, I'll take it with me.

On Monday, it was back to reality. The Grand Street station of the El was only four blocks from Henkel's dresses, so it took me only an extra twenty minutes to get to work. However, the nickel fare paid twice a day used up half my recent raise.

Wednesday, Sarah got the news that her grandmother had died in her sleep. I suspected she hadn't been well, since she didn't come down to the wedding, although I did remember seeing her face at a back window. "We weren't very close," Sarah told me. "She only spoke Yiddish, which I hardly understand at all."

Well, when you marry, you get more than a wife; you get a family. So Friday I went to the funeral service at the Polinski's *shul*. When the rabbi

135

gave some his reflections of Berta Polinski, Saul began to cry, and I thought of my own mother, back in the Ukraine. *How was she? Would I ever see her again?* It occurred to me that I hadn't written my family since shortly after Yudel died. They didn't even know about Sarah. Maybe I felt a little guilty about being so happy while they continued to suffer in Russia. In any case, I resolved to write them that very night.

After the service, the family loaded into two cars provided by the funeral director to follow the hearse on the long trip to the Jewish cemetery in Brooklyn. I excused myself and hurried to work.

Sarah and her mother were very close, and Hannah would come over several times a week with bakery products and an occasional container of some tasty dish she had cooked.

Our apartment was conveniently located. Sarah had no trouble getting to the grocery store down the block or even to the kosher butcher three blocks away—although when winter came and there was snow on the ground, her foot would get wet and cold due to her open-toed shoe.

Financially, 1912 was a good year for us. Mr. Henkel came across with the second dollar of my raise. I think he learned that Sarah and I had had Leah and Paul to our apartment for dinner, and he didn't want to seem like a cheapskate to his daughter. With the Polinskis paying the rent, which I learned from Marie was fifteen dollars a month, and supplying some food, Sarah was able to add a few dollars each week to our account in a small bank a few blocks from our apartment.

My share of the profits at Henkel's Belts was about a hundred and fifty dollars that year, which when added to our wedding money, increased our account at the Bank of the United States to over 500 dollars.

"How much would you need to start your own belt company?" Sarah asked me one night over dinner.

I thought. "Mr. Henkel started us off with 2,000 dollars."

"We're not too far from that."

"Things have gotten more expensive since then. I think I'd need 3,000 now."

"That's something we can work for." Sarah said.

I thought some more. "The problem would be: When we started Henkel's Belts we had all the business of Henkel's Dresses. If I went out my own, it would take time to get customers. We could lose everything."

Sarah nodded. "Well, keep your eyes open. Maybe an opportunity will come along."

Sarah had a good relationship with a friend of the family who published children's books, and he would occasionally give her a job illustrating one of them. I bought a table for her work and placed it in the "baby's room", much to the annoyance of Hannah, who was getting impatient for some sign that the room would soon be occupied. "So how are you today?" she would ask Sarah, casting an eye on her stomach. We wanted a baby as much as Hannah, but we found that making one was harder than it seemed—even though we tried. Boy did we try!

The Polinskis were moderately observant. Joining their family brought me back into the Jewish fold once again. Saul paid our membership dues in his *shul*, Temple Adath Israel on 169th Street. This synagogue had started off Orthodox, but switched to the Conservative tradition, which allowed men and women to sit together. It had a mixed chorus and organ music. Sarah and I usually attended only on the high holy days and special occasions, like when there was a *bar mitzvah* of a friend of the family.

During Passover, the Polinski bakery closed and my job was to pick up matzos down at the Horowitz bakery on East 4th Street. Saul would give me a large sack from the bakery, which I filled up with unleavened bread and lugged home on the subway. Sarah would spend days with her mother, helping her prepare foods for the *Seder* and the eight-day holiday. Being with the Polinski family during Passover reminded me of how much I missed my own family back in Zyvotov.

"What's this," Sarah asked one day when I returned home from work. She was holding up the photograph of Helen, which I kept in the bottom of my dresser drawer.

"Oh, it's just a photo of one of the models at work," I answered, trying to look nonchalant. "She doesn't work there any more."

"She's very pretty. Where is she now?"

"She got married and moved to Cincinnati. That's in Ohio."

"She must have been special to you, if you were hiding her picture."

So I sat Sarah down and told her about my two dates with Helen a decade earlier. I admitted she had a special place in my memory. "But not my heart," I said. "That's only for you."

Sarah thought for a moment; tap, tap, tapped her fingers on the table, and said, "I think it will bother me if you keep this. Will you be very upset if I get rid of it?"

What could I say except, "No." Sarah was my whole life now.

At that, she quickly tore the photo, which I had risked my job to steal, into four pieces. I felt like a child whose last pacifier had been thrown in the garbage.

That winter we had a chance to try out the Tremont Yiddish Theater down the block. It was the first theater I had seen since some school plays back in the Old Country.

The Tremont was showing *David's Violin* by Joseph Lateiner, one of the most famous Yiddish playwrights. The plot concerned two brothers in the Old Country. One had grown up to be the richest guy in town, while the other, David, was an itinerant street musician. When David comes back to town, he confronts his brother on the street and they argue.

The play ends with the rich brother losing all his money and getting ready to hang himself. Then David reveals to him that he has become very famous and rich during his travels. He plays a song on the violin that cures his brother's depression. Sarah didn't understand much Yiddish, and kept asking me, "What does that mean?" I translated for her, even though people kept "shushing me." Sarah thoroughly enjoyed the experience, and I promised her we would go again.

Jealous competition between brothers is a recurrent theme in Yiddish theater and in the Bible. Having only sisters, I was spared that. Maybe it was also why I'm not a jealous person. I can hardly remember a time in my life when I was jealous of someone. The few times I was, something very bad, like cancer or syphillis, usually happened to him. It seems like no

138

matter how good things look for someone, you never knew what miseries he was hiding or were waiting around the corner for him.

In the spring, Sarah took me to see the Bronx Zoo, the largest zoo in America. On a beautiful, sunny Saturday, the Polinski wagon drove us past a lake and rolling meadow and dropped us off at the main entrance on Fordham Road.

I dropped two nickels in a box at the entrance and carried the picnic basket as we walked up the main avenue to Astor Court, with its stately animal buildings and a sea lion pool. I'd never seen one of these creatures, but knew they were plentiful around the coast of Russia. A bunch of females and one large male slept on the large rocks adjacent to the pool. Occasionally one of the females would rouse herself, walk to the water on flippers and take a few lightening turns around the pool.

"I wonder if I could ever learn to swim," Sarah remarked.

"We could learn together."

While we were watching, a worker came out with a basket of fish. All the sea lions sat up and barked for their lunch. For the one male, it didn't seem like such a bad way to live—with a harem and free food.

Remembering I had never seen a giraffe, Sarah took me to a large open area where one was strutting around with a haughty look above a heard of strange looking deer. The brown-on-dirty-white creature looked pretty silly with stubs of horns, seemingly of little value in combat. The deer were browsing in the grass, but I wondered how the giraffe could get anything to eat.

"In the wild," Sarah told me, "they usually eat leaves from the tops of trees. Here they put food up on that platform." She pointed to a platform on a fifteen-foot pole at the back of the enclosure. On another tree there was a lower platform, which I guessed was for the two younger giraffes in the enclosure.

Next we went into the primate house. A half dozen apes and monkeys looked down at us from the carving above its front door. Inside, the stench was worse than what I remembered from the toilet back in the

139

tenement. The only monkeys I had seen before were those with street organ grinders or accordionists. They were trained to hold out a cup to passers-by for coins. Some of the monkeys in the house were similar to the ones I had seen on the street, but others were very different. As soon as you walked into the enclosure, we heard a loud "whooping" sound. "Those are howler monkeys," Sarah told me, "They're from South America." If an organ grinder had had one of those large hairy beasts, he would have scared everyone away.

A large glass-enclosed area contained monkeys not too different from the ones I had seen on the street. "About ten years ago," Sarah told me, "I came here with my father specially to see an African pigmy the Zoo had living in there with the monkeys. He'd play with them and shoot arrows at a target. I don't know whether they let him out at night."

It seemed very strange to me that a person would be locked up in a cage at the zoo. Even in the Ukraine they didn't do things like that.

Chapter 18

"Who are you going to vote for?" I ask Bessie, after reading an analysis of the last Carter-Ford debate on the editorial page of the newspaper.

"Why, Mr. Jimmy Carter, of course."

"I always vote Democrat," I say. "But this year, it doesn't look like I'll get to vote at all. Left in a hurry and didn't get an absentee ballot."

"I should get back just in time to vote."

"What do blacks think about the possibility of a southerner being in the White House?" I ask.

"Not all white southerners are racist. Lyndon Johnson did some good things for us colored folk. Carter's a good man. He's not like that racist George Wallace, who's governor in my home state of Alabama."

"I saw something about Wallace in this newspaper." Turning back a few pages, I read her the headline, "Wallace Pardons Last of Scottsboro Boys."

"Scotsboro Boys...," Bessie says, "I remember them. It was back in the depression. A bunch of colored boys were riding the rails. Lots of people did that back in those bad times. They got in a fight with some white boys, and then two white girls said the colored boys had raped them on the train."

"I never heard about that."

"Yeah, those white girls were prostitutes. But back in those days, all you needed was a white woman to say a colored man raped her, and he'd be hanging from a tree 'fore the sun came up. And these boys didn't have a lawyer...Oh, they had one, but he wasn't a trial lawyer, and they only gave him a couple of days to get ready."

"Did any of them get hanged?"

"No, they called out the National Guard to make sure that didn't happen. They got the death penalty, so the crowd didn't think they had to take the law into their own hands. But then a couple of days before they were s'posed to die, the Alabama Supreme Court granted them a new trial."

"What happened then?"

"The Communist Party came in and got the boys a Jewish lawyer. You can imagine how well that went over in Decatur, Alabama. One of the girls changed her story—said there weren't any rape, but the other kept telling the same lie. That lawyer couldn't break her down."

"And?"

"Of course, the jury convicted them again. Not the death penalty this time."

"I just finished reading, 'To Kill a Mockingbird'," I tell Bessie. "It's also about a black man who's falsely accused of raping a white woman."

"Yes, I read that," Bessie says. "Most coloreds don't like the book. It doesn't really develop the character of the coloreds, and that Atticus is like a benevolent plantation owner."

"I never thought of it that way."

For our first anniversary, at the Polinski's suggestion and with their financial support, Sarah and I had a party. In addition to the Polinskis, the guests were Mina and Naomi, Leah and Paul and two of Sarah's friends with their husbands. Izzy, apparently cured of syphilis, showed up with his new girl friend, Rebecca, who was a secretary in a lawyer's office. I thought she looked familiar to me. About halfway through the party, I recalled seeing her picture in Irina's book and thinking she didn't look very intelligent.

The Polinskis brought over folding chairs we spread around our apartment, as well as trays of delicatessen and rolls and pastries from the bakery. There was lots of wine and schnapps. About the only thing that Sarah and I supplied was the coffee.

"We're moving to Rochester," Mina told me. "Naomi's son opened up a dry-goods store, and we'll both work behind the counter."

"I'll miss you," I said, and I meant it. Mina had been a wonderful substitute mother for me in America. A little later I was surprised to see her holding Naomi's hand on the couch.

142

Izzy's law practice was going well, and he had purchased a Model-T touring car. "It was sooo wonderful driving up here with the wind blowing in my hair," Rebecca said. "It's sooo much better than the train."

The car had cost Izzy twelve hundred dollars, but he also had to pay two dollars a month to garage it up in Harlem. Every fifteen minutes he looked out our front window to check on it, and twice he had to run out to shoo neighborhood kids off the seat. It didn't seem to me it would be worth that much trouble just to have the wind blow through my hair.

While their husbands discussed business, Sarah's friends were comparing notes about their babies. Hannah listened to them, while looking wistfully at Sarah. Sarah ignored her and listened to Paul's description of the May Day festivities in Union Square a few days earlier. "There must have been five thousand people there," he said. "Gompers and Cahan spoke, and William Haywood from the IWW, came down from Lawrence, Massachusetts. The mill workers up there had a long strike earlier this year. It was a bloody affair; the troops were called out. A lot of children were sent down to New York to avoid freezing or starving to death while it went on. The workers finally got some of their demands and went back to work. But some of the union organizers are still in jail. They passed around a collection box for their lawyers and families."

"I guess it's not only in New York that the workers are oppressed," Leah said.

I was on the verge of saying that even though I was considered a "boss", I felt more like an oppressed worker, when I remembered that Leah was Mr. Henkel's daughter. So I kept my mouth shut.

"Do you think they'll ever have to call out the troops here?" Sarah asked.

"I can't think of anything the city police couldn't handle," Paul answered. "God knows there's enough of them."

"I don't see why the unions celebrate on May Day anyway," Rebecca said. "They have Labor Day in September. May Day should be for celebrating spring—dancing around the maypole and all that."

"Labor Day is just an attempt by the government to separate American unions from the international workers movement," Paul answered.

After the guests had left and Sarah and I lay in bed, I asked her, "Did you see Mina and Naomi holding hands on the couch?"

Sarah gave a long yawn and said, "I did. It looks like they're involved in a lesbian relationship."

"Really, you think so? I didn't think Mina was like that. She's been married twice."

"Don't be such a prude," Sarah snickered. "Women can switch back and forth. The important thing is to have someone to be close to. Gender isn't that important."

Just how experienced is Sarah? I wondered. "Maybe she just got tired of burying husbands," I said.

"There's a parade on Friday I want to go to," Sarah informed me in November of that year.

"Is it in the neighborhood?"

"No, it's down on Fifth Avenue. They're planning a huge demonstration to get women the vote. I want to support them."

Knowing women like Sarah and Leah and having seen women on picket lines, I thought they were as qualified to vote as men. "It's probably going to be pretty cold."

"I don't care. I'll dress warmly."

After work on Friday, I took the Sixth Avenue El up to 42nd Street to meet Sarah in Bryant Park, behind the imposing marble building of the New York Public Library. We bought some hot dogs from a stand in the park, and then walked over to Fifth Avenue. Along with tens of thousand of other people, Sarah and I watched thousands of women, mostly dressed in white dresses and no coats, march down Fifth Avenue. Many of them pushed baby carriages. They carried signs indicating the states already allowing women to vote. "What about New York?" one sign said. You could tell by the way they were dressed that these were not poor women. I was impressed they would brave the cold to march for their right to vote.

"I wish I could march," Sarah said.

That was one of the few time I saw Sarah upset about her disability. I looked at her face and felt her pain. If only there was something I could do, besides saying, "You'll find some other way of supporting them," and putting my arm around her shoulders.

Chapter 19

Somewhere in South Carolina, I notice Bessie dozing off. "I'd better shut up and let you sleep," I say. She doesn't object, and soon I hear her rhythmic breathing.

The guy across the aisle from me starts his coughing again. I wish he would cover his mouth when he coughs. Someone my age gets a cough, and it can be downhill from there. Oh well, maybe it's just a nervous cough.

During my conversation with Bessie, I had, for the first time since Ida left, been able to stop obsessing about her. Now with Bessie asleep, I am reminded of how much I miss Ida sleeping next to me. I'm glad I embarked on this mission to find her. Anything is better than sitting down in Florida, waiting for a telephone call or letter.

Imagining that Bessie's breathing is Ida's, pretty soon I'm asleep myself.

I've barely opened my eyes when the bus pulls in next to a small cinderblock building somewhere in North Carolina. "This is where we change drivers," the bus driver says. He takes his hat and a small bag and leaves the bus. I glance at my watch; it reads 12:30. Then I go back to sleep.

One morning in June of 1914, on my way to work I heard a newsboy call out, "Extry, extry: Assassination in Europe." The size of the headline, and the photos on the first page of the *Times* caught my eye, so I paid my two cents for a paper. **HEIR TO AUSTRIA'S THRONE IS SLAIN WITH HIS WIFE BY A BOSNIAN,** it said. The photos showed Franz Ferdinand, the heir to the Austrian throne, with his upward curving handlebar moustache, and his attractive wife Sophie. They were shot in Sarajevo, after escaping from a bomb that was thrown at their car.

I didn't know where Sarajevo was, so after work I took my *Times* over to the Seward Park Library, opposite the Educational Alliance Building. As usual, the place was packed with Jews of all ages, with their noses in every type of book. I pulled *The Atlas of the World* off the shelf. Sarajevo

146

was in Bosnia, in Southern Europe, and a long way from the Ukraine. It didn't seem like there was any immediate danger to my family, but I wasn't so sure about the Jews, who usually ended up being blamed for most calamities. The *Times* had a half-dozen articles giving the background on the assassination. I discovered Sarajevo was in a part of the world where there had been a lot of trouble in previous years, mainly because it hadn't been decided who was in charge there: Kaiser, Czar or Sultan.

The headlines over the next few days suggested this time the murder of a few thousand Jews wouldn't be enough to calm the world. Within a few days, armies were mobilized all through Europe. Germany, Austria and Turkey, the Central Powers, faced off against Britain, France and Russia, called the Entente.

The war went on and on. Over the next year, it began to look like a basketball game where the teams were very well matched and you had to win by two points. However, in this case, bystanders like America, looked on in horror, rather than excitement.

Even though most Jews were pro-German and anti-Russian, most Americans were of British, Irish, or Italian backgrounds and supported the Entente over the Central Powers. Jews, remembering their history of political vulnerability, decided it was best to keep their mouths shut. This attitude was reinforced by the lynching of Leo Frank, a Jewish factory foreman, outside of Atlanta in 1915. *If it could happen in Atlanta, why not in New York?*

Because of the British blockade, America's business community could only trade with the Entente and swung its support solidly behind Britain and France. Since American trade included lots of war material, German U-boats sank several American merchant ships. This outraged politicians, such as Teddy Roosevelt. President Wilson, however, resisted their calls to bring America into the war.

In September of '15, Mr. Henkel called me up to his office to tell me Henkel's Belts would have a salesman; his name was Eddie Hamburger, and he would start in about a month. I was excited: at last we would be able to get some outside business, not to mention set a fair price for our belts. I thanked Mr. Henkel and turned to leave, but before I could reach the door, he said, "Abe, I'm having some influential people over to my apartment this Sunday evening. I think you might enjoy meeting them. It would please me if you could come."

What could I say? It's not every day your boss invites you to meet influential people. "I'd be glad to," I answered, even though that meant I would have to excuse myself from the regular Sunday night dinner at the Polinski's. "What time?"

"Oh, about seven. We're going to have an informational session about the war."

Sarah, who at that time kept up with the news more than I did, said, "The Germans are afraid America will join England and France in the war. Because so many Jews have German backgrounds, they think American Jews might be able to influence America to stay neutral. That's why Mr. Henkel is inviting you over."

I was skeptical; I never had heard of Jews being able to influence any government.

The Henkel's apartment was packed when I arrived on Sunday night. I felt like a greenhorn, wearing the only tie in the room. The other guests reminded me of the men at Leah's graduation—a few younger guys, but mostly older, prosperous-looking men. The only women I saw there were Mrs. Henkel, Leah and Rosalyn Henneker, Henkel's union representative. The Henkel's plush living-room furniture had been moved against the walls, and about thirty folding chairs were lined up in three rows across the room.

Glasses of white and red wine and assorted pastries were arranged on a table on the side of the room in front of a waiter in a starched white jacket. I took a glass of white wine and a *ruggela* and sidled over to Leah's husband, Paul, who was standing by the window. He was wearing a flannel shirt and a pair of denim pants, at that time clothes worn almost exclusively by lower-class workers.

"I must be the only non-Jew at this shindig," Paul said.

I looked around; he seemed correct. "I don't know about that waiter."

He laughed, "Why do you think Isaac called us here?" He nodded toward his father-in-law, who was talking to a tall, immaculately tailored, blond man, wearing frameless glasses.

"Sarah says he's probably going to try to convince us not to support America joining the war on the side of England and France."

Mr. Henkel rapped a spoon on the side of a glass and said, "Please take your seats everyone." The guests filed into the rows of chairs. I sat down next to Paul, with Leah on his other side. When everyone was seated, Mr. Henkel said, "I know some of you wonder why I invited you here. I believe our country, under the direction of President Wilson, is increasingly showing signs of heading in the wrong direction—the wrong direction for America and especially the wrong direction for America's Jews. Before it commits itself to supporting the Entente, I think that we Jews should have a chance to hear from the other side, so that each of you can decide how you might want to exert whatever influence you have. For this purpose, Martin Shenkman, from the German Consulate has agreed to come and talk to us." He nodded at the tall, blond man to whom he had been talking.

Shenkman was perfectly at ease. "My fellow Jews," he started, although from the way he looked, I wondered whether Shenkman didn't really end in the two n's, common in German names, rather than the single one, used by most Jews.

"I know many of you have come here from Germany and Austria and are well aware of the high regard to which Jews are held in these countries. Let me just take a moment to remind you of some of these esteemed German and Austrian Jews.

"I'm sure those of you who belong to reform congregations know of Rabbi Samuel Adler, who played such a prominent role in the reform movement. In commerce, need I mention the Shiffs, Strauses, Seligmans and Rothschilds, the founder of this last dynasty having even been made a Baron of the Austrian Empire. And it is not only in business that Jews have prospered. Albert Einstein and Sigmund Freud are just two examples of Jews who have reached the pinnacle of their respective fields in Germany and Austria."

"Contrast the respect with which Jews are treated in the Alliance with how they have suffered in the Russian Empire, where Jews are not even

149

allowed to live in many cities. The influx of Jews to America from Russia over the last thirty years is testimony to how they have been persecuted and sometimes even murdered in that part of the world.

"And what of Russia's allies, England and France? Have they spoken up for the Russian Jews? Not at all. In fact, they have persecuted Jews on their own—the French making Captain Dreyfus a scapegoat for their own failings only being the most visible example of this."

Shenkman went on and on about the love of Germany and Austria for Jews and their mistreatment in Russia, England and France. He told of how Germany and Austria were peace loving and had only been driven to war by Russia's expansionist aims in the Balkans. He concluded with his hopes that the Jews of New York would do everything in their power to keep America from supporting the Entente and then called for questions.

An elderly gentleman asked about the treatment of Jews in Turkey, an Islamic country and the third member of the Central Powers. Shenkman assured him that the Turks' treatment of Jews was good. "In fact," he said, "several of the Sultan's closest advisers are Jewish."

Mr. Henkel then asked Shenkman for some specific things Jews could do to help keep America out of the war. Holding small get-togethers and letters to newspapers were a couple of his suggestion. He then nodded in our direction. I hadn't realized that Leah had her hand up for a question. "Herr Shenkmann," she said, pronouncing the name with the accent on the final syllable, as the Germans did. "If Germany is so peace-loving, why has it been leading the arms race in Europe for the last ten years?"

Shenkman was taken aback. I guess he hadn't expected an unfriendly question, especially from a woman. "On the contrary," he said, "Germany has not led the arms race, it has just responded to buildups by members of the Entente." He then enumerated the large battleships recently completed in England. "It's the Alliance that wants peace and Russia that's forced them into war."

Leah continued, "But didn't Austria start the war, using the murder of the Archduke by a crazy anarchist as an excuse, by giving its ultimatum to Serbia—including demands that no sovereign nation could possibly accept?"

"I think the demands were quite reasonable after the assassination," Shenkman answered.

150

There were some murmurings in the audience. "Why did you torpedo the *Lusitania*?" a white-haired man said. "I lost some good friends on that ship."

Shenkman started to answer, but Mr. Henkel, sensing the tide was turning, said, "I'm sure that most of us have sat here long enough. If there are further questions, I believe Mr. Shenkman would be glad to answer them privately." That brought the meeting to a close. Somehow Shenkman hadn't convinced me that Germany was a peace-loving supporter of Jews.

When a few months passed and Eddie Hamburger didn't show up, I asked Mr. Henkel about him.

"He's my wife's cousin. He's coming from Germany, but because of the English blockade, he has to leave from Amsterdam. It'll take him a little longer to get here."

I was crestfallen. Mr. Henkel was going to stick a relative on our payroll. I wasn't sure he could even speak English. He'd hardly bring much business to us, and his salary would lower our profits and my annual share of it.

Mr. Henkel must have sensed my disappointment. "Don't worry; I'm sure he'll work out."

I was worried, but Sarah was furious. "How could you let him do that? You should have said something."

"I don't know," I said. "Maybe he'll be all right. If he gets us even a few orders, he'll pay for himself. I'll wait a while and see how it goes." I was keeping my fingers crossed.

"Well, you better not wait too long," Sarah said, looking me straight in the eyes. "I think I'm pregnant."

It took a few seconds for what she said to sink in; then I grabbed her. Maybe Sarah didn't dance, but I had to dance, and dance with me she did.

It was almost six months until Eduard Hamburger, alias Eddie, arrived in New York. About forty, slightly built, with straight hair combed over his expanded forehead, Eddie talked in a high-pitched voice and had a nervous tic. He had been a teacher in Dusseldorf, and was an "intellectual,"

151

an expert in German philosophers. *Not exactly what I need for a belt salesman.* At least his English was good.

Mr. Henkel told me to teach him what he would need to know to get us some business, and Eddie quickly learned what price to ask for different types of belts. "You can go ten percent lower without asking me," I told him. "Now go get us some orders."

He gave me a perplexed look. "You mean I just go around and knock on doors? I don't know if I can do that."

Just what I needed: a shy salesman. "Try," I said. "It sometimes helps if you bring refreshments, cookies or something, with you. I'll pay you back for them."

My only salesman left with a glum look on his face.

Eddie came back later that day with a list of dress companies in the neighborhood. "Tomorrow I'll try some of them," he assured me.

"How are things in Germany?" I asked him.

"They're not good at all. The casualties in the trenches on the western front are enormous. Marcus, my best friend, had his leg blown off. Anyone of draft age isn't allowed to leave the country. They passed over me in the first round, but they were getting desperate and drafting everyone. With my health, I wouldn't have lasted a month in the trenches, so I bribed a border guard to cross into Holland."

"And how are things for Jews in general?" I asked, remembering Shenkman's talk.

"It's funny. By law, Jews are equal citizens. Jewish leaders feel if we act very German, the public will accept us. Services in reformed synagogues have changed. Now they're mainly in German—with choirs and organ music, just like in the church. Our leaders encourage us to join the army and fight for 'our country.'"

In a voice half an octave higher, Eddie went on, "But it's not our country at all. Most Germans hate us. They blame us for everything. Jews are beaten. Can't rent apartments. Can't get jobs." He glanced around, afraid he had been overheard. *Maybe he doesn't yet realize he's in America.*

Eddie continued talking loud and fast. "I could only teach in a Jewish school." He stopped and started to wheeze and gasp for breath.

Afraid Eddie might die, I helped him to a chair. After a few minutes, his breath returned to normal. He said in a much lower voice, "Sorry, but I get a little asthma when I get excited."

That evening I told Sarah all about Eddie.

"What are you paying him?" she asked.

"I don't know. He gets his pay directly from Mr. Henkel."

"It doesn't sound too good," Sarah frowned. "What are you going to do?"

"Next time Arthur comes around to do the books, I'll try to find out."

I was in a bad position. As the boss of Henkel's Belts, I didn't have a union bargaining for me. My salary was less than most of the sewing machine operators who I supervised, and I had to rely on my share of the profits to bring me up to a fair wage. The previous year I had done well, with a year-end check of three hundred dollars—almost equal to my annual salary. But with the ups and downs of the business, I couldn't count on that. I'd passed my thirtieth birthday and wasn't doing as well as I hoped. Now I had a child on the way. The last thing I needed was to pay a salesman who didn't bring in any business. I wasn't sure that Eddie was trying very hard, since he often talked about coffee shops where his fellow intellectuals hung out.

I couldn't get a straight answer from Arthur about Eddie's salary; Mr. Henkel must have told him to keep me in the dark. Yes, things were looking grim.

Surprises aren't always bad, however. One day Eddie came in excited. He had been at a party at the Henkels' the previous evening and had met a Mr. Schwartz. They had talked for almost an hour about Hegel, a German philosopher. It turned out Schwartz owned a dress factory that made its own belts. He needed room to expand and was receptive to Eddie's suggestion he contract out the belt business. He invited Eddie to drop around and see him. Two days later Eddie brought in a large order at a good price.

Sarah's pregnancy was an excuse for Hannah to load us up with even more food. "You're eating for two now," she said to Sarah, who put on a lot of weight until her doctor scolded her.

153

Hannah came over several times a week to do the heavy housework. "You don't want to strain yourself and lose the baby."

Sarah's brother, Benjamin, wasn't married, so this would be Hannah's first grandchild. "I hope the baby is normal," she said. I knew what she meant, and was annoyed. To me Sarah was completely normal, and I adored her.

When I came to work on a Monday in May 1916, the streets of the Lower East Side were packed with orthodox Jews. I could hardly push through the crowds to get to work. "What's going on?" I asked a bearded fellow in a black hat and jacket.

"It's the funeral for the most famous Yiddish writer, Sholem Aleichem.
Have you heard of him?"

"Vaguely," I answered, remembering the name, since it was very similar to "shalom aleichem" the Hebrew greeting, which means, "Peace unto you."

"He wrote about the old country," he continued. "Tevye, the milkman; Mottel, the cantor's son; Menahem-Mendl. Very funny stuff."

"Oh," I said, and I continued pushing through the crowd. I was almost at the factory when it hit me. "Menahem-Mendl!" That was the person Papa had told me not to be like, as I was leaving the old country. I was excited; now I would find out what Papa meant. On my way home that evening, I stopped at a bookstore and bought a copy of *The Adventures of Menahem-Mendl*, by Sholem Aleichem. It was in Yiddish, of course.

The next day I read in the paper that more than 100,000 people had lined the streets of New York for Sholem Aleichem's funeral. It was the largest funeral crowd recorded in the city up to that time.

Since for 15 years, I had made a point of reading only English, my Yiddish had become rusty. But as it came back to me, I had some good laughs reading about Menahem-Mendl, a *luft-mensch*, who got in over his head speculating in financial markets. Individual letters between Menahem-Mendl and his ever-patient wife, Shayne-Sheyndl, were originally published in the Odessa Yiddish newspaper, which was where Papa probably read them, since I didn't remember him ever reading a book. I also learned

154

Sholem Aleichem based Menahem-Mendl on his own experience, having squandered his wife's dowry on stock markets in Kiev and Odessa. Papa's advice was good: I'd try not to be like Menahem-Mendl.

Chapter 20

"How long are they going to keep us here?" a woman says in a voice loud enough to wake me up. My watch reads almost three. Damn, we've been sitting in front of this bus station for more than two hours. Everyone in the bus is getting restless, but no one is doing anything. Bessie is fast asleep.

I've got to go to the toilet. The one in the back of the bus smelled last time I was there. Maybe the facilities in the station are cleaner. But first I have to get off the bus. Gee, it's cold in here. Door's closed...isn't that a little dangerous. What if there was a fire while we were waiting for the new driver?

That toggle switch to the right of the driver's seat—maybe that's for the door. I'll flip it. There's a hiss and the door opens. The woman in the front seat jumps up. "I'll be right back," I whisper to her before descending the stairs.

A number of incidents were making it difficult for America to remain out of the war. For example, two months before Sarah had given birth, we were awakened by what we thought was thunder, which was surprising on a night with the sky filled with stars. The next day, I read in the newspaper that a massive explosion had occurred at a munitions dump on Black Tom Island in New York harbor. The explosion had been so powerful it damaged the Statue of Liberty. No longer could visitors go to the top of the torch. It didn't take long to find out German saboteurs were behind it. A similar explosion occurred in New Jersey a few months later. We weren't at war, but it began to feel like we were.

Our son, named Meyer Henry in honor of Hannah's father, Mendel, was born August of 1916. "Hannah had told Sarah, "You'll give birth in a hospital. I've heard of too many things going wrong when a doctor or midwife came to the house." So when Sarah's water broke one evening, I ran two blocks to the nearest pay phone and breathlessly told Saul, "She's ready." Polinski's had recently replaced their wagon with a truck, so it took Saul only ten minutes to get to our apartment and another fifteen to Bronx Hospital, about a half mile away.

At the hospital, I filled out some papers and Sarah was taken away in a wheelchair, while Saul drove home and brought Hanah to the hospital. Then, Hanah and I paced the waiting room floor for more than six hours until the nurse came in and told us that mother and son were both doing well.

The *bris*, on the eighth day of Meyer's life, was held at the Polinski's, so that men from the bakery and building could provide a *minyan*. As Meyer's father, I took him from his mother and carried him to the *Sandak*, a position of great honor, given to Saul. Placing Meyer on a pillow on Saul's lap, I stepped back and the *mohel* came forward and said, "'This is my covenant, which you shall keep,' saith the Lord, 'between me and you and your offspring after you: Every male among you shall be circumcised.'" Then the *mohel* bent over, and Meyer let out a little cry, which made me wince. Saul then handed the baby to Sarah, who gave him a drop of wine on her finger, before putting him to her breast. Every one said *mazel tov* and grabbed a glass of wine and a few *ruggela*. Then the bakery workers went back to work.

As best as I could tell, with hardly ever being able to get close to him, Meyer was a beautiful, healthy baby. For the first month, Hannah slept in his bedroom on a mattress she brought over and placed on the floor. She and Sarah were always hovering over him. Never before or since has a baby had so much attention. At the first sound of a cry, Hannah would rock him or Sarah would take him to her breast.

"Can I hold him?" I asked.

Hannah looked at me askance. "Okay, but be careful." She passed Meyer to me.

"Not like that. You have to support the head." She took Meyer back and showed me how she cradled him in her arm. Before I could take him back, she said to Sarah, "I think it's time for him to be fed." Sarah started to open her blouse.

"Do you need anything in the store?" I asked.

"No, I got everything on my way over," Hannah said.

Well, if I wasn't needed at home, I might as well resume my walks. I don't think Sarah or Hannah realized I was gone.

I walked a lot during Meyer's first month. Since it was late summer, and the weather was stifling. I stayed in the shade whenever possible. One of my favorite routes was along the Grand Concourse, which was three blocks west of our apartment. Set on top of the ridge that bisected the Bronx, this newly constructed road was reputed to be one of the grandest avenues in the world. Some compared it to the Champs-Elysees in Paris. Having never been to Paris, I can't comment on that. The Concourse was actually three parallel roadways, separated by tree-lined, grassy dividers. It ran for almost four miles, all the way up to Van Courtland Park. The six-story apartment buildings springing up on both sides of the road were rapidly becoming *the* place to live for fairly well off New Yorkers who couldn't afford the even more elegant buildings around Central Park.

I fell in love with the graceful white marble Lorelei Fountain at 161st Street. The fountain is set in what was then called Concourse Plaza Park and later renamed Joyce Kilmer Park, in honor of the *New York Times* editor who wrote that poem ending with "But only God can make a tree." Although I couldn't hear the songs of the four sirens at the base of the fountain, I was drawn to their perfect breasts—probably because Sarah and I hadn't yet resumed our sex life after she had given birth.

Leah told me the Empress of Austria commissioned the fountain in honor of the poet Heinrich Heine. She presented it to the city of Dusseldorf, Heine's birthplace, but Dusseldorf refused to install it because of Heine's Jewish origin, even though he had converted to Lutheranism in order to get a university position. So much for Germans loving Jews. German Jews in America purchased the fountain and brought it to New York. Dusseldorf's loss was New York's gain. Nowadays, as an added bonus, you can peek at Yankee Stadium baseball games from the fountain.

If instead of going west to the Concourse I walked east and south, I came to Crotona Park, where a weekend Communist or Socialist was often sounding off on a soapbox. One day, as I passed a speaker, a man handed me a leaflet. We stopped in our tracks, looked each other over, and then

158

recognized each other almost simultaneously. It was Dovid, my landsman, who I hadn't seen since Yudel's wedding, fifteen years earlier.

"Avrom," he said. No one had called me that in a long time.

"Dovid, what are you doing here? Where's your pushcart?"

He laughed. "I haven't had a pushcart in ten years. I'm an organizer for the Communist Party now."

Dovid had cleaned himself up a lot since I had last seen him. His hair was still long, but now it was tied behind his head. He wore a tee shirt with CPUSA in large letters on its front.

We sat down on a bench and exchanged stories of our lives in America. Dovid was David now. He wasn't married, but he had a girlfriend in the party. He had been involved in many strikes and had been beaten up by "goons" hired by the bosses several times. He pointed out the scar on his head that had resulted from one of the beatings. When he found out that I managed a factory, he said, "I guess you won't be interested in getting the workers to rise up," and took his flyer back from me. Finally, we shook hands and wished each other good luck, although I guess that would have been contradictory.

The East Bronx, on the other side of the park, reminded me of the Lower East Side. Here tenements mixed with shoddy apartment buildings. Crowds thronged through the streets, patronizing stores with signs in Yiddish. I was glad I wasn't living there, but it was a fun place to visit.

One Sunday, I crossed the 145th Street Bridge into Harlem. On my last visit to this area, about five years earlier, it had been all half-empty apartment houses, where many poor Jews lived. Now it was fast becoming the center of an upscale black neighborhood. Everywhere, black people were strolling around in their Sunday best. Everyone seemed to know everyone else. I felt conspicuous, not only because of my skin color, but also because of the shabby way I was dressed.

When Meyer was one-month old, Hannah moved back to her apartment, leaving Sarah the job of taking care of the baby. With our privacy restored, Sarah and I were able to have sex again, and I found that motherhood hadn't diminished her appetite for it at all. Hannah had left us a

159

magnificent baby carriage, which we used to take the "little prince" to the park on Saturdays. Marie allowed us to keep the carriage in the ground-level storeroom around back, so Sarah didn't have to lug it up and down the stairs and could take Meyer on her shopping outings. A couple of days a week, Hannah would return to clean our apartment or go with Sarah and the baby to the park. Hannah had an annoying habit of using her key to enter our apartment without knocking. Sometimes this was at very inconvenient times, and Sarah and I often had a good laugh over it, but I really didn't think it was funny.

In 1917 the Czar was overthrown and Russia settled with Germany. In the process, the Germans occupied the Ukraine. I was worried about my family, but there was no possibility of contacting them. I hoped Shenkman was right, and Germany would treat Jews better than Russia had.

Meanwhile, French soldiers had had enough of the carnage in the trenches and were refusing to fight. That would leave only Britain and her empire to fight the Central Powers. Things didn't look good for the Entente. But then Americans read in the newspapers about a telegram intercepted and decoded by the British. Supposedly, it was from Arthur Zimmermann, the German Foreign Minister, to the German Ambassador to Mexico. The telegram told the ambassador to offer United States territory to Mexico, if it would join the German cause.

"Don't believe it," a worried Mr. Henkel said when I met him on the stairs. "It's obviously British propaganda designed to draw America into the war."

I just nodded.

Mr. Henkel was wrong. A few days later, Zimmermann himself admitted the telegram was genuine, and on April 2, President Wilson asked Congress for a declaration of war on Germany. A month later, the United States, which didn't have a large standing army, instituted a draft, with registration of all men 21-30 years old. Four million Americans were to be drafted. Since I was almost a year past my thirty-first birthday, I didn't have to worry. What a relief! It would have been awful if, after leaving the old country to escape the Czar's army, I were drafted into America's. I also think Shenkman's arguments had had some effect on me; I wasn't sure that Germans were any more my enemy than Russians.

Sarah's brother, Benjamin, wasn't as lucky as me. Being 25, he had to register, and after passing the physical, he was told to report to Fort Dix in Wrightstown, New Jersey. The night before he left, the Polinskis had a party to send him off. Not being used to all the attention, Benjamin sat quietly, except when his friends got him up to down a shot of liquor after a toast. I wondered what Ben would look like after the army shaved off his beard and cut his long hair. Mr. Polinski was confident that Benjamin would be assigned to the quartermaster corps and serve as a baker. He toasted Benjamin with, "At least I know America's soldiers will be well fed before they go into battle."

I could see Benjamin was very apprehensive about the changes about to occur in his life, so I went over, put my arm around his shoulder and said, "Good luck, Ben."

"Thanks Abe," he answered. I guess the liquor had loosened him up a bit, because he confided in me, "I'm scared...It's not so much the war. But I've never been away from home before."

Having myself been sent away from home at age 16, I could understand how Benjamin was feeling.

The only other guy I knew who went into the army was Terrence, a good-looking Irish lad, who delivered packages and did odd jobs around the factory. On his last day on the job I took him to lunch. "Where would you like to eat?" I asked him.

"Ooo, hows 'bout that big place on Houston—Katz's I think it is. Never been there."

Terrence's eyes lit up when he saw the huge sandwiches the waiters were bringing out. He ordered a corned-beef sandwich, a plate of potatoes and a beer. "Hope ya don't mind my drinking on the job," he said with a laugh.

"Sorry to lose you, Terrence. Too bad you were drafted."

"Drafted? Oh no, Mr. Abe," he said. "I enlisted. "Go'n see the world. I'll learn to shoot a gun and drive a truck. Go'n be plenty use for truck drivers when this thing's over."

161

It didn't seem like the worst career choice Terrence could make. I can only hope he survived the war, since I never saw him again after that day.

On a Sunday in November 1917, Hannah watched Meyer, and Sarah met me at Bryant Park at noon. We bought lunch from pushcarts and then walked over to Times Square to join a big war rally. There was a band and jugglers, but the highlight of the entertainment was Harry Houdini, magician extraordinaire, son of a Hungarian rabbi, doing one of his tricks. Houdini was wrapped in a straightjacket and then lifted, head down, about ten stories by a large crane being used in one of the nearby construction projects.

"Oh, I can't look," Sarah said and covered her eyes. However, I saw she was peeking out from between her fingers.

A roll of drums and a blast from the trumpets was the signal for Houdini to start contorting. In less than two minutes, he was out of his straightjacket and upright. Everyone cheered as the crane lowered him to the ground. I guess the message was: if an American could do that, certainly we could defeat Germany in the war.

The war caused a serious labor shortage in the garment industry. Besides workers volunteering or being drafted into the military, others quit for better-paying jobs in defense industries. The flow of immigrants from Eastern Europe virtually stopped. Fortunately, large numbers of blacks were migrating north at this time, and a few younger blacks responded to the "Help Wanted" sign I put up next to the entrance of the building. The first two that came to the door spoke a dialect so unfamiliar to me, I couldn't hire them. But communication was possible with the third, Andrew, a seventeen-year-old boy, who had come up from Alabama with his family. I have to admit I offered him half what Terrence had made, and he took the job. Andrew was extremely polite, always saying, "Yessa, Mr. Abe," but he had a lot of trouble finding his way around the city. Whenever he went out on an errand, it would take him forever to come back. He would say he got lost, but I suspect, like me when I first came to New York, he found out there was a lot to see in the city.

The labor shortages and government spending on the war resulted in severe inflation. Even Andrew got another job offer, and I had to give him a raise to keep him from leaving. Sarah had been trying to put a dollar a week into our bank account, but finally said in frustration, "I just can't manage it anymore. Everything is so expensive. You'll have to ask Mr. Henkel for a raise."

Her push got me to approach Mr. Henkel. As usual, he tried to talk me down, but I came away with a two-dollar increase. Now I made ten dollars a week, five times what I did when I started, not to mention a share of the profits. *Why wasn't I feeling rich?*

With a lot of young teachers being drafted, I lost my salesman, Eddie Hamburger. He was able to get a job, teaching math at Stuyvesant High School, a massive building on 15th Street. Before he left, he took me up to meet Mr. Schwartz and his foreman, Harold, who sent out the orders at Schwartz's Dresses.

"I'll miss our discussions," Mr. Schwartz said to Eddie.

"I'm sure we'll meet at the Henkel's again," Eddie said. "This is Abe, I don't think he knows much about Hegel, but he makes good belts."

Mr. Schwartz shook my hand. "Isaac has spoken very favorably about you. I heard you used to be a champion basketball player. Do you still play?"

I blushed. "I was on a good team. Now that I'm married and have a child, I don't get much chance to play any more."

"It's good to see that Jews can excel in physical as well as mental endeavors," Mr. Schwartz said. "We've been happy with your work and I'm sure Harold here will continue to give you orders."

Harold hadn't said anything, but I held out my hand and he shook it.

On the way back to the factory, Eddie said, "Keep your eye on Harold. Someone else might approach him. I suggest you give him a bottle of Canadian Club for Hanukah and something else in the middle of the year to keep him on our side."

"I sure will." I said, amazed at how well Eddie had picked up the art of salesmanship in the short time he'd been in the country. "Anything you can do to keep us on the good side of Mr. Schwarz will help. I'll give you a small percentage of their orders at the end of the year."

"Isn't he the most perfect baby?" Sarah beamed, when Meyer was about a year old and crawling after a ball that I rolled to him.

"Absolutely perfect."

"What do you think he'll be when he grows up: a doctor, a lawyer, or just a filthy rich capitalist businessman?"

"Definitely a filthy-rich businessman—so he can take care of us in our old age, or maybe he'll be an opera star from the way he cries."

"I wonder if his brother or sister will be just as perfect," Sarah said.

I jumped up and kissed her, but I have to admit I wasn't quite as enthusiastic at this announcement as I had been at the first one.

It turned out Meyer wasn't as perfect as we had thought. When he stood up and tried to walk, it wasn't difficult to see that there was something wrong with his right foot; it had a tendency to turn like Sarah's.

"Fortunately, we can treat clubfoot nowadays," the doctor told us. "With wrapping and exercise, he should be able to walk almost normally and wear regular shoes, but he'll never be a champion runner."

For three months, Sarah took Meyer to the doctor's office once a week to have his foot unwrapped and exercised. After that he was given a first pair of shoes that provided additional support, and we only had to check in with the doctor once a month. The Polinskis paid for these treatments, which allowed Meyer to walk with only a slight limp for the rest of his life.

Chapter 21

The door of the bus depot is open, but no one is there. Inside there's a single room with a counter, two benches, a small ticket office behind glass and a bathroom. I go to the bathroom; it's cleaner than the one on the bus. On my way out, I notice a telephone on the counter. I pick it up, hear a beep, and then silence.

"Hello, this is Abe. Is there anyone there?" I say, much too loudly and then wait.

"Express Lines, Charlotte," a woman's voice finally answers.

"This is Abe. We've got a busload of people freezing to death out here. Over two hours now since we were told there would be a new driver."

"I'm very sorry, sir. There must have been a mix-up. I'll get someone out to you as soon as possible."

"How long?"

"I'm not sure, but it won't be too long. I'll get to work on it as soon as I get off the phone." And she hangs up.

I walk through the frigid air and find the bus door closed. Probably a passenger had closed it to keep the cold out. I knock on the door, and a woman in the front row flips the switch to open it. I make my way back up the aisle; Bessie is still fast asleep. I take my overcoat down from the rack, cover myself with it in my seat and try to fall asleep.

Benjamin did his basic training at Fort Dix in New Jersey and then was shipped overseas. His letter to Sarah from France said he had made the voyage safely but had been horribly seasick. The troops traveled in huge convoys, escorted by destroyers, which greatly reduced the possibility of being sunk by a U-boat. With about 10,000 American troops reaching Europe every day, Germany realized it had a short window to achieve victory and started a massive offensive in the spring of 1918. Successful at first, the offensive soon ran out of steam, and the Allies began to make gains.

The same year, articles about a serious influenza epidemic appeared in *The Times*. Initially, the reports were from Spain, which not being in the war, had no reason to suppress the information. It was not long before the "Spanish flu" reached New York. People got sick and many of them died. We didn't complain; it was our part of the war effort. Upstairs, at Henkel's Dresses, there were a half-dozen cases and one death. I felt fortunate that initially none of the belt-factory employees got sick.

Sarah was about seven months pregnant, when Yossi, one of the workers at the bakery, appeared at our door and told her, "Mr. and Mrs. Polinski have flu. Doctor came and said they're both getting better. They're sleeping now and say, ' You're absolutely not to visit in your condition.'"

Sarah paced around our apartment, while we waited for news. I held her hand and tried to assure her that everything would be fine. Two days later, we learned both patients were up and walking around. They had opened the windows to air out their apartment, so that we would be able to visit in a few days.

The next morning, shortly after I had arrived at work, Saul telephoned. He told me he was almost fully recovered, but during the night Hannah had suffered a relapse. The doctor had just left and said she had pneumonia. The prognosis was not good; she was having trouble breathing. He didn't want me to tell Sarah. If she found out, she would visit and endanger herself and the baby.

It was about four o'clock when Saul called again. He told me Hannah had passed away. He would come over to tell Sarah about six. "Please be there," he said. "She'll need you."

I rushed home. I knew that Sarah and her mother were so close this would hit her hard. I came in the door about two hours earlier than usual. Sarah took one look at my face and said, "What's wrong?"

"Uh...uh." I couldn't come out with it.

"It's my parents. I know. Have they gotten worse? Have they died? Tell me." She squeezed my upper arm until it hurt.

"Your father's recovered," I said. "He'll be over in about an hour."

"And my mother?" She held her breath.

"She had a relapse...and died," I stammered.

166

At this, Sarah let out a wail like I never want to hear again. She pulled her hair, beat her chest and looking down at her swollen stomach, said, "It's this baby that kept me from visiting her. I hate it." She made a fist, and raised her arm. I wasn't sure she would actually hit herself, but I didn't take a chance. I grabbed her in a bear hug. Her piercing scream had been so loud a few minutes later Marie knocked on our door. We both helped Sarah over to the couch, where she sobbed and shook uncontrollably. I stroked her head and tried to comfort her, to no avail. I had never seen someone so overcome with grief, and I felt useless not being able to help her.

I heard a truck pull up in front of our apartment, and a few minutes later Yossi helped an ashen Saul to our door. While Saul and Sarah hugged and cried in each other's arms, I went into the kitchen and made some tea. I brought the cups in, and Saul and I sat down and talked, while Sarah continued to sob.

"They've already taken Hannah away," Saul said. "The funeral is tomorrow. The authorities are pushing quick burials to help reduce transmission of this plague."

"I'll stay home tomorrow," I said. "But I don't think Sarah can be alone for a while."

"I agree," Saul said. "I'll have one of the girls from the bakery come over every day until she feels better."

At five o'clock the next morning a Chevrolet limo provided by the funeral director, arrived at our front door. Marie took Meyer into her apartment, and I helped Sarah squeeze between her father and me in the limo. We started the long drive to the cemetery in Brooklyn. On that September morning it was freezing in the limousine with open sides, and the director had provided a heavy blanket to keep us warm. Polinski's bakery truck, loaded with its employees, trailed behind us.

Although a quarter of million Jews lived in the Bronx, it had no Jewish cemeteries. Woodlawn, adjacent to the Bronx Botanical Gardens, was the largest cemetery in New York. It was non-denominational, and many reformed Jews were buried there, but more traditional ones shivered at the idea of being buried next to a grave marked with a cross. So Hannah would be buried in Brooklyn.

We followed the hearse across the bridge into Manhattan and down Park Avenue to 59th Street, where we took the bridge to Brooklyn. The sun was just rising as we crossed the bridge, and I was taken by the view. "What a beautiful sunrise," I said. Sarah turned her head and looked at me strangely; I realized I had made a mistake. Sometimes words cross your lips, and you'd like to take them back, but it just can't be done. There was no way Sarah could appreciate beauty at that time, and I should have realized it.

The Mount Carmel cemetery was only about a ten-minute drive from the bridge. When we pulled up at the gate, some neighbors of the Polinskis greeted us. They must have left very early to get there so early by train and bus.

Listening to the rabbi eulogize Hannah by the grave, Sarah huddled next to her father. I would have preferred to have my arm around her. On the way home, she rested her head on my shoulder. It looked like she had forgiven me for my slip.

Usually when a traditional Jew dies, the spouse and immediate relatives sit *Shiva* in her house for seven days. During this period, friends, relatives and members of the community come to the house and console them, bringing food to spare the mourners the job of caring for themselves. Everyone reminisces about the life of the deceased most of the day and night. This ritual helps the mourners stave off loneliness and speeds their return to the world.

But these were not normal times. Because of the flu, people avoided congregating, especially in homes in which there had recently been infected. There was a very minimum *Shiva,* and Saul wouldn't allow Sarah to come to his apartment until after the baby had been born. So Sarah was denied this outlet for her grief.

It was especially difficult for Sarah to endure the last two months of her pregnancy in her depressed state. She was thankful to finally give birth. The child, named Harry Joseph, in Hannah's memory, was beautiful, with dark curly hair. However, it didn't take long to find out he was endowed with excess energy. He didn't cry, he screamed, delighting in the sound of his own voice. Even holding him down for diapering was difficult.

"He's too much for me to handle," Sarah said. It was true: she didn't have much energy any more, and at night she often sat around staring into space. Sex was rare and was without its previous gusto when it did occur. With Sarah so depressed, I began to feel almost as lonely as I had when Yudel had died.

Germany was the last of the Central Powers to surrender. The combatants scheduled the armistice to come into effect at the eleventh hour of the eleventh day of the eleventh month of 1918. That was clever, but of little consolation to the loved ones of the thousands who were killed between when it was signed and when it came into effect—including one American soldier who was killed at 10:59. The Treaty of Versailles officially ended the war in June of 1919.

The world had suffered tremendously in the war: 15 million soldiers lost their lives, and a generation of women was without husbands and children without fathers. Only America, which had entered the war at its very end, had emerged relatively unscathed. With its manpower and economy intact, America was ready to become the world's leader.

In September, Benjamin was released from the army and returned home, as shy as before. However, he decided not to regrow his beard and long hair.

During the war Benjamin was assigned to the Quartermaster Corp. of the First Army. "It wasn't much cooking," he said. "Just heating things up." Fortunately, he usually was far behind the front lines.

Upon returning to New York, Ben moved back into his old room and resumed working at the bakery. His living with his father helped them both recover from Hannah's death.

It was another year and a half until the flu epidemic relented. It had killed between 50 and 100 million worldwide and left few families, including ours, unscathed.

At the end of the war, I wrote my family several times, but it was almost a year until I received this letter from Leena:

169

Dearest Avrom,

We haven't heard from you in a long time. We all hope you are well. I wrote a few times during the war, although I doubt whether the letters got to you.

The war wasn't good for Zyvotov. As reprisal for the resistance killing several soldiers, the Germans ransacked our town. Raisa's husband tried to tell them that Jews weren't involved, and they shot him. Then they went through the house and took everything of value and, of course, all the meat from the shop. We hid in the woods until it was over. They also did other things that are too horrible to talk about.

When the Russians got rid of the Czar and the Germans left, we thought things would be better. But things are never better for Jews. First, the Whites came through. They hate Jews and stole all the food in the town. Then the Reds came through and shot the rich Jews. A few young men joined up with them, impressed with their ideas of sharing the wealth. I suspect they'll be disappointed.

Mama's health is failing. She's blind and very weak. It would cheer her up if you wrote. Me, I'm still single. I'll probably be a spinster teacher for the rest of my life. However, I find my fulfillment in teaching the children, and I don't need any of my own.
Love,
Leenitchka

Leena's statement about "things too horrible to talk about" made me sick to my stomach. I immediately pulled out pen and paper and wrote a long letter. I explained I had written, but probably the postal service had been messed up by the war. I told her about Meyer and Harry and life in America during and after the war. For two dollars, I bought my first camera, a Kodak Brownie, model 2a, so I could include pictures of the whole family and, of course, New York City. I assured Leena she could accomplish wonderful things single or married, but I remained certain that someone would snatch her up, as I had Sarah.

Chapter 22

Without the rocking of the bus, I can't put my anger at the bus company away and fall asleep. Imagine: leaving us out here to freeze to death. Bet they wouldn't try that with a bunch of businessmen. They'd sue the pants off them.

It takes almost another hour before a new driver arrives. He's in a better mood than all the passengers. "Sorry folks," he says. "A little mix-up on the schedule. And thank you Mr. Abe, whoever you are, for letting us know that you were all sitting here."

Those passengers who are awake applaud.

"I heard that," Bessie says, half asleep, "You're the hero of the bus."

It almost makes the whole incident worthwhile.

The twenties started with a bang...literally. In July of 1920 a wagon packed with a hundred pounds of explosives blew up in front of the J. P. Morgan Bank on Wall Street. Thirty-eight people were killed and more than four hundred injured. I remembered that Morgan was the guy that got us out of the panic of '07. I didn't understand why anyone would want to kill him.

Anarchists, people who were anti-government and the rich, were suspected, but he police were never able to arrest anyone for the Morgan bomb. It was an Anarchist who had provided the spark to start the World War, and now they might be invading America. Since many Anarchists were also Communists, many people who had supported the Communists switched their allegiance to the Socialists. The Communist Party never again played an important part in the political process in the U.S.

Mr. Henkel's son Sammy, who was now called Sam, had been drafted into the army. After the war, Mr. Henkel turned the day-to-day running of the dress factory over to him.

In 1920, a severe recession began, as the country stopped making goods for the war, and all the returning soldiers were dumped onto the job

171

market. However, most of the soldiers hadn't been able to spend all their pay in Europe, and arrived in America with money in their pockets. Many of them bought their wives a new dress. I had picked up a couple of outside accounts and was able to show Sam that Henkels hadn't been paying market price for their belts. We reached an agreement that he wouldn't pay less than 10% below what I could get for the same item from another customer.

Things were not going too well at home. Taking care of Harry became increasingly difficult as he crawled, walked and then ran. He would get into everything, pulling items off the furniture and putting things into his mouth. He needed to be watched constantly—just the opposite of Meyer, who was upset having his calm existence destroyed by his hellion of a brother. Sarah was getting increasingly frazzled and would often scream at Harry.

Saul saw his daughter was having a bad time. To help with baby sitting and cleaning, he would send over Anna, one of the clerks at the bakery, whenever he could spare her. Anna was about eighteen and delighted in playing with Harry, who would usually go to her, rather than his mother.

Sarah was so depressed she had little interest in the 1920 national elections, the first after passage of the woman's suffrage nineteenth amendment. "Why should I register to vote," she said. "What difference will it make?"

I had to embarrass her into it. "Do you remember those women in white marching down 5th Avenue? You said you wished you could march, and now you won't even vote."

"Okay," she said. "But you'll have to arrange for babysitting and some way for me to get over to the county office."

I made the arrangements: Marie watched the boys and Polinski's truck took` Sarah to register. However, maybe Sarah was right. It was an extremely dull election. Both, James Cox, the Democrat, and Warren Harding, the Republican, followed the isolationist trend in the country and hedged on Wilson's League of Nations, which was supposed to end all wars. Harding's call for a "return to normal" resonated with the country and he won by a landslide. We didn't realize it at the time, but Cox's running mate, Franklin D. Roosevelt, would later become the savior of our nation.

One Friday afternoon in 1921, Mr. Henkel dropped in to Henkel's Belts. "Abe," he said. "I don't know whether you've heard, but Albert Einstein, one the most famous Jews in the world, is coming to New York tomorrow. I'm going to be in the delegation that greets him at the Battery at about two in the afternoon." He puffed out his chest.

"I've read about him," I said. "They say he's the smartest man in the world."

"Maybe the smartest that's ever lived," Mr. Henkel responded. "Although I can't say I understand any of his theories about space, time, and gravity. They say that there are probably only ten people alive who can understand his theory of relativity."

"Why is he coming here?" I asked.

"Chaim Weizmann is bringing him. Weizmann is a Zionist. He thinks Jews need a homeland of their own; that they'll never be safe in another country. During the war, he and Lord Rothschild got the British Foreign Secretary, Balfour, to sign a declaration supporting a home for the Jews in Palestine. I think the British were trying to get Jewish money to support their war effort. At the end of the war, the League of Nations put the British in charge of Palestine."

I knew there were Jews living in Palestine, but I didn't know the details. Wouldn't it be a little too hot for black coats and hats? "How many Jews are living there?"

"About 50,000. The Zionists want more Jews to move to Palestine—especially Russian Jews. Einstein is trying to raise money from American Jews to start a university there—in Jerusalem."

"That sounds like a good idea." I offered.

"I'm not sure. It's difficult living there, especially since Britain is expected to respect the rights of the Arabs. Many Jews have tried it and then moved to America. It's good that Einstein will see what a wonderful life Jews have in America. Maybe he won't be so enthusiastic about moving them all to some other place." As he turned to leave, Mr. Henkel added, "You might want to see his arrival. It's going to be quite an event."

I didn't relish giving up my Saturday with Sarah, so I asked her if she wanted to go. "You go ahead," she said. "I don't feel up to trekking all the way down there."

About noon on Saturday, I made the long subway trip down to the Battery. Mr. Henkel was right, this was quite an event. Thousands of people, many who didn't look Jewish, were standing around. A drum and fife band in uniforms entertained them while they waited. I bought a hot dog from one of the many peddlers who had set up stands for the occasion. There were lots of signs welcoming Einstein, and one, decorated with crosses with their arms bent to the right, that said, "Don't believe Einstein." This was the first time that I saw those hateful swastikas.

At about two, the murmuring of the crowd increased to a roar, as a boat, transporting passengers from a transatlantic liner pulled up to the pier. In the front stood two men, one with a large bushy beard, and the other with a mustache and unkempt hair. "That's him," the man next to me said, pointing to the guy with the mustache.

The band began to play what I believe was either the Austrian or German national anthem, and Einstein disembarked. Various dignitaries got to shake his hand; I didn't see Mr. Henkel among this group. In not too long, Einstein was hurried into one of a group of six limousines waiting at the curb, and following the band, the cars and most of the crowd headed north.

There's something about a fife and drum band that gets men to march along with it. That was one way they used to get fools into the army in the old country. For about two hours, I joined several hundred people following the caravan: first through the deserted financial district, then past City Hall and into the narrow streets of the Lower East Side. There we picked up other marchers, mainly young boys. Pushcart peddlers gave fruit to Einstein and sprinkled his car with flowers. I'm sure some didn't even know whom they were honoring. Finally, I noted that the sun was beginning to go down and I hurried to find a subway to return to Sarah.

After the recession of '20-'21, the country entered into a prolonged period of prosperity. The fashions of the twenties deemphasized a woman's waist and as a result, most dresses came without belts. This was fine with Sarah, who had put on quite a few pounds since we got married, but it wasn't so good for Henkel's Belts. Fortunately, belts were still being bought as accessories for sportswear. In order to keep us going, I was able to get a few orders from department stores, which made up in quantity what they lacked in price. Even with all our sewing machines running, we sometimes had difficulty in getting the work out. I often found myself staying late several nights a week. As a result of all the business, my yearly share-of-the-profits payment increased considerably.

In '23 I was approached by a couple of men with a proposition. They were planning to set up a company to service the apparel industry: belts, buckles, buttons and bows, they said. Would I be interested in setting up and running the belt part of the operation—at double my salary and ten percent of the profits? I wasn't sure I trusted them, so I took the offer to Sam. After he spoke to his father, I got a nice raise to stay at Henkel's.

Financially, we were doing well. I would take three dollars out of my salary for spending money and give the rest to Sarah for household expenses. Since Saul was paying our rent, each week she was usually able to put a few dollars in the Tremont Bank, down the block.

My bonus checks, which were sizeable those years, went right into the Bank of The United States on Delancy Street, a few blocks from Henkel's Belts. This was one of the largest banks in the country. Most Jews saved there because it was one of the few banks run by Jews. Sarah and I hoped the money would provide a down payment for the house we were planning to buy.

Our good financial situation, however, was overshadowed by Sarah's depression. She was still having a hard time recovering from her mother's death.

It didn't help that about a year after Hannah's death, Saul took up with Gita, a woman with three children. Gita was only about five years older than Sarah. I think Saul was drawn to Gita because she too had lost her spouse to the flu. With Gita and her children in the apartment, there no longer was any room there for Ben, so he moved into "an efficiency," one room and a kitchen.

Gita's oldest was Hirshel, who she called "the little genius." One year past his *bar mitzvah*, Hirsh always had his nose in a book. "He'll be a

175

doctor," Gita told us, "and go to Harvard." She showered all her attention on Hirsh and didn't spend much time or money on her two younger daughters, who were both lovely girls. Gloria, a seven-year old, would laugh and play with Harry whenever we visited the Polinski apartment. Elizabeth, who was nine, had an artistic bent and would excitedly show Sarah her drawings.

Gita had little sympathy for Sarah's prolonged depression. At one Passover *Seder*, after Saul had explained the symbols of the holiday on the Seder plate, Gita said, "You see Sarah, the Jews had terrible sadness when they were in bondage in Egypt, but we remember it only eight days during the year. The rest of the time we get on with our lives—like you should. Your husband and your children need you. Anyway, if your mother died, it was *bershert*. God has his reasons." Sarah bit her lip.

Serving the matzo-ball soup, Gita announced, "I didn't put any salt in the soup this year. Saul has high blood pressure, and the doctor said he should stay away from salt. You'll all have to salt it to your taste." The soup was tasteless and the saltshaker quickly made its way around the table.

Sarah was concerned. High blood pressure was a common and serious ailment among Jews, who liked salty and fatty foods. "How long have you known about your pressure, Daddy?" she asked.

"Only a few weeks," Saul said. "I had this bad headache, so I went to the doctor. He put this thing around my arm that measures it."

"Are there any medicines for it?" I asked.

"Only rest and stay away from salt."

When we got home, Sarah said, "That *klafte* should mind her own business. My mother's dying wasn't *bershert*. God was just so busy with the war and everything that he just let it slip by. I don't see how my father could take up with Gita after having lived with my mother all those years."

"*Klafte*, I didn't know you could speak Yiddish."

"I heard my grandmother say it enough times. Mother had more patience; she didn't call people that. Maybe I should try to be like her."

I saw Sarah had tears in her eyes.

"At least Gita seems to be watching his diet," Sarah said.

Anna's visits to help Sarah became much less frequent after Gita moved her family into the Polinski's apartment. Sarah blamed her influence for the falloff.

I guess I should have stayed home with Sarah on Saturdays and helped her with Harry and cleaning the apartment. However, on my one day off a week, I needed some relaxation, so I resumed my walks around the city. There are lots of interesting things to see in the Bronx: the Botanical Gardens, Van Cortland Park, Woodlawn Cemetery and, of course, the Zoo. A delightful wooded path ran through northern Bronx along the Hudson River. I found that country walking could be just as enjoyable as city walking.

I don't think Sarah was too happy about my going out, and that was why she would lash out at me for things I had little to do with. "This baby's always running around—just like you," she said, and, "I'm stuck in this apartment all day, taking care of your children." When I saw her slap Harry for a minor infraction, I decided to spend more time at home.

In 1923, I got a letter from Leena.

Dearest Avrom,

I am sorry to tell you that Mama has died. She had had a couple of bad years with cancer and didn't mind ending her unbearable pain. We were able to have a nice funeral service for her without interference from the authorities. Usually, they discourage any outward show of Judaism. Freyda's husband ran the service. He had been the rabbi of the local shul. Now he just usually sits around and studies Torah. They won't even allow him to give lessons.

As you know, the Communists are completely in power here. All the people are supposed to be equal, but some, I mean Jews, are less equal than others. That is because they are widely dispersed in the Soviet Union, and thus "foreigners" in any region in which they live. Because of this, some members of the government feel that the Jews will always be "subversives." This is ironic, since many of the top officials were born Jewish.

Of course, Russian peasants remain fiercely anti-Semitic, no matter what government is in power. So I don't expect things here will improve much for Jews.

Give my love to your beautiful wife and children. Mama loved the photos of them you sent us. I hope to meet them some day.

Love

Leenitchka

Leena's words cut through me like a knife–just to think of Mama suffering like that, while I was enjoying myself in America. I counted up the number of times I had written in the almost quarter century I had been away from the family. Could it have been that few?

For a while after that, Sarah and I were on the same wavelength. I understood how her grief could be much deeper than mine, with her being with her mother almost every day of her life. "Do you feel guilty about anything you didn't do for you mother?" I asked her while we lying in bed one night.

She thought for a minute. "I feel guilty she spent so much time caring for me and worrying about me that she didn't enjoy life as much as she could have."

"I guess that was her choice."

"But I just miss her so much."

"I feel guilty for not writing home more often," I confessed.

Sarah held me, and we cried together.

The darkness soon lifted from me, but it continued to enfold Sarah. Not every day; she'd have good days and bad. One day I'd come home and find her sitting by the kitchen table and staring at the wall, and on the next she'd seem to be her old self, with lots of energy and even a bit of that wonderful smile of hers.

To try to help, I tried to get Sarah out of the house as much as possible. On Saturday night, we occasionally went to the Tremont, which had converted from a Yiddish theater to a cinema showing the latest American movies, which were silent at that time. Watching them and listening to the bantering of the audience during the performance would take Sarah's mind off her troubles for a while, and their romantic content would sometimes restore her interest in sex.

Leena's "hoping to meet my family some day" in her letter suggested she might want to come to America. I was ecstatic at the idea of seeing her again, but knew she would need financial assistance for the cost of the trip to America. With some trepidation, I broached the idea to Sarah.

"My sister, Leena, sends her love," I told Sarah.

"She sounds very nice."

"With Mama and Papa dead, nothing is really keeping her in the Zyvotov. I think I could convince her to move to New York."

"It would be great for you to have family in America."

"Of course, she doesn't have much money. We'd have to help out with her transportation costs."

That stopped Sarah in her tracks. But she didn't seem totally against the idea. "I'd really like to meet your sister," she said.

I think the similarity of their disabilities was a bond between Sarah and Leena.

Sarah and I sat down and looked over our finances. A few days later I checked the price of third-class passage at a trans-Atlanta steamship company. We decided that we could afford to pay Leena's fare. I was wonderfully excited when I wrote to her about our decision.

It was almost six months until I received another letter from Leena.

Dearest Avrom,

Your offer to pay my fare to America is most generous, and I when I received your letter I immediately started to find out what would be involved.

Unfortunately, the information I've gathered indicates my moving to America is not possible. It is not as easy as it was when you went a quarter of a century ago. Now, you need what's called an immigration visa, which you get from the United States Consular Office in Kiev. I'm told that they are suspicious about Jews from the Russian Empire being Communists. In addition, my disability would almost definitely rule out my getting a visa.

179

America, it seems, is very concerned about maintaining the quality of its "race."

I recently bought a camera. Since I won't be able to join you in person, I hope the enclosed photos will be some consolation for you.
Love,
Leenitchka

One of the two photos showed Leena standing in front of the school where she taught, surrounded by a group of children. She seemed happy, and to me, still pretty enough to find a husband.

Chapter 23

At about seven in the morning, the bus pulls into a gas station next to a McDonald's in Virginia.

"We'll take twenty minutes here, folks," the bus driver says. "That means we'll leave at seven twenty five. Make sure that you and the person sitting next to you get back on time. I wouldn't want to drive off and leave someone here."

I've been in McDonald's a couple of times. It's pretty basic: hamburgers and stuff. I couldn't understand why, when Queen Elizabeth visited the White House last year and the kitchen was being renovated, Nixon took her to a McDonald's in Maryland. I don't even think Sarah would have been enthusiastic about that. She did like Horn and Hardart though...and Chinese restaurants.

I smile to myself. I've only recently been able to remember Sarah without thinking of the horrors of her last year.

Right now, the last thing my legs want is more sitting, so I pick up a cup of coffee in the gas station and drink it standing at their counter. Then I walk back and forth the length of the station trying to restore my circulation.

"You da man who called the bus company?" a young black passenger from the bus asks me.

"That was me."

"Thanks man. We could'a froze to death in dere." He pumps my hand.

"Glad to help out." I'm feeling pretty good. Maybe I will be able to get Ida to come back to Miami with me.

When Bessie and most of the others come out of MacDonald's, I join them getting on the bus.

"Didn't you want any breakfast?" Bessie asks me

"I'm not much for breakfast. Just grabbed some coffee."

181

"I had an egg McMuffin," Bessie says. "Breakfast is the most important meal of the day." Then she laughs. "I guess that's just an excuse."

Ben and I became close friends, and he often joined me on my walks around the Bronx. We would stop at the Oval, a park made by filling in what had previously been a reservoir for northern Bronx. There we would occasionally join a pickup basketball game. By that time I was approaching forty, and had slowed down considerably. Ben was a half-dozen years younger, powerfully built, but short and not very graceful. He excelled at the pushing and shoving parts of the game. Rarely did we win more than once, which was fine considering our limited endurance.

In 1923, after the Giants kicked them out of the Polo Grounds, the Yankees moved to their new stadium at 161st Street off the Grand Concourse. Being avid Yankee fans, Ben and I would often spend our Saturday afternoons there. For fifty cents you could get a seat in the bleachers and hope Babe Ruth would hit a ball your way. According to the newspaper, Babe's salary was $52,000 a year, about fifty times mine. That made him one of the richest men in New York. He was worth every penny of it.

I suggested to Ben that he should see a *shadchan* and find a wife, but even the thought of it made him blush. So I was surprised when one day at Yankee Stadium, coming back from getting us a couple of sodas, I found him talking with a woman with red hair who was sitting next to us in the bleachers. I looked at Ben and he blushed.

We watched the Yankees complete their 3-1 defeat of the Philadelphia Athletics. When we rose to leave, the woman sitting next to Ben motioned her head to her two friends and said, "We're going to get drinks at the Yankee Tavern. It's on 161st Street. Would you gentlemen like to join us?"

"Sure." Ben stammered, and I nodded my assent. I knew Sarah would be furious at my returning late, but hey, this was her brother, who as far as we knew, had never talked to a woman before. "Her name is Betsy," Ben told me. "She works at a bank."

We followed the women to the Tavern, a long, narrow, corner establishment, with a bar running its length. The place was overflowing when we got there, but we managed to push our way in. It didn't seem that we would even be able to order, but I succeeded in plunking my ten cents down on the bar and getting a beer. "This tastes like real beer," I said to Natalie, Betsy's friend. Only "near beer", with less than half percent alcohol was legal during Prohibition. A popular remark was, "Whoever had named it 'near beer' had lost their sense of distance."

"They serve real beer whenever the Yankees win…and sometimes when they lose," Natalie informed me. "You can get stronger stuff in the back room."

I had seen a fellow in the back letting select customers through a door. In the front, some patrons were augmenting their drinks with liquid from their personal flasks. Against the wall, I noticed that Ben and Betsy were deep in conversation, with her face close to his—so she could hear him over the din, I suppose.

Suddenly everyone in the bar let out a roar, as a big guy swaggered through the front door. No mistaking him—it was the Babe—taller and broader than I had realized. A place was cleared for him at the bar.

"How come no home runs today," one of the patrons called out.

"Gotta give the other guys on the team a chance," the Babe quipped, and signaled the bartender for a beer. "Get mighty thirsty out there in right field." He gulped the whole mug down in a couple of seconds and replaced it on the bar for refilling. A half-dozen girls crowded around him, and after fifteen minutes he left with his arms around the shoulders of two of them, leaving the Tavern in a state of exhilaration. Ben and Betsy resumed their conversation.

On the way home, Ben said to me, "I'm going to meet her at next Sunday's game. I guess that's a date."

"I guess it is," I answered. "You're on your own now."

"Really?" Sarah said, when I told her of Ben meeting a woman and his upcoming date. Her face lit up like it hadn't for quite a while.

Sarah seemed to be finally coming out of her depression. To continue lifting her spirits, I would take her out to a Chinese restaurant a few

183

blocks from our apartment almost every Saturday night. Marie would watch the boys. For half a buck we could get soup and a dish of Chop Suey or Chow Mein large enough to split. It was fun trying to eat it with chopsticks. Instead of paying Marie, we'd bring her back a container of food.

The happy period didn't last. One day when I came home from work, Sarah hit me with, "I think I'm pregnant again." There was no dancing this time. Both Sarah and I knew she was still close to her breaking point. I wasn't sure she could handle the added stress of taking care of another child. "I hope this one's a girl," Sarah said. "They're easier to take care of." I vowed to myself I would try to give her all the help I could. We even got a telephone in the apartment, so Sarah could call me, if there were any problems. She made frequent use of this new device.

Sarah did her best, but I would often find her crying to herself. "What's going to happen to me?" she asked me.

"We'll make it through," I assured her.

For the last three months of her pregnancy, Saul sent Anna over a couple of times a week. Ben told me this was against the advice of Gita, who thought that Sarah should grow up and assume her responsibilities.

Sarah had her wish: in April '24, she gave birth to a girl, who we named Esther. It was a good thing Saul continued sending Anna for several months after the birth, since Sarah needed all the help she could get.

About six months later, Leah and Paul came up to see the new baby. They brought their son, David, who was about Harry's age, with them. The two boys had a great time running around the apartment, while Meyer, as usual, sat reading a book.

"How's it going?" Leah asked.

"It's tough," Sarah said. "I can't wait until Harry starts school next year. Three's at least one too many."

"You should get a diaphragm," Leah remarked.

"What's that?" I asked.

"Something women wear, so that they don't get pregnant. It's the most reliable means of birth control. I use one."

That sounded fine to me.

"Where do you get it?" Sarah asked excitedly.

"You have to be fitted for it," Leah said. "The only place is a birth-control clinic run by Margaret Sanger down on Tenth Street. It used to be in Brooklyn, but the police there arrested her. The new one is staffed by doctors, so the Court of Appeals says the authorities can't do anything about it. The Catholics are up in arms; they picket it almost every day. But loads of women from the tenement brave their insults. It's the only way they can be saved from the horrible fate of having babies they can't feed."

The very next week, with Marie watching Esther and Harry and Meyer in school, Sarah traveled by subway to Margaret Sanger's clinic and got her diaphragm. Although not without inconvenience, it was a great boon to our sex life. Sarah didn't have to worry about getting pregnant again. I kept my fingers crossed.

Ben's courtship of Betsy, or should I say Betsy's courtship of Ben, was progressing. "A shy fellow is just what I want," she said. "I'm tired of those guys who think too much of themselves." In just a few months they were engaged. Since Betsy was Irish Catholic, the wedding would be in a church, and Ben would have to agree to bring the children up Catholic. Having a son or daughter marry outside of Judaism and agreeing to bring up the children in a different religion was a great disgrace for a Jew. Some fathers refused to ever see their sons or daughters after that. Saul, however, had become very close to Ben after Hannah died and he was counting on him to carry on the family business. He had begun to worry that Ben would be alone all his life. He would moan, "How can you do this to me?" to Ben about his marrying in a church, but I think this was mainly for the benefit of the community, and he was secretly pleased at the prospect of having grandchildren who would carry on the Polinski name.

Betsy's and Ben's wedding, in the spring of '24, was at Saint Joseph's Church on Bathgate Avenue, walking distance from our apartment. I was Ben's best man. The Polinskis had lots of Jewish friends and many of them showed up at the church and sat on the "groom's side" of the aisle. Noticeably, that side of the church didn't kneel for the prayers, go up to the front for communion, or "amen" the prayers that included "Jesus" or "Christ."

Saul sat in the back row of the small church, and observed the Latin rituals. He put on a good show of being dejected, but I think I observed a twinkle in his eye several time during the ceremony.

A good indication of Saul's acceptance of the marriage was the great wedding present he bought Ben and Betsy. It was a Chevrolet sedanette costing about $500. This was about $200 more than the cheapest Ford. Jews, however, stayed away from Fords, because Henry Ford, an American industrial hero, was a rabid anti-Semite. Ford railed against Jews in his newspaper, the weekly Dearborn Independent. The newspaper even published The Protocols of the Learned Elders of Zion. Papa had told me about those phony protocols, which supposedly was a plan by Jews to take over the world. In the old country they had periodically been used to justify mass extermination of Jews. Jews taking over the world: can you imagine a more ridiculous thing?

Several times Marie watched the kids while Sarah and I drove with Ben and Betsy up the Saw Mill Parkway to see fall foliage or spring flowers. The scenery on the parkway was breathtaking, and the rides invigorated Sarah.

Since Betsy was an avid Yankee fan, she and Ben would take in a game almost every weekend, and occasionally I would join them. "You should take the boys to the game," Sarah said, when Meyer was eight and Harry five. "They don't get to be with you very often." I thought I'd give it a try.

We sat in the bleachers, of course. The boys' admission cost me only twenty-five cents each. Meyer wiped off his seat and commenced studying the statistics in the program. "Is .327 a good batting average, Dad?" he asked.

I explained the mysteries of baseball to him, pointing out the infield, outfield, dugouts and bullpens. Then I discussed the stars on the Yankee roster: Ruth, Bob Musel, Wally Pipp and a young kid, Lou Gehrig, who we all thought would be great. I thought Betsy was playing with Harry.

186

However, when I looked up, there was no sign of him. Knowing how he enjoyed hiding, I searched all the nearby rows of seats. No sign of Harry. I panicked. Ben and I both called out, "Harry, Harry,"—no answer. "You stay right here," I said to Meyer, knowing he wouldn't move.

"I'll stay with him," Betsy said. Ben and I ran up and down the aisles. Two ushers helped us.

For two innings we searched: in the bathrooms, at the refreshment stand, anywhere we could think of. As the Yankees were coming to bat in the third, the loudspeaker blared, "Mr. Sokolovsky, please pick up your son at the security office."

A wave of relief flowed over me. An usher accompanied me to the office. By the time I got there, I was pretty angry with Harry for running away. In the security office, I found him sitting on a desk, eating ice cream and being cooed over by two secretaries. "He's so beautiful," they said, and indeed he was. I started to chew him out, but then gave him a big hug.

"I didn't see any bulls in the bull pen," he said, on the way back to our seats.

With three kids, I didn't get much chance to walk around the city during the next few years. Without walking I didn't feel completely alive. The kids grew up fast: Meyer always at the top of his class, Harry always getting in trouble and Esther being admired by everyone...except Sarah. It was as if Sarah had used up her maternal instincts on her first child, and all she could do was scream at the other two. "I can't wait until Esther starts school," she said. "Then at last I'll have some time for myself."

We put Esther's crib and then her bed in the living room. "It's too dangerous to have her in with the boys...especially Harry. I don't trust him," Sarah said. "She'll need a room of her own when she gets a little older...for privacy."

In '25, Marie told us that the apartment directly above ours was becoming available. "It has three bedrooms," she said. "Esther will be a young girl soon. She'll need a room of her own. The rent is only five dollars a week more than yours."

187

Esther was our baby, only four years old. I certainly didn't picture her as a "young girl", but Sarah and I agreed that Marie was right.

"I can manage one flight of stairs," Sarah said, and it was decided. A month later we hired two strong guys to carry all our stuff up to the second floor. The apartment had a fire escape from the window of the boy's bedroom. On sweltering summer mornings, I would sometimes find Harry asleep out there. At first Sarah and I scolded him for that, but with people in the adjacent buildings doing the same, we finally decided it was a reasonable way to beat the heat. Meyer, of course, sweated it out in his bed.

I guess Saul would have paid the five-dollar extra rent for the new apartment, but I didn't ask him. In those flush times, it felt good to be paying for at least part of our housing.

In '27, tragedy struck the Polinski household. Hirsh, "the little genius," was turned down by both Harvard and Columbia Universities and had to enroll in City College. The Boards of the Ivy league schools had decided that as a result of Jews "cramming" for the entrance exams, they were beginning to make up an uncomfortably large percentage of their student populations, changing the very nature of the institutions. Harvard and Columbia's losses were City College's gain. Not only were Jews the best students, but they were also the best basketball players at that time. City College's basketball team dominated the collegiate leagues in the late twenties and early thirties.

"Anti-Semites," Gita said. "May they rot in Hell."

I think Saul was relieved at not having to pay the high tuition of the private schools.

In '29 the clothing unions bargained for and got a two-day weekend. Thereafter, Henkel's Belts was no longer open on Sunday, but, as the boss, I had to occasionally go in to finish an order. However, it was great to usually have an extra day to spend with the family and occasionally a chance to walk around the city again.

Izzy invited Sarah and me to a big party to see his new house in Forest Hills, Queens on a sweltering July evening in '29. It was so hot in the

188

train I carried my jacket. "We should get a car," Sarah said. "Then we could get a breeze on a trip like this." I ignored her comment.

Izzy had been married to Diane for about five years at the time, and they had two girls. Diane was distantly related to the Strauss's, who manufactured work clothes including Levi's jeans. I guess the connection brought Izzy's law firm lots of business. His house didn't match those on Fifth Avenue, but it was quite impressive: three stories, about ten rooms with a large high-ceilinged front room that easily accommodated the fifty-or-so guests at the party.

As far as I could tell, I was the only one there from Izzy's Lower-East-Side days. Both Sarah and I felt out of place at the party. Our best clothes were seriously out of date. Short, shapeless "flapper" dresses were in style on the young girls, but didn't fit Sarah's now abundant figure, and my sport jacket was over ten years old. I was standing by myself while Sarah went to the bathroom, when a young man introduced himself. "I'm Charles Dixon, from Isador's firm."

"Abe Sokolovsky, I used to play basketball with Izzy." We shook hands.

"Yes, I heard he used to be very good."

"He was the best," I remarked.

We both looked over at Izzy; prosperity had added quite a few inches to his waistline.

"Hey, Charlie," another young fellow said, "You still into Radio?"

"Yes, making a killing. Got any new tips for me this week? Oh, by the way, this is Abe. He used to play basketball with Izzy."

"Bernie Malkovic, I'm a stockbroker." He gave me a vigorous handshake. "You into the market, Abe?"

"No, not yet."

"What you waiting for? Everyone's cleaning up. Here's my card, in case you want to take the plunge." I put his card in my pocket.

"Do you think the Fed's rate hike is going to slow the market?" Charlie asked.

"Don't worry," Bernie replied. "There's plenty of money out there. You might just have to pay another point interest on your margin account, that's all."

What was the Fed? And what was margin? I wasn't sure, but it seemed like these were things I should look into.

"I see you've met some of the boys," Izzy said, on his trip around the room. "Glad you could make it, Abe."

"Great house you have here, Izzy," I said, and I meant it.

"Thanks," Izzy said, with a quick wave, as he continued his circulation around the room. I excused myself from Bernie and Charlie and went over to pick up a few more hor d'ouvres.

Most of the conversation was like that: investments, stocks and trusts—things I usually skipped over in the *Times*. Almost everyone said they made a "killing" on the market, even the girls who were secretaries in Izzy's firm. Unlike most gatherings I had previously gone to, the crowd didn't segregate into sexes, with men talking business and women discussing recipes and their children. Here the women actively engaged in the financial discussions. I found a glum Sarah in one group.

On the train back home, she said to me, "Everyone's making a lot of money on the stock market. Why not us?"

In my distant memory, I recalled 1907, when the bottom came close to falling out of the market. "I don't know. I'm not sure it can go on much longer, especially with the Fed going to raise interest rates. We need our money for a down-payment on a house."

Sarah looked at me with new respect.

"Maybe, we can put just a bit of it in the market," she suggested. "At least, it will give us something to talk about at parties."

"I'll think it over," I told her.

At the end of the month, when Arthur came around to do books, I asked him about "margin" and the "Fed."

"Margin is just borrowing," he told me. "It allows you to increase your bets on the stock market."

"You mean a stockbroker would lend me money to buy stocks?" The concept seemed strange to me; ordinary people like me usually only borrowed when they got sick or lost their job. Only a very good friend, a relative or a *landsman* would put up the money, although I heard the unions had funds with which they would sometimes help out a worker. "Why would they do that?"

"For the interest," Arthur said. "The Fed sets the rates... and for the commissions. Of course, you have to put up most of the money, and if the price of the stock goes down, you can lose it all."

That didn't sound too good to me. It reminded me of Menahem-Mendl, who Papa had told me not to be like.

Sarah and I didn't have any time to think about stock market during the next few weeks, since we were getting ready for Meyer's *bar mitzvah*, when he would officially become a man and be responsible for his adherence to Jewish law. Before this, Sarah and I bore the responsibility for his adherence. To mark the occasion, Meyer would be called up to read the daily portion from the *Torah*, the Five Books of Moses; and the *Haftorah*, the Book of Prophets. Meyer was the star pupil in his Hebrew class at Adath Israel, and we had no doubt he would perform his responsibilities exceptionally well.

Meyer's chanting of the Torah at the Saturday service was beautiful to me. As was custom, he also gave a discussion of the Torah portion, and related the statement that "The enemies of Israel will be punished by God," as it related to the massacre of the Jewish community of Hebron by Palestinian Arabs the previous week. I hadn't even known about this latest tragedy that befallen the Jews. I was glad we were living in America and very proud of my son.

After the service, there was a small party at our apartment. My job was to get wine to toast the *bar mitzvah* boy, or should I say man. Since it was during prohibition, I went down to Eldridge Street, where a grocery store sold bottles of kosher-style wine under the counter. It was obtained from a winery in California under the fifty-gallon exemption provided for rabbis. Just about everyone in the neighborhood claimed to be a rabbi and then resold the wine to the store.

A *bar mitzvah* for Harry was not something I had to think about. It was difficult enough to get him to do his homework for public school, without trying to get him to learn Hebrew and prepare to read the *Torah*. By the time he was ten, we began to get reports of truancy from his teachers. With a group of like-minded friends, he would skip school and roam all over the Bronx. Then when Harry was eleven, something really bad happened: while I was at work, a policeman brought him home, a local candy store proprietor having caught him shoplifting.

"What were you thinking?" I asked. "Do you want to go to jail?"

"It was just a dare," he answered. "I won't do it again."

I felt guilty. I had worked too hard and hadn't spent enough time with the kids. Meyer had been self-sufficient, but it looked like Harry really needed my attention. I decided he would become my project. Maybe I could interest him in basketball, and he would join a team at the Jewish Community Center. That would keep him out of trouble.

For the next few months, almost every Saturday morning, I took Harry out to the schoolyard for basketball practice. I was in my forties, but still in good enough shape to play a few games of three-on-three with the kids. Harry was an excellent athlete, smooth and quick. He could drive around whoever was guarding him. The trouble was that in basketball, like in everything else, he was undisciplined, and would often miss his layup when he got to the basket. However, he did seem to relish my attention, and in the winter he joined a Community Center team. I think all the attention I focused on Harry had an effect on his brother. Meyer seemed to become more aloof and wouldn't even raise his nose out of his book when Harry and I returned from our basketball outings.

With Meyer's *bar mitzvah* out of the way, I began to watch the stock market. I even started to put down my two cents for the Times each morning. I'd read it on the crowded subway, folding the paper to keep it compact, like the guys in business suits did. The stock market was wild: up two percent one day, down three percent the next. Out in the Midwest, where farmers were doing very poorly, a couple of banks failed every week. I told Sarah I'd worked too hard for our money to gamble with it, and reluctantly she agreed.

Chapter 24

When we cross the Potomac, I remember that, back in the 50s, Sarah and I took the bus to D. C. and spent three nights there in a cheap hotel over a Labor Day weekend. The temperature was in the nineties, and we sweated while we toured the museums. Walking and standing was rough on Sarah, so we sat a lot on benches or in cafes. As a result, I didn't have nearly enough time in the Museum of Science and Industry to satisfy my curiosity about how things worked and in the National Gallery to see the world's works of art. I vowed to come back, but never did. Well, maybe it's not too late for that.

The twenties ended like they began: with a bang. In the last week of October, the stock market crashed.

On Thursday, October 24, 1929 *The Times* headline ran, **Prices of Stocks Crash in Heavy Liquidation**. I didn't worry. First of all, I had managed to resist Sarah's arguments that we should get into the market, and second, I'd seen things like this before, and they didn't last too long: a week, a month or six months at the most. Moreover, *The Times* assured us: *There is hardly a single item of news that might be construed as bearish.* I thought it might be a good time to take the plunge and buy some stock and made a mental note to look into it.

However, little did I know that on that day, while we were merrily making belts up on Essex Street, about a mile south, the turmoil continued. The stock market plunge accelerated. Crowds formed in the street and the police were called out to protect the stock exchange.

The next day *The Times* told us that, **Treasury Officials Blame Speculation**. I didn't mind if a few speculators suffered losses. Moreover the newspaper assured their readers that some of the richest bankers in the country were pooling their funds to come to the rescue of the market. Like they did back in '07, I thought.

Sure enough, Friday was a pretty good day down on Wall Street, and those of us who weren't invested didn't think much of it over the weekend. However, over the next few days I learned a lot about that word "margin," I had first heard at Izzy's party. Many people were speculating in stocks with borrowed money, paying up to 20% interest. They would put down the minimum collateral, and when prices fell, their brokers would ask them for more. If they didn't hurry to their broker's office with cash, their stocks would be sold, aggravating the downturn. That's what happened on Monday, and even more so on Tuesday, which they called "Black Tuesday." No longer could anyone believe statements by certain "experts" about it being a new era where the market would rise indefinitely. Something was wrong—basically wrong—with the markets and maybe the economy.

To tell you the truth, I wasn't completely displeased by the stock market crash of October. I remembered everyone at Izzy's party lording it over us hardworking non-investors. Not to mention I had risen in Sarah's estimation by keeping us out of the market. She didn't have to know that I had starting following the stock pages, and if the crash had delayed a month or so, I might have also bought some stocks. The market itself gave an indication that all was not lost. November was poor, but December was pretty good, and that continued into early 1930.

But the real question on everyone's mind was whether the crash would just hurt the speculators or would it spread to the economy in general. President Hoover was called the "Great Engineer," and he went to work engineering a recovery. He assured us, "Our national capacity for hard work and intelligent cooperation is ample guarantee of the future." More importantly, he called business people and government leaders to Washington, where they pledged to start lots of new projects. The Fed lowered rates. I wasn't sure what this would do, but since at Izzy's party people had worried about their raising rates, I assumed it would be good.

Back in those days, it was hard to know just how the economy was doing. They didn't publish all the data that's available now. But in my daily life, I began to collect my own data. Henkel's Dresses' orders began to slide, and Sam complained that he was having trouble collecting some of the money owed him. I'd pass stores that were closing and selling off their inventory at rock-bottom prices. A few shuttered stores were taken over by church groups giving out free bowls of soup and a chunk of 5-day old bread. And there were even worse sights, like people searching through garbage cans outside of restaurants for something to eat. "Can you spare a few

194

cents," became a constant refrain on the streets, and few people could. It didn't seem like America was still the golden land that Yudel had written us about.

In 1930, the stock market started off well. By April, most of the losses of the previous year were recovered. I began to hope that maybe the country wouldn't have to suffer too much. Then things took a nasty turn, with an unrelenting market drop through the summer, fall, and into the winter. By December, a dollar invested in the market in the summer of 1929 was worth about forty cents.

But I was doing okay. Although it didn't look like I'd have much of a bonus check that year, my salary was enough to live on. Even if Sarah hadn't regained the lightness of spirit that had first attracted me to her, her depression was greatly reduced. She was able to manage our household and take care of the kids. Each day she'd tell me about the great buys she'd find in stores, which enabled her to put even more money into her account.

Even I found some great buys. One day on the way home from work, I saw a radio in the window of a pawnshop. It was a Radiola brand table model in a faux mahogany cabinet, with three tuning knobs. The proprietor was asking twenty dollars for it, but I was able to bargain him down to twelve, which I estimated was a tenth of its original price. Even without batteries, it must have weighed about 40 pounds. I managed to lug it home on the subway. That weekend, I bought batteries, and with Ben's help got it running. I was delighted to see Sarah's face light up when it filled our living room with music.

They called it the Great Depression, but for the Sokolovskys, the Depression didn't start until December 10, 1930, a date I'll remember until I die. It was warm for December but raining on that Wednesday, when I got the call from Sarah about eleven. "Daddy called," she told me. "His truck just made a delivery at a restaurant on Southern Boulevard. The driver said there are about a thousand people outside the Bank of the United States up there. They say the bank's run out of money."

I thought quickly. What Sarah told me was hard to believe. Just this morning I had picked up yesterday's paper, which talked about a merger of the bank. I couldn't take a chance. I banked at the Delancy Street branch of the Bank of the United States. Maybe they still had money, even if the Southern Boulevard branch had run out. "Maybe I can still get our money out down here," I told her. But then I remembered: my passbook was home—no passbook, no money.

"Listen," I told Sarah. "I can't get our money without the passbook. It's in my top drawer. I'll go over to the bank and get in line, if there is one. Meanwhile you bring me the passbook."

Sarah understood the urgency of the situation. "I'll look for you on the line," she said.

Grabbing my hat and jacket, not bothering even to take my umbrella, I rushed down the stairs and up Essex Street as fast as my 46-year-old legs could take me. When I turned the corner onto Delancy, my jaw dropped. From three blocks away, I could already see the crowd in front of the bank. As I got closer, I saw there were about fifty guys and a couple of women in the line, which was growing longer every minute. Two guards stood at the door, and about every five minutes they'd let three more customers in. One guy tried going directly to the front of the line; he was almost killed. A man in a suit was in front of me. "What are our chances of us getting our money?" I asked him.

"I don't know," he said. "But if I don't, I won't be able to pay my workers on Friday. I guess I can give them checks, but that won't do them any good, if the bank goes under. I'll probably have to close down my factory."

Close down the factory. Now that was something to worry about. But then I remember that the Henkels kept their money in the Bank of New York. *Why hadn't I done that?*

The rain drenched most of us; only one in three had stopped to pick up his umbrella. There was a lot of comradery on the line, with several people huddling under each umbrella. After about a half hour, they closed the doors of the bank and put up a sign, **Bank Closed for Today**. Neither the rain, nor the sign got most of the crowd to leave. I think I could tell about how much each person had lost. The small losers went to get a drink, but those who were wiped out, just stood there shell-shocked. I kept my eye on the subway exit across the street, until Sarah limped out. She could see from the look on my face that things were not good. She hurried over and we hugged each other. I think at that moment, she finally put her mother's death behind her.

I knew that tomorrow we might have to cut back, but this was today, so I said, "Let's get some lunch at Katz's."

Warming up over bowls of hot matzo-ball soup, Sarah and I analyzed our future. "Don't worry," she told me, holding my hand. "It's only money. You've got your job and health. Daddy pays our rent. We're in a lot better shape than most people."

Seeing I wasn't convinced, she continued, "I've got a few hundred in my account. We don't really need a house anyway."

"What about college for Meyer?" I asked.

"He's still has two years of high school to go, and City College is free and excellent. Look, we're all healthy. That's the most important thing."

Sarah was strong then when I really needed her to be. It reminded me of how much I loved her.

A lot of people thought their lives were over when the Bank of the United States went under. One woman with $20,000 in the bank hanged herself. But it wasn't too long before the newspapers reported that all was not lost. Although the bank was not, as some people had believed, part of the United States government, it did have lots of assets, and depositors were told they should eventually get most of their money back. In the mean time, to keep businesses from failing, the State of New York set up a fund from which people could borrow up to half of what they had in their accounts at a low interest rate. Sarah and I discussed the offer. Since we had no immediate need for the money, we decided to pass it up.

Even though there was no change in our income, the Bank of the United States failure got Sarah to take up the banner of frugality with gusto. No longer did we have meat every night. Our diet became heavy with sandwiches made with Polinski Bakery bread. We ate out or went to the movies very rarely. Our entertainment was mainly limited to listening to the radio. We laughed at *Amos and Andy,* and Sarah hardly ever missed an episode of *The Goldbergs*, which being about a Jewish family in the Bronx, was a little too close to home to laugh at. Gertrude Berg read the part of Molly Goldberg so realistically we all worried with her about the members of her family. "You see what a Jewish mother goes through," Sarah would say. To tell you the truth, I identified a little with Molly's husband, Jake, who everyone seemed to take advantage of.

Sarah cut back all our expenses: Meyer occasionally got new clothes, but Harry had to do with his brother's hand-me-downs. I brought home an old sewing machine from the factory, and Sarah used it to sew dresses for Esther. Sarah didn't worry much about style; to me Esther started to look like something out of one of those pictures of farm families in the dust bowl, although anyone could tell that she was really quite pretty.

By nature a docile girl, Esther was cowed by her mother, who could explode if she was lax in doing her multitude of chores around the apartment. As she approached her teenage years, Esther became more and more depressed, not wanting to go out to play or even go to school. "Can't I have something decent to wear?" she asked me, which melted my heart. When I passed a rack of clothes on sale in front of a store down on the East Side, I would look for something Esther might like. Sarah would glower at me when I brought my purchases home, but the happiness in Esther's eyes more than made up for Sarah's anger.

Finally we reached a compromise. I'd buy Esther fabric, and she learned to make her own clothes on the sewing machine. She threw herself into sewing, and made a few things for her mother, as well as herself. I think making her own clothes gave her more satisfaction than she would have gotten if they had come from a store.

The big problem with the Bank of the United States failure was that it piled a panic on top of a depression. All around the country, people lined up outside their banks to withdraw their money. More than 300 banks failed during the month after the Bank of the United States went under, although thankfully, none of them were big New York City banks.

In the papers I read that the auditors were looking over the books of the Bank of the United States. Some of the dealings of the Marcus family, who ran the bank, were very shady. I was waiting to see how much of the almost $3,000 in our account we would get back. It would take more than ten years to find out, and by then the money wasn't worth very much.

A side effect of the Bank of the United States failure was a rise in anti-Semitism. Since Marcus was Jewish, it gave every anti-Semite in America an excuse to come out of the woodwork and find Jews to persecute.

As the depression ran on, people exhausted their savings and landlords lost their patience. More and more, I'd see a pile of furniture sitting in the street, not only in the poorer neighborhoods, but even up on the Grand Concourse. If the evictees were lucky, it wouldn't be raining, and they could try to sell some items while trying to find another place to live. I'd occasionally buy something, much to the annoyance of Sarah. Even if we didn't need my purchase, it felt good to put a few dollars in the pocket of a frightened woman with children.

In the newspaper, I read of people starving to death in New York City; not everyone could make their way to a charity soup line or stand there for hours with hundreds of men. Governor Franklin D. Roosevelt tried to set up a more extensive relief effort in the City, but was thwarted by the Tammany machine and the mayor, Jimmy Walker, who they controlled. Dapper, "do-nothing Walker," who had been an acceptable mayor for the twenties, now didn't seem to want to help. Most of the money the state sent to the city got stolen by Tammany and never reached the people. It was really bad times.

During the twenties there had been a huge building boom in New York. The buildings got taller and less light filtered down to the street, especially in Midtown and on Wall Street. Now there was a depression, with empty stores and factories all over New York, but that didn't stop the builders from reaching for the sky. Two buildings, both planned during the good times, were racing for the distinction of becoming the tallest building in the world.

The Chrysler Building at 42nd and Lexington had been started in '28 and was finished in the summer of '30. With 77 floors, it was certainly the most beautiful building I had ever seen. Seven successively smaller crowns and a tower that seemed to be reaching to the heavens topped the building.

For eleven months, it had the tallest-building trophy. I spent many lunch hours on the roof of Henkel's building watching it rise.

They started the Empire State Building at 34th Street and 5th Avenue at about the time the Chrysler Building was finished. The work proceeded at a feverish pace—one or two floors were added every week. I didn't know why; by that time anyone could see there wasn't a lot of demand for office space. By May of '31, it was finished. Herbert Hoover threw a switch in Washington, and the lights went on in the new champion.

On a sunny Sunday in July of '31, Sarah and I took the subway downtown to get a look at the city from the observation deck of the Empire State Building. We waited on line for about two hours, paid our dollar admission, and were whisked up to the 86th floor by one of the dozens of elevators. The elevators didn't stop between the 45th and 85th floors; an elderly gentleman told me that those hadn't been finished. They were just large empty spaces. In fact, most of the building was empty. I later learned, in its first year the Empire State Building made more money from observation deck admissions than it did from office rents.

The elevator deposited us on the observation deck, where we joined over a hundred other gaping visitors and at least that number of pigeons on the ledges. On each side of the deck the views were spectacular. With all my walking around the city, I had never gotten a good feeling for its scope until I looked at it from up there. Sarah, of course, hadn't done much walking around New York; this was like her first visit to the city.

To the east we could see the Chrysler Building, the point of whose tower was at just about at our eye level. Sarah looked over the wall. "Oo, I'm dizzy," she said. "Is that narrow street down there Fifth Avenue?"

"Yes, it is, but be careful by the wall." I guess it would have been difficult to fall off. However, climbing over the wall seemed possible and, in fact, was done in 16 suicides during the next 15 years. When the last of these, in '47, hit a pedestrian below, they finally put a chain-link fence around the deck.

I showed Sarah the bridges over the East River: the 59th Street Bridge going to Queens, and three bridges going to Brooklyn, which seemed to go on forever.

Walking to the right, I focused on the lower East side, and finally was able to pick out Seward Park, where I had played many basketball games. Looking beyond the tip of Manhattan, we could see so far that the horizon was curved. "Now I really believe the Earth is round," Sarah said. The Statue of Liberty seemed lonely, standing by herself in the harbor.

To the west, we could see over the buildings of the riverside communities in New Jersey to rolling farmlands.

Up north was Central Park, and beyond, the bridges going to the Bronx. "Can you see our building?" Sarah asked. I pointed in its general direction.

Toward the center of the deck, a couple was feeding breadcrumbs to the pigeons. An army of them gathered around their feet. Other pigeons, attracted by the activity, were converging on the scene. They better watch out, I thought, since I had read in the newspaper that people were trapping them for food. To me, t hey looked like dirty birds and not too appetizing to eat. I guessed that anyone who could afford the admission to the deck wouldn't have to eat pigeon stew for dinner.

During the twenties, magnificent movie theaters were built all over the country. In the Bronx we had the Loews Paradise, at 188th Street and the Grand Concourse. The theater, with 4,000 seats, opened two months before the stock market crash. It was like an Italian palace plunked down in the Bronx. Every hour, Saint George popped out of the clock on the top of the façade and slew the same dragon.

When Sarah and I went to the Paradise in '32 to celebrate our twentieth anniversary, even with ticket prices reduced to thirty cents, there were only about a hundred people in the audience. We saw *Grand Hotel*; that's the movie where Greta Garbo says "I vant to be alone." She was one great actress!

Sarah and I had never been in such a grand building. It had a huge lobby, decorated with statues, with a wide marble staircase leading up to a promenade. You could imagine a queen coming down that staircase. The auditorium was designed like a courtyard garden of an Italian palace, with carved columns, decorated arches and a garden scene on the stage curtain. The stars that twinkled in the ceiling amazed us the most. It didn't look like

201

Sarah and I would ever get to go to Italy, but after that night we felt that we had experienced a little of what it would be like. What did we care that it was plaster of Paris instead of marble, an illusion like the prosperity of the twenties.

Even bad times couldn't stop the frenetic building in New York City. At the beginning of the Depression, the Rockefellers, probably the richest family in the world, starting building Rockefeller Center, a dozen buildings around 50th Street between Fifth and Sixth Avenues. The complex included the Radio City Music Hall, the largest theater in the world, where the Rockettes, a group of 30 long-legged, high-stepping beauties performed. During the depression, Sarah and I didn't have the money to spend on admission to the Music Hall, but it didn't cost anything to watch the skaters at the outdoor ice rink in the complex.

By early '32, Saul was in pretty bad shape. There were no medicines to control high blood pressure in those days, and his went on until it damaged his kidneys. "He hardly pees at all, and he sleeps all the time," Gita told us.

Saul had long since turned over the running of the bakery to Ben and would hardly even go downstairs to see how things were going. "My legs burn like crazy," he complained.

In fact, Ben confided to me, things weren't going too well at the bakery. People were cutting back, and would wait to buy three-day-old bread for half price. Not too many families could afford the pastries and cakes on which the bakery made most of its profit. Ben had to let go a few workers and he and Yossi handled all the baking by themselves.

A few months later Marie knocked on our door. All but one of her children had left home, and now she took in a boarder, as well as taking care of the building. "Mr. Shineson said he didn't get your rent last month. He asked me to check on it."

"I'll have Sarah speak to her father," I told her.

Sarah visited her father the following day. She was very upset when I got home. "He just laid there in bed, with his eyes practically closed. I'm not sure he even recognized me. And he smells funny, like ammonia."

202

"How's Gita doing?"

"She doesn't seem upset; she just says it's *bershert.*"

"I guess you couldn't ask him about the rent," I said.

"I asked Gita about it. She put a guilt trip on me. 'Is that all you can think about when your father's dying?' she said. I don't know what we'll do about the rent."

"We'll have to pay it ourselves until things get settled," I said, recalling Izzy warning me twenty years earlier that the Polinskis should buy the apartment for us.

I paid Marie the thirty-five dollar monthly rent the next day. Since this was about a third of my monthly take-home salary, Sarah and I both kept our fingers crossed.

The depression years were a time of moving. So many families doubled up that landlords had a lot of empty apartments. They would offer two, or even three, months of free rent as an inducement to get people to move in. Some families would move every few months. I hoped we never had to do that.

About a week later, Saul died in his sleep. The good news was Sarah didn't take it nearly as badly as she had when her mother died. I think she felt she had lost most of him when he remarried. The bad news was that it didn't seem likely Gita would continue the rent payments. When I mentioned it to her about a week after the funeral, she said, "Your rent? What about my rent? Saul didn't leave me a pile of money."

In fact, we never learned how much Saul had left her. There wasn't a will and Gita wasn't planning to account for his finances. Ben took over the bakery. It wasn't worth anything without his running it. "If I have a good month, I'll pay your rent," he told me. I guess he didn't have too many good months in the next few years.

I asked Marie's opinion about what I should do.

"Maybe I can get you a deal," she said. "Apartments are pretty hard to rent nowadays, and you're good tenants." Two days later she got back to me. "Mr. Shineson says he'll take twenty-five until the economy improves." That was a relief to Sarah and me.

Meyer was due to graduate high school in June of '32. Attending City College, which was tuition-free, was his obvious next step. However, when Arthur, Henkel's accountant, who was approaching eighty, paid us his monthly visit, I had an idea how Meyer could jump start a career. During the Depression one didn't pass over any opportunity to do that.

After talking it over with Sarah and Meyer, I made an appointment to see Arthur at his apartment on 74th Street, off Eighth Avenue, on my way home from work.

He greeted me with, "Abe, to what do I owe this pleasure? No problem with the accounts, I hope."

"Oh no, I wanted to buy you dinner and make you a proposition."

"Dinner sounds good. I'll have to hear the proposition. I'm glad you don't want to come in. The place isn't so clean since my wife died two years ago."

"Where should we go?" I asked.

"I like Fine and Shapiro's, we can walk there."

Arthur, who was about 80, walked slowly but enjoyed the three-block trip to the restaurant.

When we were seated at one of the wooden tables in the delicatessen, he told me, "Now that I'm alone, I eat here almost every night. You should try one of their soups. They're outstanding."

Arthur was right: the barley soup was fantastic, and so was the corned beef sandwich that followed.

"So Abe, what's this proposition you've got for me?"

"Arthur, I think it's time you had an assistant. Someone to help you…and also someone to whom you could pass on all your accumulated knowledge about accounting."

"Is something wrong with my stamina, or do you have a suggestion for who should be my assistant?" he asked with a wink.

"Oh no, there's nothing wrong with your stamina. And yes, I have the perfect assistant for you: my son, Meyer. He's graduating from high school—an all A student."

"And how much will this genius cost me?"

"Try him out for a couple of weeks with no charge. If he's of use to you, pay him twenty-five cents an hour. He'll be starting an accounting program at City College night school in the fall. As he learns, you can increase his salary."

Arthur thought for a minute and then said, "Doesn't seem like I have anything to lose. Tell him to meet me at Henkel's this coming Tuesday."

Of course, Arthur was more than satisfied with Meyer, and within a month he began paying him. As Meyer progressed in his accounting courses at City College, he took over more of the responsibilities of the audits, and his salary increased. He was even able to give Sarah a few dollars a week for his room and board. He did much better than most other young people did during the depression.

Sarah's newfound energy extended beyond saving money. She also became involved in a number of activist movements that were sweeping the Bronx in the dark days of the Depression. Not long after Saul died, we heard about rent strikes that were occurring in the North Bronx. Led by Socialist and Communists, people were demanding that their landlords reduce rent in line with their reduced salaries. The landlords had mortgages to pay and refused the demands. The tenants withheld their rent. When the marshals showed up to evict tenants, they were met with crowds on the street and stuff thrown at them from windows of the apartment houses. As soon as they carried someone's furniture out into the street, the tenants would carry it back in. Pretty soon police, some on horseback, showed up, and a real riot broke out.

When Sarah heard about this, she told me, "I'm going up there tomorrow. Our rent was reduced. Why not theirs?"

I tried to talk her out of it. "You can get hurt. Let them fight their own battles."

But she wouldn't be dissuaded. "If we don't stick together, we'll all starve," she said.

The next day at work, I worried about Sarah. I called her all day, but there was no answer. I hurried home at about six, but only Esther was there. No dinner was on the table. About half hour later, a tired but elated Sarah came through the door. "We drove the police off," she told me.

I suspected it had just been time for the police to change shifts and they would be back. Actually, the next day evictions resumed, but the landlords finally agreed to some concessions.

During the Depression things were so tight, we couldn't justify keeping up the payments for our synagogue membership. For the High Holy Days, and especially Yom Kippur, I, like all Jews, felt it would be bad luck not to pray to God to inscribe us in the Book of Life. Temple Adath Israel sold tickets for the Days of Awe services for ten dollars. They would even wave that for those who claimed extreme hardship. Thankfully, we weren't in that group. The tickets, however, didn't get you into the main sanctuary, which was filled to capacity by the regular members. You had to sit in one of the three classrooms in the basement, and listen to the service on speakers. Speakers were not very reliable at the time, and the one in our classroom stopped working in the middle of the service. Orthodox Jews are not allowed to do "work," such as fixing a speaker, on the High Holy Days. For that purpose, the synagogue employed a non-Jewish maintenance man, who was able to get it going again.

Adath Israel's cantor at the time was a young man by the name of Reuben Tucker, and even through a speaker his voice was mesmerizing. Sarah gave up mingling with other women outside the *shul*, and sat next to me, entranced by his singing. It was hard to believe that God wouldn't respond to Tucker's prayers on behalf of the congregation and inscribe us all in the Book of Life.

When I saw Tucker, he looked familiar to me. I later found out that during the week he ran a silk business and had often paid sales visits to Henkel's Dresses. A few years later, Tucker changed his first name to Richard and began a successful career with the Metropolitan Opera Company.

The presidential election of 1932 was the first time I had strong political feelings. I had always been a Democrat, resisting Mr. Henkel's advocacy of the Republicans and Leah's favoring the Socialists. To me voting for a Socialist was throwing your vote away.

In '28 I had almost voted for Herbert Hoover. He seemed so competent, with his engineering and management skills. But what swung me over to Al Smith, the Governor of New York, was Hoover's support of prohibition. What a stupid idea prohibition was—especially for Jews, who didn't tend at all to drunkenness.

Smith, of course, didn't have a chance. The country wasn't ready for a Catholic president. In the South, Protestant ministers railed against him, and the Klu Klux Klan burned crosses along the route of his campaign train. His running, however, had one good result. When Smith resigned as New York's governor to run for President, Franklin Roosevelt ran for his job. Roosevelt squeaked by and was a great governor. The position helped him launch his bid for the presidency in '32.

By election time, almost everyone was tired of hearing from Hoover that good times were just around the corner. We even called the shantytowns that had sprung up in Central Park and along the East River "Hoovervilles." With Hoover's urging, in '32, Congress passed a big tax increase to control the deficit. The lowest individual tax rate went from 1% to 4%. That was probably the worst thing they could have done.

In July of '32 there was a march on Washington by about 50,000 World War I veterans and their families. The veterans had been given bonus certificates for their service. There was only one problem: they couldn't cash the certificates until 1945. The government called out the army with tanks and gas to clear the veterans off government property. Two of them were shot dead.

Ben was running the bakery by then and had two kids, a six-year old son and four-year old daughter. He didn't participate in the march, but hoped that it would be successful. "I could really use that bonus money," he said. "I don't know why they won't give it to us when we really need it."

Ben and all the other ex-military men were horrified at how the veterans were treated. "It reminds me of why I would never vote for a Republican," he said.

Roosevelt's campaign song went:
Happy days are here again
The skies above are clear again

207

So let's sing a song of cheer again
Happy days are here again

I sang that song so many times at his rallies, I couldn't get it out of my mind when I went to sleep at night. We all felt that by singing it enough, happy days, or at least days that weren't so sad, would return to America.

The night of the election, Sarah and I were glued to the radio. When it became obvious that Roosevelt had won by a landslide, I made her get up and dance around the living room with me.

"I sure hope he does something soon," Sarah said. "This country is going down the drain."

While Americans waited for Roosevelt to take office, Hoover bad-mouthed him, saying he would ruin the financial system.

"No one could do a worse job than Hoover," Sarah said.

I agreed. It didn't seem that things could get much worse: a quarter of the work force was unemployed and two thirds of the states had closed their banks. I noticed that some of the lines at the soup kitchens were three deep and stretched around the block.

With great hope, on Saturday, March 4, 1933, Sarah and I listened to Roosevelt's inaugural address on the radio. We heard, "the only thing we have to fear is fear itself," and, "Happiness lies not in the mere possession of money."

"Doesn't he realize how bad things are?" Sarah asked when it was over. "'The only thing we have to fear is fear'—Ha! What about mothers who can't feed their children?"

"I think it was just a pep talk," I said. "Like a coach does when his team is twenty points behind at half time."

"It's okay for him to say having money doesn't bring happiness," Sarah continued. "He's got lots of money."

"It sounds like he's going to do a lot," I said. "Let's give him a chance and keep our fingers crossed it will work."

Roosevelt did get right to work. A bank holiday was declared for the Monday after the inauguration. No one in the country could cash a check or withdraw money from a bank. That Friday I finally found out what the Henkels had in their safe in the office: enough cash to meet our payroll. I was relieved that the workers and I didn't have to go home that weekend without any money.

On that Sunday night, Sarah and I, like everyone in the country who could get to a radio, anxiously listened to what the President had to say in his first fireside chat. Roosevelt tried to reassure us: The government had been busy printing money, which would be used to back the banks. Most of them would be reopened in the next few days, starting with the most solvent ones on Monday. He put the blame for the failures on dishonest and incompetent bankers. He implied that depositors who took more of their money out of the bank than they needed were unpatriotic "hoarders".

"At least he's doing something," Sarah said.

"I sure hope it works," I said, not being sure there was enough cash in Henkel's safe to cover another week's payroll.

There was a flurry of activity during Roosevelt's first hundred days in office. Almost every day there was a new program. Congress went along with all of them and added a few of its own, including federal insurance of bank deposits up to $2,500 in 1933. For Sarah and me it was closing the window after all our money had blown out.

Roosevelt's program was called the New Deal; anti-Semites referred to it as the Jew Deal, in reference to all the Jewish members of his administration. Roosevelt's fireside chats kept the country abreast of how things were going and gave people hope that their lives would be getting better. Even the stock market began to react favorably.

America wasn't the only country suffering a depression. It was a worldwide plague. The Germans, burdened with payments of reparations for World War I, had a particularly difficult time of it. In January 1933, they appointed Adolf Hitler Chancellor, and by March he and his National Socialist Party took complete control of the country. To celebrate, the Nazis

209

beat up and imprisoned a large number of German Jews and even killed a few of them.

When news of the atrocities reached America, leaders of the Jewish community held meetings and rallies all over the country. Politicans and religious leaders from other denominations participated in many of these. I heard that a huge rally was planned for Madison Square Garden, and after work, I took the Eighth Avenue subway up to 50th Street to attend. Unfortunately, when I got up there, the Garden was already filled to its 20,000 capacity. Thousands more were milling around in the surrounding streets, and leaders of all stripes were up on soapboxes working the crowd.

I heard that the speeches in the Garden would be broadcast outside on speakers set up at 48th Street, so I worked my way over there and listened for about an hour. Ex-Governor Al Smith spoke as well as religious leaders. It seemed like everyone was very careful to only blame Hitler's Nazis and not the German people as a whole. I wasn't too sure about that. Finally I got back on the subway and went home, where Sarah warmed up my supper and made me tell her everything that had gone on.

"Look," I said to Sarah several weeks later, pointing out an article in the *Times*. "Albert Einstein has decided to stay in America."

"That guy with the bushy hair?"

"Yes, and under that hair is the smartest brain in the world, maybe the smartest that ever lived. That's what Mr. Henkel said."

"I didn't know he was here," Sarah said.

"He was giving a lecture tour in America. When he heard what was happening in Germany, he decided not to go back."

Einstein wasn't the only famous German Jew to move to America; quite a few musicians and artists, who I had never heard of, but read about in the paper, also came. They probably found it a lot easier to get visas than Leena had. Famous professors from German universities arrived in America and were snapped up by schools like Columbia and Harvard. I guess they didn't think having too many Jewish professors was as bad as having too many Jewish students.

One day in the winter of '34, Eddie Hamburger stopped by Henkel's Belts. He was uncharacteristically disheveled, with bags under his eyes. "Got a hot lead for me?" I asked him.

"No, I was upstairs, borrowing some money from Sam," he told me. "I just got a letter from my sister. Things are getting very bad for Jews in Germany. I'm trying to get her to leave with her family."

"I read of all the horrible things happening there," I said. "The Germans are worse anti-Semites than even the Russians. It makes me sick."

"You can't imagine. Since Hitler and his National Socialists have come to power, Jews have been excluded from more and more professions. My sister's husband was fired from his job in the tax office. Hindenburg, the President, was the only restraint on Hitler, and now that he's dead, I can't imagine what's going to happen."

I told him about my going to the rally at the Garden.

"A lot of good that will do," Eddie said.

I agreed.

"They even burned all books by Jewish authors," he added, and then, "You wouldn't be able to spare a little, would you, Abe? I'm trying to get boat passage for four people."

I promised him fifty dollars.

Sarah wasn't happy when I told her. "Are you trying to save all the Jews in Europe?" she asked.

"Look," I reminded her. "It would have cost much more to bring Leena over."

"That's different. She's family. And anyway that was in good times."

I went ahead and gave Eddie the fifty dollars, but I knew that if I gave any more, I'd have to face the ire of Sarah. Until things got better in America, it would have to be the rich Jews who tried to save the Jews of Europe.

Food, especially meat, was taking up an increasingly large share of our falling income, so in '35, Sarah joined the kosher meat boycott. For three weeks, not one piece of meat or chicken was served in our home and in those of thousands of other Jewish families in the City.

211

Although Sarah made a good vegetable soup, I was getting pretty tired of a diet of potatoes, beans and cabbage. "You'll have to put up with it," she told me. "We can't let the butchers rob us blind."

The boycott did result in a small rollback of some prices, and its success encouraged other ethnic groups in the city to try similar tactics.

About a month later, Sarah said to me, "I think it's pretty silly for us to continue keeping kosher. It's so expensive."

"It would be fine with me, if we stopped," I said. "I'm sure those hot dogs I buy on the street aren't kosher. And we've been eating at the Chinese restaurant for years."

Keeping kosher was something that Sarah had done to carry on a family tradition. It helped her hold her mother's memory close. I guess she didn't need that any more.

On a Friday in April, '35, Sarah told me I had to be home by seven, so we could go to a party at Esther's school. When I opened the door, the apartment was dark, and when I switched on the light, screams of "Surprise!" came from everywhere. Crepe paper was strung across the living room, and on a large banner was written, *Happy 50th. You're over the hill.* It hadn't been difficult for Sarah to surprise me, since this was the first birthday party I had had since I left the old country.

"Didn't you wonder what I was cooking?" Sarah asked. She had made stuffed cabbage, blintzes and a noodle pudding.

"I thought you were making stuff for Esther's party."

Besides Sarah and the kids, Leah and Paul, Diane and Izzy, and Betsy and Ben were there. I hadn't seen Leah since her father's funeral the previous year. "How's your mom doing?" I asked her.

"She's pretty frail. Paul and I moved into her apartment to help her."

"The same place on Broadway?"

"Yes, still the same place." Leah smiled. "We're not used to all that elegance. But the real estate market is so bad now, we can't sell it."

"Who takes care of your mom when you're working?"

"Megan watches her during the day."

"Megan? That pretty redhead who served us at *Shabbos* dinner thirty years ago."

212

"Yes, she left us when she got married, but she lost her husband in the war and her only child to the flu."

"That's sad," I said.

"It was," Leah said, "But Megan's a strong woman. She recovered and came back to my parents. Over the years, she's saved quite a bit of money. When my mother no longer needs her, she's going to move back to Ireland and buy a cottage."

"And how's you sister," I asked.

"Ruth is married to a doctor. They have four grown children and live in Connecticut."

"Little Ruth. How time flies," I said. "And are you still a visiting nurse?"

"Yes, things are really bad down on the East Side now. Thank God for Relief," Leah said, "or there'd be mass starvation."

"I know, when I go out for lunch there's somebody begging on almost every corner."

"No one can doubt Roosevelt's doing every conceivable thing to get us out of this hole," Leah said. "But it just doesn't seem to be enough."

"Do you think he's going to be able to anything about the situation in Germany?" I asked.

"I don't know. It doesn't seem to be his highest priority. I heard that Rabbi Wise, the Zionist, and a delegation spoke to Morgenthau. He's the Secretary of Treasury and a very close friend of Roosevelt. Maybe he'll be able to get him to do something."

"Remember that guy from the German consulate who spoke to us in your apartment?" I asked Leah.

She laughed. "Shenkmann—great friend of the Jews. My father would turn over in his grave if he knew how his beloved Germans were treating their Jews."

"Announcement everyone," Paul called out. "Leah is having another child...actually three more children."

I looked at Leah. Triplets would be most unusual at her age.

She laughed. "They're coming from Austria, a girl of seven and two boys, age nine and eleven. Siblings. Their parents are sending them here to get away from the Nazis."

213

"How did you work that out?"

"I'm their distant aunt. They're coming to America to attend the Sachs' schools. The authorities assume that since their parents aren't with them, they'll be going back when they finish their schooling."

"Will you still be working?" I asked her.

"No, I told the Henry Street Settlement I'd be leaving when they arrive. Three young children in addition to David and my mother are all that I can handle."

"Stop hogging the birthday boy," Izzy said, putting his arm around my shoulders.

"What's that you've got under your shirt?" I said, noticing that he had put on quite a bit of weight since we had last been together.

"That's the good life," Izzy answered. "How do you stay so thin?"

"Worrying about money does it. How's the law business?"

"Not too good. Can't sue anyone, because they don't have anything. I had to fire half my staff."

"Food's ready," Sarah called from the kitchen, where she and Esther had been taking stuff out of the oven. The smell of cinnamon from the noodle pudding made everyone's mouths water. We all formed a line to fill our plates and take them back to the living room.

I was stuffing my mouth with the good food, when Meyer escorted a young lady over to me. She was thin with dark straight hair.

"Dad, I'd like you to meet Florence," he said, "a very good friend of mine."

"Glad to meet you," she said, and made a little motion that looked like a curtsy. I hadn't seen many of those in my life. I smiled at Florence and shook her hand, and then they left to get in the food line. My impression of Florence was that with a little makeup and a different hairdo and dress, she'd be quite attractive. But, I guessed that if Meyer brought a girl home to meet the family, he must be pretty serious about her.

That night in bed, I said to Sarah, "That's a wonderful thing she's doing. Taking in those three children."

"She can afford it, with all her money."

"Still it's a lot of work, on top of taking care of her mother."

"She's got what's-her-name to help?"

"Megan."

"What do you think of Meyer's girlfriend?" Sarah asked.

"She seems nice…very polite."

"I think Meyer could do better…much better," Sarah offered.

"She was just nervous," I offered. "As she gets to know us, she'll be more at ease."

"I hope he doesn't decide to marry her."

I don't think there was anything I could have said that would have helped Sarah accept the fact that soon she'd no longer be the most important woman to her first born.

A few months after my birthday party, Roosevelt signed the Social Security Law. Since salary made up almost all my income, I was classified as a worker and was eligible to join the system. Social Security took a big burden off my mind. I was fifty, with practically no savings. Now it looked like, at least I wouldn't starve to death when I retired.

The WPA was one New Deal program that was very popular. Not only did it give a lot of young people jobs in projects like building roads, dams and parks, but it also fed them nutritious food and got them working outdoors. Without the program, we would have had a generation of skinny runts, ill prepared to fight the Second World War.

The Bronx, like just about every other place, had lots of WPA projects that enhanced our quality of life. On one of my walks, I was impressed by the magnificent swimming pool complex they were building in Crotona Park.

Crotona Park Pool opened in July of '36. Harry and Esther had already been there, when, shortly before Labor Day, I said to Sarah, "Let's go. We'll get away from this horrible heat, and, who knows, maybe we'll learn to swim."

"I don't know."

"Do it, Mom," Esther said. "I've seen lots of women from the neighborhood there."

"What women?"

"Mrs. Slavinsky from the next building, for one."

"Mrs. Slavinsky? Hmm, She's no bathing beauty. Okay, I'll try it. But I'll have to buy a suit."

"Don't wait too long," Esther informed us, "It closes after Labor Day."

On scorching hot Labor Day, Sarah, Esther and I walked the eight blocks to the Crotona Park Pool. They charged ten cents for admission, which in the depression was enough to keep the "undesirable" poor away. At the entrance, a group of black children were staring through the fence at the almost exclusively white swimmers. I felt sorry for them, but was glad that the pool was no more crowded than it was on that holiday.

The pool had separate locker rooms for men and women, where we changed into our suits and checked our clothes.

"You look great in that suit," I said to Sarah.

She beamed, and then we found a free space in the wading pool, which was about waist deep. It was much more crowded than the large swimming pool, because at that time, few residents of the Bronx knew how to swim. We held on to the side of the pool and kicked our feet, and then I supported Sarah while she floated. It was wonderful to feel her completely confident that I wouldn't let her sink.

"What a wonderful feeling not to be walking on my foot," Sarah said. "Next year, we'll have to come here a lot."

We did come back a half-dozen times. I watched the swimmers and tried to imitate them. In the big pool, I would start at the shallow end and then, bit by bit, extend further into water over my head. Finally I had enough confidence to swim across the width of the pool. Sarah never did learn to swim, but with my help she lost her fear of the water.

In subsequent years, we occasionally took the bus to Orchard Beach on the eastern end of the Bronx. It was at the end of Long Island Sound, so the waves there were very mild, and Sarah wasn't afraid to splash around in the water.

With the New Deal, the country was making slow progress pulling out of the depression. Roosevelt was reelected in 1936 by a huge margin. However, in '37, the President and Congress suddenly got nervous about

216

budget deficits. They cut spending and raised taxes, throwing the country back into bad times.

On November 11, 1938, the headline in the *Times* was, **Nazis Smash, Loot and Burn Jewish Shops and Temples Until Goebbels Calls Halt**. It was called *Kristallnacht*, the night of broken glass, for the windows of all the Jewish shops, apartments and synagogues that were smashed by the Hitler Youth, the Gestapo and the SS, in retaliation for the assassination of a German diplomat in Paris. Hundreds of Jews were killed and thousands were hauled away to detention camps. Most disturbing was that it seemed to be organized by the government, rather than being a spontaneous outburst by the people, as had occurred in most East European pogroms.

Like most New York Jews, I hoped for some action by our government. However, we underestimated the anti-Semitism in our own country; the last thing most people wanted was more Jews in America. Congress voted down a bill to allow entry of 20,000 Jewish children into America in addition to the annual German immigration quota. Typical of American's views was a statement by FDR's cousin, Laura Delano Houghteling, wife of the U.S. Commissioner of Immigration, that "20,000 charming Jewish children would all too soon grow into 20,000 ugly Jewish adults."

Unlike what had happened in '33, American Jewish leaders organized very few rallies or marches to protest these new atrocities. I think they were afraid of inflaming American anti-Semitism and making things "uncomfortable" for American Jews.

America wasn't the only country that turned a deaf ear towards the cries of European Jews for help. Britain, now in charge of Palestine, valued Arab oil more than Jewish money, and limited Jewish immigration to Palestine to pitiful low numbers.

I think what was happening in Germany emboldened some of our homegrown anti-Semites. I had a painful demonstration of this during one of my walks later that year. After watching a couple of basketball games at the Oval, I was cutting across 207th Street to Bronx Park, when I came across a pitiful sight. Two young orthodox Jewish boys with *peyes* and *tzitzits* were

217

being attacked by four bullies in a vacant lot on the quiet street. The Jewish boys were tall and heavy and obviously had had some experience with similar occurrences, since they were standing back-to-back, so neither of them could be jumped from behind. The bullies looked like they hadn't been as well fed, but they were older and mean looking. As long as the Jewish boys stayed on their feet, they had a chance. Meanwhile the bullies were taking turns jumping in for a quick punch or kick. It looked very bad for the Jewish boys.

Maybe at some other time I would have just gone my way, but combined with what I had recently heard about *Kristallnacht*, the sight made my blood boil. If there had been rallies or marches where I could have expressed my anger, I might have been able to restrain myself. But now I jumped to the boys rescue. "Leave them alone," I yelled at the bullies, grabbing the shirt of one and pulling him away. I guess I expected the intervention of an adult would scatter them, but I was wrong. These were budding anti-Semites, who wouldn't pass up the opportunity to pummel a Jew.

"Mind your business," one said; "Jew lover," a second. "He's a Jew," the third. All four of them turned their attention to me. The two Jewish boys used the opportunity to run off down the street.

Now the four surrounded me, and I didn't have anyone to protect my back. I swung my fists whenever one of them got too close. Suddenly all four rushed me simultaneously. One jumped on my back, while another grabbed my lower legs. I knew once I hit the ground, they'd have their way with me, so I tried to remain standing…to no avail. Now I was face down on the ground with my arms protecting my head. With my most vulnerable parts protected, most of their kicks landed mainly on my ribs. One blow managed to catch the side of my face. Only their wearing sneakers saved me from some very serious injury. "Dirty Jew," one of them called out, just before someone jumped on my back.

They were only bullies—little more than children—but in my mind's eye, they were the brown-shirted thugs they might become. Would they haul me away to jail or a detention camp? Would they kill me?

"They're beating up that man," I heard a woman call from a window.

"I'll call the police," another woman called out.

"Get out of here, you *drek*," the first one said.

Fear of police intervention brought the bullies out of their blood lust. "Let's get out of here," one said.

"He's a Jew. He must have some money," a second answered. Hands were in my pocket. Better my wallet than my life, I thought.

The blows stopped and I peeked out from under my arms. They were gone. I sat up and inspected the damage. Not much blood...but boy did I hurt.

Belatedly, several rescuers from the apartment building approached me. A white-haired guy carrying a baseball bat asked me, "You all right?"

"I think so," I said, trying to get up, but having trouble.

"It was those toughs from Saint Brendan's School," he told me. "They're always beating up Jewish kids, but this is the first time I've seen them go after an adult. It's that Father Coughlin egging them on with his radio program."

"Maybe you need an ambulance?" a bald guy asked.

"I don't think so," I said. "But I could use a hand standing up."

The men each took hold of one of my arms and helped me to my feet. I tried to walk, but could only hobble due a particularly nasty kick to the side of my knee. A police car pulled up at the curb and two of New York's finest strolled across the lot.

"What happened here?" the first cop, a large redhead, asked me.

"I saw four bullies picking on two Jewish boys. When I tried to break it up, the four turned on me."

"How old were they?"

"Probably thirteen or fourteen."

"Where are the two Jewboys?" he asked me.

I looked around. "I guess they ran away."

He snickered. "So you interfered in a kids fight and got hurt. Not surprising. What do you want us to do?"

"Nothing...I didn't call you."

"Okay," he said. "Mind your own business from now on."

They started to walk back to their car, when I remembered feeling a hand in my pocket. Sure enough my wallet was gone.

"They took my wallet," I called after them.

"Damn!" said the big cop. He turned around and took a pad out of his pocket. "Your name and address," he asked, and after taking that down, "How much was in the wallet?"

"Three dollars."

He looked at me incredulous—*a Jew with only three dollars in his wallet.* "Do you think you could identify them?"

"I'm not sure."

"Don't count on getting it back," he said and then handed me the police report to sign.

"I've got a truck," the white-haired guy with the bat said after the cops had left. "Let me get it and give you a ride home. You don't look like you can walk."

"That would be great," I said. The bald guy supported me, while the other went to get his truck."

"My name is Larry Gershowitz," the white-haired fellow said. "Used to be in vegetables. Bought 'em down at the market and hauled 'em around the city in this truck."

"Abe Sokolovsky, I'm in the garment industry."

The truck was a Chevrolet pickup, about ten years old and badly rusted.

"I had a new motor put in five years ago," Larry bragged. "Automatic starter too. You wouldn't be interested in buying a truck, would you?"

"I don't think so."

"No question where that cop's sympathy lies," Larry said. "I'll bet he went to Saint Brendan himself, and it hasn't been too many years since he was beating up Yeshiva kids."

"I wouldn't be surprised."

"I'd like to get a chance to work over that Father Coughlin with this baseball bat," Larry continued. "Do you know what he said at a rally last week?"

"No I don't," I admitted.

"He said, 'When we get through with the Jews in America, they'll think the treatment they received in Germany was nothing.'"

I gulped.

220

"What are you trying to do," Sarah said, as she looked over my wounds, "take on all the anti-Semites in the world by yourself?"

"I sure won't get any help from the New York City police," I said and told her about my experience with the Irish cop.

She swabbed the bruise on my face with iodine. I cried out "Ow."

"If you're going to play Superman," she said, "you'll have to learn to take a little pain."

The red bruises down my side were beginning to turn purple. I tried to smile, but it was difficult with my face swollen. I was hurting, but, in a strange way, it was worth it.

"Someone has to do something to stop them," I said. Then I told Sarah what Father Coughlin said would happen to American Jews.

"I don't think that could ever happen here," she said, but her brows furrowed.

"What happened to your face?" Esther asked at the dinner table that night

"I had a little run-in with anti-Semites."

"Anti-Semites, I didn't think there were any around here," Harry said, reflecting the fact that our neighborhood was overwhelmingly Jewish.

"Not around here. Up in the North Bronx, near the Oval. Four bullies were picking on two Jewish boys and I tried to intervene."

"Picking on an old man," Harry said. "What say I get a few of my friends and we go up there? You could point them out to us."

"Just what we don't need, a religious war," Meyer said.

"Listen *feygele*, you can let them push you around, but I'll fight back?" Harry replied.

Meyer reddened. *"Feyg... "* I thought he was going to throw his soup at his brother, so I intervened.

"I agree with Meyer. These were kids—Esther's age—but they probably have older brothers. Who knows where it would lead."

"We don't want to start a war," Sarah said.

221

"There's nothing to be gained by escalation," I continued. "There'll always be anti-Semites. Jews outnumber them around here, but not in the world and probably not even in America."

"Like when Hirsh didn't get into Columbia?" Esther asked.

"That's an example of what happens in America. But it's a lot worse in other parts of the world. Have you heard what's been happening in Germany?"

Meyer had read all about *Kristallnacht* in the newspaper, but Esther and Harry knew very little about it. So I started to go into the details.

"Don't get them nervous," Sarah said.

"I think it's time to stop protecting them. They should learn what the world is really like," I insisted. I went on with the gruesome details.

When I finished, Harry sat there with his mouth open and Esther asked, "What do people have against Jews?"

"I really don't know," I said, and I didn't.

Things were becoming increasingly worrisome. Mussolini had become an avid supporter of Hitler and the British and French were showing little appetite for slowing the German expansion into Austria and Czechoslovakia. Maybe it was time to start taking Father Coughlin's rants more seriously.

Early in '37 I got a letter from Leena, bringing me up to date on events in the old country.

Dearest Avrom,

Your not hearing from me in a while is the result of international correspondence not being allowed during the very bad times we had here in the Ukraine during 1932-35, when there was much hunger, and even starvation. Somehow, everyone in our family survived this period, although we all lost a lot of weight. Things have improved a lot since then.

It's now three years since I moved to Kiev. Freyda and her family also live here. Jews are no longer restricted on where they can live. I love living in a city. There are so many more things to do here than in Zyvotov. I take a lot of books out of the library, although they are quite limited in what they carry.

I teach in a state school, (there aren't any Jewish schools, anymore) and have an apartment (actually just a room, with the bathroom in the hall) just two blocks from the school, so I don't have any trouble getting to work.

It's not only the Jewish religion and all Jewish observances that are suppressed, so is the major occupation of Jews in Kiev, that of shopkeeper. Shopkeepers are now considered capitalists and enemies of the people. Many of them have been arrested, tried and sent away—to Siberia, I hear.

As you know, under Communism resources are shared equally. However, since there are no resources, everyone suffers. The government tells us that things are even worse in America, but I doubt that.

Please write and let me know how you are doing. I don't have much contact with family members besides Freyda since I moved. I hope you and Sarah and your children are doing well.

Love.

Leenitchka.

Although Leena had tried to be upbeat in her letter, I sensed that things were no better for Jews in Russia under the Communists than they had been under the Czar. However, at least it wasn't Germany.

I immediately wrote back to Leena, letting her know that, although America had been going through some bad times, things had been relatively good for my family and me. It saddened me to know that she'd probably never be able to come to New York.

Chapter 25

"I'm going to find a phone booth and call my daughter, so she can pick me up," Bessie says when the bus pulls into the D.C. terminal.

I follow her off the bus and do a half-dozen laps around the waiting room to stretch my legs. Then I go back to my seat on the bus.

Old yellow skin across the aisle hasn't gotten off the bus. When he starts one of his coughing fits, I decide I've had enough. He's been talking in Spanish to the woman next him, so I don't know whether he understands English. But what have I got to lose. I lean over and say, "Would you mind covering up your coughs?"

He looks at me, blinks his eyes, then reaches into his pocket and takes out a handkerchief.

Pretty soon there's another coughing fit. This time it's into the handkerchief. It's a small accomplishment, but it makes me feel good.

"Were you able to reach your daughter?" I ask Bessie when she comes back to her seat.

"Yes, She's going to meet me at the Port Authority."

A few minutes later the bus starts up, and we're off on the last stretch of our journey.

After *Kristallnacht*, I became obsessed with world affairs and began to read the *Times* every day. Hitler's taking over Austria and Czechoslovakia depressed me. When would the world stand up to him?

When, in August of '39, Hitler and Stalin, the world's two worst tyrants, signed a trade and non-aggression treaty, I knew we were in for big trouble. A couple of weeks later, the *Times* announced **Hostilities Begin**, as Hitler invaded Poland from the west. This was a move that France and Britain couldn't ignore, and within a few days they declared war on Germany.

"Maybe now they'll stop that madman," Sarah said, while chopping vegetables with unusual vigor.

Thinking back to World War I, I said, "I don't think Britain and France will be able to stop him by themselves. Now Hitler won't give a damn about international opinion. Only God can save Jews of Germany and Poland."

"Just as long as we stay out of it," Sarah said. "I wouldn't want Meyer or Harry fighting over there."

"I don't know," I said. "Maybe if we just threatened to get involved, Hitler would back off."

"What if he didn't?" Sarah asked.

I didn't have a good answer for that.

If the Sokolovskys, a typical Jewish American family, couldn't agree on stopping Hitler, you can imagine how the rest of the country felt. Congress had already passed an Act proclaiming America's neutrality, and we weren't surprised when Roosevelt in his first fireside chat after the invasion said that America would remain a neutral nation.

It didn't take the Germans long to roll over most of Poland from the west. Meanwhile, with his dream of spreading communism, Joseph Stalin invaded Poland from the east. Within a month Poland was divided up, and since fascism, communism, and democracy were conflicting ideologies, the world was set up for some very bad times.

Everyone remembered the First World War and got ready for a long war of attrition. For a while that seemed what was happening. The French sat behind the massive fortifications of their Maginot Line. Britain shipped almost a half million men to northern France, where they just sat and waited. Britain controlled the oceans and German U-boats prowled everywhere. There was some bombing, but not much fighting. We called it the "Phony War."

America began ramping up its production of war material. When I looked across the East River from Henkel's roof, I could see lots of activity at the Brooklyn Navy Yard. The destroyers built there were being "lent" to Britain and Canada to help patrol the Atlantic. Such activity put money in people's pockets and they were starting to feel more prosperous. In '39 my share of the profits of Henkel's Belts was the best it had been in a decade.

Unemployment, however, remained scandalously high throughout the country.

"What should we do for our anniversary?" Sarah asked me in the spring of '40. She knew if she didn't tell me it was on the way, I'd forget all about it.

"How about dinner and a movie?" That was our usual mode of celebration.

"What should we see?

"Is *Stagecoach* still playing? We can't go wrong with John Wayne."

"I think I'd like to see *The Wizard of Oz*."

"The Wizard of Oz—isn't that a kid's movie?"

"Mrs. Rizzio upstairs said it's good for adults too."

So we went to see the *Wizard of Oz,* which was partly in color, an amazing advance. I had trouble, however, enjoying the evening. While Judy Garland had a golden voice and I knew I'd be humming *Somewhere over the Rainbow* for a while, the newsreel before the movie showed Hitler and Mussolini screaming to their fascist fans. Not even Roosevelt could work up a crowd like they could. I had a foreboding of bad things to come and didn't think it was only from my experience as a Jew.

The very next week, the "Phony War" came to an end, with the Germans attacking Denmark and Norway. In May they invaded Holland, Belgium and Luxemburg. The reports of the battles in the newspapers were sketchy, so one night on the way home from work I stopped at Times Square to watch the electric zipper bulletin board. I was surprised to find thousands had had the same idea. In one headline, the French claimed to have made advances, but I tended to believe the one that said, *Border Resistance Broken, Nazis Claim.* The man standing next to me exclaimed, "Damn Krauts, ve should have finished dem off in der last var."

When I got home Sarah could read the concern on my face.

"What's wrong?"

"It looks like the Nazis are taking over the world. I don't see how we can stay out of it."

"Bite you tongue," Sarah said.

I only vaguely knew where all these newly conquered countries were, so at lunchtime the next day I walked over to the Seward Park Library, opposite the Educational Alliance Building where I had played basketball more than thirty years earlier. Back in those days the place had always been packed with Jews, soaking up every type of knowledge. Now it was much less crowded, and few of the occupants seemed Jewish. In fact, the entire Lower East Side wasn't as crowded as it had been in my youth.

I took Goode's World Atlas up to the roof garden and poured over a map of Europe. Most of the countries Hitler had invaded were pretty small. Maybe things weren't as bad as they seemed. I decided that an Atlas would be useful to have around the house, so I bought a used one on my way home from work that night.

Sarah and I were invited to Ben and Betsy's place for dinner that Sunday. Since Ben had been to Europe in the First World War, I looked forward to hearing his thoughts of the situation.

With the aroma of cooking corned beef and cabbage filling their apartment, Sarah went into the kitchen to help Betsy, while Ben and I looked over a scraggly map of Europe he had had since the First World War. "That's Strasbourg," he said. "Near where I was stationed."

"Forget about where you were stationed," I said impatiently. "What's going on now?"

Ben made an "X" on the map. "That's Fort Eban Emael, one of the strongest in the world. The Germans took it in a few hours on Friday by landing gliders on its roof. I'm not a fan of Germany, but that was an impressive operation."

"What do you think will happen?" I asked.

Ben thought for a minute. "There's a pretty strong British force in the West. If they join up with the Dutch, they should be able to stop the German advance. Further East is the Ardennes, a very thick forest. I don't think the Germans will try to bring their tanks through there."

"Dinner's ready," Betsy called, poking her head in from the kitchen. "Timothy...Moira, come to dinner."

Dinner was at the kitchen table, which usually sat four. With the six of us, we only had room for our plates and glasses on the table. The first course was Betsy's excellent bean soup. She filled the bowls at the stove and they were passed down the table.

"None for me," twelve-year-old Moira, a redheaded beauty, said. "It gives me cramps."

"It doesn't affect me at all," Sarah said.

"Your mom's bean soup is worth cramps," I said.

"Could I have the ham bone?" fourteen-year-old Timothy asked. His short, solid physique took after his father's.

"You can have it for tomorrow's dinner," Betsy said.

We had finished the soup and passed our bowls to Betsy, when I asked Ben, "What happens if the French can't stop the Germans?"

"Let's not talk about Europe," Sarah said. "The thought of us getting involved and Meyer or Harry getting drafted will spoil my dinner."

"Timothy perked up. "Drafted?" he asked.

"Don't worry," Betsy reassured him. "You're too young to be drafted."

I didn't bring up the subject during the rest of the night. We all set to work on the corned beef, cabbage and boiled potatoes, followed by a carrot cake that Ben had brought home from the bakery. We ate royally. Betsy put all the leftovers into the refrigerator. I imagined they would feed the family for the rest for the week.

Ben was wrong: the Germans did manage to bring their tanks and troops through the "impenetrable" Ardennes Forest into northern France. We'd read about counterattacks by the Allied force, but they never seemed to get anywhere.

"It's starting to look pretty bad," Sam said to me, when we met on the stairs in May. Unlike his father he hadn't the slightest loyalty to Germany.

"I hope the French can hold," I said.

"If they go down," Sam ventured, "I don't think Britain can hold the Germans by themselves, even with Churchill the new Prime Minister. I think we'll have to get involved."

"I agree."

"I haven't heard from my relatives in Germany for two years," Sam said. "I fear the worst. Thank God Leah was able to get their children out."

"Now it's all the Jews of Europe that have to be afraid," I said. I was thinking about my family. Right now, it was probably good that they were in Russian territory and Russia and Germany were friendly. But I had little confidence that Russia had any interest in protecting its Jews from Hitler's anti-Semitism. If Germany were to be stopped, America would have to get involved.

Sarah didn't agree with me about our intervening.

"Look what happened with the First World War," she said when I brought it up. "Wilson told us it was the 'war to end all wars', Ha!"

"This is different. Hitler is a monster."

"That's what they always say. It's none of our business."

The French couldn't hold. By the end of May, the German columns had reached the North Sea, cutting the British forces off from most of the French. While Americans were preoccupied with baseball and graduation speeches, a quarter of a million British and French troops were evacuated from the beach at Dunkirk, using anything that floated the British could muster.

Every day we read of further German advances. Then Mussolini joined Hitler and grabbed a bit of southeastern France.

When the German columns advanced on Paris, the French forces withdrew to avoid destruction of the city that Leah had called "the most interesting in the world." By June the French had surrendered and set up a German controlled government at Vichy in Southern France.

I knew the news must have hit Leah hard, so I called her. "Oh, it's so horrible," she said. "The French hate those sausage-eating Germans. So many of my relatives are at risk. The kids haven't heard from their parents in months."

"How are they holding up?" I asked.

"As well as can be expected," she said. "They're old enough to know what's going on."

229

More than ever before, Leah seemed to have a need to talk, and I let her go on.

"I occasionally correspond with a Jewish girl I met on my visit there thirty years ago," she said. "I write in French and she answers me in English. She lives in Lyon now and has two sons...I can't imagine what will happen to her and her family."

"We can only hope America gets into it pretty soon," I said.

Everyone was in awe of the Germans conquering all of Western Europe in just a few months. Maybe they had become the master race after all. American Jews, however, were despondent and afraid. Now Jews throughout Europe would be subjected to Hitler's torments. We didn't yet know how horrible his plans were.

And what of our own safety? True, the Atlantic was a wide ocean, but the *Luftwaffe* was bombing London every day. Could German planes reach New York...maybe from aircraft carriers? Thankfully, Britain still had control of the oceans. If Germany could get Britain out of the war, America would be in trouble as the last major democratic power. I guess that was why Roosevelt seemed inclined to send the British anything they needed. Too bad we hadn't joined Britain and France the previous year and stopped Hitler before he got started.

Germany was massing its superior forces on the English Channel. Every day we read that the invasion was only days or even hours away. Only one thing delayed the Germans: a successful Channel crossing required control of the air. Throughout July and August of '40 the *Luftwaffe* and the Royal Air Force duked it out over the English Channel and Southern England. German planes bombed England and British planes bombed Dutch and German factories. Somehow the fliers of the British RAF got the best of it, and we all agreed with Churchill that, "Never in the field of human conflict was so much owed by so many to so few." After a few months of sporadic bombing of Britain, Hitler turned his attention elsewhere. In June of '41, Germany, with its new allies: Hungary, Romania, Slovakia and Bulgaria, invaded the Russian Empire.

On a Sunday in June I sat by the open living room window reading the newspaper. The weather was great, but the news was definitely not good. The Germans were advancing into Russia.

"Oh, no!" I groaned.

"What's wrong," Sarah asked.

"This map…it shows the Germans heading right for Kiev. Leena and Freyda live there now, and the rest of my family isn't far away."

"That's bad. Maybe the Russians will be able to stop them."

"I hope so," I said, but I really had little hope. It looked like the period of "relative safety" that Leena had written me about, would be coming to an end, and she and the rest of my family would be subjected to Hitler's depravities. I had a horrible foreboding of being cut off from my family perhaps forever. If only now there was some way I could tell them, "Get out of the way. Evil is coming!"

Seeing how low I was, Sarah tried to console me by saying, "Maybe some members of your family got to Israel or some other safe place."

Her naivety annoyed me. "I doubt it. And anyway, what good would that do. The Germans are taking over the world. They've moved into Africa to help the Italians. They'll be in Israel in no time."

"Do you think there's any chance they'll attack us?" Sarah asked.

I thought. "Not for a while. But if we don't get involved now, they'll eventually get around to us."

"Maybe you're right," Sarah said. "We probably should get into it."

She seemed to be starting to agree with me.

Things kept getting worse in '41. By September, the Germans had engulfed the Ukraine and had captured over 600,000 Russian troops. I had no information on what had happened to my family, and I imagined the worst.

You'd think America would react quickly to the German conquests, but it took until September for Congress to pass a Selective Service Law. At that time there were fewer than a half million men in our armed forces, not nearly enough to stop Hitler if he came over here, not to mention to take back Europe. Only the Navy was being built up—to protect American ships in the Atlantic from German U-boats.

After its invasion of Poland, Germany had few open supporters in America. Those who previously had extolled Hitler's efficiency and racial ideas, such as Henry Ford and Charles Lindbergh, shifted their efforts to keeping America out of the war. Lindbergh spoke at a number of rallies of the America First Committee, a large noninterventionist organization. Most Americans were still against any sort of intervention. About all that Roosevelt could do was start a Lend Lease Program, which sent Britain and Russia vital supplies.

American Jews pined for Roosevelt to do something to help European Jews, or at least intervene to stop German advances. However, the leaders of the Jewish community believed in not making *rishis* by demonstrating, since it would be counterproductive for the country to feel it was a Jewish war. In fact, Senator Gerald Nye held hearings on the "Yiddish influence" in Hollywood, which he felt was trying to drag America into the war in Europe.

On a Saturday in August of '41, Sarah and I went to see the movie, *The Grapes of Wrath*, in a theater in Times Square. The movie was about the dust bowl during the depression. Conditions there were so horrible, New York seemed prosperous by comparison. The movie starred Henry Fonda as Tom Joad, whose family is among a group of "Okies" trying to migrate to California. They face repression and exploitation every step of the way. At the end, Tom goes off to organize farm workers. Those members of his family who haven't starved to death end up living in a railroad boxcar with another family. For the two hours we were in the theater, I was able to escape thinking about what was going on in Europe.

"I never knew Christian Americans discriminated against each other like that," Sarah remarked as we exited the theater into a balmy spring evening.

"I guess when there aren't any Jews around, they'll persecute anyone they can."

After the movie we stopped at the Horn and Hardart Automat around the corner, putting our coins in slots to get baked beans, macaroni and cheese and creamed spinach from behind the little windows. Sarah delighted in the "magical" process where food was provided seemingly without human intervention.

It was so pleasant when we got outside after eating that we took a cab over to the West Side docks, where the world's fastest and most luxurious ocean liners, the Queen Mary and Queen Elizabeth and the Normandie, were berthed. Seeing the Queen Elizabeth reminded me of what I had read about it in the *Times*. The ship had literally sneaked out of South Hampton, where it had been constructed, to avoid being attacked by German bombers. In order to trick German spies, it hadn't even been outfitted with lifeboats, putting its skeleton crew at great danger during its perilous trip across the submarine-infested Atlantic.

Because of security concerns, viewers were limited to the embarkation area, a considerable distance from the ships. The large crowds had brought out peddlers, and we bought ice cream cones to munch on while looking over the ships.

"Do you think we might someday be able to take an ocean cruise?" Sarah asked. "After the war, of course, when there aren't any submarines."

"I don't want to go anywhere near Europe," I told her.

"We could just go to the Caribbean."

Remembering my ocean voyage and what had happened to the *Titanic*, I said, "I'd be happy just to take a walk through one of these ships."

In the next few years, the Queen Mary and Queen Elizabeth would be converted into huge carriers for transporting American troops to Europe. A similar conversion was begun on the Normandie. However, in the process, a welder accidently started a fire on the ship, and it burned and sank in New York Harbor.

With all the ships berthed at Manhattan piers and war materials being shipped out of New York, a German U-boat slipping into the harbor could have had a field day. A couple of months later, I read that huge nets made of metal cables had been strung across the entrance to the harbor. It was reassuring to know some preparations were being made for the war with Germany I believed was fast approaching. Most New Yorkers, however, were more concerned with Joe Dimaggio's hitting streak or Joe Lewis's defense of his heavyweight title.

In '41 my sons were called to the draft board for classification. By that time Meyer was thinking of marrying Florence and wasn't happy about the idea of going into the service. Harry, on the other hand, was anxious to fight the "Huns." They both got their wish: Harry was declared 1A, fit to serve, and Meyer 4F, due to his somewhat misshapen foot.

I still remember Harry coming to me shortly after receiving his classification.

"I'm going to enlist in the Navy, Dad."

I wish that there had been someone around to tell him of the horrors of war, but I had never served, and his uncle Ben's experience in the Quartermaster Corp wasn't much of a guide.

"Why don't you wait until they call you?"

"Because, as you know, I've pretty well messed up my life—no career, no prospects. If I wait to be drafted, they'll put me in the infantry. Not much to learn in the trenches. I spoke to the Navy recruiter. He said I could learn to be a radio operator, which will be a good trade for me when I get out. Maybe I'll be able to do something with my life besides helping out in the bakery."

I didn't have a good answer for that.

Three weeks later, our whole family went down to Penn Station to see Harry off for the long trip to Camp Callen, near San Diego in California. Sarah gave him a large bag of food, reminding me of my own departure from the *shtetl*, when I went to America. My gift was a pocket World Atlas, which would help Harry see where his ship was going.

"All aboard," sounded the loud speaker.

"Good luck," Meyer said. He shook Harry's hand and then, almost as an afterthought, gave him a quick hug.

"Next time we see you, you'll be in uniform," Esther said with tears in her eyes. "The girls will be all over you, with those deep brown eyes of yours." She gave him a long hug and a kiss. Esther and Harry were particularly close, in reaction to Meyer being their mother's favorite. Next it was Sarah's turn. She looked a little sad as she kissed and hugged Harry. "I really love you," she said.

"I know that, Ma," Harry said and hugged her tightly.

"Good luck, son," I told Harry just as the train whistle blew. I grabbed him for a quick hug. He picked up his bag and was gone.

With Harry out of his room, Meyer wasted no time. About two weeks later he brought Florence up to the apartment one evening. "We're married," he announced.

Sarah wasn't happy about this at all. "What do you mean you're married? Don't I get a to see the ceremony and cry like any Jewish mother does? When did this happen?"

"This afternoon down at City Hall," Meyer said. "We'd thought we save everyone a lot of trouble and expense. Florence's sister Agnes and her boyfriend, Artie, were the witnesses."

Sarah looked over at Florence. "Don't tell me you're pregnant," she said disapprovingly.

"Oh no!" Florence said. Her hand shot up to her mouth.

"Florence's sister, Agnes, is moving to Buffalo. Artie's being transferred there by his company," Meyer explained. "We thought this would be a good time to do it."

Florence and Agnes were orphans. They lived in a nice apartment on the Concourse, with Agnes paying most of the rent, since she had a good secretarial job. Florence was just a typist and didn't make much.

"So what's the matter?" Sarah said. "We're not even good enough to be witnesses?"

"We did it on the spur of the moment," Meyer said. "Artie had to leave right away."

"Where are you going to live?" I asked the newlyweds.

"We'll stay at Artie's apartment until the end of the month," Meyer explained. "His rent's paid up until then. After that I thought we move in here for a while, to save up money before getting our own place."

"That seems like a good idea," I said.

After they left, I tried to explain to Sarah that her comment about Florence being pregnant wasn't a good way to welcome her into the family.

"It's their fault. They shouldn't have sprung that on us," she said.

I never had much luck in getting Sarah to think before she spoke.

Florence hardly ever said a word. Perhaps having such a strong mother, Meyer had chosen a wife with whom he could be "the boss." Maybe Meyer was the boss, but he couldn't stop Florence storing up resentment against Sarah, and I guess, by association, against me.

From the very beginning, the arrangement of Meyer and Florence living with us didn't work out. Sarah was anxious to prove that she could take better care of her favorite than his wife could. After Florence "straightened" the bed when she and Meyer left for work in the morning, Sarah would go into their room and make it up "properly." She would also wash, dry and iron Meyer's clothes better than she ever had before he was married. Florence's stuff stayed in the laundry basket. "What am I, her slave?" Sarah said, when I asked her about it.

"Can I cook tonight?" Florence asked.

"I'm going to make a nice pot roast," Sarah answered. "Meyer needs to eat well."

Florence glared at Sarah.

In about four months, Meyer and Florence found a one-bedroom apartment of their own, two blocks from ours. Two months later, Florence announced she was pregnant.

Chapter 26

"Did your wife ever work?" Bessie asks as the bus gets back on the road.

"No she didn't. Taking care of the three children and me was a full-time job."

Bessie nods. "I can see that. And how are your children doing?"

"Meyer, my oldest," I tell her, "had his own accounting firm. He retired about ten years ago and moved down to Boca. That was one of the reasons I moved to Florida. Thought I would see him more, but it didn't work out that way. Maybe I see him twice a year."

"That's too bad," Bessie says. "Does he have any children?"

"Two. Michael, he's my oldest grandchild, lives in New York—Jamaica Estates in Queens. That's where I'm staying when I get to New York. He's a successful lawyer, so I imagine he's got a nice house. He was always Sarah's favorite grandchild when he was a kid. He's got two children of his own now."

"Sounds like Sarah tended to favor the oldest boy," Bessie says, and she's right, I tell her.

"Samantha is Michael's kid sister; she's almost thirty now. Got a degree in psychology and lives somewhere out west...Denver, I think. Haven't seen her in about ten years."

"What about your other children?" Bessie asked.

"My daughter, Esther lives in New York. I had a big fight with her husband Milton a while ago, and we stopped talking."

"That's too bad," Bessie says,"You know, you can probably keep talking to your daughter and ignore her husband."

"I guess you're right."

A little later Bessie asks, "How many grandchildren do you have?"

"Only four. We run to small families."

"They don't have big families anymore," Bessie says. "Gets in the way of their lifestyles."

"Didn't you say you had three children?" Bessie asks.

"Oh yes...Harry...I have some pictures of him up here," and I stand up and bring down my scrapbook from my suitcase.

Pearl Harbor hit us New Yorkers from out of left field. We had our eyes fixed on Europe. It was Sunday, December 7, 1941, and I was sanding down a table, while listening to the Dodgers-Giants football game on the radio. The announcer said, and I remember his words to this day, "We interrupt this program to bring you a special news bulletin. The Japanese have attacked Pearl Harbor, Hawaii, by air. Now we return you to the Polo Grounds." *Did I hear what I heard?* I was paralyzed as thoughts of everything it implied raced through my mind.

I called Sarah in from the kitchen, but by the time she came, the radio was back on the football game. "What is it?"

"I'm pretty sure it said Japanese planes attacked Pearl Harbor."

"I've heard of Japan," she said, "but where's Pearl Harbor?"

"Hawaii, in the Pacific."

"That's far away," Sarah said. "I'm glad Harry's still in California."

I remembered the recent letter from Harry, in which he had written about San Diego's beautiful November weather and how pleased he was with his radio-operator training. Now it looked like he'd be seeing some action, although it wouldn't be the Huns he was fighting.

Most New Yorkers tended to lump all Asians in with the Chinese, for whom they had little respect. So they asked, "Who is this Japan, who dared attack the great United States of America? How long will it take for us to crush it like some insect and get back to our real concern, the menace looming across the Atlantic?"

At first the government downplayed the damage at Pearl Harbor; they told us one ship was destroyed and 100 military personnel killed. But soon it came out that that was the understatement of the century; more like 30 ships put out of commission and over 2000 killed. I guess our government didn't want Japan to know how badly they had hurt us.

The day after Pearl Harbor, Roosevelt asked Congress for a declaration of war against Japan, which was immediately granted. Very quickly all Japanese citizens and some American citizens of Japanese origins in the northeast were rounded up and confined in Ellis Island. Very few Americans objected to this; we were at war and had to protect ourselves from saboteurs.

On Tuesday we all sat around our radios, as Roosevelt told us of the gravity of the situation: Not only had Japan attacked American forces all around the Pacific, but its submarines had also sunk several American transports. There were many casualties and planes and ships were destroyed. To the satisfaction of Jews, Roosevelt linked the "gangster nations" of Germany, Italy and Japan.

Now America was going to respond he told us. Armament factories would be working seven days a week. Communications would be restricted. We could expect shortages of metals and other materials. We should consider serving in the military a privilege, not a sacrifice. With Harry soon to be in the thick of it, I had mixed feelings about that.

Two days later, Germany declared war on us. They hadn't learned from World War I, not to start up with a country as large as America, with its huge manufacturing capability. Italy immediately followed suit. I guess Hitler had some pretty big ideas: conquer the world, and, as began to leak out, get rid of all the Jews. I was frantic; I hadn't heard from my family for over two years, and now they were in Nazi-occupied territory.

With us being at war with Germany and Italy, Americans of German and Italian descent suddenly made a show of their love for America. The swastikas came down in the Yorkville section of New York, and the non-interventionist groups disbanded. Nevertheless, a few Nazi sympathizers were rounded up, and many Germans that lived near the shore were moved. Unlike with the Japanese, there were too many Americans of German and Italian backgrounds to put them all in camps. And what would they have done about the German Jews, who were among the most ardent supporters of America?

The Sunday after Pearl Harbor the telephone rang about five in the afternoon.

"Abe, it's Harry," Sarah said excitedly.

I ran over to the phone and put my head next to Sarah's, trying to hear a bit of the conversation, which was about the weather and his health. I wanted to push her away and talk myself, but, of course, I didn't. Finally she passed the phone to me.

"Hi Harry, this is Dad."

"Hey Dad, what do think about those Jap bastards."

"They're worse than the Germans. At least the Germans weren't sneaky."

"All the guys here are itching to get out on the Pacific and teach them a lesson."

"Any idea when you'll be shipping out?"

"Sometime this week, I think," he said. "They don't tell us much...for security reasons."

"I hope you'll write or call whenever you can."

"I will, but they say over and over 'Loose lips sink ships,' so I won't even be able to tell you where I am."

"I   understand."

"There goes my last dime. Have to hang up now. Give my love to Esther...and Meyer."

"Love you," Sarah and I both said.

I've replayed that conversation over and over in my mind. Because, you see, it was the last time ever I spoke to Harry.

When Harry shipped out, Sarah put a blue star in our window, indicating a family with a member in the armed services overseas. In every building in our neighborhood there was at least one of these symbols.

I didn't know where Harry was, but I followed every step of the war in the Pacific in the newspaper and on the maps in my World Atlas. For a while the news was all bad. It seemed the Japanese were everywhere. They took control of Burma, Siam, Malaya, the Philippines and other places I had never heard of, capturing loads of American soldiers in the process. A Japanese submarine even shelled an oil refinery in California, the only time in the two world wars Continental America was attacked.

Towards the middle of '42 things started to improve, or at least not to get worse. We heard of American victories in the Coral Sea and near

Midway Island. These were naval battles in which the ships never saw each other. Planes from aircraft carriers did all the fighting and destroyed each other's ships. It seemed that aircraft were dominating sea battles as much as they did the land battles in Europe. And in manufacturing planes and the ships to carry them the U. S. had a tremendous advantage, with huge shipbuilding facilities in the Gulf of Mexico and auto assembly lines in the Midwest that were converted to producing aircraft. I've heard that the U. S. produced over 300,000 military aircraft during World War II.

We received three V-mails from Harry in the next few months. A censor read V-mails, then they were photographed. The rolls of film were airmailed to post offices all over the country, where they were developed to one quarter their original size. One of Harry's letters had two lines blacked out. It indicated that he was somewhere out in the Pacific and was still itching to give it to the Japs. He couldn't, however, tell us anything about the ship he was on or where he had been. I've wondered what could have been in those two lines.

With our son in the military, Sarah and I tried to do our part to aid the war effort. I purchased blackout shades and painted the edges of the windows black to block the light that went around the shades. Air raid wardens would go around and point out any place where light was showing. There never was an air raid on an American city during the war, if you don't count the time an American bomber on a practice run accidentally dropped six bombs on Boise City, Oklahoma. Fortunately these were practice bombs, 90% filled with sand, and they didn't do much damage or kill anyone.

For coastal cities, such as New York, the real reason for having blackouts was so ships moving out of the harbor or along the coast wouldn't be silhouetted against the glow of the city, making them an easy target for U-boats. Most of the time, the city was under dimout restrictions, which meant no lights or the use of shades in homes and buildings and every other streetlight off with the lit ones at reduced power. Autos used hoods to direct their headlights downward. Stores kept their awnings down at night. Even the electric billboards at Times Square, including the zipper that we had so

241

often relied on for the most recent news, was shut off for the duration of the war.

Periodically, different parts of the city had blackout drills, in which no lights were permitted to show outside. This was similar to the restrictions that held all the time along the shore.

Baseball was affected by the war. Night games, which were the only ones working people could attend during the week, were not allowed. In addition, a lot of the best baseball players went into the service. Joe DiMaggio, my favorite Yankee, enlisted, and Hank Greenberg, the Jewish star of the Detroit Tigers, was drafted.

Sarah collected every drop of kitchen fat for explosive manufacturing and went through our closets and the basement storage area for anything made of metal she could donate for the war effort. I didn't mind losing the old bicycle that I hadn't used in twenty years, but I was sure I could have found use for the tools that she placed in the collection box.

When Sarah found out that the military was training WAVES, the women's auxiliary to the Navy, at nearby Hunter College Campus, she offered her services. All week she baked cupcakes to bring to their Saturday afternoon teas. She'd take a cab to the bakery, pick up unsold pastries and have Polinski's truck take her up to the base. There she mingled with the recruits and often came back with tears in her eyes, after hearing the stories about how so many of their brothers and boyfriends had been lost in action.

Esther did her part by going to the USO and dancing with the soldiers who were in New York getting ready to ship overseas. While Sarah and I were proud of her patriotism, we were both worried she might get "in trouble" cavorting with these young men.

"Remember, only dancing," Sarah would tell her on her way out. But she was almost twenty, and we had little control over her.

Esther and I would usually have breakfast together before we both left for work. One morning, after a night of dancing, bleary-eyed Esther announced over her cereal, "I've met somebody."

"Oh," I said. "Tell me about him."

"His name is Milton Cantor. He's from Brooklyn. He's off to France in a week."

"Are you serious about each other?" I asked.

"I think so."

"Be careful," I said. "A soldier off to war isn't always in complete control of his emotions."

"I will," she said, before grabbing her coat and heading out the door.

Esther was out every night that week and was hardly able to drag herself to work in the morning. Friday, she was out all night.

On Saturday Esther slept till noon, and when she got up, I asked, "How's Milt?"

"He's off. I walked him to the ship last night," she said, waving her hand in front of her, until I could no longer ignore it.

"What's that?" I asked.

"I thought you'd never ask: an engagement ring. It's his grandmother's"

"Let me see." It looked real. I guess I was wrong. Milt was serious, and God be willing, he'd make it back and in not too long I'd be losing my baby."

"Great news," I said as I hugged and kissed her.

About every second week, Esther would get V-mail from her Milty. She never let Sarah or me read them.

Chapter 27

The scrapbook probably contains more about Harry than Bessie is interested in knowing, but I haven't looked at it for a while, and it makes me feel good to show it to her. Since I always get a little teary-eyed when I show someone Harry's scrapbook, after putting it away, I fake going to sleep, so that I can recollect my times with Harry.

August 12, 1942—a date I'll never forget: No lights on in the apartment when I came home. Sarah sitting on the couch, like a statue. Piece of paper in her hand. Held it out to me. When I switched on the lamp, I saw it was a telegram. It read,

The Secretary of War desires me to express his deepest regret that your son, Harry Joseph Sokolovsky, has been reported missing in action since ninth of August, near Guadalcanal. If further details or other information are received, you will be promptly notified.

William Franklin Knox

Secretary of the Navy

I sat down and put my arm around Sarah. She put her head on my shoulder and began to sob. "I was such a bad mother to him," she said.

"Don't say that," I said, although there was some truth to it. "Look, it doesn't say he was killed." Who was I kidding? Being missing in the Navy wasn't like being missing in the Army. There was only one place you could be.

Sarah and I remained in limbo for over a month until we got the official notification. Harry had been on the *USS Quincy*, a cruiser that was sunk shortly after the American landing on Guadalcanal. He was presumed dead.

I felt guilt as well as grief over Harry's death, since I had been the one who had supported American intervention since the beginning of the war in Europe. Perhaps that had influenced Harry's decision to enlist. Until recently, Sarah had been against our getting involved in the war.

The loss of Harry left a hole in my heart. Because he was always getting in trouble, I was more involved in his life than in Esther's or Meyer's, and our playing basketball together had created a bond between us.

We received the telegram about Harry on a Thursday and began *Shiva*, the seven-day Jewish period of mourning, that night. Following tradition, we drew the shades and covered the two mirrors in the apartment with black cloth. Both Sarah and I pinned black ribbons on our chests, instead of ripping our clothes as done by the more orthodox Jews. Replacing the blue star in the window with a gold one, which indicated the home of a war casualty, showed the neighborhood that our son had died. After a call to Sam, notifying him of the situation, I tried to keep all thoughts of work out of my mind for the week.

Except for Saturday, when we went to *shul*, Sarah and I stayed in the apartment for the entire week. Sarah neither shopped nor cooked, but Betsy and Gita brought over hot meals and neighbors stopped by to see if we needed anything from the store.

A constant stream of visitors came to our apartment, including, for the first time, Sam and his wife, Debra. Several of Harry's friends, some of whom we had never met before, dropped by, and their stories of Harry's antics managed to give us a few laughs, as well as bring more tears to our eyes. Dan Bernstein, a long-time friend of Harry, who had dined with us several times over the years, sat with us two entire evenings. He told us Harry had lots of other friends who couldn't visit because they were serving overseas.

On his second visit Dan brought a longhaired beauty with him. "This is Sylvia," Dan told me. "I don't know whether Harry ever told you about her, but she was his girlfriend."

Sylvia started to cry; tears flowed from her grey eyes over her symmetric face only enhanced by the small mole on her right cheek. Sarah put her arms around her and I helped her over to the couch. She dabbed her eyes with a handkerchief.

We sat and talked...and cried for close to an hour.

"He said wonderful things about you both: how much you loved him and put up with his antics." I think that made Sarah feel much better.

Sylvia also felt guilty. "I think the reason he joined up," she said, "was to learn a trade, so we could get married."

"I think he just got to a point of his life where he got serious," I said. I was beginning to shed my own guilt.

At the end of the *Shiva* mourning period, Sarah and I went for a walk around the block, symbolic of our "rejoining the world." The sun blinded us, after being inside the dark apartment for a week. I held Sarah's arm, and we both felt noticeably older than we had on our last walk around the block several months earlier.

If Harry had been killed in Europe, there would have been a grave somewhere that I could at least think I might some day be able to visit. With him lying at the bottom of the Pacific, I needed some other sort of memorial. I bought a scrapbook into which I pasted all the photos of Harry that we had taken over the years. Sarah, Esther, Meyer and I wrote up our remembrances of Harry and put them into the scrapbook. When Sylvia came back for a second visit, I took out my Brownie and added two photos of her. Esther, who had some of Sarah's artistic ability, made a sketch of Harry with Sylvia. I added the photos and sketch to the scrapbook.

Ironically, about a month after receiving the official notice of Harry's death, we received a V mail from him. The censors must have fallen behind. When it came, Sarah became hysterical. "He's still alive," she said.

I looked at the date on the letter. It was written two days before the invasion of Guadalcanal.

I became obsessed with finding out more about Harry's life in the Navy and the details of his death. It took a long time to get the facts, and they made me sick. They were even more shocking than Pearl Harbor, where we had ignored signs of the impending Japanese attack, which could be explained by our not being at war with Japan. But at Savo Island, just north of Guadalcanal, there was no excuse for not being alert and taking basic precautions.

About half of the *Quincy's* crew had survived her sinking. One sailor, C. W. O'Dell, a good friend of Harry, wrote me a lovely letter of their time together, which I added to the scrapbook.

246

Dear Mr. Sokolovsky,

    Harry had the next bunk to me on the Quincy. He were my best friend.

    I'm thinking of Harry a lot, since that night when the Japs surprised us. It's hard to believe that they could sneak up on us like that. Somebody musta been sleepn at the wheel.

    The Quincy was a fine ship. Too bad it only saw action once after Harry and me joined up. We had a good day shelling the oil refinery at Lunga Point and supporting the marines during their landing. The refinery were in flames when we moved over to Savo Island for the night.

    I'm sleepn when the bells rang. When I hit the deck, it were so bright from searchlights from the enemy ships. A minute later their shells began to land. We didn't even have a chance to fire back.

    We went down so fast I could only grab a life vest and jump overboard. Lucky the water were warm cause I spent four hours in it before a boat picked me up.

    Harry were on duty in the radio room that night. That part of the ship got a direct hit so I don't have much hope for him. I ended up back at Pearl Harbor for almost four months. I asked a lot about Harry there and finally got the word he was MIA.

    Harry were a great guy and the first Jew I ever know. Theres not a lot of Jews down in Meridian Mississippi where I come from. I only remember Mr. Goldstein who owns the hardware store. Theres not a lot of Catholics like me either.

    Harry were a great kidder. He said he'd fix me up with his kid sister when the war was over. Do you think she'd like to move down to Meridian?

With Great Sadness,
Charles W. O'Dell (Charlie), GM
U. S. Navy

When I showed the letter to Esther and Sarah, it brought tears to their eyes. I wrote Charlie, thanked him for his letter and informed him that Esther was already taken.

"Asleep at the wheel," that must have been a very deep sleep to allow eight Japanese cruisers to sneak up on the Allies. Not to mention, to allow them to escape from the scene without being pursued by any of the US carrier aircraft that were nearby. The only consolation was that on their way back to their base the cruisers passed by a US submarine, which sank one of them.

For a while there was no mention of the engagement in the US press. The Japanese trumpeted the victory in their newspapers. The battle for Guadalcanal dragged on for almost six months, with the Allies finally victorious. Gradually details came out, some of them not until the end of the war: How the Japanese Navy, having lost control of the air, developed tactics for fighting at night. How the admiral in charge of the US carriers withdrew them for refueling when it wasn't necessary. How air patrols of the sea-lanes were called for but never carried out. And finally, how the Japanese ships were sighted twice on their way to Savo, but no action was taken on those reports. All these I documented with articles in my scrapbook.

This time it was Sarah who recovered from grieving first. Three months after Harry died, Florence gave birth to a boy, who was named Michael. She and Sarah declared a truce, so that Sarah could help out at her apartment. Going there every day took Sarah's mind off Harry's death.

"He's the cutest baby," Sarah told me. "He takes after Meyer."

"And how's Florence doing?"

"She acts like a queen and lets me do everything."

After Harry's death I began to feel tightness in my chest. "It's about time you had a physical," Sarah said. "You're almost 60."

"I'm only 57. Don't rush me." But nevertheless I made an appointment with Morris Bernstein, a family physician Sarah had used several times.

"What's bothering you, Abe?"

I told him about not being able to sleep and getting winded going up stairs.

"Okay, we'll do some tests." He took my blood pressure, stuck me with needles and laid me down and put rubber things all over my body. "It's called an electrocardiogram. It measures the electrical signals of your heart."

"So far, so good," he said after looking at the paper rolling out of the machine. "Come back in a week; I'll have the results of your blood analysis then. It will be 15 dollars for today."

When I came back Bernstein told me, "Abe, from all your tests, you're in great shape. I can't find anything wrong with you physically. Sometimes symptoms like this result from psychological factors. What's going on in your life?"

I told him about Harry's death and how I was finding out what a mess-up the whole thing had been. As I talked, I got more and more agitated. Finally I had to stop to catch my breath.

"Relax, breathe slowly," he told me. "It sounds like you've got a lot of anger in you. Don't keep it inside; scream, if you feel like it. Exercise sometimes helps. That will be ten dollars for today."

Twenty-five dollars was a lot of money in those days, about half our monthly rent. But it took a load off my mind. Following Bernstein's advice, I increased my walking, sometimes going as far as ten miles on a weekend day.

For a while, I was practically oblivious to where my feet were taking me. When I got home, Sarah would ask where I had been, and I couldn't give her a good answer. She would look at me suspiciously.

On a beautiful Saturday in May of '43, I walked across the University Heights Bridge into upper Manhattan. After wandering around the local streets in the area, I found myself in Fort Tryon Park, one part of New York I had never before visited. The land there was hilly, but I found a path that headed up to the top of a ridge. Somehow I was able to make the climb without getting winded, and when I reached the top, I was rewarded with a magnificent view of the Hudson River and wooded areas of Jersey on the other side, just coming into bloom. With a cool breeze off the river blowing in my face, I felt renewed. There were places in New York that could move me, and this was one of them. Harry was dead, but I was alive and could still appreciate moments like this.

Fort Tryon Park was a spot I returned to several times in subsequent years. The Park contains a museum called The Cloisters, which was built by John D. Rockefeller and donated to the city. Once, I paid the admission and wandered past the archways of covered walks surrounding the peaceful gardens of its park. I was told it was common to attach cloisters to churches in Europe, so monks could escape from the problems of the world and contemplate God. I felt at peace with the world when I left the cloisters; those monks were really on to something.

In November '43 my heart dropped when, on the train going to work, I read on page 3 of the *Times*, **50,000 Kiev Jews Reported Killed**. The article said 50,000-80,000 men, women and children were told they were going to be relocated. They were removed of their possessions and stripped naked. Finally they were machine-gunned at Babi Yar, a ravine outside the city. The report came from, among others, Soviet soldiers, who had been prisoners of the Germans, and had been forced to dig up and burn the bodies as Russian troops were advancing on the city. The Germans had intended to kill all the prisoners, but three out of about 300 had escaped.

The article said the evidence for the massacre was "scanty", but the descriptions were so graphic, I was sure they were true. It was clearly the slaughter of unresisting civilians.

With horror I remembered Leena had moved to Kiev. She was probably one of the victims. I imagined her lying naked on a pile of dead Jews. Of course it wasn't her sixty-year old body I pictured, but her teenage body I had peeked at in my youth. That was an image that recurred in my dreams and sometimes even when I was awake for the rest of my life. It was one reason I could never forgive the Germans.

Leena had said that Freyda was also living in Kiev. How many members of my family been killed at Babi Yar? I didn't know, and there was no way for me to find out. In a daze, I got off the subway at 59th Street and sat down on a bench in Central Park, where visions of the massacred Jews flitted through my mind. How big would a pile of 50 to 80 thousand naked bodies be? *My God, that was the capacity of Yankee Stadium.* Only once, had I been to the Stadium when it was sold out. Crowds of fans had pushed

250

through the gates. Imagine them all dead, filling up the field. I pushed the image out of my mind and burst out in tears.

It was almost two hours before I realized how cold I was and went to call Sam to tell him I wasn't coming to work that day.

Actually, as far back as the end of 1942 Stephen Wise, a Reform rabbi with close ties to Roosevelt, had started informing the American Jewish community of something he had known for a while, but was asked to keep secret by the State Department: Hitler's plan for the Jews of Europe was to exterminate them all. Concentration camps and the Warsaw ghetto were only stations on the way to extermination camps to which Jews were being transported for Hitler's "final solution" to the "Jewish problem."

It took a while for Wise's information to filter down to the Jewish community. When we realized what was happening, we were horrified. What could be done to stop the German massacre of the Jews? Rumors flew: We'd bomb the trains taking the Jews to the camps. We'd pay Romania to release 70,000 Jews. But where would the Jews go? Nobody wanted them. Palestine? The British vetoed that idea, since they needed Arab support to protect their oil supplies. Cuba? It had taken as many as it would. America? Congress authorized additional visas for Jews, but damn Brekinridge Long, Assistant Secretary of State in charge of visas, was a notorious anti-Semite and instituted administrative obstacles that kept Jews from our shores.

Roosevelt and Churchill agreed the first goal was to win the war, and only then would those responsible for heinous crimes be punished. Of course, that would be too late for the Jews. Millions of them already had been killed, and millions more would be expendable before the war was over.

Chapter 28

"Three of my nephews served in the Second War," Bessie *tells me. "They were all in segregated units. One of them was a Tuskegee airman and learned to fly a plane."*

"Did they get through the war okay?" I ask.

"Thank God they did. I guess being colored helped them. At first they weren't trusted, and their units were kept out of the serious action. It was only toward the end of the war that they began to be respected by the generals. Too bad my nephew wasn't able to get a job flying commercial jets after the war. It took a Supreme Court decision in '63 to get the airlines to hire black pilots. By that time his flying skills had gotten rusty. He works in a grocery store now."

The war years were difficult for Henkel's Dresses and Belts. Manufacturing for the military put money in people's pockets and ended the depression once and for all. However, material for clothing was limited, and after June '41, women had to turn in a number of their margarine rationing coupons for each item of clothing, depending on how much material it consumed. As a result, Henkel's produced garments using the minimum amount of material. The "little black dress", with hemline at the knees became popular during this time, because with different accessories it could be made to look like different outfits. Henkel's upscale business, however, wasn't hurt too badly. I guess rich women found ways to obtain rationing coupons.

Since most of our employees were women, we didn't have to worry about their getting drafted. Several of them, however, left for higher paying jobs in the defense industry, and we had to give raises to the others to keep them. The two young men in the factory were both drafted, and in their place I hired Manuel, a short, powerfully built 45-year old, from Puerto Rico. Manny was a reliable worker who spoke excellent English. On a cold winter's day, I asked him why he immigrated to America.

"I'm not an immigrant," Manny said indignantly. "Puerto Rico is a colony of the United States. We've been citizens since 1917 and drafted in both world wars. One of my sons is over in Europe right now."

"Okay, but why did you leave the warm climate of the Caribbean to come to cold New York."

"A warm climate is great for growing things. But you need more than sweet potatoes to raise a family. There aren't any jobs in Puerto Rico. We've never recovered from the Depression. None of the manufacturing for the war has come to the island. I don't think we're trusted since the Ponce massacre."

"Ponce massacre—what's that?"

"Haven't you ever heard about how they shot twenty peaceful marchers in '37? It happened in Ponce, that's in the southern part of the island."

"I guess I haven't," I said, embarrassed by my ignorance.

Most of the garments for the military were being produced in large factories in low-wage Southern States. In '42, through a "connection," Sam got a contract to produce woolen skirts for the WACs. These came with a buttoned closure made in our factory. An order for 20,000 of these kept us busy most of that year. With higher costs and low-price contracts like this one, my share of the profits was modest during the war years. This was offset, however, by the thought that, in our way, Henkel's was also contributing to the war effort.

Only a fraction of the ten million men in America's military was fighting in Italy or the Pacific. We Jews wanted a Second Front to be opened in Europe to bring relief to European Jewry. In July of '43, Stalin sent a Jewish delegation to America to generate support for an invasion. The rally at the Polo Grounds at which they spoke was on a Thursday, so I couldn't attend, but Sarah went with a few other women from our neighborhood.

"It was exciting," she told me. "There must have been 50,000 people there. Rabbi Wise and Newbold Morris, the President of the City Council, spoke. Albert Einstein even said a few words."

"What did they say?"

"They all said we should invade the continent as soon as possible. The Russians told us about all the Jews they had been able to evacuate before the Nazi invasion."

I thought back to Leena's letter from Kiev, probably the last one I would ever get from her. Were the "evacuees" the Russians talked about the Jews they sent to Siberia she had mentioned? Now Russia, like Germany before it, was claiming to be the friend of the Jews. I had my doubts.

At the end of '43 articles in the *Times* reported significant advances by the Allies. In the Pacific, Guadalcanal was taken, and islands off Alaska were attacked. At Stalingrad, the Russians had held and were starting a counter offensive. In Italy, Sicily was taken, but as soon the mainland was invaded, the Italians, under the direction of King Victor Emmanuel, sued for peace. Mussolini set up a new Italian government in northern Italy, under the protection of the Germans, who disarmed any Italian unit that didn't pledge loyalty to him.

In June of '44, three million Allied troops on six thousand ships invaded the Normandy coast of France. It was the largest armada ever assembled. General Dwight Eisenhower directed the invasion.

You would think that against a force like that and with their factories and cities being bombed into oblivion, the Germans would throw up their hands and surrender right away. However, even though Paris was liberated by August, German resistance stiffened. In December, they launched a massive counter attack from the Ardennes, designed to split the Allied forces and break their supply lines. Fortunately the "Battle of the Bulge" petered out by the end of January, and pretty soon the Allies were in Germany. Unlike the Italians, the Germans didn't immediately surrender when their homeland was invaded.

I remember being with Sarah in the movies, when, in the newsreel, we saw pictures of Dresden on fire and bombed into rubble by the Allies. For just a moment I felt sorry for the Germans. However, the next reel showed prisoners liberated from concentration camps. *Were any of those skeletons members of my family or people I had known in the old country?* I didn't know, but seeing them made my sympathy for the Germans quickly evaporate.

Just as Moses was allowed to see but not enter the Promised Land, FDR lived long enough to see the invasion but not the surrender of Germany. Like the attack on Pearl Harbor, FDR's death was one of those things everyone remembers where he was when he heard about it. We had the factory windows open on that warm Thursday in April '45, when the noisy street below suddenly became silent. Then a woman cried out, "Oh, no," and others began to wail. I leaned out the window and saw men standing motionless with their hats off. Some held them by their hearts. One woman was helping another to sit down on the stairs across the street, while a third was hysterically banging on a wall.

"What happened?" I called down to a man on the street.

"The President is dead."

I repeated his words out loud and the six operators stopped sewing, held each other and cried.

It was almost five, so I announced, "That's it for the day."

It was a gloomy ride home. Roosevelt had been president for 13 years—so long, it was hard to imagine the country without him. He was like a father to the whole country, or at least to the Democratic-leaning New York area. Who was that guy, Truman, who'd be taking over? I seemed to remember that he'd run a clothing store. I was in the clothing business myself, but didn't feel it was good training for the most important job in the country…and the world.

When I arrived home, Sarah and most of the other women in the building were congregated on the front steps. Tears were in their eyes. We all needed to be with others at that time.

"I think I'll miss him more than my own father," Sarah said.

"My father was a drunk, I don't miss him at all," remarked Mrs. McClosky, who had moved into our first floor apartment.

About a month after Roosevelt died, we learned that Adolf Hitler had committed suicide. I didn't get any satisfaction from this. The little jerk with a mustache had already done his damage; more than 50 million were dead, including six million Jews. I saw him in movie newsreels several

255

times. There must have been something fundamentally wrong with the German people to make such a ridiculous character their Fuhrer.

The big news we were all waiting for came on May 7, a Monday morning. About an hour after I got to work, church bells began to ring all over the city, announcing Germany's unconditional surrender. Workers poured out of buildings on both sides of our street, bound for church or *shul* to give thanks, or to bars or the street to celebrate. There was no way the bosses could stop them. I didn't even try. I put up a "Closed" sign on the door and joined the throngs on the street. The crowd waiting to get on the El was huge; I had to wait for three trains. Almost everyone got off at 42nd Street. We were all heading for the same place, Times Square, but I could only get to within three blocks of the place.

It didn't take long for Esther's fiancée, Milton Cantor, who she called Milty, to get back to the U.S. In June, he and 15,000 other American servicemen pulled into New York Harbor on the Queen Mary. Milty was given a two-day leave in the city and then transferred to Fort Dix in New Jersey. Esther took off from work and we didn't see her both those days.

"So when are we going to meet Milton?" Sarah asked her, when she got back to the apartment.

"The next time he gets leave, I'll bring him for dinner. I hope they don't ship him off to the Pacific now."

I was glad to see that "the deal still seemed sealed."

With the defeat of Germany, blackout restrictions were eased on the East Coast. The Times Square billboards and the Zipper stayed on at night. New Yorkers, however, had a big scare when, in July of '45, a B-25 bomber got lost in fog and crashed into the 79th floor of the Empire State Building. For a couple of minutes, people in the street or in adjacent buildings thought we were attacked. Fortunately the plane wasn't carrying any bombs, and, since it happened on a Saturday, only eleven office workers, in addition to the three crewmembers of the plane, were killed. Despite the damage on the upper floors, offices were open on the lower floors on Monday. It took about three months for the damage to the building to be repaired.

There was still the matter of unfinished business in the Pacific. For most Jews, Germany had been the evil enemy. I, however, was seething with anger against Japan and wanted revenge for Harry's death. I'm not proud to say it, but I even felt joy, when I saw a photo of the atomic bomb blast at Hiroshima.

"That's beautiful," I said to Sarah, and I wasn't just talking about the symmetry of the mushroom cloud.

"Yes it is," she answered. "Maybe that will get Japan to surrender and we won't have to suffer lots of casualties invading them."

"I think the Japs deserve anything they get," I said.

Later, when I saw the pictures of how the bombs had reduced the cities to ash and rubble and the people to char or bones I began to change my mind. Those women and children with their skin peeling off were not the real culprits. They had just followed their leaders. Those bombs should be put away and never used again.

The Japanese vowed to fight on to the last man, but on Sunday, August 14, Sarah and I were listening to the radio, when we heard, "Japan accepts surrender terms of the Allies." This was immediately followed by "Ladies and gentlemen, please disregard that flash."

I looked at Sarah and she looked at me; we both had puzzled looks on our faces. "It can't be far off," I said, and we hugged each other and began to cry. It wouldn't bring Harry back, but at least it felt like he died for a purpose.

The official announcement came on the following day, when Japanese leaders signed surrender documents on the USS Missouri. New York went wild. Work was out of the question. All over the city there were celebrations. Men in uniform had a free ticket to kiss any girl they chose.

Remembering how crowded Times Square had been on V-E day, I decided to confine my walk to the Lower East Side. In Chinatown, just a few blocks down on Canal Street, the celebrations were particularly exuberant. The Japanese occupation of China had been brutal, with atrocities approaching some of Hitler's in Europe. In just about every tenement window in Chinatown, people were waving American or Chinese flags, and the dragons, usually only brought out to celebrate their New Year, were snaking through the streets. Several stores put out trays of delicacies, just for the taking. I tried a few very tasty things that I had never had before. I should bring Sarah down here some time, I thought.

In September of '45, American Jews got something to be proud of: Bess Myerson—Jewish, a talented musician and a graduate of Hunter College, was voted Miss America. It was good revenge for that nasty comment made by FDR's cousin about "charming Jewish children becoming ugly Jewish adults."

Chapter 29

The New Jersey Turnpike doesn't smell any better now than it did on my bus ride down to Florida six years ago. Looking out Bessie's window, I see a few houses among the chemical plants. Those poor people must have to breath this stuff 24 hours a day. When they get into clean air, they probably think it's polluted.

Through the haze, I start to make out the skyscrapers of lower New York. It raises my heartbeat; I've been away from the city too long. I wonder how it's changed. The weather in the winter may be better for walking down in Florida, but, to tell you the truth, there's a lot more to see in New York City than there is in Miami Beach.

After struggling through the horrors of the war, you'd think the world deserved a break. But it wasn't in the cards. Soviet troops remained in Hungary, Romania and Bulgaria, countries that had joined the Nazis in the war, and in the eastern part of Germany. Maybe the Soviets could justify that, but they also stayed in Poland and Czechoslovakia, two countries that had been conquered by the Nazis. At several conferences before the end of the war, Stalin had promised to allow the citizens of those countries to choose their own government, and Roosevelt, in his weakened condition, had taken his word for it. Now it seemed that, in stages, Stalin was converting each of them to Communist rule under domination of the Soviet Union. I guess with the atomic bomb, the Allies could have forced the issue, but no one had the stomach for that. A Cold War was better than a hot war.

After the war I tried writing Leena, my family in Zyvotov and even the rabbi of the *shul* in the town, but no one responded. Zyvotov wasn't even shown on a post-war map of the Ukraine I looked at when I went to the library. When the Iron Curtain came down, it became increasingly difficult to get any information. I was desperate for news about my family, and I remembered that Dovid Fenkel had been active in the Communist Party. Maybe, with his contacts, he might be able to find out something about

Zyvotov. I figured I had nothing to lose by trying to contact him, so I telephoned the New York office of the American Communist Party and asked for him. They weren't able to identify anyone by that name, but said they would check and call me back. I called once more and came away empty handed. Maybe I had the wrong last name.

I passed through Crotona Park several times, hoping that I might see Dovid handing out communist literature. However, Communism had become America's enemy, and the Communists had mainly gone underground. There wouldn't have been much patience with a Communist speaker at that time; he would have been pelted with garbage. Finally, I gave up trying to find out about my family, and consoled myself with the thought that perhaps a few of them, sisters, nieces or nephews, had made their way to Israel or some other safe place.

With the war finally over, Milton was discharged, and we got our chance to meet him at a Friday night dinner at our apartment. Meyer and Florence joined us. Sarah made chicken, pot roast and two different pies for the meal.

"I haven't eaten this well in three years," Milton said, and I believed him, from the way he packed it away at that meal. I didn't know where he put it all in his lanky six-foot frame.

Sarah was beaming.

"What will you be doing now?" I asked him.

"I'll join my father in his house-painting business. With all the soldiers coming back and getting married, the country's going to need a lot of new houses. Most of the old ones need painting, since people couldn't get paint during the war. I'm going to make a lot of money and take care of your little girl real good." He put his arm around Esther's shoulders and squeezed her. She smiled at his show of affection.

"And we want to get married as soon as possible," Esther said.

"I hope there's no emergency on its way," Sarah said.

"Oh no!" Esther laughed.

After dinner, Sarah asked Esther, "So what type of wedding do you want?" She gave a disapproving look at Meyer, to remind him that he denied her a wedding.

"I'm not sure," Esther said, "but there will be a lot of people to invite. Milty has a sister and two brothers and other family in Brooklyn."

I gulped; a big wedding would cost big dollars, and it was the bride's family's responsibility.

A few weeks later, Milty gave us his list of people it would be absolutely necessary to invite—about 60, and those who it would just be nice to invite—about 80 more—forget about them.

Since there was now a row of garages behind Polinski's Bakery, we couldn't have the wedding there. Any way, Esther was horrified at the idea. "What if it rains?" she asked. What had happened to my little Esther, who had suffered through the Depression so valiantly?

Sarah and I had saved a little money during the war, and now it looked like it would all be gone. At age 60, I was starting to think about retirement, and this didn't help.

Out of desperation I called Sarah and Esther to a meeting around the kitchen table. "Okay, this is the bottom line." I placed our two bankbooks on the table. Their sum came to a little more than six thousand dollars. "It would be nice if we had a little left over for the rest of your mother's and my lives," I said to Esther.

Ester laughed. "Oh Daddy, I wouldn't think of spending your last dollar. I'm sure Mom and I can work it out to save you some." That wasn't totally reassuring to me.

On a warm Sunday in May of '46, Sarah and I took the B train to have dinner with our *machatunim*, Philip and Gloria Cantor, at their house in the Midwood section of Brooklyn. On our walk from the Kings Highway station we saw kosher butcher shops and pizzerias in the mixed Jewish-Italian neighborhood.

The Cantors owned their own house. In the driveway were two vans with Cantor and Sons, House Painting written on their side, and retractable ladders on their tops. Through the open door of the double garage, we saw

261

paints, ladders and drop cloths stacked to the ceiling. *They look prosperous…should have no problem contributing to the wedding…probably invited us over to talk about it.*

We climbed the porch steps. The front door was open, closed only by a screen door. Sarah and I gave each other a final look-over. She had already started a diet to get ready for the wedding and I thought she was looking very pretty in a flowered dress from Henkel's. I was wearing a sport shirt and slacks. I pressed the bell, and was surprised by a loud gong. *I guess they need a loud noise to hear it all over this large house.*

"Abe, Sarah, I've heard so much about you," a tall guy called out as he approached the door. Except for much less hair and a fifty-pound belly, he looked a lot like Milty. "I'm Phil Cantor; come right in." "Gloria," he called loudly, "The Sokolovskys are here." Over beltless pants, Phil was wearing a beach shirt, fastened only with its center two buttons, so his naval looked right up at us.

"I'll be right down," a woman called from up the stairs.

"Join the family," Phil said. He pumped my hand and slapped me on the back and then hugged Sarah, who seemed uncomfortable at the naked protrusion he pressed against her.

"Hello, hello," said Gloria, carefully coming down the stairs in high heels, tight pants and a low-cut top, that really didn't flatter her fifty-something, mildly overweight figure. Her hair was dyed a whitish-blonde, although its dark roots called out for retreatment. "What are you drinking? I'm doing gin and tonics today." From her unsteadiness, I guessed she had already done more than one.

"Gin and tonic sounds good to me," I said.

"I'll just have some soda or seltzer," Sarah said.

"Coming right up." Gloria left for the kitchen.

"Let me show you around the house," Phil said. He ushered us into the living room. Above the mantle was a mounted swordfish. "Caught it down in the Keys before the war. Ever been there Abe?"

I had no idea where these Keys were, so I just said, "Not yet."

"You should try it. The fishing's great."

"Here are your drinks." Gloria said.

Phil toured us around the room, pointing out other trophies and knick-knacks from their travels, mainly along the East Coast.

I have to admit the Cantors entertained us very well. They were outgoing people and fun to be around. Phil cooked up chicken and steaks on an outside grill, and Gloria continually filled our glasses. Even Sarah started to do gin and tonics. Esther and Milty showed up about an hour after us, followed twenty minutes later by other members of the Cantor clan. I was happy that Esther would be joining such a friendly family.

We had such a good time that after we left and I was helping a somewhat tipsy Sarah walk back to the subway, it occurred to me that I didn't remember anything being said about Milt's folks paying for any of the wedding.

"Did you hear them offer to pay for any of the wedding expenses?" I asked Sarah.

"I don't remember. You really should have brought it up," she said, but she was more interested in keeping her balance.

"It was hard to get serious, when everyone was having such a good time. I guess it really is the bride's parent's responsibility. Maybe they'll come across with something later on."

The Cantors never did volunteer to pay for part of the wedding, although they did give the kids money for a Florida honeymoon and for furnishing their apartment in Brooklyn. Sarah and I weren't too happy about Esther being so far away, but with Milty working with his father, he would have to live close to his parents.

Even though Sarah did her best to keep the costs down, the wedding cost us a pretty penny. I wasn't a veteran, but Ben was and belonged to the American Legion post up on 223rd Street. He got us good deal on renting their hall and also provided the wedding cake gratis. Rather than a sit-down dinner, we had the local deli bring in trays of food.

"Young people want to dance," Esther informed me. Fortunately she had friends who had recently started a band. In order to get exposure, they wouldn't charge us much.

With a wedding, however, there are expenses you don't anticipate. For example, to have the ceremony at Adath Israel, I had to rejoin the congregation and make a contribution to their building fund. We passed on having their new cantor, Mario Botoshansky, sing at the ceremony, which would have cost $200. If Henkel's had made wedding dresses, Sarah could have gotten one free. However, since they didn't, we had to shell out $150. It seemed to me a lot of money for something hopefully Esther would only wear once.

On a Saturday in September '46, Adath Israel had three weddings scheduled after regular services. With all the soldiers coming home, it was a busy time for weddings. Esther's was the middle one, from four to six. A half hour to get the guests seated, 45 minutes for the ceremony and then another half hour to get everyone out. Not like when Sarah and I were married in Polinski's back yard.

All thoughts of money left my mind when Esther, radiant in her gown and veil, took my arm in the anteroom next to the synagogue entrance. I hadn't realized she looked so much like Sarah did when we'd wed almost 35 years earlier. The organ struck a cord and we followed the three ushers and three bridesmaids down the aisle. One of the latter was Sylvia, with whom Esther had become close because of their shared grief over Harry's death.

The ceremony started with the reading of the *ketubah*. In keeping with Adath Israel becoming a Conservative synagogue, instead of the requirement that the groom have sex with his wife, the marriage contract now read that "he be attentive to her emotional needs." There was enough flexibility in the ceremony so that Esther and Milty could compose their own vows. Sarah had been working with Esther for weeks on hers. After the vows, the rabbi blessed the couple in both Hebrew and in English, Milty did the "break the glass" thing, and then we were on our way back down the aisle. There were some hugs and kisses by the door, the bride and groom got into a limo and most of the locals into a bus I had rented for the ride to the reception. The crowd from Brooklyn had their own cars.

The music that Sarah often listened to on the radio was big band stuff: Harry James, Les Brown, Xavier Cugat. There was a chance that she would try to dance with me to those tunes. That was not what Esther's friend's band was in to. It consisted of a saxophone, two guitars and a drummer and mainly played new types of music that were coming out of the South. One of the guitarists attempted to sing. Only rarely was there something that someone over 40 could dance to.

I filled my plate, sat down and watched the young people on the dance floor, until Esther headed my way. "Come on Daddy you can do it," she said.

Oh well, I was paying for this shindig—might as well try. So I followed Ester's lead and made an attempt. The raucous applause when I finished suggested I hadn't done badly. I guess Esther had warned Milty not to try to get Sarah to dance.

The Brooklyn bunch, especially Phil and Gloria, were hitting the bottles pretty hard, and I had my doubts whether they'd be able to drive back to Brooklyn, but Phil assured me he'd be okay. "Come out and see us again, Abe," Phil said. "Don't be a stranger." He slapped my back on the way out the door.

We weren't strangers, mainly because Esther and Milty found an apartment a half dozen blocks from the Cantor's house. When we went to visit them, we'd often end up going over to Phil and Gloria's for barbecue. A lot of new homes were being built out on Long Island at that time, and Phil's company appeared to be doing very well. The extended Cantor clan would gorge themselves on barbecued steak and chicken every weekend.

Chapter 30

The bus comes out of the Lincoln Tunnel into the blinding sunlight of a New York afternoon. A few ramps later, we pull into our berth in the Port Authority Terminal. Bessie presses her nose to the window, looking for her daughter.

"Port Authority–New York City, last stop," the driver calls out. He opens the door, and Bessie and I follow the other passengers down the steps. We stand by the side of the bus, while the driver pulls suitcases out from the luggage compartment. Bessie's red suitcase and my black one soon are sitting on the ground.

"Well Abe," she says. "My daughter's either inside, or she'll be there in a while. I certainly enjoyed talking to you on the trip. It made the time fly."

"I enjoyed talking to you, and I loved your fried chicken," I say.

Bessie laughs and holds out her hand. "The sandwich was pretty good too. When you get back to Miami come visit me in Brownsville." She shakes my hand and looks into my face like she really means it. "That's Bessie Warner, on Northwest 52nd Street, Brownsville. I'll make you a cup of tea, and, who knows, maybe even some fried chicken."

Bessie takes the handle of her suitcase and rolls it away into the waiting room. I rehearse her address, so there's a chance I'll remember it.

Sarah and I were proud of how well Meyer had been doing. When Arthur died in '37, Meyer had inherited most of his clients and now had his own thriving accounting business. He had moved to a three-bedroom apartment off Mosholu Parkway in the swanky Bedford Heights section of northern Bronx. The building had a lobby, an elevator and laundry facilities in the basement. On Friday mornings he played golf with some of his business acquaintances. It amazed me that in one generation, the Sokolovskys had gone from the Lower East Side to playing a rich-man's game like golf. Although, to be fair, Meyer mostly played on the Van Cortland Park course, the first public golf course in the country.

"Golf is important for my business," Meyer told me. "I play with clients. They become my friends, and then they're less likely to dump me and sign up with another accountant."

In the years immediately following the war, inflation was bad, especially in rents, with all the soldiers returning home and starting new families. Mr. Shineson, who had owned our building, had died in '42, and soon we got a new landlord. The rent control law put into effect in '47 only applied to buildings with at least six rental units. Our landlord found a way around it by moving his cousin into Marie's old apartment, leaving only five rental units in the building. Then he hit us with several big rent increases.

Sarah showed me a letter from the landlord. "They're raising our rent to 80 dollars."

I thought for a minute. "I don't think we need three bedrooms, now that the kids are gone. We should start looking for a smaller place."

"Maybe we can move closer to Meyer and Michael," Sarah said.

"Bedford Heights would probably be too pricey," I told Sarah. "But maybe we could find something not too far from there."

Apartments were scarce at that time and would be snapped up as soon as they were advertised. So when on one of my walks in the North Bronx, I saw an Apartment-for-Rent sign in a window in a building on Perry Avenue, I found the super and took a look at it. It was a one-bedroom on the fifth floor of a building with an elevator and the rent was only 50 dollars a month. I slipped him a five-dollar bill to hold it, while I hailed a cab to get Sarah. Three weeks later, in August '47, we moved in.

It was an ideal location, a mixed neighborhood, with primarily Jews in the apartment buildings and Irish and Italians in single-family homes. Among the stores on Bainbridge Avenue at our corner were a Jewish bakery, a deli, a pizza joint, and even a small movie house. On our other corner were the grassy areas along Mosholu parkway. We became members of the Mosholu Jewish Center on Hull Avenue, one block over.

Two months after we moved to our smaller apartment, I returned home to find a red-eyed Esther sitting on the living room couch. Two large suitcases were in the corner of the room.

"What happened," I asked her. She burst out crying when she tried to answer.

"She's left Milty," Sarah informed me. "Something about his father's bookkeeper."

"He stayed out...the whole night," Esther managed to blurt out, before she began to cry again.

"That doesn't sound good," I said.

"You did the right thing," Sarah said. "Once you let a man away with something like that, he'll never stop." She gave me a look that said, *Don't even think of trying it.*

To tell you the truth, I never had thought of trying it. Not that I hadn't had the chance. Over the years, there had been a number of sewing-machine operators who had "given me the eye," although I had no idea just what they had in mind. Unlike Henkel's Dresses, the belt factory didn't have a private office with a couch.

Getting involved with another woman was just not in my script. You left your parents, got lonely, fell in love, got married and had children. You helped your wife through tough times and she did the same for you. You could count on her and she on you. And she would always be there for you. That's the way it was and should still be, no matter what type of experiences the soldiers had had in gay Paree, or wherever they were stationed.

Sarah sat down on the couch and put her arm around Esther's shoulders. "It's good you found out his true colors before you got pregnant." She hesitated and then said, "You're not pregnant, are you?"

"Oh, no," Esther sobbed.

Fortunately, Esther still had her job. She bore up well sleeping on the living room couch. Three days after she arrived, a dozen roses were delivered to our door. Similar offerings arrived every third day or so.

"Don't forgive him too easily," Sarah recommended. Esther agreed, and when Milty called, Sarah would tell him Esther was out, no matter what time it was.

"He should give you something," Sarah added.

"What do you suggest?" Esther asked.

"Maybe a fur coat or a diamond necklace."

After about three weeks, Esther said a few words to Milty on the phone. The next Saturday, shamefaced Milty suffered Sarah's dirty look when he came to take Esther to dinner. Esther called at about ten saying she wouldn't be home that night—a sure indication she was giving him a second chance. The next morning they pulled up in Milty's truck and took Esther's suitcases back to their apartment.

"Well, let's hope she's taught him a lesson," Sarah said.

"I've got my fingers crossed," I said. Among other reasons, the idea of making a second wedding didn't appeal to me.

A big question after the war was what to do with the millions of Jews languishing in camps throughout Europe. Although many of them came to America, most of the diplomats manning our embassies equated Jews with Communists and put roadblocks in their way. A few ended up in Britain, France or South America.

Zionists wanted the Jews to go Palestine, but the British had other ideas. In '47, we read about the SS Exodus, carrying 4500 Jews rescued from German camps and from hiding. The British turned the ship away from Palestine, killing three passengers and wounding many others in the process. Then they sent it to France, but few of the passengers would disembark there. Finally the ship was sent to Hamburg, Germany, where the remaining passengers were dragged off and returned to displaced persons camps.

Fed up with trying to reconcile the Jews and Arabs in Palestine, the British finally told the newly formed United Nations they were giving up control of the area. The UN decided to partition Palestine into a Jewish and an Arab state. The Jews accepted the plan, the Palestinian Arabs didn't, and riots ensued.

On May 14, 1948, the Jews of Palestine declared the formation of the State of Israel with David Ben-Gurion as its first prime minister. The next day, I read in the *Times* that the United States was the first country to recognize the new nation. Jews danced in the streets of New York. I was ecstatic; even though I had no plans to move to Israel, it was good to know that there was a place where American Jews could go, if things ever got bad for them. I was impressed that Truman did what he thought was right, over the advice of a number of his advisors, who thought he should protect American influence with the Arab nations.

The same issue of the *Times* that told of the formation of the State of Israel also announced **30,000 Trained Arabs Massed.** These were not some rag-tag Arab troops; they were the British-trained and equipped armies of Egypt, Jordan and Iraq, joined by contingents from Syria, Lebanon and Saudi Arabia. The Jordanian troops were even led by British officers.

"I'm worried," I told Sarah. "It could be another massacre of Jews."

"What about the British?" she asked. "Won't they protect them?"

"They're just interested in getting their troops out. They're not going to interfere."

"I can't see them just sitting around while the Jews are all killed," she said.

"Don't count on it."

I had many sleepless nights during the next year worrying about the fate of the Israeli Jews. However, when it became clear that the Jews were getting the upper hand, a cease-fire was declared and a line of separation drawn between the combatants. Jordan ended up controlling the West Bank and Egypt the Gaza strip. Three quarters of a million Arabs left or were expelled from what then became the State of Israel. Israel was accepted as a member of the United Nations on May 11, 1949.

I was very proud of the Israeli Jews. Jews putting up a fight…and winning, that hadn't happened since biblical times.

As the 1948 elections approached, the Democratic Party was a mess. Truman was nominated, but his support of civil rights—including an order to racially integrate the military—led Strom Thurmond to run as the candidate of the State's Rights Democratic Party. Henry Wallace, a former Secretary of Commerce also split from the Democratic Party to run as the candidate of the Progressive Party.

A few months before the election, the Russians gave Truman an opportunity to enhance his reputation as a strong president. After the war,

Germany had been divided up into sections under the control of Britain, France, Russia and the United States. The capitol, Berlin, was divided up in similar manner. Berlin, however, was located completely within the Russian section of the country. In June of '48, the Russians blocked access to all the roads leading into Berlin, attempting to starve the city into becoming part of its section of the country. There was some talk of the Allies forcing an armored column into the city, which scared me out of my mind.

"I don't think the Russians will back down," I said to Ben over dinner at our place. "We've removed most of our troops from Europe. The Russians have clear superiority on the ground. This could escalate to nuclear war."

"I'm sure they'll find another way around it," Ben assured me.

Ben was right. Britain and America decided to supply Berlin by air. What audacity—trying to bring in enough food, coal and supplies for a city of two and a half million people. The Russians didn't believe it could be done, and I had my doubts.

America at that time, however, didn't accept failure. By the end of August, C-47 cargo planes were landing at the Berlin airport at a rate of one every three minutes. Truman was credited with successfully standing up to the Soviets, and Russia got an early lesson on the difficulty of competing with the industrial might of America.

Meanwhile, the Republicans for the second time chose Thomas Dewey the New York governor as their candidate. In '44, Dewey had captured 46% of the vote against Roosevelt and a unified Democratic Party, so with the Democrats split this time, he was considered a shoo-in. Dewey was from the progressive wing of the Republican Party. He had been a fine governor of New York, and I considered voting for him, but Truman's support of Israel kept me a Democrat.

The initial polls told us that Dewey was far ahead, and I guess he believed them, because he ran a lackluster campaign, designed not to offend anyone. He was like a basketball team that gets ahead and decides to run a defensive game. Usually they end up losing. Truman on the other hand was a fighter. He barnstormed the country from the back of his campaign train. On Election Day, against all odds, he beat Dewey. Much to their

271

embarrassment, several big newspapers hadn't waited for the final results and had declared Dewey the winner in their early edition.

I became a big Truman fan. However, years later, I heard a sad story: After Truman was president and he and his wife, Bess, moved backed to her family house in Independence, Missouri, she wouldn't let any Jews in the house. I hope it wasn't true, but if it was, I can't blame Truman, because, as I know, some wives do their own thing regardless of its effect on their husbands.

Chapter 31

No one answered Michael's phone. *Not surprising with the bus being three hours late.* *Can't expect him to stay around all day waiting for my call.* *The Port Authority isn't too far from Times Square.* *I haven't been there in ten years.* *While I'm waiting, I'll see if it's changed.*

Real chill in the air. *It hardly ever gets this cold in Miami Beach.*

Think I'll take a look at the Zipper. *First, I have to brave 42nd Street from Eighth to Times Square, New York's sleaze district.* *This suitcase with wheels is one of the best investments I ever made.* *I used the old one to store my stuff at the Sun Spot.*

I'm hungry now. *Better get something to eat; don't know when I'll get to Michael's.* *There's Romeo's—I remember: slice of pizza and a soda for a buck.* *Can't beat that.*

Didn't realize I was so hungry. *Decided not to get a second slice.* *Michael probably will offer me something when I get to his house.*

More seedy types around here than I remember. *They probably think I'm a greenhorn, pulling this suitcase.*

"Hey mister, wanna buy some postcards?"

"Let's see what you got." *Oh, oh.* *Don't think I want those.* *They'd probably arrest you, if you mailed them.*

"Buddy. *Can you spare some change?"*

I looked at him. *Seems like if he cleaned himself up he could get a job.* *I walked on.*

Let's see what's playing on 42nd Street: Blood Splattered Bride, The Centerfold Girls. *I'll pass on those.*

"Hey mista, help you with dat suitcase?"

I shook my head. *If that guy ever got his hand on my suitcase, I'd never get it back.*

"Hey Pops, want to party?" *says a buxom blonde.*

I'll pass on that.

I wonder why the Zipper's dark. It used to be such an important part of life in New York. It was where you went to get the news as soon as it came it out. Even though they have instant TV coverage nowadays, they should get it up and running again. It's just not New York without it.

Must be 500 people waiting on that line. Maybe it's for something worth waiting for.

"Excuse me Ma'm, what's this line for?"

"It's for half-price tickets for shows."

"Thank you." Half-price—that's something I can relate to. That lady's wearing a mink jacket. You'd think she'd be able to afford a full-price ticket.

Okay, I've wasted enough time. I'll try to call Michael again.

In the winter of '48, Meyer and Florence had a second child. They named her Samantha. When the baby was six months old, Florence got a part-time job. Sarah volunteered to baby sit for Michael and Samantha three days a week. Meyer would pick Sarah up Monday, Wednesday and Friday morning and take her over to his apartment. He'd bring her back about five.

"How's the babysitting going," I asked Sarah.

"Samantha is delightful and so smart. She can eat a banana by herself."

"It must be a little messy."

"So what?" Sarah said. "Someone has to give that baby some good food. She's so skinny."

About a month later, I noticed Sarah didn't get out of bed on a Wednesday morning.

"Aren't you sitting today?"

"I've been fired. Florence decided she didn't want me to babysit any more."

"What did you do?"

"Oh, nothing."

"Nothing?"

"Nothing, except when Florence told me to be careful about getting banana on the furniture, I told her, 'Someone has to give the baby good stuff to eat, and I should report her to the authorities.' She should have known I didn't really mean it." Sarah wiped the tears from her eyes.

I usually didn't interfere in Sarah's "business," but this time I made an exception. I called Meyer and explained to him his mother's tendency to blurt out anything that crossed her mind and how she really loved him, Florence, Michael and Samantha. She just came from a generation where parents stuffed their children with food, thinking that was the way to keep them healthy. I hoped that he and Florence could find a way to forgive Sarah and let her spend more time with the baby. I was sure Sarah would apologize for what she had said.

"Me apologize? Never," Sarah said.

"Do you want to spend time with your grandchildren?" I asked.

She thought, bit her lower lip and said, "Okay."

A compromise was reached. Sarah watched Michael and Samantha on Fridays, while Florence brought them to a woman in her building on Mondays and Wednesdays.

Occasionally, when Meyer and Florence went to a movie or restaurant on a weekend, Sarah and I would go over to their place and babysit for their children. That was a lot of fun! Even though I was a prejudiced grandparent, I found them both extremely good natured and intelligent. Sarah would play with the baby, while I worked on teaching Michael his letters.

"Read me a story," he would insist, before agreeing to go to bed. I picked a book out of his collection called "And to Think I Saw It on Mulberry Street" by Dr. Seuss, mainly because I thought it was about the Lower East Side. The story was about Marco, who uses his imagination to make up a story to tell his father about what he saw on his way to and from school, when all he actually saw was a horse and cart. If Mulberry Street had been the one in the New York, Marco wouldn't have had to make up anything. I remembered it as one of the most crowded and interesting streets in lower Manhattan.

Michael and Samantha loved Dr. Seuss books, and I would often buy them one for their birthdays.

275

1949 was a depressing year for America. Communists took control of China and its population of over a half a billion. In addition, America lost its position as the sole nuclear power when the Soviet Union tested its atomic bomb. We were amazed. How could the Soviets, devastated by the war, progress on a bomb so quickly? It didn't take long to find out that they had had some help along the way, and much to our chagrin, the help was Jewish. Ethel and Julius Rosenberg, along with Ethel's brother, David Greenglass, were among those who had helped provide information about the American nuclear weapon program to the Soviets. In '51 the Rosenbergs were tried for espionage, and in '53 they were executed.

America was involved in two wars in the '50s. The one we read about in the newspapers was in Korea. It was a remnant of the Second World War. When the Japanese were defeated, Russia occupied the northern part of the Korean peninsula and the U. S. the southern part. The communist government Russia set up in the north invaded the south in June '50. Unlike what had happened in Eastern Europe, America felt it had to put up a stand. Once again, American boys were taken from their families and sent far away to fight for something they hardly understood. They were doing pretty well until Communist China decided to get involved, and then it got real messy. After about 40,000 Americans and a few million Koreans were killed, everyone agreed to go back to their respective sides of the 38th parallel— exactly where they had been before the war had started.

The war you didn't read much about in the newspapers was in Puerto Rico. More than half the workers at Henkel's had recently migrated from that island. They had arrived in New York just in time, since after World War II, most of the Irish and Italian women who had previously worked in the city's garment industry, were reluctant to take up their old jobs, after receiving much higher wages in defense industries during the war.

The Puerto Ricans were very industrious workers, although many of them couldn't speak English. Since I knew only a few words of Spanish, Manny would relay my instructions to the operators. At the end of October 1950, the radio that usually played music in our factory was tuned to a

Spanish-speaking news station, and during lunch hour the Puerto Rican workers all huddled around it.

"What's going on?" I asked Manny.

"There's an uprising on the Island, led by the Nationalists."

"Who are they?"

"One of a few parties that wants complete independence from the United States."

"Why do they want that?" I ventured. "Right now they have American citizenship and don't have to pay any taxes."

"That may be, but it's very expensive to live there and there are few jobs. They get drafted, but don't have any representation in Congress. And worst of all, there isn't free speech. You can be arrested for just waving a Puerto Rican flag."

In the *Times* I read the claim by the governor of the Island that there was only a small number of Nationalists. But if that was the case, how could they take over so many towns and attack so many police stations? At first we were told that only the Island police and National Guard were involved in the fighting, but later we learned that the U.S. Air Force had attacked several buildings where the Nationalists were held up.

"Look, I don't agree with those crazies," Manny told me. "But they have some good points."

A few days later, the uprising came to the mainland. Three Nationalists, having heard the uprising on the Island had failed, walked up to Blair House, where President Truman was residing during repairs to the White House. Two of them were killed during a shootout. Hearing the shots, Truman opened a window and looked out. At that point he was only 30 feet from one of the would-be assassins.

On a beautiful Sunday in August of '52, Sarah and I went with Esther and Milty to Jones Beach in Milty's van. Sarah and Esther squeezed in the front with Milty, while I sat on a bench in the back that usually accommodated two or three Puerto Rican painters. Extra windows had been cut in the back for ventilation, so I had a good view on the trip. We took the Belt Parkway, which went along the shore close to Idlewild Airport. As we passed the airport, a plane was taking off. I couldn't imagine how something that heavy could get up in the air.

The traffic moved at a reasonable speed on the Belt and Southern State Parkways, but after we turned south towards Jones Beach on the Meadowbrook, it was one big traffic jam. Robert Moses, New York's construction czar, had been putting up parkways right and left, but he couldn't keep up with the increase in automobiles. He had even begun construction on an expressway crossing the Bronx that would link Long Island to New Jersey via the George Washington Bridge.

Jones Beach had a huge parking lot. We paid our dollar and then lugged our cooler, blankets, chairs and beach umbrella about a quarter mile to the sand, where we set up our own encampment, only a few feet from the next blanket on the crowded beach.

Sarah took a look at the waves and said to Esther and Milty, "You go in the water first. We'll watch the stuff."

When they ran towards the water, she said to me, "It looks rough today, I'm not sure I want to go in."

"The waves are a lot bigger here than they are at Orchard Beach," I agreed. "But we'll stay close to the shore."

Jones Beach faced the Atlantic, so its waves were much stronger than at Orchard Beach in the Bronx, which Robert Moses had created on a landfill at the western end of Long Island Sound. Sarah and I had been there several times. We had also gone to Coney Island Beach in Brooklyn once with Esther and Milty. Howver, that was so crowded that you could hardly find a place to stand, and putting down a blanket was impossible. By comparison, Jones Beach was practically empty.

Next to us a three-year old girl wearing a floppy hat and a pink bathing suit was using a shovel to pile up sand.

Sarah smiled at her and said, "Are you making a castle?"

"I'm making a cake."

"Is it a chocolate cake?" Sarah asked.

"It's vanilla. Don't you see it's white."

Sarah laughed and said to me, "I'd like a granddaughter like that."

"The water's great," Esther said, grabbing a towel after running up from the water. You should try it before we eat, so you don't get cramps."

278

"Where's Milty?" I asked.

"He's way out there. He's a great swimmer."

Sarah and I got up and snaked our way between blankets, down to the water, where the waves appeared even more formidable. However, a little way down the beach a thick rope had been strung out to a buoy, giving poor or non-swimmers, like Sarah and myself, some confidence in the water.

Sarah and I stayed near the rope and walked out to where the water was about waist high. That was where the waves were breaking, and after being pummeled by them a few times, we ventured a little further out. But not every wave is the same. One, somewhat higher than its siblings, broke just where we were standing. It crashed down and threw us both under the water. I quickly got up. Where was Sarah? Ten seconds and no sign of her. A foot kicked above the water and moved away from the beach. Sarah must be in an undertow.

Walking would have been too slow. I wasn't much of a swimmer, but I was propelled by my panic. I splashed to Sarah in just a few seconds, grabbed hold of her foot and pulled her to me. She had swallowed some water and coughed in my arms while I bobbed my way back to shallower water.

"I thought I was going to die."

"I wouldn't let you die," I said. I didn't let her know how terrified I had been. What would happen to me if I lost her?

When we got back to our blanket, Milty had returned and Esther was spreading out our lunch. There was baked chicken, potato salad and sodas. "I almost drowned," Sarah said.

Esther put her arm around her mother. "Are you okay now?"

"I guess so."

Milty was busy helping himself to food. "I put a special treat into the cooler," he said. He reached in and pulled out a bottle of champagne. "We have an announcement."

"I knew it. I knew it," Sarah cried out. "You're pregnant. When did you find out?"

"I missed my period a couple of weeks ago, but the doctor only verified it on Thursday."

279

Sarah was deliriously happy the rest of our time on the beach. She forgot about almost drowning and the sunburn that was starting to hurt her by the time we got back to the car.

The traffic on the return trip was almost as bad as it had been getting to the beach. I sat in the back for the trip, and when we arrived in Brooklyn, I noticed Sarah was more subdued. "Is it your sunburn?" I asked her.

"No, Esther said they're going to look for a house on Long Island. I'm afraid I'll hardly ever get a chance to see the baby."

Esther and Milty bought a house in Levittown, Long Island, a community planned for GIs returning from the war. The houses originally sold for $8,000, but by the beginning of '53, resales were going for $10,000. "The original owners put in some improvements," Esther informed me, when we lent them $500 for their down payment.

Getting out to see the house was quite a *schlep*. It made me half-seriously consider learning to drive and buying a car. First we took two subways to get to Penn Station at 34th Street, where we purchased Long Island Railroad tickets to Hicksville and telephoned Milty to tell him what train we would be on.

"What's a 'hick'," Sarah asked me, during our half-hour wait for the train.

"It's like a greenhorn, but from an American farm, not from a foreign country."

"I'm surprised they'd name a town that."

It being Saturday, the train was fairly empty, and we had a good view out the window. "Is this the train that had that horrible crash?" Sarah asked me.

I remembered reading two years earlier about a train plowing into the rear of one that was stalled on the track. Seventy-nine commuters had been killed and scores more badly injured. It had been the deadliest passenger train accident in America.

"I think it was. But that was at night. I don't think it could happen during the day."

"We'd better come back before it gets dark," Sarah said.

With her mind at rest, Sarah enjoyed looking at the farms in Nassau County, so different from the apartment buildings that stretched to the horizon in the Bronx. I remembered that only fifty years earlier, the Bronx also had its share of farms.

Milty was waiting for us alongside the Hicksville station in his new Buick. "I don't have the truck anymore. My brother uses it to bring workmen from Brooklyn."

"I'll give you a quick tour of Levittown on the way to our house," he said. He wound his way around curving streets lined with small houses, each appearing to be slight variations of three basic models. "They leave some room on the side—for expansion." He pointed to one that had added a garage topped with some living space.

"There's the pool," he told us. "It's closed now for the winter...and here's our house. It's the Cape Cod model."

As soon as she heard us pull into the driveway, Esther came waddling out of the house and hugged us both. She looked very pregnant, although Sarah had told me she had two more months until her due date.

The Cape Cod style seemed pretty basic to me, two floors with a steeply sloped roof from which two windows projected out. It seemed large from the outside, but from the inside, it had about the space of a two-bedroom, one bathroom New York apartment. There were stairs up to the second floor, but that space hadn't been "finished." It had rough wooden floors and walls had not been installed over the insulation. "We'll fix this up, as our family grows," Milty told us.

"Most of our neighbors are our age," Esther told us over the pot roast dinner she had prepared. "I have loads of friends."

"And there aren't any Blacks," Milty added. "You're not even allowed to sell your house to one of them."

I was surprised. I knew things like that went on in the South, but I didn't think it happened in New York. "It sounds like back in the Ukraine, where Jews weren't allowed to live in certain areas."

"Oh, it's not the same thing, Daddy," Esther said.

I wasn't sure why.

Sarah expressed her concern about being on the train after dark, so Milty drove us to the station, to get the 5 PM train back to the city.

281

Two months later, Sarah was able to retrace our steps, when she stayed with Esther for a week after her baby, a girl they named Doris, was born. It was the first time Sarah and I had been apart since she went to the hospital to give birth to Esther in 1921. I found it very lonely sleeping by myself. Several times I rolled over and put my arm around the empty space where she usually slept.

For every misfortune there's someone waiting to take advantage of it. In the case of Russia getting the atomic bomb, it was Joseph McCarthy, a Republican Senator from Wisconsin. Taking advantage of American's fear of the expanding Soviet Union, in '50 he had announced, during a talk to a women's group, that he had a list of 205 Communists who were employed at the U. S. State Department. Even a Senate committee discrediting these accusations didn't stop McCarthy from becoming more powerful. He accused other members of the Truman administration of being Communists, including George Marshall, the Secretary of Defense, who had previously been Secretary of State and Army Chief of Staff.

In '52 the Republican candidate for president was Dwight D. Eisenhower, who had been in charge of the Allied forces in Europe during World War II. The Democrats chose Adlai Stevenson, although it seemed as though he had to be dragged into accepting their nomination.

Sarah and I were on opposite sides in this election.

"Can't you remember what happened under Hoover, the last Republican president?" she asked me.

"But Eisenhower isn't a real Republican. The Democrats almost chose him to run in '48. He's for getting us out of Korea. That's why I'm voting for him. Anyway, Stevenson doesn't seem like he wants the job."

The press called Stevenson "an egghead," for being overly intellectual and for his receding forehead. However, Eisenhower's hair had also made a strategic retreat, and looking in the mirror, so had mine.

When Eisenhower was elected in a landslide, I hoped for some relief from the anti-Communist hysteria. However, McCarthy was also reelected in '52 and was made the head of the Senate Permanent Committee on Investigations. With his assistant on the Committee, Roy Cohn, a Jew, I'm sorry to say, McCarthy attacked various American institutions, such as the

282

Voice of America and the State Department. As a result of Cohn touring the libraries of the American Information Agency in Europe, the State Department ordered them to remove all books by authors who sympathized with communism. Some of the libraries actually burned the books, reminding me of what had been done by the Nazis. We were all waiting for Eisenhower to speak up against McCarthy, but the only thing he ever said was, "Don't join the book burners. Don't be afraid to go in your library and read every book."

McCarthy wasn't the only lawmaker to make his reputation by ferreting out Communists in American society. As early as '47, the House Committee on Un-American Activities had conducted an investigation into Communist influence in movies, radio and television. This led to setting up an informal "blacklist," whereby many performers and directors could no longer be employed in those industries.

For our fortieth wedding anniversary in 1952, Sarah and I splurged to see the musical South Pacific. It was about WAVES serving as nurses on an island in the South Pacific, and starred Mary Martin and Ezio Pinza. Wow, could they sing! We came away from the performance with tears in our eyes when we realized it was about the Guadalcanal battle in which Harry was killed.

For that anniversary, Meyer and Esther chipped in to get us our first TV set. It was a GE tabletop model. Now Sarah could see her beloved Molly Goldberg twice a week on TV. The show had missed the '51 season because Phillip Loeb, who played Molly's husband, Jake, had been put on the blacklist. Gertrude Berg had initially refused to accept a replacement, but finally was forced to accept Harold Stone as a substitute. Sarah had previously watched the program on the set of a neighbor, Estelle Bernstein.

"He just doesn't seem like Jake to me," she remarked about Stone.

A few years later, Loeb, his career destroyed, committed suicide.

As usual, in '52 we went over to Ben and Betsy's for Christmas dinner. Ben wasn't his customary cheerful self when he showed me a letter. It was signed by Robert Moses and informed Ben his building had been condemned for construction of the Cross Bronx Expressway. Ben had ninety days to vacate the premises.

"How can they do this?" Ben asked.

"Moses is pretty powerful," I said. "I don't think anyone has successfully resisted him."

"A joke going around," Ben said, "is that Moses thinks he's God, but he's only Moses."

"I'm not sure that's true," I said.

"He thinks the automobile is the future of the city, " Sarah offered. "Everyone will live in the suburbs, have a car and be able to get to work in no time at all."

"I don't know about that," Betsy said. "Have you seen some of the tie-ups on the expressways."

I remembered our trip to Jones Beach. "Yes, I have."

"The expressway is going to pass right across the street from the bakery," Ben informed us. "They've already started knocking down buildings. Business is down and it's pretty hard to keep the dust off the food."

"What are you going to do?" I asked Ben.

"I guess we'll join the 1500 other displaced families and look for a rent-controlled apartment. I doubt whether I'll be able to find one within walking distance of the bakery."

Although some families followed Moses's directive and moved out of the East Tremont neighborhood, Ben was encouraged by reports that Moses did not yet have title to the land for his proposed route for the Expressway. Lillian Edelstein, a housewife in the neighborhood, organized the East Tremont Neighborhood Association, which recruited lawyers and engineers to thwart Moses's land grab.

"They've found a different route for the Expressway," Ben informed me when I stopped by the bakery a few months later and viewed the huge ditch being dug across the street. "If they move the Expressway two blocks south, it can run along North Crotona Parkway. That way they'll only have to knock down two buildings instead of 54. I hear that Lillian has support for the new route from James Lyons, Bronx Borough Chairman."

Ben was an optimist, but trying to get Robert Moses to change his plans was like butting your head against one of the massive walls of the Expressway. By the end of '53, Moses had all the politicians lined up on his side, and his route was approved. Soon after, Ben moved to a tenement in the East Bronx.

I think it was the rats pouring out of the construction site that was the final straw for Ben. That, and the loss of Jewish families from the area led him to close Polinski's Bakery, which had been in business for more than fifty years. He found work in a bakery nearer to his new apartment.

As an example of how far the anticommunist hysteria inspired by McCarthy went, in '53 two young men came through the door of Henkel's Belts. Their suits and ties were not what I usually saw on the scruffy types in the garment district, and they certainly didn't look Jewish. I wondered what they wanted.

"We'd like to speak to Abe Sokolovsky," the tall blond one said.

"That's me."

He flipped open his wallet to show me a badge and said. "Agent Peter Thomas—F. B. I. This is Agent Charles Fallow." The other guy just nodded. "Is there some place private we can talk?"

I felt a chill go down my spine. Maybe it was because, after centuries of being persecuted by the authorities, Jews have inherited an instinctive dread of being questioned by them.

"There's a storeroom in the back."

"That'll be okay."

We walked to the back of the factory. When he saw there was only one chair in the storeroom, Agent Thomas brought a second one in. "Have a seat," he said. I sat down. He closed the door—not a good sign—before sitting on a table adjacent to my chair. He towered over me. Agent Fallow moved the second chair to a corner, where he sat down and pulled out a note pad. He never said a word, but I could hear his pen scratching all my answers on the pad.

"What's this about?" I asked.

"We'll ask the questions." He extracted a photograph from his pocket. "Do you know this man?"

285

I looked carefully at the photograph, which was what is called a "mug shot," taken when someone is arrested. The man in the picture seemed to have blood on his forehead that had streamed out of his grey hair, which wasn't reassuring.

"It looks like Dovid."

"Is it Dovid or David?"

"I know him as Dovid; that's Yiddish for David."

"Dovid who?"

"I'm not sure of his last name," I said. "I think it's Fenkel."

"And how often do you get together with Dovid Fenkel?"

I thought. "I haven't seen him in twenty years."

"Twenty years!" the giant boomed. "It was much less than twenty years ago when you left a message at Communist Party headquarters for Fenkel to contact you. What did you want to tell him?"

The giant was playing cat and mouse with me. I was sweating and not enjoying it at all. *When had I tried to contact Dovid?* Then I remembered. "Dovid was my landsman…from the same Jewish village in the Ukraine as me. I just wanted to find out if any of my family had survived the war. I thought…with his Communist connections, he might be able to find out something."

"Hmm," the giant said. "Who was with Fenkel the last time you saw him?"

"It was in Crotona Park. Dovid was handing out leaflets while some Communist, I don't who, was talking."

"And this woman, have you ever met her?" He pulled another photo out of his pocket. It was of an attractive woman, somewhat younger than Sarah.

I looked over the photo. "I don't think so."

The questions went on for almost hour: Did I know any other Communists? Was I member of the Communist Party? Was I a member of any of thirty other organizations on a list he gave me. Then he asked me the same questions about Dovid all over again. I told him I was a loyal American, who lost a son in the war. I wanted to, but I didn't, ask him whether he had been in the service.

Finally with, "Thank you for your cooperation," and, "If you hear from Fenkel or the woman, contact me," he left me his card, and he and the note-taker were on their way.

I was shaking. Did they really think that Communists had nothing better to do than to infiltrate the belt business? With the thin walls of the storeroom, I was sure all the workers had heard my interrogation. Sam would get the word in no time.

Sarah didn't take my run-in with the F.B.I. seriously. "Maybe you'll be called in front of McCarthy's committee and be on TV," she said.

Actually McCarthy was too busy to get to my case. In '54 his committee started an investigation of Communist influence in the Army. It didn't turn up anything. The Army retaliated by using the same committee to investigate the charge of undo influence having been exerted by McCarthy on behalf of David Shine, a member of his staff who had been drafted. These hearings were broadcast from start to finish on TV and were chaired by Senator Charles Mundt. Sarah, who blamed McCarthy for getting rid of her beloved Jake Goldberg, was glued to the set.

"That McCarthy is a regular Hitler," she told me. "But Welch, the Army's lawyer really got him today."

"How did he do that?"

"At one point Welch backed McCarthy into a corner, and he tried to get out of it by accusing a member of Welch's staff of being a Communist. Welch answered by asking, 'Don't you have any sense of decency, sir?' Everyone in the audience applauded."

As a result of the hearing, a large majority of the Senate voted to censure McCarthy. He lost his power, and his reign of terror was over.

Chapter 32

My God, the subway has changed since I last rode it six years ago. There was occasional graffiti then, but now every car is covered with it. There are lots of names in fluorescent paint, with outlines, and some funny pictures. The overall effect, if you're not used to it, is a bit scary. I'm glad to get out of there.

"Over here, Gramps," Susanna calls out from the window of the Buick that pulls up to the 179th Street Station of the E Train. "Just throw your suitcase in the back seat."

I put the suitcase in the back, next to a toddler in a pink jacket in a car seat, who seems excited to see me. "Gran...pop!" she says, waving her arms.

"Michael is sorry he couldn't meet you. He had to take Kevin to a birthday party. They should be home by now."

Susanna, in her mid-thirties, is as pretty as I remembered she had been at her wedding. Her face is framed in a short haircut, and, as best as I can tell, she hasn't put on any weight in the intervening six years. I guess that with their appliances and maids, women nowadays have more time to keep their selves looking good.

"How old are your children?"

"Kevin's five and Amanda back there is two." She turns into the driveway of a three-story brick house. It seems much too large for a family of four. "The guest room is on the third floor. I hope you don't have any trouble with stairs."

"No, that'll be fine." I lie a little.

"There's Michael; he must have heard us coming."

"Hey Gramps. Long time no see," Michael says, coming down the front steps, very unlawyerly in jeans and a flannel shirt. Except for a receding hairline, he looks very much like the college student that slept on my couch the summer after Meyer and Florence moved to Florida.

288

"Come meet Kevin," Michael says. "He'll be able to brag to his schoolmates about having a great grandfather in such wonderful shape."

Over dinner that evening, I tell Michael about my mission to find Ida.

"She just left...without saying goodbye, that's horrible," Michael says. "Contact Ida's son. If he won't tell you where she is, I'll threaten him with legal action."

Dwight Eisenhower's first term as president was from '52-'56. He got us out of the Korean War, and during both his terms, the country was reasonably prosperous. I would have voted for him again in '56, if he hadn't chosen Richard Nixon to be his running mate for the second time. Nixon had been on the House Un-American Activities Committee and had gone after Alger Hiss for Communist sympathies. Hiss had been convicted of perjury on what, to me, seemed like pretty flimsy evidence. Nixon reminded me of that FBI agent who tormented me about my non-existing relationship with Dovid Fenkel. Eisenhower was my age, so the possibility he wouldn't complete his term and Nixon would become president had to be considered. No way was I going to vote for that, so I joined Sarah and cast my vote for Stevenson. I guess Nixon didn't scare the rest of the country as much as he did me; Eisenhower was reelected by a landslide.

In '56, New York City decided not to continue collecting trash from businesses. It didn't take long for the Mafia to move into the vacuum. Two burly guys came to the factory door.

"Yes?" I asked them.

"Carloso Haulage," the shorter one said. He was my height, but twice my weight—all muscle. "We want to discuss your signing up for trash removal." He handed a business card to me. "I'm Jimmy Miloti." I took the large hand he offered. His handshake had just enough pressure to suggest he could easily break my hand if he pleased.

"Mr. Henkel upstairs takes care of that," I told him.

"Well then, take us upstairs and introduce us to Mr. Henkel," he said.

"I'm sorry, but I'm too busy now."

"You hear that, Gino," Jimmy said to the monster behind him who was cracking his fingers, "the man doesn't have any time for us."

I reconsidered. "Okay, I'll be right back."

I told Manny I was going upstairs and led the two guys up to Sam's office.

"What's up?" Sam asked as we came through the door.

"These gentlemen…," I started to say, but Jimmy interrupted me.

"Jimmy Miloti from Carloso Haulage, we'd like your trash business." I could see Sam was also impressed by his handshake. "Give me the contract, Gino."

Gino pulled some papers out of his jacket pocket. Sam put on his glasses and took a look at them.

"This is pretty expensive," he said.

"A premium price for a premium service," Jimmy bragged. "Some other companies don't charge so much, but they don't do such a good job. Sometimes fires break out in the trash."

"I'd like to think about it," Sam said.

"We'd like a decision right now," Jimmy said. He stood there and tapped his foot.

Sam stared at the contract on his desk for a few seconds, and then took his pen out of his pocket and signed it.

A few months later Sam asked me to come up to his office.

"Abe," he said, "as you know, it's getting harder and harder to make a living in the garment industry in New York. Rents are sky high and we have to pay almost double the wages they do in the South. That business with Carloso Haulage was the last straw. With Debra's health not being good, I figure we'd be happier in Florida than in New York. I'm planning to close down Henkel's."

I gulped. "Close down? Henkel's Dresses…and Belts?"

"Dresses, yes. Belts? That will be up to you. We can sell all the machinery and furniture. I don't know what they will bring—maybe $5000. It's all yours. Or if you'd like, you can try to make a go of it on your own. I'll turn Henkel's Belts over to you."

I thought. That was a pretty big decision. I'd better not make it on my own. "I'll talk it over with Sarah and get back to you."

"Five thousand is a lot of money," Sarah said.

"We won't be rich. Do you think we can make it on our savings and what I'll be getting in Social Security?"

"We'll survive," she said.

"I'd try to keep it going, but with losing the 80% of our business that comes from upstairs, I don't think I'd be able to pay the rent."

"Do you think you could pick up some new accounts?"

"Maybe—but it would take a while."

"It sounds too risky."

So it was decided: Henkel's Belts would shut down with the dress company at the end of the year. I called around and got Manny a job comparable to what he had with Henkel's. But my real question was: *What would I do?* I was 72 years old. Except for a few emergencies, I'd gone to work five days a week for the last 35 years, and six days a week before that. Sitting home with Sarah all day would drive us both crazy. Walking aimlessly around the city every day also didn't appeal to me.

I had an idea. I had a few outside customers. Probably I could negotiate with another belt company to service them. I could go downtown almost every day, pick up and deliver orders and get a small commission. I'd be a salesman. That didn't seem too bad to me.

Mercury Belt Company, up in the garment section on 8th Avenue and 38th Street had been a competitor to Henkel's. Their name signified that they could provide fast delivery. Of course, so could Henkel's when it was required. I'd never heard anyone complain of Mercury's product, and I'd met the owner, Nat Brownstein, several times over the years. We worked out an arrangement: I'd get ten percent of any business I brought in, but would be responsible for picking up the orders and keeping the customers happy with gifts during the year. I wasn't going to make a lot of money, but I'd more than cover my subway fares and lunches. Fortunately for me, Congress, two years earlier, had eliminated any restrictions on earnings for those over 72 collecting social security.

Spending a couple of bucks on lunch was important. There was no better place to get a lead than sitting at the counter of a luncheonette in the midtown garment district. I became adept at striking up a conversation with the guy on the next stool, who occasionally worked at a dress or sportswear company. If he had any influence sending out belt orders, I might pick up the tab for his lunch. I acquired several new customers by that route.

After lunch, I often had little to do and plenty of time to continue my walks around Manhattan.

They put up a lot of new building in New York in the fifties, but in my opinion, most of them were tacky glass-and-steel structures, with no personality. Not at all like the Empire State or Chrysler Buildings. An exception to this was the United Nations Building on the East Side. Maybe it was because this simple "box" stood alone, or perhaps because we had such high hopes for the organization at that time.

One of the first things I did in retirement was to have my hernia repaired surgically. It had occurred about five years earlier when I lifted a large roll of buckram.

"It won't be much of an operation," Doc Bernstein had told me then, but when he saw me hesitate, he had added, "If you'd prefer, you could get a truss."

"What's that?"

"It's a strap you wear, that pushes the wall of your intestinal cavity back where it belongs. Not too comfortable, especially in the summer."

I was so panicked about an operation that I convinced myself I was too busy to take time off for the procedure. But now, after five years of discomfort, I no longer had an excuse. The Bernstein-recommended surgeon performed the operation up at the new Jacobi Medical Center on Pelham Parkway.

"That didn't take very long," Sarah said at my bedside, when I awoke from the anesthesia. It was true: a one-hour operation, one night in the hospital, a week resting up at home, and I was "fixed." I could have kicked myself for not doing it sooner.

The cold war with the Soviets continued during Eisenhower's terms, and in '57 it took on a new dimension with the launch of the first Sputnik by the Russians. On the TV we could hear the distinctive beeps the satellite made as it passed overhead. Some of the neighbors claimed that, on the roof at night, using binoculars, they could see the two-foot diameter sphere as it passed overhead. I had my doubts.

"Does Sputnik worry you?" I asked Sarah.

"That little ball in the sky—why should it worry me?"

"The Russians could watch everything we do."

"What's to watch? I clean the house. I go shopping. They want to know about that, they can send around someone to help with the bundles."

"Well, we're going to spend millions to match them with our own little ball in the sky. That'll probably raise our taxes."

"That's scary," she admitted.

The Republicans nominated Nixon to be their candidate in the '60 election. I'd never vote for him. The Democrats chose John F. Kennedy, an inspiring speaker and war hero. Kennedy was only 43 and had serious back problems, which we only learned about later. The campaign featured the first televised presidential candidate debates.

"What's wrong with Nixon?" Sarah asked me when we sat down to watch the first debate on TV.

"He looks pretty sickly," I opinioned. On black-and-white TV, Nixon looked pale. With his stubble, I would have shied away from him, if he approached me on a street corner.

The election of '60 was a squeaker; it was probably decided by Nixon's bad (or lack of) makeup in that first debate. But hey, I'll take my candidate winning for any reason. Now America had a young vigorous president-elect, with a spiffy wife, who I had to admit wasn't much of a speaker.

Shortly after the election, a bad cold went to my chest, and before I knew it, I had pneumonia. I don't know whether walking around in cold, wet weather had anything to do with it, but for the first time I began to contemplate moving away from New York to a warmer climate. I was 75, an

293

age when, a decade earlier, getting pneumonia had been greatly feared. But now penicillin and a number of other antibiotics were available, and pneumonia was less serious. Doc Bernstein came to our apartment, put his stethoscope to my chest and gave me an injection in my buttocks. The miracle drug didn't seem to help very much. For two days, I ran a fever of 103 and coughed my insides out. Then the fever subsided, but the cough went on for two more weeks. I strained a muscle in my chest, making each cough extremely painful. I think the tea with lemon and honey and chicken soup that Sarah made me helped more than the injection. She also put mustard plasters on my chest, which helped the cough, but left my skin red.

Gradually I improved, and after a week was able to walk around the apartment. However, I was still very weak, and Sarah wouldn't even consider allowing me to go out in the raw winter weather.

"But what about my customers?" I asked her.

"I called Nat and told him you wouldn't be coming in for a while," Sarah said, "He'll have another salesman service your accounts until you get back."

I wasn't too happy over that arrangement, since it meant I was a dispensable part of the loop. But Sarah wouldn't even consider letting me leave the apartment.

"Don't you want to go over to Meyer's and see your grandchildren," I asked her.

"No way. I know as soon as I leave, you'll be out in the street. I don't want to be a widow. I hardly know anyone in this building."

So I sat and watched TV with Sarah. Shows like: *I Love Lucy, The Price is Right* and *Truth or Consequences.* I have to admit to having a few good laughs, which at the beginning were horribly painful, but it didn't take long for me to decide that watching TV was a big waste of time. I hoped it would never become my major pastime.

Six weeks later, in March, the weather improved, and Sarah allowed me to venture outside. At first I could just make it over to one of the benches on Mosholu Parkway, where I would watch the cars go by and occasionally get in a conversation with a guy from the neighborhood. Most of these were *alta cockers*, who just talked about their physical ailments, which didn't hold my interest. However, on a windy afternoon, a tall, distinguished-looking man with a halting step approached my bench.

"Mind if I share your bench?" he asked.

"Not at all," I said.

"My name's Aaron Salkind."

"I'm Abe Sokolovsky."

"Let's see how they're messing up the world today." He took the *Times* out of his coat pocket and tried to unfold it. But the wind threatened to blow it away, so he gave up and said, "I guess the world can wait until I get back inside."

"I gave up I said," pointing to the *Times* in my pocket.

"What brings you out here watching the cars go by," Aaron asked.

"I'm recovering from pneumonia. Waiting to get my strength back so I can do some walking."

"I'm afraid that walking down here to watch the cars is about all I'm ever going to be able to do," he told me. "I had a heart attack about a year ago and it left me pretty weak."

"Sorry to hear that. I guess you don't work."

"I had to retire. Couldn't even handle a cushy job at a university."

Aaron told me about being a professor at NYU. Fortunately, his attack had occurred at the university and they were able to get him to the hospital right away. Even though we were from different strata of society, we hit it off well. I guess our mutual interest in the *Times* had something to do with that.

"Haven't I seen you at the synagogue," he asked me.

"I haven't been there since I got sick."

"Are you a member?"

"We were for a year, but I let the membership lapse a while ago. My wife and I found we hardly ever went. Now, we just pay to go to the High Holy Day services. Sometimes we go on *Shabbos*, if there's a *bar mitzvah* of someone we know."

"You should really rejoin," he said. "It's not expensive, if you don't have children in Hebrew School. We really need new members, so many of

295

the old ones are moving upstate or to Long Island. I should know: they made me the membership chairman." He chuckled.

"I'll consider it," I said.

I talked it over with Sarah.

"A professor," she said. "He was probably friendly just to get you to join. But..." she thought for a minute. "It could be a good idea. I'd probably meet more women in the neighborhood."

We did rejoin the Center, attending either Friday night or Saturday morning services about once a month. I enjoyed listening to the rabbi's sermon. Rabbi Schachter was a man of the world. I heard that the Nixon administration sometimes called on him for advice on Jewish matters. His talks dealt with important world issues, as well as religious ones.

I didn't make any new friends at the services, just acquaintances, with whom I'd exchange a *Good Shabbos* and a handshake after it was over. Sarah, however, did become friendly with a number of women up in the balcony and even took on some small responsibilities in the Sisterhood.

As my strength returned after my illness, I resumed my walks, at first only in the North Bronx. I'd always start out going down to Mosholu Parkway, and if I found Aaron sitting on a bench, we'd exchange a few words about the world situation.

When I finally got around to getting downtown, I found, that as I had feared, my job had pretty much disappeared. Mercury's regular salesman, Sid Shapiro, had gotten pretty tight with my customers. For a while, however, each quarter of the year, Nat would send me a small check, in recognition of my getting him the accounts.

Meanwhile, a large part of the Bronx had become too dangerous for walking. The biggest problem with the Cross Bronx Expressway was it had divided the Bronx into two separate communities. As the project drew close to completion, it became obvious that, in the eastern part of the Bronx, the neighborhoods south of the expressway were rapidly being transformed into slums populated by the poorest groups in New York: Blacks and Puerto Ricans.

These problems were exacerbated by Robert Moses's vision for those New Yorkers who couldn't escape to the suburbs. No longer would they live in the three or four story, tenement-like buildings that were predominant in various neighborhoods throughout the city. These would be replaced by "projects," groups of eight to fifteen floor buildings, built around playgrounds, benches and other amenities. Unfortunately, the families living in a neighborhood were usually not the ones that were allotted apartments in the project that was built there when the buildings were torn down. Puerto Ricans, had populated the tenements, and having only recently come to America, were generally at the bottom of the list for public housing. They were forced out on the street on their own. Since apartments were scarce, quite often they just moved in with relatives in the South Bronx. The area became overcrowded, teeming with children, who more often than not, were allowed to play unsupervised on the streets.

The warring gangs in these neighborhoods made the area very dangerous. It wasn't only a matter of getting mugged or beaten up; they would just as likely stick a knife in you.

Chapter 33

At first Ida's son won't tell me or Michael where she is. "She's recuperating from an operation and shouldn't be bothered," he says.

Michael tells him, "She should be able to make her own decision on whether she wants to see the man she's lived with for two years." When he threatens to get a court order, he finds out that Ida is at Beth Abraham rehab facility in the Bronx.

Michael and Susana have gone out of their way to treat me great. I haven't eaten this well since Sarah got sick. This morning, Susana told me she invited Esther and Milty over for dinner next Saturday. She probably doesn't know I haven't spoken to them in six years. Dinner conversation should be a little strained. I'm surprised they accepted the invitation.

Beth Abraham Hospital is near the Bronx Botanical Gardens. Michael thinks very highly of it. He said Oliver Sacks, a very famous doctor, is at the hospital.

Kennedy's presidency didn't start out well. He was like a sub, who comes into a basketball game and immediately throws the ball away a couple of times.

In '58, Fidel Castro overthrew a corrupt regime on the island of Cuba, just 90 miles from Florida. By '60, Castro had confiscated much of the private property on the island, including a lot belonging to Americans. He shut down the independent newspapers and mafia-run gambling casinos. Thousands of the islanders were imprisoned and large numbers left the island and settled in the Miami area.

In April '61, less than three months after Kennedy was inaugurated, I read in the *Times* a force of Cuban exiles had landed at Bay of Pigs not far from Santiago in southeastern Cuba. I put down my morning cup of coffee and said to Sarah, "Uh, oh, a bunch of guys have invaded Cuba. It looks like we're sticking our nose in where it doesn't belong."

"Is that going to affect us?" she asked.

"I'm not sure."

298

The United Nations debated Cuba's claim the invasion was directed by the United States, and we bombed airfields on the island. We claimed defectors from the Cuban Air Force did the bombing, and we were not involved in the invasion in any way.

"It has nothing to do with us," Ben said, when I spoke to him on the phone.

"I'm suspicious," I answered. "I can't imagine some Cubans down in Miami deciding to invade their country without help. I think the CIA has something to do with it."

The invasion was spectacularly unsuccessful. It never received any support from the people on the island. For three days, Castro's forces pounded the invaders, until those who hadn't been killed, surrendered.

I had been right. We soon learned the CIA had trained the force and planned the invasion during the last year of Eisenhower's presidency. Kennedy stupidly agreed to allow the invasion to proceed.

Those members of the invading force who weren't executed by the Cuban government were ransomed and sent back to the U. S. in '62. We were told the fifty million dollars for the ransom was raised from private donations. Fat chance! The whole incident was a tremendous failure for the CIA and for the new Kennedy administration.

Even worse, the Cubans took the invasion as a threat to their independence and invited the USSR to install nuclear missiles on the island. By September '62, the Soviets had built missile installations on the island, and a ship was on the way to Cuba with the missiles. New York City would certainly be a top target. It was only ninety miles between Cuba and Florida. I remembered the newsreels showing the devastation of Hiroshima. Americans wouldn't have much time to get to a place of safety, if in fact there was such a place. I was envious of families in the suburbs who were digging their own underground bunkers.

"Now you see what that invasion had to do with us," I said to Sarah.

"What can we do?" Sarah asked me.

"Nothing, but pray."

We later heard that Kennedy had considered a full-scale invasion of Cuba, before the ship delivered the missiles. However, he settled for a naval embargo of the island. There were some tense days until the Russian ship turned around, and then everyone let out a sigh of relief. We proved we could intimidate the Russians, but the incident may have been the closest the world ever came to all-out nuclear war.

As "part of the deal" Kennedy agreed never to invade Cuba. It seems like both sides gained something from the experience, but it was too close for comfort.

The second time Kennedy threw the ball away was when he increased our involvement in Vietnam. Robert McNamara, Kennedy's Secretary of Defense, believed in something called the Domino Theory: if South Vietnam fell, other governments in Southeast Asia would topple. He proposed sending a huge American force to defeat the Vietcong and save the Indochina peninsula for Democracy. McNamara was supposed to be some sort of genius, but to me, that seemed like a very stupid idea. Perhaps Kennedy would have been better served by a Defense Secretary who had fought in the front lines in a war...or lost a son in one, like I had.

Kennedy didn't take McNamara's suggestion, but he did allow a ten-fold increase in the number of American "advisors" in Vietnam. Before long, they were training and transporting Vietnamese troops, as well as providing logistics and intelligence. By '63 several hundred American families had lost sons in the war.

"I hope Kennedy doesn't get us any deeper into Vietnam," I said to Meyer.

"We can't just let the Commies take over wherever they want," he said.

"I don't see how you can say that with Michael just turning 21."

"He'll never end up in the army; he's going to law school when he graduates."

"I mean: with a son of draft age and having lost your brother in a war, I'd think you'd have some feeling for all the minority families who will lose sons over there." It was one of the few times I gave Meyer a piece of my mind.   He could have used some parental feedback, other than Sarah's idolization, earlier in his life.

Since my major criterion for the success of a president was how successful he was in keeping us out of war—with the Second World War, of course, being an exception—I wasn't a Kennedy fan. Maybe he would have learned with experience, but he wasn't given a chance.

On November 22, 1963, Sarah and I were sitting at the kitchen table, having soup for lunch, when we heard on the radio, "President Kennedy has been shot in a motorcade in Dallas." I held the hot spoon six inches from my mouth for about ten seconds before saying, "What was that?"

"My God!" Sarah moaned. "I never thought it could happen in America."

"It's not America.   It's Texas. They carry guns down there.   He should have never gone there."

Who could be behind this, I thought.   The Russians?   Cubans? Southern racists?   And what about the Secret Service?   Where were they? Weren't they supposed to jump in front of any bullets meant for the President?

"It could just be a flesh wound," I said. "Let's see what they say on television."

We let the soup go cold, while we sat on the couch, our eyes glued to the drama that was unfolding in front of us.   The streets of Dallas were pandemonium. The program switched between the ambulance pulling into the hospital and police officers running around outside and into buildings.

Before long, we heard that a bullet had hit Kennedy in the head— hardly a flesh wound. "It doesn't sound like he can go on being President," I said.

"His poor family," Sarah said. "And such a young wife."

And then the news: our President was dead.   Vice President Lyndon Johnson, who had been riding just two cars behind Kennedy and wasn't harmed, took the oath of office on Air Force One just two hours after the shots had rung out. I think thereafter, our government was more careful and avoided having the President and Vice President in the same place at the same time.

Meanwhile, the police arrested a guy who they said had fired the shot that killed Kennedy from a window of the Texas School Book Depository adjacent to the motorcade route. Was he just a lone nut, or was he part of some grand conspiracy? Two days later, our chances of finding out were greatly reduced, when a second nut shot and killed the first nut. Moreover, we learned the second nut had terminal cancer and wouldn't be around for questioning all that long.

The lone gunman explanation for the assassination was so improbable that everyone had his own conspiracy theory to explain it. Many of these sprung from individual prejudices. My theory was that the assassination was a plot by Southerners to put one of their own in the White House. Just like in the old country, some people attempted to pin it on the Jews, in particular Israelis, who were dissatisfied with JFK sucking up to Arabs.

One way that America tried to mitigate the shock of Kennedy's assassination was by naming things after him all over the country. In New York, Idlewild Airport, which had been changed to New York International in '48, was renamed John F. Kennedy International Airport.

You would think that the Kennedy assassination would have cast a pall over America that would have taken a while to dispel. But in '64, the huge generation of teenagers that had been born after the war took over American culture. Two groups from England, the Beatles and the Rolling Stones, invaded America. I didn't get to see the Stones, but after seeing on TV the near riot that occurred when the four mop-tops from Liverpool landed at JFK, Sarah and I decided we had to watch them on that week's Ed Sullivan show.

"Why are those girls screaming?" Sarah asked, when Sullivan introduced the Beatles. "They're cute…but not sexy like Elvis."

The camera panned across the audience. Each girl was jumping up and down with rapt attention on the four smiling musicians with long hair and skinny legs!

"I don't know," I offered. "They sure do something to girls. But I don't think they're something to be afraid of, like some people say."

It was true, I could see little similarity between the girls in the audience and my own daughter, who at their age was involved with schoolwork, helping around the house and making her own clothes. "Maybe young people nowadays just don't have enough to do," I said.

But young Americans were doing more with their free time than developing new tastes in music for the country. Some of them were Freedom Riders, who rode buses in the South to test the Supreme Court decision of 1960 desegregating facilities in interstate bus terminals. Others were developing the conscience of the country by going down to Mississippi and participating in a drive to register blacks to vote in the summer of '64. Members of these groups were often beaten or arrested. In late June, we were shocked to learn that Andrew Goodman and Mickey Schwerner, two young Jews from the New York area, and James Chaney, a black Mississippian, were missing after having been briefly detained in Meridian, Mississippi for a traffic violation.

At first, the FBI said the disappearances were a local matter, but after 36 hours of pressure from Attorney General Robert Kennedy, J. Edgar Hoover, Director of the FBI, finally agreed to start an investigation. All summer, agents tramped around in the swamps of Mississippi, and finally, in August, they found the bodies of the three civil-rights worker buried under an earthen dam.

"I told you the South was dangerous," I said to Sarah.

"Philadelphia isn't too safe," she said, referring to the race riots that had been prominent on television news the previous few days.

A few years later the sheriff who had stopped the boys for the traffic violation and six others were convicted for violating their civil rights. They had conspired to have the local Klan grab them when they were released. I think the sheriff got a six-year sentence, which to me didn't seem like much for three brutal murders.

When he was sworn in after Kennedy's assassination, LBJ had the opportunity to get us out of Vietnam, where a succession of military governments in the South couldn't get the loyalty of the army, no less than that of the citizens. Unfortunately, he didn't take it. Bit by bit we slipped

303

into deeper involvement in Vietnam. First it was shelling of patrol boats of the North, then bombing port facilities, then bombing military installation, then indiscriminate bombing. We needed the Air Force, then the Marines to protect the Air Force, then the Marines were in combat operation—defensive at first, but then offensive, which more suited their style. To support our expanded engagement, the draft was doubled in July '65 and extended to married men without children in October of that year.

The expanded draft didn't sit well with young people. Anti-war riots sprung up along the east and west coasts and in Michigan. At some of these, draft cards or representations of President Johnson were burned.

Irving Goldstein was a regular at Saturday morning services, and his son almost always sat next to him. When the son was missing one week, I asked Irving if he was all right.

"Don't tell anyone," but he ran off to Canada. "He got a low draft number and refuses to go off to the other side of the world to kill women and children."

I didn't tell anyone, but it looked like Irving was bragging about it, rather than keeping it a secret.

As someone who had left home to avoid the army, the draft resistors, dodgers and protestors had my sympathy. However, the young Quaker who doused himself with gasoline and burned to death outside Robert McNamara's office didn't have my sympathy—especially since he had a wife and child.

America's involvement in Vietnam created another problem: we didn't have the resources or energy to become involved elsewhere in the world. In May of '67 tensions between Israel and the Arab states of Egypt, Syria and Jordan accelerated, with Egypt finally expelling a United Nation peacekeeping force from the Sinai Peninsula. The population of these Arab countries was more than thirty times the number of Jews in Israel, and their armies had been fortified with Russian equipment. Gamal Nasser, the president of Egypt, dreamed of becoming the leader of the Arab world; what better way to achieve that than to destroy Israel? Without protection from America, would this be the end of the State of Israel, a Second Holocaust?

Jews felt a need to huddle together at this time. The Saturday morning service at Mosholu Jewish Center was as packed as it usually is only during the High Holy Days. We prayed for God to come to the assistance of his Chosen People. Afterwards we stood in groups in front of the shul.

"What do you think will happen?" I asked Aaron Salkind. "You were a professor."

"It's not exactly Russian literature," he said. "But when Estelle and I were in Israel last year, we were very impressed by their military preparedness. I think they'll be okay."

Aaron was right: they called it the Six-day War; it was more like the Six-hour War. Israel didn't wait until the Arab armies attacked. Its planes swept in from the Mediterranean and destroyed the Egyptian Air Force on the ground, quickly deciding the outcome of the conflict. Facing complete Israeli air superiority, Nasser tried to bring his army back across the Sinai, which ended up littered with the charred remains of his tanks and trucks and the bodies of his soldiers. The Jordanian and Syrian military were also overcome. In six days, Israel ended up taking the Sinai from Egypt, East Jerusalem and the West Bank from Jordan, and the Golan Heights from Syria. American Jews exhaled and puffed out their chests. It felt good to be a Jew.

Chapter 34

I'm really nervous about seeing Ida. What if, as her son said, she doesn't want to see me? That's why I didn't telephone before I came up here. I was afraid she'd tell me our two years together was just a diversion for her. That would be hard to take. I have to see her face-to-face.

I switch from the E train to the IRT #2 at 42nd Street. This train is elevated in the Bronx—one of the few El's left in the system. Too bad they phased them out; elevated trains are fun, although I remember it could get pretty cold waiting for the train in the middle of the winter. I can't wait for the train to come out into the open, so I can see a bit of my old neighborhood.

My God, the South Bronx looks horrible! So many buildings are burnt out. I see smoke rising from three different places. They're burning it down. I wonder who's doing it: the drug addicts who camp out in empty apartments or the landlords who want insurance money?

Things get better when we cross the Cross Bronx Expressway, and up here at Allerton Avenue, there's no sign of a war zone.

Beth Abraham is about four blocks from the station. No problem, but my knees don't like walking down the steps. That's been creeping up on me the last couple of years. Hey, I'm not complaining. I'm happy to get around as well as I do at my age.

And now we come to the saddest part of my story. On an August evening in '67, Sarah and I were watching the Ed Sullivan show on TV, when she called out, "Ow!"

"What's the matter?"

"A sharp pain right here." She pointed to her left cheek.

"Sounds like a tooth ache." Unlike me, Sarah still had almost all her teeth. "You should make an appointment to see Doc Brennerstein."

Brennerstein, our new dentist, had his office down the block, so Sarah went there by herself. "What did he say?" I asked when she returned that evening.

"He didn't see anything. Told me to come back on Friday when the X-rays are developed."

Sarah cried out in pain several times before her appointment, so I decided to accompany her to Brennerstein's office to see what the trouble was.

"The X-ray doesn't show anything, but sometimes there's decay in the root that doesn't show up. I suggest we just remove the tooth," Brennerstein said.

I looked at Sarah. "Anything that will take the pain away," she said.

Brennerstein removed her molar. It didn't help. The pain was occurring more often. The following week, Brennerstein pulled the next tooth. That also didn't help. The pains and the extractions were taking their toll on Sarah; by our next visit to his office she was looking decidedly washed out.

"I don't know what the problem is," Brennerstein admitted. "There's no sign of infection." And then, when Sarah wasn't looking, he whispered to me, "Maybe it's in her mind." He made a little circle at his temple with his finger.

I should have said something. I knew Sarah; she wasn't prone to psychosomatic illnesses. I didn't believe Brennerstein knew what he was doing. On a recommendation from Leah, we made an appointment to see an oral surgeon across the street from Beth Israel Hospital in lower Manhattan.

"You have some sort of nodule in your jaw," Dr. Karlson informed us.

"A nodule, what's that?" Sarah asked.

"A little bump. I don't know what it's from. I think one of the facial surgeons at the hospital should look at it."

So we made an appointment with Dr. Levy at Beth Israel Hospital for the following week.

"I think the biggest problem when you get sick is getting to see the right doctor," I said to Sarah.

"I hope we see the right one soon. This pain is beginning to wear me down."

Sarah was convinced Dr. Levy was the right doctor. He was about 40. "Young enough to be up with the latest techniques, but old enough to have a lot of experience," she said.

She put herself in the hands of this tall Jew in a white coat, with just a bit of grey in his hair. We became regulars in his office. First there was a needle biopsy. The Novocaine injections didn't keep Sarah from screaming while it was performed.

On the next visit, Dr. Levy said, "The biopsy indicates it's a carcinoma."

"What's that?" Sarah asked.

"A type of cancer. It should be removed as soon as possible."

Sarah turned white and didn't hesitate. "When can you do it?"

"Let me check my schedule."

When he left the room, Sarah looked at me with fear in her eyes. The unspoken possibility had been on both our minds, and now it had been uttered. I put my arm around her shoulders. I wished there was something more that I could do.

"I can do it two weeks from tomorrow—first thing in the morning," Levy said on his return. "I'll schedule you for two nights in the hospital. Medicare will cover just about everything."

I hadn't even thought about how we'd pay for the operation. Thank God Medicare had gone into effect two years earlier!

"You'll have a scar and an indentation," he said.

"So I'll never be a beauty queen." I was glad to see Sarah hadn't lost her sense of humor.

The next two weeks were hell for Sarah. Chewing any food became increasingly painful for her. Now that the pain had a name, she felt it more intensely.

The operation was scheduled for "first thing in the morning" on Friday, April 5, 1968. That meant that Sarah had to be at the hospital at 6 A.M. We probably could have taken a taxi at five, but I was worried it wouldn't show up at our door. For just a little more money, we were able to

308

take the subway down the night before and stay overnight in a hotel across the street from the hospital. Sarah's instructions said she could only have clear liquids for dinner and nothing after that, but she told me, "You don't have to fast. Go down to the restaurant and get yourself dinner."

I wouldn't think of leaving her, so I just ate the apple I had brought with me and we switched on the television, trying to get our minds off what was to come. That was no problem. Martin Luther King, the charismatic leader of the Civil Rights Movement, had been assassinated just a few hours earlier by an unknown white male.

"Oh, my God," Sarah said. "What is it with this crazy country?"

"I think it's all the guns people have."

We watched as Attorney General Bobby Kennedy, who was campaigning for president at the time, announced the assassination while standing in the back of a flatbed truck. Kennedy called for the crowd to strive for unity between blacks and whites and to respect King's call for nonviolence. Fat chance! By the time we turned off the television, it was after midnight, and riots had started in the nation's capital. Getting up at five for Sarah's operation wouldn't be easy. But we had no choice, so I set the alarm clock I had brought from home, and the one in the room, and told the front desk to call us.

In the morning, we checked out and left our small suitcase with the bellman. First Avenue was still dark when we entered the lobby of the hospital at 5:30. The receptionist directed us to the surgery department, where Sarah signed in.

"Here, you hold this," Sarah said to me, struggling to remove her rings from a finger wider than when we were married. "I've heard of people waking up and finding their jewelry missing."

I thought they'd have to amputate Sarah's finger to get her rings off, but with a little saliva and superhuman effort, she managed to remove them. "Put them in a safe place," she told me.

It didn't take long until they called Sarah. "It will be several hours before you can see her in the recovery room," the nurse said.

I gave Sarah a hug and a kiss and then headed for the hospital cafeteria, where I had a huge breakfast. I told myself I shouldn't feel guilty having such a good appetite, since I had missed dinner the previous night.

309

Then I went back to the surgery waiting room, where I paced the floor and thumbed through every magazine on their table. It was after noon when they called me in to see Sarah. A large bandage was taped to the left side of her face and she was very groggy. I held her hand, and she opened her eyes for a moment. After giving me a weak smile, she fell back into a deep sleep.

"She did just fine," Dr. Levy said when he came to look at Sarah. Then he whispered to me, "The tumor was more extensive than I thought. I think I removed it all."

Thinks he removed it all—that didn't reassure me at all.

About an hour later, a nurse woke Sarah and told her she was being moved. Two orderlies put her on a gurney and I followed them up an elevator and down hallways into a double room. The second bed in the room was empty.

I sat by Sarah's bed all afternoon while she slept, watching the liquid in the bag attached to her arm. About dinnertime she woke up moaning. "It hurts so bad," she whispered to me.

I called a nurse, who gave her a pill and a few sips of water through a straw. "Do you feel like eating anything?" she asked Sarah.

Sarah shook her head, "No, not yet."

"That pill will probably put her out for a while," the nurse told me. "You might want to go home and come back in the morning."

I wasn't ready to leave Sarah yet, but the odor of disinfectant in the hospital was starting to get to me, so I decided to get a little fresh air and then come back and see how she was doing.

Across the street from the hospital was Stuyvesant Town, a bunch of redbrick buildings, which was built right after World War II. I remembered that veterans were supposed to have first digs on the apartments, but Metropolitan Life, the owner, interpreted that as meaning only white veterans. I had read there had been some token integration, but the place was still overwhelming white. I would have enjoyed walking through the complex, but a gate surrounded it, so I walked around the periphery, gazing through the gate at its playgrounds and wooded pathways.

Throughout my walk, Dr. Levy's words kept going through my mind. *What if he hadn't gotten it all, and how much of her face did he have to remove?*

310

Back at the hospital, Sarah seemed to be in a deep sleep. "What time will she be up in the morning?" I asked the nurse.

"The doctors come in around around six and the patients have breakfast at about seven."

"I'll be back then," I told her, and then I left, picking up my suitcase at the hotel. By that time, I was so tired that, after transferring to the D train, the rocking of the subway car put me to sleep. Fortunately, my station was the last one on the line, and a kind woman woke shook my shoulder.

"Last stop," she said.

I jumped up and started off the train and then remembered my suitcase. But it wasn't there. Someone had taken it while I was sleeping. *Oh well, it was just some underwear and pajamas, not important compared to my other problems.*

At home I grabbed a sandwich before setting the alarm and hitting the bed. In two minutes, I was fast asleep.

The next morning I was back at Sarah's bedside at 6:30. "Where's my rings," she mumbled through her bandages as soon as she opened her eyes.

"I left them on the dresser at home. Has Dr. Levy been by yet?"

"Yes. He said I was looking great. I don't feel so great."

"Are you in much pain?"

"I'm horribly sore, but I don't have those sharp pains I had before. Did Dr. Levy say anything to you?" Sarah asked me.

I had decided against sugarcoating, so I told Sarah Dr. Levy's words.

"'I hope he got it all', that doesn't sound so good." she said.

When they brought Sarah her breakfast, I was able to feed her a few spoons of oatmeal through the right side of her mouth.

"Have you had any breakfast?" she asked me.

"No, I rushed out of the house."

"Why don't you finish mine? I'm really not hungry. Think I'm going to go back to sleep."

I ate Sarah's cold scrambled eggs, bacon and toast, and then dozed off in the chair next to her bed. Later that morning a nurse removed her catheter and the tube attached to her arm. She suggested I try to walk her to

311

the bathroom. "The more walking she does, the better," she said. She helped Sarah up and I held her arm while she shuffled to the bathroom.

"Was she able to urinate?" the nurse asked me a little later, and I told her Sarah had been successful.

At lunchtime, Sarah managed to eat her mash potatoes and her Jell-O. When she fell asleep, I went down to the cafeteria and had lunch.

In the afternoon, Sarah managed two more trips to the bathroom and one down the hall to the nurse's station. She was getting steadier on her feet. "Do you think she'll be leaving in the morning?" I asked the nurse.

"I think so, but the doctor will have to check her out."

I left right after Sarah's dinner that night, so I'd be sure of being back early enough to catch Levy the next morning.

It seemed like the middle of the night when I took the subway back to the hospital. At a little after six, Dr. Levy looked over Sarah and pronounced her fit to go home. "She should rinse her mouth with salt water four times a day. Change her bandage every night and dab her wound with hydrogen peroxide."

He told Sarah to make an appointment to see him in his office in two weeks. After I helped her dress, an orderly pushed Sarah to the front entrance of the hospital in her wheel chair and a taxi took us home. By the time we arrived, Sarah was exhausted and went right to sleep.

I was very busy the next two weeks. Besides shopping, cooking and cleaning, I had to help Sarah dress, bathe and go to the bathroom. We got quite a shock the first time we changed her bandage. Sarah's lovely oval face had become markedly unsymmetrical, with a large indentation on the left side. As Sarah had said, she'd "never be a beauty queen." However, she was still my Sarah, and I loved her. It wasn't long before I no longer noticed her "imperfection."

Even though she now had three children, Esther made several trips from Long Island to give me a hand taking care of Sarah. "You need help, Daddy," she told me. "Somebody to come in at least once a week for cleaning and maybe preparing a couple of meals." I asked around in the building, and one woman suggested Maria, from Puerto Rico. Even though her English was minimal, Maria was a hard worker, and in one day she would clean the house, help with Sarah and cook enough food for two or three meals, which she would wrap up in the refrigerator. Also, Florence would occasionally bring over a casserole, probably at the urging of Meyer, since she had remained "cool" to Sarah since their big fight. Maria's food was too spicy for Sarah's taste, and she was happy in the spring to take over cooking and reduce Maria to just cleaning, every other week.

Gradually Sarah's strength returned, and Dr. Levy declared she was coming along very well. One day Sarah took my arm and we walked to a bench on Mosholu Parkway at our corner. On the way back, a little boy looked at Sarah's face and slinked behind his mother. Sarah noticed his gesture and said, "I think from now on I'll get my fresh air by sitting at the window." That was the last time she went out for a walk.

Whatever optimistic things Dr. Levy said, to me, it seemed like Sarah didn't have much of an appetite, and like all Jews, I took that as good evidence something was still wrong with her. Turns out, my diagnosis was better than his. It was May of '68, almost a year after the first pain in her face that Sarah discovered the lump in her breast. I telephoned Dr. Levy, who referred us to Dr. Carter, who was also at Beth Israel.

We had to wait almost a month to see Dr. Carter, and by the time Sarah got out of the taxi at the hospital for her appointment, she was so weak that she didn't reject the wheelchair offered by the doorman.

"She doesn't look good to me," Dr. Carter said. "I'd like to keep her overnight in the hospital for some tests. We should have the results by tomorrow afternoon."

For months, I had been so busy taking care of Sarah that I hadn't had a chance to assess her condition. Dr. Carter's words hit me. What Sarah needed now was a miracle, and I didn't think that many miracles were given out to those over eighty.

The next day, I brought fresh clothes to the hospital and sat by Sarah's side while we waited for Dr. Carter to make his rounds. He came in the room carrying several large X-rays. "The news is not good," he said, putting one X-ray up against the light. "There are malignancies in both breasts." He pointed to several dark areas on the film. "That's where the cancer probably started. But more serious, it's spread to the liver." He

313

changed films, and pointed out additional dark regions. "There's nothing I can do for you," he said to Sarah, whose hand covered her mouth in horror. Then Dr. Carter turned and left the room.

I held Sarah, while she sobbed uncontrollably on my shoulder.

I hated Dr. Carter then. *How could he deliver such horrible news to Sarah, and not show any compassion?* However, over time, I began to pity him. He must have to deliver news like that several times a day—sometimes even to women in the prime of their lives. His job had probably robbed him of his humanity.

In the taxi on the way home, something else Dr. Carter had said, came into my mind. "That's where the cancer probably started," he had said about the dark areas in Sarah's breasts. Did that mean that all the medical attention that had been directed towards Sarah's jaw had been futile? It seemed that in medicine, getting to the right doctor early enough was crucial.

Now there was no hope. While she still had some strength, Sarah alternated between depression and rage. When Meyer's daughter, Samantha, now a student at New York University, came to visit, bearing a bouquet, Sarah threw the flowers on the floor. "What use do I have of flowers," she said before bursting into tears. Samantha, one of Sarah's favorite grandchildren, was studying to be a psychologist and knew just what to do. She held Sarah while she cried, knowing how ashamed Sarah was for what she had just done.

However, Sarah didn't completely lose her sense of humor. Seeing her image in the mirror when I was helping her to the bathroom, she said, "Look, I've always wanted to lose weight, and now I've succeeded."

As Sarah's condition worsened, it became apparent that taking care of her in the apartment, even with Maria's help, was becoming too much for me. "You'll either need a full-time aid in the apartment or have to send her to a nursing home," Esther advised, when she, Milty and their two youngest children visited on a Sunday afternoon.

"Aren't both of those pretty expensive?" I asked. "I don't think Medicare pays for them, and it wouldn't take long to use up all our savings."

"There's an alternative," Milty said. "Medicaid."

314

"Medicaid, that's for poor people—we wouldn't qualify for Medicaid until we used up almost all our own money."

"I've heard of people with a lot of money giving it away so they could get on Medicaid. And then later they get the money back."

"Is that legal?"

"Who would know?"

"What sort of nursing homes takes Medicaid?" I asked.

"Some pretty good ones," Esther said. "In fact, most nursing homes have both paying and Medicaid patients. Many of the Medicaid ones started out paying, then got on Medicaid after all their money was used up."

So I turned $10,000 over to Milty, leaving me with about $3,000. The woman at the Medicaid office said I could keep $2,000 of that for my own rent and food, while the other $1,000 would be used for the first monthly nursing home payment. Then Medicaid would take over. With her help I found a facility in Riverdale, about three miles from our apartment. On a lovely day in October, an ambulance arrived to transport the now bedridden Sarah to the North Riverdale Nursing Facility.

After Sarah's move my life became very regular. For the next few months I didn't miss a single day at the nursing home. Our apartment seemed so empty without Sarah, that as soon as I woke, I would hurry to see her. Usually, I rode the B10 bus, which took me almost door-to-door. At the nursing home, I would wheel Sarah up to the third floor lounge, where the window provided a view of the surrounding neighborhood. Sometimes that would cheer her up a little.

On the weekend, Meyer and Florence or Ben and Betsy would often drop by. Florence visited once a week, raising my hopes she had softened towards Sarah. Leah even managed to make the long trip up from Manhattan. Although we had talked on the telephone, I hadn't seen her in several years, and we hugged when she came to Sarah's door. I noticed that she walked with a cane.

"It's just varicose veins," she told me. "Painful, but not serious."

"How's Paul?" I asked. Leah had kept me abreast of Paul's condition since he had had a stroke six months earlier.

"Not too good. He has no control over his right leg, although his speech is slowly coming around."

"Do you still have an aide living in your apartment?"

"She's there six days a week. I don't know what I would do without her. Twice a week a physical therapist comes to exercise Paul."

As Sarah became weaker, she'd sleep most of the day. When the weather turned nice, I couldn't resist getting some fresh air by taking an alternative route to visit her. Getting off the B16 bus at 233rd Street, I'd walk through Van Cortland Park, past the tennis courts and the golf course and over Tibbett's Brook.

The nurses took care of most of the things that had to be done for Sarah, but sometimes they had to be alerted to her needs. In addition, I got great pleasure out of helping her drink a few sips of water or feeding her some applesauce or Jell-O. While Sarah slept, I'd sit at the side of her bed and hold her hand, as if that could somehow keep her from leaving me.

During those long hours, I couldn't keep questions about Sarah's cancer out of my mind. *What if we hadn't wasted all that time seeing Sarah's dentist? And, if we had gone to Carter before Levy, could she have been helped?*

There was also one thought that went through my mind of which I'm not proud: *Who was Sarah's first sexual experience with?* Was it a man or a woman and under what circumstance. I considered waking her up and asking her, but, of course, I didn't.

Towards the end, there were three whole days during which Sarah didn't wake. She took in no food, and as far as know, had no bowel movements. Occasionally, she would mumble something in her sleep. She'd call my name, and our children's and her mother's once or twice.

I was up and having breakfast at 7 AM, on May 8, 1969, when the phone rang. I had a pretty good idea what the call was about, since Sarah's breathing had been labored the previous night when I left. After almost six months at the nursing home, Sarah had died during the night. Now they wanted my plans for her body.

316

Well, there were no plans, since I had never accepted the obvious reality that Sarah would soon be gone.

"Unless you tell us otherwise in 24 hours," the director told me, "your wife's body will be turned over to the City."

"What will happen then?"

"The City will probably inter her in the pauper's cemetery on Hart Island run by the New York Department of Corrections. You or anyone else who will want to visit the grave will have to apply to the Department, since there are prisoners on the island, who perform the burials."

I panicked; that would be horrible. Fortunately, when I called Ben to tell him about his sister, he informed me that the family plot in the Brooklyn Cemetery had space reserved for Sarah and himself. He gave me the name of the funeral home that could handle all the arrangements.

Even with Sarah's burial plot paid for, and only a simple pine box being preferred for burials at the orthodox Jewish cemetery, the funeral arrangements would cost about $800. The funeral home would need $500 before they would send an ambulance to pick up Sarah's body at the home.

On Bainbridge Avenue, I caught a taxi to take me to the bank. I had the taxi wait while I went in and withdrew $500. Then it took me to the funeral parlor, where they said they would send an ambulance to pick up Sarah immediately. I had managed to keep her from being buried in a pauper's grave, but I felt so stupid for not taking care of the arrangements earlier.

That evening, back at the apartment, I called Milty. "Take $800 of my money and send a check to the funeral home," I told him.

"Don't you have enough left to pay it?" he asked me.

What? Was this jerk going to give me trouble getting my own money? "Put Esther on," I said.

"Don't worry," Milty said. "I'll send a check right out."

I had been running around so much that day, I hadn't had a moment to think of what had happened. Now it hit me. *Sarah was gone and she wouldn't be back!* I sat down at the kitchen table, where Sarah and I had so many of our conversations, and sobbed.

Chapter 35

*The woman at the information desk tells me Ida is in room 329.
When I look into the room, the bed is empty. A nurse in the hallway tells me,
"I saw Ms. Blinsky in the lounge." She points to the end of the hall.*

*There's a slight smell of Lysol at the doorway of the large room. I
see eight patients: five in the couches and chairs in front of the TV—no Ida
there, two dozing in their wheelchairs; also not Ida. She might be that
woman in a wheelchair looking out the window with a turban wrapped
around her head. She's wearing a blue bathrobe like the one Ida had. I can't
tell from here. I'll have to go over by the window to make sure. Suddenly my
shoes seem nailed to the floor.*

*The window has a southern view. Through it I can see the smoke
rising above the South Bronx that I saw from the train.*

*"It looks like they're burning it down," I say, when I finally get my
feet to take me across the room.*

*"Yes, it does...Abe, my God! How did you get here?" Her hand
pulls her robe more tightly around her.*

"Didn't your son tell you I was coming?"

*"I haven't seen him in a week. You know how it is with children."
Tears flow from her eyes. "Oh Abe, I've missed you. Give me a hug and a
kiss."*

*I want this to last, so I move a nearby chair next to her wheelchair. I
sit next to her, encircle her with my arms and gently pull her to me. She
presses her lips against mine and then pulls them away, after repeating this a
few times, she says with a laugh, "We're making a scandal. They'll kick me
out of the hospital." She pulls back and says, "How are you, Abe?"*

"I'm fine, Ida, and you?"

*"Not too good. I've had a very extensive operation and now I'm on
chemotherapy. It makes you sick as a dog and all your hair falls out. That's
the reason for this fancy headdress."*

"I'm so sorry for you."

"Are you disappointed after coming all this way?"

318

I can feel my heart beating in my chest. "Ida, I missed you so. I didn't know what happened to you, and when you didn't call or write, I just had to see you again." I think there are tears in my eyes. Hope I don't start bawling. "Why didn't you contact me? I felt you didn't really care for me, if you could just ditch me like that."

"Oh Abe, I can't tell you how many times I was on the verge of writing or calling you, but then I thought: I know Abe. If I contact him, he'll be up here sitting at my bedside. And then he'll lose his nineties caring for me, just like he lost his eighties caring for his wife. You've got so much energy, Abe, I couldn't see doing that to you."

"I would have gladly taken care of you, Ida. I love you. You're all I have left."

"No I'm not," she says through the tears rolling down her face. "You have your kids. You should still be able to reconcile with them. And your grandchildren. And the walks in the early morning in Miami Beach you love so much. I couldn't take that away from you."

"But being with you would have been more important to me than all those things."

We both stare out the window in silence for several minutes. Then I ask Ida, "What's going to happen to you now?"

"I'll be here for a few more weeks. Then, if I continue to recover from my operation, they'll release me. There's a building across the street with efficiency short-term rentals. Patients often stay there when they leave Beth Abraham. Makes it easy to come back for post-operative treatment. They clean the apartment and serve one meal a day downstairs in a dining room. My son has put me on the list for one of those, in case it comes available. If not, I'll stay with him for a while, although I'm not sure that will work out. He has a pretty small place."

"And us?" I ask. "Do you think we still have a chance to get back together?"

"I'm afraid my South Beach days are over. I'm not the same woman I was. There's nothing for you to hold on to if we sleep together anymore." She pulled her bathrobe tighter to show me how flat she is.

"That wouldn't make a difference, I just want to be with you."

319

"Abe, you're great to say that, but I think we'll have to play it by ear. I'll write and call you...I see now I made a mistake not contacting you. Maybe things will change or we'll be able to visit each other; we'll have to see."

Just then a nurse comes by. "Would you like your lunch out here, Miss Blinsky, or should I bring a tray to your room?"

"Out here will be fine. Would you like to share my lunch, Abe? They always give me more than I can eat."

"You need to eat and get your strength back. Is there a cafeteria, where I can pick up a sandwich?" I ask the nurse.

"Take the elevator down to the lobby and follow the signs."

I go downstairs, buy a sandwich and soda and bring them back to the lounge. All my anger at not having heard from Ida has evaporated on hearing what she went through.

After eating, we talk a little about To Kill a Mockingbird, the book Ida gave me before she left, and Bessie's comment about the book. I notice Ida's head is nodding. She says, "I'm sorry Abe, but I'm going to have to take a nap now. Since the operation, I sleep most of the day"

Before I leave, I kiss her again and tell her I'll be back.

Sarah's funeral was on Sunday morning. Although it was probably quicker to get to the cemetery in Brooklyn using Robert Moses's highways, I asked Meyer to take the route we had used when we had gone to Hannah's funeral fifty years earlier. We drove down Park Avenue in Manhattan and took the 59th Street Bridge to Brooklyn. When we crossed the bridge, even though the sun was already high in the sky, I silently asked Sarah again to forgive my calling attention to the sunrise on the way to her mother's funeral.

The rabbi at the grave looked exactly like the one at Hannah's funeral. *Could he be his son?* I was so involved with this question, I hardly heard what he said about Sarah. *What could he know about Sarah: about her strength, her grief and her suffering?* After we said the *Kaddish*, I threw the first shovel of dirt on the grave. Meyer, Esther and Ben were next, and after them the twenty-or-so people around the grave followed suit. Even Leah, who had come by taxi, put down her cane to shovel some dirt. When we finished, we hugged all around and I told everyone that the *Shiva* would be at our apartment. Meyer took the shorter highway route home, so we could get there before everyone else.

Sunday afternoon, the apartment was packed with Meyer's, Esther's and Ben's families. Several couples we knew in the neighborhood and a few men from the *shul* also dropped in. The kitchen table overflowed with casseroles and food from the delicatessen and bakery. I was going through the motions: thanking everyone for coming and making sure they had enough food and drink, not really aware of why they were all there.

Everyone left that night, except for Esther, who let Milty go back to Long Island by himself.

"What are you going to do now, Dad?" she asked, while wrapping the leftovers to put in the refrigerator.

The question shocked me out of my torpor. I felt a sudden constriction across my chest and sat down on one of the kitchen chairs to catch my breath.

"Do? Why...I haven't had a chance to think about that. It'll take a while for me to get my life in order."

"I wish I could invite you to come out to live with us," Esther continued. "But the house is so small, there really isn't enough room."

That shocked me. Going to live with Esther and Milty out in the sticks, walking through blocks of nearly identical houses, didn't seem like a remote possibility to me. Being turned down for an option that I wasn't even considering was extremely embarrassing.

"Esther, I just want you to know that my moving in with you and Milty is not something I was or will be contemplating," I said. "Now that the funeral is over, I'll have more time to make my plans."

Of course, what my plans would be depended on whether I'd get my money back from Milty. It didn't seem like this was the best time to ask Esther about that.

Over the years, among less-observant Jews, *Shiva* had become foreshortened to less than the mandated full week. On Monday, Meyer and Ben stayed with Esther and me. In the evening, Esther went back to Long

Island, and I was alone in the apartment. I tried to sleep, but thoughts kept going through my mind. *Would I be alone in this bed...in this apartment for the rest of my life?* Finally I rose and flipped on the TV. I can't remember the movie I was watching when I fell asleep on the couch.

On Tuesday, Meyer went to his office. Ben came over in the morning, but by noon, we were both getting antsy. "I don't think anyone else is going to drop by," I said. "Why don't we go out for a walk? I'd like to see the old neighborhood where Sarah and I used to live."

It was over a mile back down to 179th Street. Ben had put on quite a few pounds over the years, so we couldn't walk as fast as we had when he first came home from the war. It was a good way to talk about the old times and remember Sarah.

"I'm so glad my sister married a great guy who would be my best friend," Ben said. "If you hadn't gotten me to go to Yankee Stadium, I wouldn't have met Betsy."

"Then you would have been a wild bachelor all your life."

"Not quite." He laughed and then confessed to having been jealous when he was young over all the attention his sister had gotten from their parents. But he finished on a positive note with, "She really was the greatest sister a guy could have."

Thursday, when it seemed no one else would be dropping by, I went down to Mosholu Parkway and sat on my usual bench. I began to count the number of friends I had left. Izzy had died two years earlier—on a trip to Paris no less. It was questionable whether Paul would recover from his stroke. That left Ben and Betsy, Leah and a few guys in the neighborhood I occasionally chatted with—not much to fill the void left by Sarah's death.

Aaron Salkind wasn't around, and it occurred to me that he hadn't dropped by to the *Shiva*. *Maybe he moved or is on vacation. But his wife is a professor. He couldn't leave in the middle of the semester.* Then I remembered something I had overheard at the *Shiva*. Two guys from the shul were talking and one had said to the other, "We'll need a new membership chairman, now." I knew that Aaron previously had had a heart attack, and I feared the worst. The next Saturday, at *shul*, I learned that Aaron had passed away two months earlier. I'd really miss him.

I remembered that by walking, I had finally broken out of my depression after Harry's death, so I tried another dose of the same remedy. It also served to get me out of the apartment, with all its memories of Sarah.

I quickly found that walking was easier said than done. Besides being older, I had spent more than a year sitting around the nursing home or the apartment. It's amazing how fast you go downhill at my age, if you don't keep moving. Besides reduced endurance, it seemed that every joint and every muscle hurt after I returned from even a short walk. I spent many nights tossing in bed with pain. A new over-the-counter medicine, Tylenol, seemed to help, and I resolved to keep walking. At least it would get me out of the house, and maybe I could return to my former condition.

At first my walks followed a circuit. I would stop at various benches along Mosholu Parkway, in the Oval and in Van Cortland Park to rest. Only occasionally would I notice the brilliant colors of the autumn foliage. By the time I got home, I was so exhausted that after a quick bite to eat, I'd collapse in bed.

When October stretched into November, I wore a sweater and wrapped myself in my overcoat. On one particularly chilly day, a homeless man lay under a blanket on a bench not far from me in the park. We both shivered. He had no place to go, and I was fleeing my Sarah-haunted apartment. *This is stupid! Come December, I'll freeze to death. Better to face my memories.*

I began to spend more time at home with the ghost of Sarah. I'd mumble to her at the kitchen table, and we'd laugh together in front of the TV.

"This place is a mess." Esther told me when she visited, and she was right. Every dish I had lay dirty in the sink or on the furniture. The bed linen hadn't been changed in over a month, and balls of dust were building up in every corner. Esther and I went to work. I wasn't experienced in housework; Sarah had always taken care of that. But under Esther's direction, we got the place cleaned up.

"You really need a haircut," Esther told me as she left.

I looked at myself in the bathroom mirror. She certainly was right. And it wasn't only the hairs on my head that needed trimming.

The next morning I headed up the block to Ralph, the barber who formerly had cut my hair every third week. While Sarah had been in the nursing home, I had only occasionally gone out while she was sleeping and used a barber across the street from the nursing home.

It being Saturday, a few customers were already waiting for Ralph's services. I was in no hurry, so I grabbed a seat and picked up a *Newsweek* magazine from the table where various reading material was strewn. It turned out to be the issue in which the magazine reviewed the previous year.

I was mortified. How could I not have known that students were taking over university buildings and blacks were rioting in cities all over America?

And Bobby Kennedy had been assassinated! I thought of Kennedy's mother and father, who had lost one son in the war, like I had, but now had had two more of their sons assassinated. I don't think I could have recovered from that. In fact, Joseph Kennedy, Bobby's father, died just a short time after his assassination.

For years, I had been intensely interested in everything that was happening in the world. I had first scavenged and then bought copies of the *Times* and at least skimmed the entire paper. Now, America appeared to be coming apart and I had been oblivious to the entire drama. *Who was the president?* I thought. *Was it still Lyndon Johnson? Let's see: it's March of '69. That means there was an election. Who ran? Who won?* I had a funny feeling it was that communist-baiter, Richard Nixon, but I wasn't sure. I resolved then and there to get back in the world.

"Mr. Abe," Ralph said, " I haven't seen you in quite a while." He motioned me into his chair. "How's life treating you?"

"Not too good, my wife died last year."

"I'm sorry to hear that. I hope she didn't have a hard time of it."

I didn't answer. I think I decided it was time to stop focusing on Sarah's death.

Ralph started with a shampoo and scalp massage. Under his fingers, I felt much of the tension flow out of my mind.

"You need some fixing up," Ralph said, and he went to work on hairs protruding from my nose and ears. How about a shave?"

The mirror showed I hadn't done a good job that morning. "Sure, go ahead."

After lathering and shaving me, Ralph covered my face with a hot moist towel. "It opens the pores," he always said. However, now the towel did more than open my pores; it also opened my mind. When he removed the towel, I was ready to go out into the world once again.

Interesting things were happening in the world. Just as I had anticipated, we had gotten deeper into the Vietnam quagmire, and young people were protesting our involvement.

In July, something really interesting happened. Two American astronauts set foot on the Moon. "One small step for a man, one giant leap for mankind," Neil Armstrong said, when a human for the first time set foot on a heavenly body. Space programs had come a long way from the beeping ball I remembered.

I didn't do much to keep the apartment clean. Probably subconsciously I believed that if it was messy, Esther would return to clean it. I was lonely and needed her visits.

"This place is a filthy again," she said, rolling up her sleeves to do some serious cleaning. Milty sat down in front of the TV to watch a football game. After about two hours the place was looking presentable.

"Could you go to the deli and get us some sandwiches?" Esther asked Milty.

"When the game is over."

"When's that," she asked.

"The fourth quarter just started."

"Okay, I'll go. Give me some money," she said.

Milty handed her a ten, and she stormed out of the apartment.

I figured that with Esther gone, this would be a good time to press Milty for my money. I waited until there was a time out.

"Hey, Milt. You remember that ten grand I gave you to hold."

"Yeah."

"It's time to give it back."

"Can't do that—things are slow right now."

"What do you mean, 'things are slow?' It's my money."

"Well it's your daughter who wanted to have her kitchen redone."

"How much can you give me?" I asked.

"Don't know. I'll have to check my bank balance," he said. And then, "Let's watch this. The Giants only have a three-point lead."

Milty had me in a bind. I couldn't sue him to get the money, since I had probably committed fraud in giving it to him to get Medicaid to pay for Sarah's nursing home. Now that he'd shifted the blame to Esther, I couldn't complain too much, without alienating my only daughter, whose help I needed in getting over Sarah's death. Anyway, how could I begrudge Esther a new kitchen, after how much she'd been deprived during the Depression?

Esther came back with the sandwiches, and we ate them in front of the TV, watching the Giants win the game by ten points. As soon as it was over, Milty stretched and said, "We'd better get started. It's a long drive home."

Esther looked at me with concern. "Will you be okay, Daddy?"

"Sure, I'll be fine."

"I'll call Florence." Esther said. "Maybe she can come over once in a while to make sure things don't get out of hand."

I hugged Esther and ignored Milty, which didn't seem to bother him. And then they left for their drive home.

Florence did occasionally come over to clean and provide the human contact I needed to get through that very bad winter. I had always gotten along well with Florence; it was only with outspoken Sarah that she had had trouble.

"Would you like some tea?" Florence asked me.

"That would be nice."

Over our cups of tea, Florence and I rambled about our early years. My memories of Zyvotov were getting a little fuzzy, but I tried to recreate life in the town for her. My eyes teared when I told her about the probable death of Leena during World War II.

326

Florence told me how difficult it was being financially dependent on her sister, Agnes, after their parents died.

"She treated me like a slave. I had to do all the cleaning and make the meals."

Chapter 36

The smell of pot roast filling the house brings me downstairs to the living room. I'm looking forward to dinner.

As soon as she sees me, Amanda waddles over carrying a book. "Read book," she says, climbing up on the couch and cuddling next to me.

I think of Sarah and how excited she had been with her grandchildren. Too bad she couldn't see this next generation.

"Sure, I say. I don my glasses and look at the book. It's the Cat in the Hat, by the same Dr. Seuss who wrote the book I used to read Michael. Writing popular children's books for more than thirty years, I think Dr. Seuss must be doing better even than regular doctors.

I start, "The sun did not shine. It was too wet to play. So we sat in the house all that, cold, cold, wet day." I really ham it up, waving my arms and shaking my finger. Amanda loves my performance. Attracted by her screeches, Kevin leaves his jigsaw puzzle and kneels down next to her with his elbows on the couch.

When I finish reading the book, Kevin asks me, "How old are you Grandpop?"

"I'm 91."

Kevin counts on his fingers. "That means when I'm fourteen, you'll be one hundred."

I'm amazed. The kid's a genius.

The bell rings and I hear Susanna answer the door. A few minutes later she comes into the living room. "Look who's here," she says.

It's Esther and Milty. God, I haven't seen my daughter in a while. She's attained plumpness similar to her mother's at her age. Doesn't look bad on her at all.

"I'm going to feed the baby," Susanna says. "Come get your dinner, Amanda."

Amanda waddles into the kitchen.

"Esther." I struggle to my feet to give her a big hug.

328

"Daddy, it's been so long." She squeezes me back. "We haven't heard from you in ages." She steps back and looks me over. "You look great!"

"How are you, Abe?" Milty holds out his hand. I hesitate a moment before shaking it.

"Healthy but poor." He ignores my answer.

"Tell me all about your trip," Esther says.

"It was long, and they stranded us in North Carolina."

"Stranded you?" Milty says.

"Yeah, the bus driver left. He said another one was coming. But he never showed up."

"What did you do?" Esther asks.

"I yelled at them over the phone."

"Good for you." Milty seems impressed.

"And I sat next to a very nice black lady on the bus," I add. They don't seem to react, so I say, "Do you still live in that lily-white town? What's it called?"

"Levittown," Esther says. "But it's not lily-white anymore. We've got a black family living on our block. The woman's very nice and a lot of fun."

I'm glad Esther is losing her prejudice. "Do you know this little genius? He can do math."

"I've met you, Kevin," Esther says. "But it was when you were just one year old. I don't think you remember me, do you?"

"Sure I do. You're Esther, like in the Purim story."

"He is a genius," Esther squeals.

"Dinner's ready," Susanna calls out. "Michael, get off the phone."

We take our seats at the large, oval dining-room table and are half way through our chopped-liver appetizers when Michael comes in and apologizes, "Sorry, but I had a very upset client on the phone." He looks over the table and says, "Let me get the wine."

He uncorks the bottle and pours some in each glass, even giving Kevin a drop.

The wine seems great to me. Kevin tastes it and makes a face. "Can I have some juice please," he says.

"Of course, honey." Susanna says to Kevin, and then to Michael, "Help me bring out the food."

"Let me help," Esther offers. She gets up and follows them into the kitchen.

That just leaves Milty, Kevin and me at the table.

"How's business, Milty," I ask.

"Not all that good. With gas prices shooting up after the Arab oil embargo, a lot of people out in the suburbs are hurting. They're putting off painting their houses."

Esther returns with a large bowl of potatoes, Michael with two of vegetables, followed by Susanna with a tray of sliced pot roast. We all fill our plates and start to eat. Conversation is mainly about Kevin and Amanda and then turns to Esther's children.

While we're waiting for Susanna to bring in the dessert, Esther says, "I hear you came to New York to find some woman. Tell us about her."

Now, talking to your daughter about your girlfriend is not pleasant, so I play down my relationship. I hope I'll be saved by the reluctance of young people to imagine any sexual interactions among those of us advanced in age. "Her name is Ida. She's a very nice lady. She was a good friend of mine down in South Beach; we lived in the same hotel. One day she just disappeared; her son took her to New York. She didn't even leave a forwarding address. Michael helped me find her."

Michael goes along with my underplaying. "Yes, her son said she had cancer and was at Beth Abraham hospital in the Bronx."

"That's a good hospital," Esther says. "I hope they can do something for her."

Dessert is hot apple pie that Susanna baked herself. Vanilla ice cream is optional; I take it. We're washing it down with coffee, when I decide to take the bull by the horns. "Well, Milty," I say. "When will you be returning the money you're holding for me?"

Silence envelopes the table. Milty stares down into his coffee like he'll find the answer to my question there. It's Esther who answers. "Oh Daddy, we don't want to keep your money. You never asked for it."

"Like hell I didn't. You try living on $400 a month social security."

"It's just that its pretty bad times right now," Milty ventures.

"Don't give me that bad times business. That's what you said last time I asked you. I can't wait forever; I'm 91. What can you give me right now?"

"I guess I can manage $500."

"And $200 every month until it's all paid back. I figure you owe me $9200. You can keep what's left over when I die."

"Oh Daddy, don't say that. You'll never die," Esther says.

"That sounds like a fair deal," Milty says.

Milty will never send me that money I think. "How about you mail my check to Michael every month and he can deposit it in my checking account. If that's okay with you, Michael?"

"Sure Gramps. I'll do that for you."

Milty doesn't seem too happy about having a lawyer make sure he pays up.

One Sunday in May after Sarah died, Meyer and Florence took me out to dinner at a Chinese restaurant. This was so unusual I suspected something was up.

"I've had an interesting offer," Meyer started out.

"What's that?"

"A large accounting company has offered to buy me out."

"Are you interested?"

"I think so. My firm is doing fine right now, but accounting is changing so fast, I don't think we can keep up with it."

"What do you mean?"

"Have you heard of computers?"

"I've read about them in the newspaper."

"Well, they're very expensive. But they're taking over accounting. I'd have to make a huge investment to keep my firm competitive. At my age, I don't think I want to do that."

331

I did a quick calculation. "You're only 54."

"Actually 53. But this offer would give me enough to retire right now."

"What would you do?" I asked.

"I like to play golf. Maybe we'd move down to Florida, where I could play year round."

"That sounds nice. Maybe I'll come visit sometime."

"Even better, why don't you move down there now? You wouldn't be stuck in the house all winter."

"I'll think about that," I said as I started on my soup.

In only a few months, Meyer had sold his business, and he and Florence moved to a house on a golf course in Boca Raton.

About a month after Meyer had moved, I had a telephone call from his son, Michael, now a law student at the University of Pennsylvania.

"I've got a favor to ask you, Gramps."

"What's that?"

"I've got an internship at a law firm in Manhattan for the summer."

"An internship, what's that?"

"It's like a job, except they don't pay you."

"That doesn't sound good."

"It's often a way to get a job at the firm after you graduate."

"Oh, what's the favor?"

"Well, I was going to live at home during the internship, but now that my parents have moved, I've got no place to stay. How would you like a roommate for the summer."

"I'd like it, but I only have one bed. You'd have to sleep on the couch."

"That would be fine. I've got a girlfriend in New York, so I'd be spending a lot of time with her."

"I warn you," I said. "The apartment isn't too clean right now, but maybe the two of us could get it into shape."

"I'll be rolling up my sleeves as soon as I get there."

My summer with Michael was totally enjoyable. His girlfriend, Susanna, was a law student at N.Y. U. She had a summer job—one that paid money—in another law office in Manhattan. Her job kept her pretty busy, so Michael and I had a lot of time to "hang out." On nights he slept in the apartment, he'd often get up early and go for a run along Mosholu Parkway. He'd pick up a couple of danish and the *Times* on the way back, and we'd have breakfast together. We'd trade sections of the newspaper and discuss world news and the 1970 Yankee team's prospects, which weren't too good. None of their players even had a .300 batting average. They had come a long way down from the days of Ruth, Gehrig and DiMaggio, and even those of Maris, Mantle and Yogi Berra.

Michael brought Susanna up to the Bronx for me to meet, and we went to a night game at Yankee Stadium. Even in slacks and a sweatshirt, you could tell that she had an excellent figure. Over our pre-game hot dogs, I asked them, "How did you two meet?"

Susanna almost choked on her dog. Michael slapped her on the back and said, "We met at Woodstock last year."

"Where's that?"

"It's off the Thruway, not far from Kingston."

"Sounds like farm country. What were you doing up there, milking cows?"

"Milking cows?" Michael exclaimed. "They had the biggest music festival ever up there last year—a half million people. Where have you been, Gramps?"

"Mainly at the North Riverdale Nursing Home," I answered. "What kind of music did they play?"

Susanna, having recovered, said, "There was Joan Baez, Arlo Guthrie, the Grateful Dead, and about forty other performers. Mainly people involved with the Peace Movement. It went on for three days."

I vaguely remembered hearing those names. "Three days...where did everybody sleep."

She laughed. "We all slept on the ground...I should say on the mud, in sleeping bags."

"That doesn't sound like fun."

333

"It was wild, really wild," she said. From the look in her eyes thinking back on it, it must have been.

The summer was very therapeutic for me; my mood picked up. However, the apartment seemed empty again when Michael went back to school in August. Shortly after, I packed up my clothes, sold my furniture to various neighbors, and took a bus south to Miami.

The next summer, when Michael was married, Meyer and Florence drove up from Florida to New York for the wedding, and I went with them. They stayed in a hotel, but I was invited by Susanna's parents to stay at their apartment on West 64th Street in Manhattan. They were very gracious and well-off people. I thought that Michael had found a good match.

Chapter 37

Here I am, back at the Port Authority Terminal again. I told Susanna and Michael I was heading back to Miami, but when I got here, I wasn't sure. I guess without Ida I'm not drawn to that lonely room at the Sun Spot, no matter how nice the weather is down there.

I visited Ida again Sunday. Her son, Alex, was with her. He was nicer than I had expected. Seemed very concerned about his mother. It puts my mind at ease to know someone is looking after her up here.

I waited around for Alex to leave before trying to talk about the future with Ida. She said she has to take it day-by-day, and was adamant that I shouldn't wait around at her side. She's probably right: my watching her go downhill is something neither of us wants. It would break my heart to go through that again. She promised to write and keep me up to date on her condition.

Ida's young. I hope she'll come through it okay and come back to Florida. I don't think that's what she expects to happen. When it warms up in the spring, I'll make another trip up here. She'll probably be in an apartment by then, so I'll be able to stay with her.

Susanna washed my clothes and Michael cashed Milty's check, so I have everything I need for my trip. My wallet's loaded, and I also taped a couple of hundreds into my shoe. Too bad Papa isn't around to sew the money in, like he did when I came to America over seventy-five years ago.

Three quarters of a century, what a long time! All the people I've known who have passed away: Mama, Papa and Leena, Yudel and Mina, and, of course, Sarah and Harry. Well, not everyone is gone. I can still visit Leah down in Coral Gables and yell at Meyer in Boca for not visiting me more often; I should have done that a long time ago. Maybe I'll even take Bessie up on her offer of some tea. She might even have some more of that fried chicken.

I sit in the coffee shop studying the bus schedules for almost an hour before I decide to buy a ticket for only as far as D. C. There's a lot of stuff in the museums down there that I missed on my trip there with Sarah, 20 years ago. I don't know where I'll sleep...maybe that little hotel where Sarah and I stayed, if it's still there. If not, there are probably others just as cheap.

After D. C.? I'm not sure. Richmond, Nashville, Memphis, maybe even New Orleans. There are lots of other interesting places for me to see in America before I wind up back in South Beach.

Yesterday, I remembered that a couple of months after his stroke, Yudel said something very wise to me, "Avrom, a man should stay alive, if only out of curiosity."

Glossary of Hebrew and Yiddish terms

Alta cocker (Y) – old man

Bershert (Y) – meant to be

Cheder (H)– traditional Jewish elementary school

Chuppah (H) – canopy under which a Jewish couple stand for marriage vows

Dreck (Y) – dirt, excrement

Feygele (Y) – homosexual

Gonif (Y) – thief, dishonest person

Hamotze (H) – blessing over bread

Kaddish (H) – prayer in Jewish service

Ketubah (H) – Jewish marriage contract

Kiddush (H) – blessing over wine

Kittel (Y) – a white robe used in certain religious occasions

Klafte (Y) – bitch

Le'chayim (Y) – to life, cheers

Machatunim (Y) – parents of your child's spouse

Macher (Y) – important person

Mazel tov (H,Y) – good luck, congratulations

Mezuzah (H) – a prayer written on parchment, in a box Jews affix to their doorpost

Minyan (H) – minimum of ten men required for public worship

Mitzvah (H) – commandment, worthy deedNebbish (Y) – loser

Peyes (H) – sidecurls worn by some orthodox Jews

Schmuck (Y) – stupid person

Schnapps (Y) – hard liquor

Shadchan (H) – matchmaker

Shidduch (H) – meeting of Jewish singles for the purpose of matchmaking

Shiksa (Y) – non-Jewish woman

Shiva (H) – week-long Jewish period of mourning

Shlemiel (Y) – fool

Shtetl (Y) – a town with a large fraction of Jews

Tallis (H) – ritual shawl

Tefillin (H) – small boxes containing verses from the Torah worn by Jews during morning prayers

Tzitzit (H) – cloth fringes worn by some orthodox Jews

www.ingramcontent.com/pod-product-compliance
Lightning Source LLC
Chambersburg PA
CBHW070208260626
47160CB00002B/483